The Black Orchestra

A Novel

BY R.J. LINTEAU

Based on Actual Events

The contents of this work, including, but not limited to, the accuracy of events, people, and places depicted; opinions expressed; permission to use previously published materials included; and any advice given or actions advocated are solely the responsibility of the author, who assumes all liability for said work and indemnifies the publisher against any claims stemming from publication of the work.

All Rights Reserved
Copyright © 2021 by R. J. Linteau

No part of this book may be reproduced or transmitted, downloaded, distributed, reverse engineered, or stored in or introduced into any information storage and retrieval system, in any form or by any means, including photocopying and recording, whether electronic or mechanical, now known or hereinafter invented without permission in writing from the publisher.

Dorrance Publishing Co
585 Alpha Drive
Pittsburgh, PA 15238
Visit our website at *www.dorrancebookstore.com*

ISBN: 978-1-6376-4125-5
ESIBN: 978-1-6376-4764-6

The Black Orchestra is a work of fiction. Any relationship to actual individuals, places, and circumstances, unless intentional, is purely coincidental.
Printed in the United States of America.
Author email: rjlinteau.author@gmail.com
Cover Design by:
Fedota Design Consultants
Atlanta, GA

THE BLACK ORCHESTRA

The following is a work of fiction but depicts numerous historical events that happened in 1943 and 1944. The dates of certain events have been changed slightly to integrate them into the storyline.

All of the German characters lived during that time, including Claus von Stauffenberg, Wilhelm Canaris, and the other German officers and conspirators in The Black Orchestra.

Father Jonathan Strauss and the Americans portrayed as part of the Office of Strategic Services (OSS) are fictitious. Alan Dulles was head of the OSS in Europe.

This book is dedicated to my wife Sharon, who has been my rock for thirty-seven years.

Special thanks to Kay Olsen for her assistance in editing and proofing this work; for making me a better writer, and Jonathan Strauss a better character.

Many thanks to Ann Roecker for additional editing, and to my long-time friend, Brian Kagan for his strong support in urging me to write on.

Thank you to all the readers of my first novel for their positive, supportive comments. You have energized me to to continue writing.

Also by R. J. Linteau

Novels:
The Architect

Screenplays:
The White Rose
Second Trumpet

Short Stories:
Summer Kamp
Havana Daydreamin'

Part I

UNITED STATES

PROLOGUE

April 7, 1943
The Kasserine Pass
Tunisia, Africa

The Horsch 108 lorry lumbers down the dusty road, part of a column of half-tracks, trucks, and tanks. It seems to hit more potholes than necessary.

"Can't you avoid the ditches, for God's sake?" Lieutenant Colonel Claus von Stauffenberg is in a foul mood.

"I'm doing my best, Herr Colonel. This road's hardly a road at all anymore. It's been bombed quite a bit."

"Stay to the left. It looks better there." The two worn tracks level out, and Sergeant Fredrick Kemp shifts into a higher gear. A swirl of dust spews up on either side of the heavy, gray vehicle. Shouting above the roar of the engine, Kemp yells, "I have been your adjutant for six months, sir. You are like my older brother. So please explain to me why we are even in Africa?"

"Because we have been ordered to. We are here to save the collective asses of the Italians. Damn Hitler and his adventures."

"You know you should be careful what you say, especially about the Führer. I could be working for the Gestapo."

"If you are then I guess I'm already screwed."

"I will confess that I feel the same way. But I'm just a soldier doing my duty. I go where I am told. Fortunately, right now, it is beside you."

"The war goes badly. We should have learned our lesson here a few months ago, and now the Allies have Patton leading them. We have suddenly hit a brick wall. And this pass seems to be the only way through it. Can't you go any faster? We're an easy target here!"

"We need to stay with the column; there is safety in numbers. And you don't want the engine to overheat, do you? It's so damned hot out."

"It's not called the desert for nothing. Certainly not like Bavaria, eh?"

"No, not at all. I dream of my house in the mountains every night."

"Yes, and I dream of my home in Albstadt." Looking up, he squints, staring at the sky. He tries to focus on a distant image.

"What is it? Do you see anything?"

"No, but I thought I heard something."

He listens again, straining to hear something above the din of the convoy. Now he hears the distant roar of an Australian Kittyhawk P-40 fighter bomber, finally making out its shape above the horizon, and heading for them.

"Shit, I knew it! Here they come. Get out from this column!"

Kemp pulls out and steps full on the gas. The lorry lurches forward but outside of the worn tire tracks, the way is treacherous, with rocks, small boulders and deep ruts lining the side of the road. Stauffenberg grabs onto the top of the windshield trying to hang on. At that moment, the plane comes right at them, machine guns firing.

"Forget what I just said! Pull in behind that tank up there!" Stauffenberg shouts.

"I can't go any faster, sir!" Kemp is trying to maintain control of the cumbersome vehicle and is now alongside a large truck that kicks dust and sand on them. He attempts to wipe the dust from his goggles, while Stauffenberg turns around to look to the rear, grabbing the top of his seat for support.

"They're coming back! Get behind the tank!"

The fighter bomber closes in, shooting at the column with its four wing-mounted guns. This time the bullets hit the lorry's seats and rip into Stauffenberg's hands. Kemp is shot several times in the back and the vehicle careens out of control. Caught between the truck and a large boulder, the lorry crashes, overturns, and bursts into flames. Stauffenberg is thrown from the truck, and his face skids along the gravel road. Kemp lies dead in the wreckage of the burning vehicle. Stauffenberg rolls over, his body racked with pain. One hand is a bloody shred of its former self, the other is bleeding profusely. But he can see neither; in fact, he can see nothing out of his left eye. It is gone from his skull.

Chapter One

MARCH 1944
Von Moltke Estate
Kreisau, Poland

The grounds are dark on this moonless night, pierced only by moving beams of bright yellow light from the large headlamps of the Mercedes and BMWs—long, black conveyors of very important people. They line up in the circular drive, and then stop beneath an imposing staircase leading to a pair of front doors. The right one opens, betraying the luminescence of the elegant interior beyond. One after another, uniformed officers and dark-suited businessmen enter the large house. And then the darkness comes back; the blackout curtains have been pulled tightly closed.

The butler leads the way to a large reception hall. The silk damask walls, polished floors beneath rich oriental rugs, and electrically lit crystal candelabra create a warm and inviting atmosphere. A servant offers flutes of French champagne and hors d'oeuvres. Off to one side, there is a bar where those not interested in products from an occupied country can get single malt scotch or gin from an unconquered one. Better yet, there is good German beer. The men shake hands, some hug, others salute. Wehrmacht officers wear gold braid and polished boots. The old men in suits wear medals earned fighting for the Fatherland in the Great War.

After thirty minutes of polite discussion and small talk, great doors are opened to an octagonal dining room with a large fireplace burning oak logs. On either side, two antique Queen Anne chairs flank the roaring fire. A huge mahogany table, usually glittering with the finest china, sterling silver, and floral arrangements, dominates the center of the room. There are places for twenty dignitaries, each defined by a white rose in full bloom atop a red linen placemat. Next to the rose lies an ominous silver dagger. In the center of the table is a large bronze eagle, an Iron Cross in its upraised claw.

"Colonel, we are ready to begin."

"Thank you. I am ready."

The man slowly stands. Each movement is deliberate and painful. He is an imposing figure of noble bearing. Across his left eye is a black eye patch, at once sinister but also regal and a bit mysterious. He has no right hand, only the stitched sleeve of his lieutenant colonel's uniform. The left hand has only a thumb and two fingers. Claus Philipp Maria Schenk Graf von Stauffenberg, a son of Bavarian nobility, walks to the table with a slight limp. Recovery from his wounds in Tunisia has been slow, but his devoted wife, Nina, and his Catholic faith have sustained him.

As he approaches the large table, the uniformed officers salute him, though some are of higher ranks. The older men bow. The gathering is motionless in the presence of this new member, struck by his handsome face, thick, dark brown hair and his strong Aryan bearing. He is everything a German officer should be, minus some essential body parts. He takes the last remaining place at the great table. The butler pours Mosel wine into the glasses, and then quietly departs through a hidden side door. Now there are just twenty patriots facing each other and death, if caught. The Gestapo has assigned a name for this group, **The Black Orchestra**, a moniker that these patriots have accepted, even embraced. Von Stauffenberg waits for quiet and nods toward their host.

Peter Graf von Wartenburg, the de facto leader of the Kreisau Circle, speaks. "My friends, thank you for coming tonight. For some it was a long journey. For all, it is a dangerous one. As you know, our leader, Helmuth von Moltke, has been imprisoned. His lovely wife, Freya, is very gracious for permitting this gathering at her beautiful home tonight. She is taking a grave risk for our benefit."

Heads nod, and others murmur agreement.

"I have invited our other friends in the opposition to join us tonight to discuss the future of Germany." Von Wartenberg looks at his friend, the colonel.

Stauffenberg speaks; he is tired of talk. "My friend, thank you for including us in your meeting. But let me be frank. What is the future of Germany, Peter? The Kreisau Circle has discussed the future until you are blue in the face. There is no future unless we act now."

"Claus, we cannot resort to the same violence as practiced by the Nazis," Peter responds.

Stauffenberg shows his frustration. "We are few and the forces of evil are overwhelming. We must act! I am sorry for my bluntness, but Hitler must be assassinated. Only then can we secure an honorable peace with the Allies. After that is accomplished, we can discuss the political structure of a new Germany."

"There will be no structure at all unless we lay out a plan. That has been Helmuth von Moltke's goal from the start. That is why the Kreisau Circle was formed. Without a plan, there will be another dictator like Hitler, filling the vacuum of power." Von Wartenberg speaks with passion.

"Yes, and where has it gotten him? He is rotting in prison, writing down his ideas," Claus says sarcastically.

Admiral Wilhelm Canaris, head of Germany's intelligence-gathering arm, the Abwehr, stands and raises his glass to toast his fellow conspirator. Canaris's face is angular, steel blue eyes secondary to bushy white eyebrows and a handsome crop of combed, snow-white hair. The former U-boat commander in the Great War and recipient of the Iron Cross speaks. "Gentlemen, please. Herr Peter, thank you for allowing us to join in your group's discussions. But I am afraid all of us in the Black Orchestra are inclined to think the same way. First, we must remove the Führer, and then we can organize a new democratic government. It will not be easy. We have failed in the past, numerous times."

"Yes, but this time we will find a way and it will be done. Our past failures will not be repeated." Stauffenberg, only thirty-seven years old, has aged over the past year. A year of rest and recuperation in which he committed himself to ridding Germany of their maniacal leader. Standing, he commands the room. "At this moment, we must pledge ourselves to our just and righteous mission." Knives against glasses ring with approval.

Canaris speaks. "Gentlemen, I propose that we agree on new leadership for our group under Colonel Claus von Stauffenberg. You see his passion; he is the one to now lead us. And tonight we make a renewed, sacred pact to kill Adolf Hitler."

"Here, here! Agreed. Well said!" The voices of the soldiers and politicians drown out the head shaking murmurs of the writers, philosophers and academics.

Canaris picks up the white rose. "The white rose before you signifies the purity and righteousness of our cause." Canaris holds up the dagger and cuts his finger, blood dripping slowly onto the rose. "This honed blade is our resolve. My blood is our blood that we are willing to shed for the Fatherland in our sacred mission. I pledge my life to this cause."

Those assembled speak as one, "To Germany! To the Black Orchestra!" Many of those assembled rise and run the blade across their fingers.

Von Wartenberg slowly stands. He pierces his finger with the knife, and then raises his glass. "To the Black Orchestra. To the Fatherland!"

Chapter Two

March 1944
Fifth Avenue and 47th St.
New York City

The rain is incessant. It's almost dark at midday and the streetlights have turned on along Fifth Avenue. The top of Rockefeller Center is hidden in ominous, swirling gray clouds; it is inordinately cold and has been since winter ended. The only news of late that brightens the mood of New Yorkers is that the tide of war has turned everywhere: in Eastern Europe, in Italy and in the Pacific. Across the globe, the Axis is in retreat. Soon the Allies will land in France. The only question is when and where.

The man holds tight to his ineffectual umbrella as he crosses the street in front of the dominating statue of *Atlas* holding up the world. The rain is sideways and drenches his black overcoat. He hurries up the dozen or so steps to the great bronze doors of St. Patrick's Cathedral. Fortunately, within the great door is a smaller one, heavy still, but manageable for those wanting entrance to pray and worship.

Father Jonathan Strauss enters the narthex of the great cathedral. Shaking himself like a wet dog, he furls the umbrella, leaving a small puddle on the stone floor. He removes his black fedora and enters the main church. It is ablaze with lights from massive twin chandeliers down the nave and additional ones along the side aisles. Dipping his hand into the marble font of holy water, he blesses himself then walks up to the raised altar and genuflects, turns right and heads back to the sacristy. In the large room, filled with carved wood closets and cabinets, an ornate mahogany door leads to the second floor.

The middle-aged priest opens the door and ascends the worn granite steps. Strauss enters a large office, clad in rich rosewood paneling with hand carved scrollwork, dentils, and crown molding. On one wall is a painting of the Madonna and Child, several hundred years old. No one is seated at the large and imposing desk with its accountant's lamp at the center and bejeweled crucifix to one side. On the other end of the desk are two phones. Off on the right, a fire burns in a substantial stone fireplace.

He has been in here only a few times. It is the office of the Cardinal Archbishop of New York, his eminence, John Francis Mulrooney.

"Jonathan, is that you? Over here, by the fire." His eminence peers around the side of the winged-back chair, his face full of a broad smile. His hair is white and thick, setting off the red skullcap signifying the rank of Cardinal, a prince of the Roman Catholic Church.

"Your Eminence. I'm sorry; I didn't see you."

"I'm hiding from Sister Mary Evangeline. She doesn't like to see me drink during the day!" He raises a Baccarat crystal glass toward Father Strauss, filled halfway with twenty-year-old Jameson. "Is it still raining?"

"Oh yes, archbishop, sideways, and it's cold!"

"As my sainted mother would say: 'A perfect Irish day.' Listen, join me. On the credenza. See the decanter? It's the good stuff. The distillery ships it to me direct from Ireland. One of the perks of my job."

Strauss doesn't much care for Irish whiskey, preferring scotch whiskey, but the invitation is tempting and he's somewhat nervous in the presence of the head of the largest diocese in America. "Well, how can I refuse? Maybe it will warm me up a little. You wanted to see me?"

"Good. Yes, come and sit. I have a letter for you."

"A letter? Am I being reassigned?" Strauss dreads to think that he might lose his choice position as one of eight priests serving under Mulrooney at St. Patrick's. He doesn't want to be sent to some God-forsaken rural parish in upstate New York where the rain and snow never seems to end.

"Not by me. You're one of my best. You give the best sermons. I've been taking pointers from you."

"Thank you, but I think it's the other way around. So…about the letter?"

Archbishop Mulrooney reaches over to a mahogany table next to his chair, picks it up and stares at the return address. "It's from the War Department, Jonathan. It seems that they want to speak with you in Washington…next week."

"Why would they want to speak with me?"

"My boy, that's what I was wondering. If they want you as a chaplain, they'd have written me directly. No mention here and you're too old. Anyway, I can't lose any more priests. I'm already struggling with eight. I normally have fifteen here at St. Pat's."

"And when is this appointment?"

"It says Monday at 10:00 A.M. You better take the train after your Mass on Sunday. I think you have the 11:00 A.M. service."

"The War Department? Where are they located? I've never been to Washington."

"They just moved into a new building. I read about it in the *Times*. It's just outside the city in Arlington, Virginia. The building is shaped like a pentagon and it is massive. It says office 567, in A-Ring, whatever that is. Sorry I can't help you beyond that. Here, take the letter. I'm sure if you wear your collar, people will be happy to help you."

Strauss studies the letter intently, scratching his head. A worried look on his face betrays his mood. "I'm sure it's nothing. Thanks for the drink, Eminence."

"Jonathan?"

"Yes?"

"You were in the first war, correct? A German soldier?"

"Yes, I was a soldier, but it was a long time ago. Now I'm a priest and an American."

"Certainly, son, certainly. May God be with you." The archbishop takes a drink of his whiskey, emptying the glass.

Chapter Three

The War Department
A-Ring, Office 567
The Pentagon

The waiting room is gray and bland; the aroma of new paint hangs in the air. Father Strauss sits in one of four guest chairs, trying to concentrate on *Stars & Stripes Magazine*, the sole reading material available. The only color in the room is an American flag in the corner. The secretary, immersed in her work behind a gunmetal desk, wears a gray dress and has gray hair. Strauss puts down the magazine and stretches his arms and legs. The long trip by train, delayed by priority freight trains, and the lumpy mattress at his second-rate hotel, has left his six-foot-two frame stiff. The rains from the previous week have made the arthritis in his knees worse.

The woman looks up from her paperwork at her strange guest with his Roman collar. She thinks he is handsome. His face is ruddy like an outdoorsman, with a few deeply etched lines. His chin is square and above it is a strong mouth. He has a full head of black hair with slight graying at the temples. He has reached the middle of life, showing age, but not in a bad way. Sensing her stare, he looks up. His clear, dark blue eyes focus on her intently. He tries to smile, but he is really in no mood. The phone rings at her desk, and she immediately picks up the receiver, speaking in a barely audible voice. She looks up.

"You can go in now, parson."

"Please, Father is fine."

"Sorry, I'm a Baptist."

"Yes, well, thank you." Strauss gets up and goes toward a door with opaque glass that leads to a private office. He reads the gold and black letters:

Winslow M. Gardner
Assistant Secretary – Military Intelligence

Inside, it is yet another non-descript, cream-colored office, containing a wood desk, two more metal guest chairs, and a side credenza. The only artwork is a large photo on the wall of the president of the United States, Franklin D. Roosevelt. A man is at his desk, intently studying a manila folder. A uniformed soldier, an army major, stares out the window toward the green expanse of Arlington National Cemetery. Strauss stands by the door, not knowing whether he should sit, continue to stand, or pray.

"Have a seat, Father." Winslow Gardner speaks curtly, not looking up from the dossier in front of him. Head still buried in the file, he points toward the figure at the window. "This is Major Thomas Bourke; he works with me. He's with the War Department. Special projects."

Strauss nods toward Bourke as he settles into one of the chairs. "What is all this about?"

"It says here that you were in the German Army in the first war. Then in army intelligence; very interesting. So, were you a spy?"

"No, I wasn't really a spy. I was a…a message runner. Why am I here?"

"Born Johan Mikel von Strauss in Augsberg, Bavaria. Wealthy family. Joined the army at age eighteen in 1913. A patriot, I presume. Later taught at the German Military Academy from 1927 to 1931. What kind of messenger were you?"

"I was a private. I ran with messages from one trench to another. Then, well, I lost my nerve. Battle fatigue, I guess you'd call it. I did other work for the government. Information gathering, that's all. You still haven't told me why I'm here."

"We'll get to that. Okay, a battle fatigued solider, not a spy. I'll make a note of that, though I don't quite believe it. Do you believe it, Major?"

"Sure. And Lindbergh's no Nazi."

Strauss shakes his head. "I'm not a Nazi! I'm an American citizen for eight years now. And I'm a priest." Strauss gets out of the metal chair and turns toward the door.

"Padre, we're not done here. Sit down. I'll let you know when you can leave. You speak fluent German and some Italian?"

"Brilliant. I was born in Germany, raised in Germany, and lived in Germany until 1932. Now I know where the 'intelligence' comes into play in your title."

"Don't crack wise with me, Padre."

"It's not Padre, its Father. Father Jonathan Strauss. And I'm leaving unless you tell me what the hell this is all about."

"Father, do you know a Claus von Stauffenberg?"

"Stauffenberg. Yes, our families knew each other. His father was in the government; my father was a diplomat. They were Catholics, like us. Claus was just a baby when I was twelve or thirteen."

"But then you taught him later at the Military College?"

"The *Kriegsakademie* in Berlin. It was quite a coincidence. After the war I stayed in intell…in the army and then studied there. I earned my degree in history, and then later, like your file must say, I was hired to teach there."

"What kind of student was he?"

"What's the point of this trip down memory lane?"

"And what kind of student?"

"Very bright; very smart. He later joined his family's hereditary regiment, the 17th Calvary. But I left the college. It was getting too National Socialist for me."

"Did you see him or socialize with him after classes?"

"Yes. Sure. Our families were close. I felt somewhat like an older brother to him. I took him under my wing, you might say."

"Was he a Nazi?"

Strauss fidgets in his chair, wanting to get up. He says nothing.

"Answer the question, Father, then I'll tell you."

"He wasn't a Nazi, at least while I knew him. It was a long time ago. He may have joined the party later but I doubt it. I don't know; it's possible. I naturally lost track of him when I came to America."

"All right Father, you're here because your country, your adopted country, the United States needs you. You were a German soldier; you speak Italian and German; you know how to spy and you know things. Plus, you know this Stauffenberg fellow."

"I told you I wasn't a spy. I was in fact-finding. And I'm done with war and killing. I'm too old and I've already seen too much of it."

Major Bourke turns and walks behind Gardner's desk—reinforcements have arrived. "Strauss, you're right. You are a priest and you're too old to be a chaplain. We can't really make you do anything. You can go back to New York if you want."

"Good. Goodbye." Strauss stands when he hears Bourke's words and quickly makes for the door.

"Wait, Father. Please tell us about Anna Schmidt." Bourke tries to hide a slight smirk.

Strauss lets go of the half-turned doorknob. His face turns ashen. "What is this about?"

Bourke picks up Gardner's file, peering down. "You had an affair with Miss Schmidt when you came to the States in 1932. She had a baby, a boy, born out of wedlock. You're the father, I believe. Not very priestly behavior, now is it?"

Strauss feels his legs weaken and grabs the back of the chair; he feels lightheaded. Gardner pours the priest a glass of water from a carafe on the credenza, and places it in front of him on the desk.

"I wasn't a priest then. I was just a lonely man, alone in New York. We were going to be married, but she died giving birth. I was devastated."

"It says here that you abandoned the child." Bourke is bearing down on his prey.

Strauss drops into the chair and takes a drink of water. "I did not. It was best to give him up for adoption. I could not care for the baby!"

"You left the child in the hospital. You ran."

"I was confused, scared."

"Relax, Father, there's no crime in any of this."

"He needed a mother, a family," taking another drink. "I have confessed all my failings."

Bourke walks around to the front of the desk and stands over the shaking cleric. "You mean your sins? Well, maybe. But I bet you didn't confess the lies on your application for the seminary, did you?" He points to a yellowed form in the file. "About being celibate all your life; about never having any children?"

Strauss hangs his head and mutters: "I can't believe this." Gardner speaks. "Father Strauss, you're a good man. I'm sure of that and we don't want to see you defrocked, or whatever it is that your people call it."

"The word is 'excommunicated,'" Bourke says, not being able to resist another blow. Gardner waves him off.

"What do you want from me?"

Gardner speaks. "We just want your…no, we need your help."

"What do I need to do?"

"Go back to New York for now. Do your priestly duties. You'll receive more information there. And your government is grateful, I assure you."

Strauss rises for the last time and heads for the door. He turns. "I hate war. I saw too much so many years ago. I'm done with it, forever…is that good enough for you?"

Chapter Four

Von Moltke Estate
Kreisau, Poland
The meeting of the Black Orchestra continues.

General Ludwig Beck, former Chief of Staff of the Army, impeccably dressed in a dark blue suit, looks up from his notes. His hair is thin and gray. He has large eyes that size you up instantly, and he wears a perpetual frown. He has hated Hitler since 1938, when he was forced into retirement by the man and has been trying to remove him from power ever since. It is believed that Beck will take a place of prominence, most likely as president, should a coup succeed. One plot after another has failed and he just wants the Führer killed by any means possible.

"My friends, time runs short. The invasion of Europe will come soon. And with it our chance of securing just peace terms will greatly diminish. We must act. I think a new opportunity has presented itself." He looks toward Major General Henning von Tresckow, who has been part of the plotting against Hitler since the beginning.

"Thank you, General Beck. You all know how many times we have tried and failed. I must say that the Führer has been very lucky."

"Damned lucky! That bottle of brandy should have exploded on his plane last year," Beck reminds his colleague.

"Yes, and there have been other times. But that is in the past. We must move on," Tresckow says.

Stauffenberg now speaks. "It is all getting very tiresome. We are a bunch of amateurs. We should have succeeded long ago. What is the plan now, Tresckow, and will it work?"

Peter von Wartenburg listens passively as others talk of killing the head of state. He says nothing, taking a deep drink of his wine. The Kreisau Circle has been eclipsed by the determined members of the Black Orchestra. The Circle is now complicit in the scheme to commit murder.

"All plans have the potential for failure. Regardless, we must try until we succeed. Our man, Eberhard Breitenbuch is likely to be called to the Berghof with his boss, Field Marshal Busch, in a few days. Hitler wants an update on the disaster on the Eastern Front and we understand that Busch has returned from Russia to Berlin. Breitenbuch will be in the meeting. He'll carry a gun in his trouser pocket. It is simple. A gun usually fires. Bombs sometimes go off, but most times they don't."

"Just great! A gun. It might work if an SS bodyguard doesn't see Breitenbuch taking aim at our esteemed Führer's head! And if it does not work, we're almost out of options." Beck is getting frustrated. He looks at Stauffenberg. "Colonel, are there any further developments on your possible assignment to General Fromm's staff?"

"I'm working on it. The wheels of the Third Reich grind slowly. It may be our final option. If I can secure the position, then I will have direct access to the Führer, and I swear to heaven, I will kill him. Then we'll demand a cease fire and negotiate a just peace."

Admiral Canaris stands. He is wearing the black double-breasted jacket of an admiral in the Kriegsmarine. He has removed the detested swastika pin from his left breast. The ends of the sleeves bear a gold star, three gold stripes and a larger solid gold bar. "Let us not have any illusions about the peace we hope to achieve. The *Casablanca Declaration* stated that nothing less than 'unconditional surrender' will be accepted. The United States wants to turn us into a bunch of farmers—make us a purely agrarian society, never to produce as much as a Volkswagen.

Fortunately, the British are not convinced that is the wisest approach. They need Germany to be a strong bulwark against the Bolsheviks and communism. I understand that Churchill is now more concerned about Stalin than he is of our great leader. Anyway, you can forget about keeping Poland and Czechoslovakia, or the Rhineland."

"They'll think differently when Hitler is dead, and the lives of hundreds of thousands of soldiers can be spared," Stauffenberg says, looking hard at Canaris.

"You worry about killing the man. I'll take care of the Allies."

General Beck interjects. "Fine, fine. Anything else before we adjourn?"

Henning von Tresckow rises. He has the bearing of the son of Prussian nobility and a long line of military generals. His eyes are deep and piercing, not mean, but strong. His mouth is a thin straight line. The war has brought on a premature loss of hair.

"I've been reassigned to the Russian front, my friends. This will be my last meeting with you. Promise me that whatever transpires, you will, under any circumstances, remove Hitler."

Beck speaks. "Thank you, Henning. We all appreciate your resolve and I speak for all of us when I wish you luck in the east. Now, gentlemen, I do have one other disturbing piece of information. Our man in Brandenburg, Erich Reinenger, has been arrested by the Gestapo. It is a serious blow to us."

"Where is he now?" Canaris asks.

"Görden Prison in Brandenburg. If he talks under torture, it will be disastrous."

The corridors of the prison are poorly lit, a dim bulb every fifty feet or so. The wet walls are rough, un-hewn stone. They bleed black water; a green, slimy moss has grown on the rock, leaving a smell of old grass and mildew.

The man in polished jackboots and a green trench coat walks with military precision down the long hallway. The sounds of his wood heels resonate down the corridor. He takes a final draw on a cigarette and drops it ahead of him, stepping on it as he passes. Wilhelm Canaris turns left down another corridor, lined with hard, old wooden doors fitted with heavy steel latches and padlocks. He can hear moans emanating from the cells, pleas of "I am innocent!" followed by the dull thud of a truncheon and a scream.

"Fucking Gestapo," he mutters to himself. He finally arrives at his destination, Cell 239. A guard is standing outside the door. He snaps to attention with a crisp salute.

"Let me in. Has he talked?"

Fiddling with his keys, the soldier answers: "No, Admiral, no." He finally gets the door open, hand shaking in the presence of the high ranking official.

"Thank you. You may leave us."

"But I'm not to leave my…"

"I said leave us."

The guard relents and walks down the corridor. Then he stops and turns. Canaris has gone into the cell; the soldier gingerly takes a few steps back to the door, leaning against it to hear anything inside.

Reinenger is seated in the middle of the cell tied to a wooden chair with leather straps. They cut into his wrists and ankles, and there are small pools of blood on the seat and floor. His eyes are bound with a dirty rag.

"Reinenger, you miserable traitor to the Reich. I should kill you now!"

"I am innocent. Please believe me!" Reinenger is forcing his loudest voice.

Canaris turns, quickly opens the door and stares at the spying guard. "I told you to leave us. Must I report you?"

"No, sir, sorry," the guard mutters. "I'll grab a cigarette then." He walks down the corridor. When there is no longer any sound to his footsteps, Canaris returns to the dungeon. Canaris removes the rag covering the prisoner's eyes. They are bruised and almost swollen shut. "Erich, it's me, Wilhelm…Canaris."

"The Black Orchestra makes a beautiful sound…" Reinenger whispers.

"Yes, yes. I know, I know. Have you talked?"

"No, but the torture. I don't think I can…"

"You must be strong."

"The pain, it is awful. I wanted to tell them everything. But then they stopped." He opens his mouth; several molars are gone, blood oozing out the sides of his mouth.

"If you tell the Gestapo about us, all will be lost."

"You must end this. Once I talk, they will kill me anyway."

"Do not ask me to do such a thing."

"I beg you; you must do it now. Please! I am a weak person. I think they're going to pull my fingernails out next!"

Canaris backs away, shaking his head. "Oh, Reinenger, why did you get arrested?"

He removes a Luger from his coat pocket, thinks first to leave the wretched man to his own devices, and then looks at Reinenger again. He sighs and lifts the weapon. He pauses. Then a shot rings out through the prison, the sound traveling down the corridors. Reinenger's blood, brain and skull fragments splatter the walls of the cell. Hearing boots coming from several directions, Canaris turns to leave. As he steps out of the cell, two startled guards arrive. "He told me what we need to hear, so I executed him. He was a traitor. You may tell your superiors. Clean up this cell."

Chapter Five

APRIL **1944**
6th Avenue & 41st Street
New York City

Father Strauss adds sugar to his coffee. A lot of sugar. It reminds him of the sweet, dark coffee drinks of Bavaria. He stares out the window of Gino's Diner, which is on 41st Street and 6th Avenue. There are many other restaurants closer to St. Patrick's, but he enjoys the walk down Sixth and likes the food here, especially the donuts, evidenced by the empty plate that once held two Boston Crèmes and a jelly. A copy of the *New York Herald Tribune* lies on the red Formica table; the sports page has prominence. Strauss has glanced over the front page, but it was nothing but war reports, and he is sick of reading about the Axis and the Allies, and the goddamn Nazis. He didn't fight in the Great War to have his country taken over by a ruthless dictator who started another world war. And now the War Department wants him to get involved. Why they want him, he has no earthly idea, but the thought of it has almost ruined his appetite. He thinks: *"I'm a forty-nine-year-old priest with bad knees. What do they want with me?"* He looks to heaven and says a silent prayer of deliverance while adding sugar to his coffee.

"Like some coffee with that sugar?" A man stands over Strauss, looking down at the newspaper and the coffee cup.

Without looking up, instinctively Strauss responds: "Yeah, I do," then looks up. "Do I know you?"

"No, I don't think so." The man sits down into a red vinyl chair across from Strauss. "A black coffee over here, please," he says loudly to catch the waitresses' attention.

"So, how's your morning going? Day off, isn't it? No need to say Mass for the parishioners?" The man looks down at the newspaper, noticing the sports section. "You like the Yankees' chances this coming season? I'm a Dodger fan myself."

"How do you know it's my day off?" Strauss looks around the diner to see if there might be an off-duty policeman at the counter.

"I know things; it's my job. Oh, by the way, Mr. Gardner sends his best wishes."

"Gardner? Gardner. Oh, I get it. You're with the government." Strauss puts down the coffee cup that had almost reached his lips and stares at his unwanted guest.

"I heard you were a spy. That's why you connected the dots so quickly."

"Funny. And I wasn't a spy. Again, who are you?"

"Name is Lawrence. Jack Lawrence. I'm your contact. Your, shall we say, 'handler.'"

"Now you listen to me, and you can tell Mr. Gardner too, I'm not going anywhere. I'm a priest at St. Patrick's and I'm staying in New York. I'm done with war. And you can't force me to do anything." Strauss gulps down the rest of his coffee and gets up, reaching for his black London Fog.

"Sit down, Father. Please."

"Why? Why should I even talk to you?" Strauss stands, ready to leave the diner and his unwanted guest.

"Do you know that your son's name is Michael?"

"I don't have a son." Strauss's voice rises, losing his temper.

"Really?" Lawrence takes a drink of his coffee, blowing on it first to cool it. "Think back to 1932; you and Anna Schmidt had a baby. It was a boy, I believe?"

"He is not my son now; he's someone else's." He slumps back down into the booth.

"Father, he'll always be your son."

Strauss becomes curious. "Do you know him? Where does he live?"

"Sorry, that I can't tell you. But he's a good kid; he's handsome, strong and intelligent. He's twelve years old now. You'd be very proud." Lawrence takes another slow drink of his coffee, giving Strauss time to process the information.

"Twelve? Already? Listen, you better not hurt him, or I swear to God I'll..."

"Relax, Father. Nobody's hurting anyone. I just thought you'd like to know about your son. He wants to attend that expensive Jesuit high school on the Upper East Side. What's the name...Loyola? But, unfortunately, his parents don't have that kind of money. He'll probably have to attend public school down in his sorry-ass neighborhood of Hell's Kitchen. So, why don't we talk about your future in the OSS."

"Who are you again?" Strauss's head is spinning.

"I work for the OSS, the Office of Strategic Services. I'm a liaison, an information officer. You'll be one of us. We need your help, as Mr. Gardner told you."

"Why does the War Department need my help? I'm a priest, for God's sake." Strauss looks for a waitress; he needs another cup of Joe.

"We need you because you're German and speak the language fluently and with a German, not American, accent. You were a spy, an agent in the first war, deny it or not. And most importantly, you know Colonel Claus von Stauffenberg."

"And why is he so important to you? He's just another officer in the German army."

Lawrence finishes his coffee. "Claus Stauffenberg is trying to assassinate Adolf Hitler, that's why."

"He's what? Von Stauffenberg?" Strauss waves for a waitress.

"He is part of an underground group in Germany that opposes Hitler. The Gestapo calls them the Black Orchestra. They're high-ranking German Wehrmacht officers, some generals, a few Weimar politicians, patriots, and other veterans of the old Republic. One thing they all have in common is contempt of Nazism and Hitler. They have attempted to assassinate Hitler before, but most were bungled affairs. Now Stauffenberg has taken a leading role. He is determined to succeed where others have failed."

"That's a good thing, isn't it? I wish him all the luck in the world, but it doesn't involve me. As I said, I'm staying in New York."

"You're from Bavaria, and you know Stauffenberg and he knows you. And no one will suspect that a priest is an agent for America. I think you could be a big help."

"To help Stauffenberg kill Hitler?"

"No, we want you to stop him," Lawrence says without emotion.

"What do you mean? 'Stop him?'"

"Okay, here's the deal. Your son's name is Michael Wagner. Like I told you, his parents are good people of very limited means. If you help us, Michael can get a scholarship to that expensive Jesuit high school. A free ride. Then we will see that he goes to Fordham, or NYU or any college he likes. All paid for by the U.S. Government. And since you're a priest and took a vow of poverty, it might help. Oh, and nothing more will be said or done about your application for the priesthood. I'm sure that's a sin you didn't confess."

"You son-of-a-bitch!"

Lawrence gets up, throwing a dollar bill on the table. "Think about it." Lawrence puts on his coat, looking for any reaction from Strauss; all he sees is confusion. "You'll receive further information soon; where to go, who to see. I'll see you around, Father." He turns and leaves the restaurant.

Chapter Six

Grunewald Forest
Outside Berlin

The morning air is crisp, even chilly. Steam rises from the nostrils of the two majestic Holsteiner stallions, both seventeen hands high. Admiral Wilhelm Canaris and SS Brigadeführer Walter Schellenberg ride down the wide dirt path along the River Havel, a small part of the 7,400 acres that comprise Grunewald Forest, Berlin's largest park. It is an activity both have taken pleasure in for some years. The two men are friends, though each is wary of the other, and their respective powers. Canaris's Abwehr spies for the Wehrmacht, particularly in England and in the few remaining countries of Europe not occupied by the Nazis. Schellenberg's Sicherheitsdienst, known as the SD, handles all internal espionage work for the SS and Gestapo. Canaris wants the war to be over and retire to his estate, Valkenburg. Schellenberg is ambitious and covets control of the Abwehr, and a position equal to Himmler. His face is angular and effete. His hands, covered in riding gloves, are thin and boney. He wears a custom-designed green riding jacket with black suede lapels, adorned with the SS death head on one side and the twin lightning bolts on the other. Canaris is riding in a civilian long coat, part German and part American cowboy; he is having some difficulty controlling his horse.

"Wilhelm, your horse is quite spirited today." The Brigadeführer pulls back tightly on the reins of his steed.

"Mercury hasn't been out in quite a while. I don't ride as often as I'd like, I'm afraid. He'll calm down when we go full out in the pasture ahead."

"Yes, you have been busy with all your intelligence gathering…" Schellenberg stops his horse again. Canaris wants to ride but is forced to stop in deference to his riding partner.

"Yes…exactly. We seem to have more intercepts from the French Resistance and Great Britain than ever." The admiral glances at his riding companion. He knows there is something on his mind.

"Indeed. But I understand that you executed one of my prisoners at Görden Prison. A fellow by the name of Reinenger."

"Yes. He told me what we needed to hear. And it was clear he had betrayed the Reich."

"He was an SS prisoner…"

"I could tell. Your methods obviously did not work. Mine did. It's done."

"What did he tell you?"

"It will be in my report. I could be writing it now, but we are enjoying the morning. I can tell you this: he was a part of that Black Orchestra group, as you call it."

Schellenberg raises his voice slightly and speaks with precision. "You interfered with SS business. He was of no concern to the Abwehr. We weren't done interrogating him."

"Torturing him is more to the point…and he did have information that the Brits gave him. I needed it."

"What, are you losing your stomach for our methods of intelligence gathering?"

"No, let's just say I prefer spying." Canaris kicks his horse and takes off down the path. The sun is up and he begins to feel its warmth. Schellenberg follows, a small smile breaking out on his face; he is enjoying this game of cat and mouse. They ride to a large, green pasture. Canaris has given Mercury full rein and gallops across the field. The Brigadeführer slaps his horse with his riding crop and follows in pursuit. The admiral stops at the far end of the field. His horse is still, bending down to eat grass.

"See, I told you, Mercury just needed some exercise."

"Wilhelm, do you think the war is going badly?"

"What does it matter what I think? What do you think, Walter?" He stares intently at his companion.

"I think there are traitors and betrayers everywhere, my friend. Some have lost faith in our leader, which is a bad mistake."

"Perhaps it is the war we have lost faith in. It is not going as originally planned. What do you expect? Our great leader is perhaps... becoming unsteady."

"Careful what you say, my friend. He is still the head of state."

"Such as it is." Canaris snaps the reins and the horse raises his head and walks on.

Schellenberg smiles and follows his friend. He feels the same way as Canaris, but only because the opportunist in him thinks he can earn a high position in a new government. He dislikes Hitler and hopes he will soon be eliminated by someone's bullet.

The two riders proceed for a few minutes until Canaris stops by a small stream that feeds into the Havel to allow his horse to drink.

Schellenberg has been waiting for this opportunity. "It might interest you to know that yesterday my organization executed three Black Orchestra collaborators near Odessa. They were providing intelligence to the Russian army. As a result, we lost the city."

Canaris stiffens in his saddle. He is motionless, absorbing the deaths of three members that he knew. He lets out a sigh but says nothing.

"Canaris, you seem upset. Is something wrong?" Schellenberg is enjoying the moment; he suspects him of being a key member of the Black Orchestra.

"No, Schellenberg, not at all. I'm impressed with your efficiency. My compliments."

"The SD is nothing if not efficient. And from now on leave the interrogation of prisoners to me. Just find out where the invasion will happen, all right?"

"Agreed. But I already know that answer…the Pas de Calais."

"How can you be so sure?"

Chapter Seven

St. Patrick's Cathedral
New York City

The morning sun shines through the stained-glass window that depicts Christ preaching, Mary Magdalene and St. John at his feet. The windows, made by Polish artisans in the 1800s, splash the room with red, deep blue, magenta and ochre in a kaleidoscope of colors. On one wall are ornate maple wardrobes for the priest's vestments. Other cabinets hold gold chalices, elaborately embroidered chasubles, and drawers of fine French linen hand towels that are part of the celebration of the Eucharist. Father Strauss is removing his heavy chenille vestment after saying Mass. The door to the stairs leading to Archbishop's office opens.

"Ah, Jonathan, how was attendance today?" Cardinal Mulrooney is all business.

"Eminence, good morning. Oh, with the war it's been good for a long while now and probably will be for some time. We haven't even invaded France."

"I think that will happen soon enough."

"Not soon enough for me."

"I listened to some of your sermon. Like I told you before, you have a gift for oratory."

"You've been eavesdropping again," Strauss says taking off the white alb undergarment. He reaches for his cassock.

"I'm just taking some pointers from the pro." A slight smile comes across the archbishop's face.

"I'm hardly that," Strauss responds, slipping his cassock over his lanky body.

"Father, I received a letter." Mulrooney reaches into his black coat and removes it. "It's from the Vatican. I don't get many letters from there, and when I do its important. It's from my predecessor, Brendan Galloway. He's in Rome representing the United States."

"I've heard of him. Wasn't he the pastor here?"

"Yes, he was a monsignor but in 1942 he suddenly got promoted to archbishop; here read it."

Strauss takes the letter, noting the Vatican coat of arms embossed in gold at the top. The paper is heavy. At the bottom, below the archbishop's signature, is a red wax seal. He slowly reads it, then staggers, and drops the letter. "I've been assigned to the archbishop's staff. Rome: I don't want to go to Rome! I want to stay here."

"My son, I don't think you have any choice in the matter. You took the vow of obedience, remember?"

"I know," Strauss replies in a low voice. "But I never want to go back to Europe."

"I must say, it is quite unusual. I think you're the most interesting priest I have. First Washington, now this. By the way, I forgot to ask you about your trip to the Pentagon. What did the War Department want with you?" Mulrooney looks intently at his vicar, believing there is a connection between this letter and the last.

"To be honest, to blackmail me."

"Father, you can't be serious?"

"They need my help, or think they need it, and are holding something from my past against me."

"What could that be? From the first war?"

"No, later. Archbishop, I need to tell you something. Maybe if I do, I can tell the War Department to go to hell." Strauss looks at the archbishop. He knows his boss is a kind and forgiving man.

"What is it, my son?"

"When I first came to the States, I was all alone. I hardly spoke any English. There weren't any jobs, and it was the height of the Depression. I lived in a small hotel room on 12th Street down in Hell's Kitchen. It's a despicable place. I didn't know what I was going to do with my life. My prayers to God for some direction went unanswered. Then I met a woman, one morning in a restaurant: a German woman. I was busing the tables for fifty cents a day. Not much money, but it was a job. Anyway, this woman was beautiful. Her name was Anna, Anna Schmidt. She had a wonderful smile." Strauss looks up wistfully to the stained-glass at Mary Magdalene. "When I got off work, we had coffee. I can't believe she was willing to do so, I smelled so bad from work and the hot kitchen." Strauss takes a deep breath.

"Go on," Mulrooney impatiently looks at his priest.

"Anyway, we went out many times. She was from Hamburg. We fell in love."

"Many priests fall in love before hearing the call from the Lord, Jonathan. Sometimes that's a good thing."

"It wasn't that simple. We had relations out of wedlock."

"Well, that is troubling, but perhaps understandable. I assume you confessed this sin of the flesh?"

Strauss ignores the question. "Anna got pregnant. She wanted the child and I wanted us to get married. But there was so little money. It was a difficult pregnancy and…" Strauss is silent for a long time.

"Continue, Father, please."

"She died giving birth. The child was fine, but I lost my Anna."

"I'm very sorry to hear that. It must have been very difficult for you. And the baby?"

Strauss looks directly at his superior, tears streaming down his face. "I just left the hospital. I ran back to my apartment and then left the city. I didn't know what happened to the child. Afterwards I applied for the seminary and was accepted."

"Father, this is all very troubling to hear."

"Will you forgive me these sins?"

"My son, I didn't realize this was a confession. If you had said: 'Archbishop I need to confess my sins,' it would have been different. Father, you had intimate relations before marriage and worse yet, a child out of wedlock, and then you abandoned the child. These are very serious, mortal sins. They cannot be forgiven in such an offhand and casual manner. Particularly since you are now a priest. These serious sins have followed you, been a part of you, and all while you have performed priestly duties."

"I'm sorry, Archbishop."

"I am sorry too, but I have an important meeting and I must be going, and now you are assigned to Archbishop Galloway. So you will go serve him. He'll hear your confession and assign an appropriate penance."

Strauss looks at the stained glass again. He shakes his head. "I don't want to go back to Europe."

Mulrooney looks at his vicar with empathy. "Father, do you know anything at all about the child?"

"I was told by the government that he lives here in the city. He is fine. If I do what they ask of me, they'll pay for his education."

"Then I'd do what they want. It will help you make amends for your past failings." Mulrooney looks at his watch. "Sorry, but I'm late for that meeting with the Mayor at Gracie Mansion. I need to go. I'm sure with God's help, everything will work out. Let me know when you will be leaving for Rome, and Godspeed my son."

"Godspeed indeed." Strauss walks out of the sacristy and into the great cathedral. He finds a small, empty pew off the side aisle and kneels, his head in his hands. *"Lord, just as you spoke in the garden, Father, if you are willing, take this cup away from me; still, not my will but yours be done."* His body trembles. Europe. War. The past relived. Tears well up in his eyes and begin to stream down his face.

Chapter Eight

MAY 1944
The Berghof
Obersalzberg, Germany

The Condor aircraft makes a final turn between the mountains and then swoops down toward the landing strip, lengthened in 1938 to accommodate the many visitors to the Führer's headquarters. Crosswinds buffet the plane, but the pilot holds it steady, although the landing is rough.

"I'm afraid that landing was as bumpy as my meeting will be with the Führer," General Field Marshal Ernst Busch yells over the engines to his adjutant, Rittmeister Eberhard Breitenbuch. His aide nods but is nervous. Today he will kill Adolf Hitler and will probably be killed on the spot for the effort. A Mercedes sedan waits for them on the tarmac. The driver salutes and the two get into the auto for the long drive up the mountain to the Eagle's Nest.

"General Field Marshal Kleist will be in attendance as well. He has promised to support me in our mutual failures along the eastern front. He has disobeyed Hitler's orders by retreating, and I have lost 250,000 men by following them. Either way, we are in the man's crosshairs."

"I'm sure you can make him see the difficulty in either action, General. There are just too many Soviet troops."

"Stay close to me. I may need the intelligence reports that I brought."

"Of course, my general." Breitenbuch reaches into his pants pocket for the seven-millimeter Browning pistol to reassure him that his mission is not merely to carry his boss's briefcase to a meeting.

The car arrives at the guardhouse, a steel pipe barrier across the road. It is manned and guarded by four Waffen SS soldiers with machine guns. The two promptly exit the car and stride toward the checkpoint. A soldier approaches them.

"I am sorry. We have a new directive. No aides, attachés, or assistants are allowed in meetings." Busch looks at Breitenbuch, who is clearly surprised and dismayed.

"On whose authority?" Busch inquires in a commanding tone.

"The Führer's."

"But this man is essential to my presentation to the Führer!"

"I told you, no aides, on the Führer's orders. What further authority do you need?"

Breitenbuch feels the gun with his hand, deflated. "It is fine, my General, I'll wait here at the plaza. It is a beautiful day after all. Good luck in the meeting." He takes out a cigarette from his other pocket. His hand is shaking.

Adolph Hitler is in a rage. From a low monotone, his voice rises into a ringing tenor harangue. It is the voice that has mesmerized Germany since 1930, reaching its zenith at the Nuremberg Rally in 1938. The war has taken a toll on the man; just four short years earlier, Germany's empire stretched across Europe, from the Atlantic Ocean to the gates of Moscow, from Norway to North Africa. Now it is in full retreat in the Soviet Union and the invasion of Fortress Europe by the Allies is imminent. Soon Germany will be fighting on two fronts and Hitler knows it. He stares down at the map of Eastern Europe, his eyes dark pits of emptiness; his left hand trembles, rumored to be the byproduct of syphilis contracted from a prostitute early in his troubled youth.

"Cowards! You are all cowards. None of my generals can fight!"

"But my Führer, my men have fought well; as well as can be expected under the circumstances. The Russian forces are greater than we expected, far greater. Our intelligence estimates well over 2,500,000 men." General Busch's face breaks out in beads of sweat. He tries to loosen his tight collar. "I have already lost far too many men."

"Their army is made up of inferiors: Bolsheviks, Asian mongrels and slaves. Our men are of Aryan blood and far superior, if you would only lead them."

"Führer, I have no more men to lead. We have no choice but to retreat. Their army, whatever it might be, has re-taken Odessa and Sevastopol."

"There will be no retreat! How many times must I state that? Every German must die in his place for the Fatherland! No ground can be lost."

The generals assembled around the table look at one another and at Busch. They feel for him. Some shake their heads, aware that their fearless leader is too busy concentrating on the map in front of him. One sighs, another coughs, tired of having to listen yet again to the rants of this "Austrian corporal."

General Kleist speaks up. "Sir, if General Busch and I are allowed to retreat behind the Dnieper River, and we bring in Manstein's Panzers from the north, we can regroup, and then hold them."

"Hold them? What about taking back the land we have lost? We need the Caucasus' oil fields to fuel our tanks and trucks!"

"Führer, I do not think that is possible. They have too many soldiers. We have less than 400,000 fit men remaining on the front. The best we can hope for is to keep the ground we have left."

"Is that so? Then I am relieving you and Busch of your commands."

"Sir?"

"You heard me. I am placing Field Marshals Schörner and Model in charge of your respective forces. Now get out."

Kleist and Busch look at each other. They click their boots in unison, issue a "Heil Hitler," crisply turn around and head for the door.

"What are you going to do now?" Busch asks of his fellow general once outside the room.

"I guess I'll go home to my estate and write my memoirs."

The meeting continues. The Führer is growing weary. "Brigadeführer Schellenberg, what is your report?"

"Führer, we believe that our movements in the east were compromised. The Russians seemed to know our plans in advance. We would move to their flank, and it was already reinforced. They were receiving information from our front lines."

"Then find these traitors and eliminate them! Is that not a simple enough solution?"

"Indeed. We found three who were instrumental in our loss of Odessa. They were members of the Black Orchestra. We executed them summarily."

"Why didn't Canaris know of this? He is in charge of military intelligence."

"He should have but it is a gray area, my Führer. I can tell you he took it upon himself to execute one of my prisoners. That person was also a member of that organization."

"Canaris did that? I no longer trust Canaris or the Abwehr's effectiveness. He has opposed my policies from the beginning. What do you suggest, Schellenberg?"

"Führer, I would streamline our intelligence gathering."

"How?"

"Abolish the Abwehr; merge it into the SD. Eliminate the gray areas."

"I will consider it," Germany's leader says in a distracted tone, looking back at the map of Russia.

Schellenberg smiles. "Yes, my Führer. I should like to put my name forward to head the new organization."

"Hmmm. Give me a detailed report, a plan on how to accomplish it."

"Immediately, sir!" Schellenberg clicks his heels.

Hitler looks up from the table full of maps. "We needed the oil from southern Russia. And now it is lost." He walks toward the large picture window with an awkward gait. The majestic view showcases the Bavarian Alps, and in the far distance, the home of his birth: Austria. He looks at the magnificent scenery and knows it all may soon be lost. He speaks with a voice barely audible but rising, just as in speeches past.

"I have dedicated my whole life to the resurrection of Germany, to its Aryan purity, to our ultimate victory. I have given myself to the Fatherland with every fiber of my being! I have created Lebensraum for our people. Now, because of cowardice, betrayal, and a lack of iron will, that empire may be lost!"

Hitler is silent, peering out at the vast expanse of the Alps in front of him. His voice lowers. "We are finished here. Leave me." The tired man walks slowly to an overstuffed chair and drops into it, his hand trembling. He pulls out a handkerchief and wipes the beads of sweat from his face. He closes his eyes and thinks of a railway coach at Compiegne, France in 1940, the day when the French were humiliated by Germany and forced to sign an armistice that handed over one third of their country to him. And the rest would be a puppet state of Germany. A meager smile of remembrance breaks across his face.

Chapter Nine

USS General O. H. Ernst
The Atlantic Ocean

Father Jonathan Strauss heaves his breakfast into a bucket. Midway through a smooth sailing across the Atlantic toward Naples, Italy, a violent storm has hit. The 500-foot troopship carries over 3,000 fresh soldiers for the 36th Infantry Division and more than twenty new OSS operatives; it is rolling and dipping violently. Its top speed of seventeen knots has been reduced to a submarine friendly ten knots. Strauss's cabin is generous compared to the four-bunk-high accommodations for the average GI. The OSS personnel have their own cabins, but other than meals in the mess hall, they are not to mingle with the soldiers. There is a knock on the door.

"Come in and kill me, please!" Strauss looks up and sees Jack Lawrence, then turns back to the bucket, and heaves again.

"I see you haven't gotten your sea legs yet." Lawrence steadies himself by grabbing onto a towel bar at a small sink. The ship sways from left to right and back again.

"I really don't want them if this is what the sea is like..." Strauss coughs up the last of his breakfast, and then begins the dry heaves.

"Maybe you shouldn't have eaten breakfast," Lawrence says reaching for a towel that he can wet for his charge.

"I was hungry. I love breakfast, but what they serve here is anything but."

"You don't like oatmeal?"

Another dry heave. Strauss feels like he is going to throw up his stomach. Then the retching subsides, and he breathes heavily. Lawrence hands him a cold, wet towel. Wiping his face, Strauss decides he might just live.

"You had to cross the ocean before when you came to America. Did you get sick?"

"No. It was summer, and the water was like glass. And it was a grand ship, the *Europa*, not a little pig boat like this!"

"You're not very grateful. You have your own cabin with a sink. Anyway, only five more days until we get to Naples. Did you bring any reading material?"

"Yes, and it's a good thing, stuck on this boat. I brought *A Farewell to Arms* and a *Tale of Two Cities*, my Bible and Breviary."

"It's a nine-day trip, not a month, Strauss."

"I might have some time while I'm doing espionage work in Europe," Strauss says smirking.

"I doubt that. If you feel up to it, let's discuss your assignment." Lawrence sits down on the unmade bed, one that Strauss has found quite comfortable, given that the ship and mattress are less than a year old.

"My assignment? My assignment should be a simple parish priest at St. Patrick's."

"We're way past that, aren't we? Let me be frank with you Strauss. I was against your being assigned to this job. I don't think your heart is in it."

"How did you guess?"

"I think you're too old, too tired, and probably still too German."

"What's that supposed to mean, Lawrence?"

"Maybe you'll really want to see Hitler killed."

"I really don't care if you want to know the truth. I'm an American now. He's Germany's problem, not mine. I should be attending to my flock at St. Patrick's. At least the cooks there know how to make a proper breakfast."

"You'll have a new flock in a few days…the men on this ship. They're reinforcements for the beachhead at Anzio."

Strauss is perplexed at the statement. "I remember reading about that invasion, but it was back in January. It's May."

"Correct, the entire operation has been FUBAR'd from the start. They even replaced the commanding general, a guy named Lucas, and sent him back to the States. From the hills above the godforsaken beach, which is more like a swamp, the Germans have pounded us relentlessly." Lawrence shakes his head in dismay. "We landed too few men in the wrong location. But now, with better weather, we're building up our reserves and a breakout is planned."

"Breakout to where?"

"Rome, where you've been assigned. But first you get to join in the fighting as a chaplain. I'm sure you'll be plenty busy, administering that last blessing."

"It's called Extreme Unction, the Last Rites." Strauss lifts his hands toward heaven. "Oh, dear God, is there never an end to the killing?"

"Not until the Nazis are defeated, and right now there are a whole lot of them left in Italy."

"I need holy oil to perform the rite. I didn't plan on being a chaplain."

"Don't worry, Father, I brought you a large bottle. A priest is the perfect cover for an OSS agent, which is now what you are. But we're shorthanded for chaplains. A lot of them have been killed; the 3rd Infantry Division and the 36th, the one that these soldiers are a part of, were hit particularly hard and lost the two they had, plus a rabbi." Lawrence's voice is matter of fact, with no emotion.

"Great. Now I'm chaplain too."

"And a courier. I have some plastic explosives for you to deliver to Rome."

"A chaplain, a pack-horse. How am I supposed to get to Stauffenberg and stop him from killing Hitler if I'm busy doing all these other jobs?"

"Once we liberate Rome, and you report to Archbishop Galloway, you'll be back to your main mission."

"But he's the Papal Nuncio. What does he know about my mission or any of this? Isn't he just my cover?" Strauss is confused.

"No. Galloway's in the OSS, too."

Chapter Ten

The Bendlerblock
Reserve Army Headquarters
Berlin, Germany

"General Fromm will see you now." The secretary with a round pale face, pulled back hair, and white blouse buttoned to the neck and adorned with a service medal bearing a swastika, nods to Claus von Stauffenberg. She can't help noticing his eye patch, and the missing hand. She does her best not to seem alarmed, but it shows.

"Thank you. Have a good day," Stauffenberg stands, clicking his heels ever so slightly. He goes through the door she holds open. The office is well-suited for the head of the Reserve Army, forces kept in reserve should they be needed at any front that is in trouble, but more importantly to restore order at home in the event of a Jewish or conscripted labor uprising.

General Friedrich Fromm sits at his large wooden desk shuffling papers. Behind him, above a massive credenza, hangs a tapestry of *Tristan and Isolde* showing Isolde collapsing alongside her recently dead lover, Tristan. It is all very Wagnerian. Stauffenberg looks to a side wall and there is a large portrait of the Führer, which commands the room. On the other side of the office are large windows, heavily draped, looking down into the courtyard used for the assembly of the Reserve Army. Fromm looks up, and then stands, peering at his guest. The commander of the Reserve Army is tall at six-foot-three. His face is fat with a bulbous nose, and a protruding double chin. There is a decided midriff paunch. The wars have taken a toll on him. In front of him stands the man that many have recommended as his new chief of staff.

"Sieg Heil!" Fromm exclaims in a strong salute.

Stauffenberg hesitates, and then slowly raises his right arm showing only a sleeve with no hand to complete the anatomy. He quietly responds: "Sieg Heil, General." He is ramrod straight, six-foot-one in height. Over his perfectly combed brown hair is an angled silk sash holding the black patch that covers his eye. He clicks his heels: a true Prussian officer. Fromm is impressed, and having been told of his visitor's battle scars, shows no emotion.

"Lieutenant Colonel, a lot of influential people have been recommending you for a position that I need to fill. You obviously have served your country well, but forgive me, are you up to this task? It involves carrying a briefcase." Fromm looks at the officer's uniform.

"Herr General, I think before my accident I possessed many more digits than I needed."

Fromm laughs. "Well said; all right then, I appoint you my new chief of staff. And you are hereby promoted to the rank of full colonel. You will start Monday. My assistant will show you where your office is. Not as grand as this, but still comfortable."

"I'm used to sleeping in tents. I'm sure it will be quite suitable. What are my responsibilities?"

"Primarily, you will deliver reports prepared by me to the Führer. That will either be at the Berghof, which gives me altitude sickness, or at the Wolf's Lair, a Godforsaken place in East Prussia. The mosquitoes there are as big as dragonflies, and there are lots of them. You can slice the air with a knife, it is so humid. Why our great leader chose that place, I'll never know. But then, I can't figure him out most of the time, if you get my drift."

Stauffenberg understands. He nods. "Indeed, I do. I appreciate the opportunity to be in the presence of my Führer. I will not let you down."

"Fine, then we understand each other. When you report to him, be brief. He doesn't like, or have time for, a lot of details about the Reserve Army. He is too busy fighting a war with Russia." Fromm returns to his desk stacked with official folders and letters. "You are dismissed," he says without looking up.

Claus von Stauffenberg salutes, clicks his heels, and turns. As he leaves the spacious office, he places his cap on his head and nods in satisfaction.

Part II

ITALY

Chapter Eleven

JUNE 2, 1944
142nd Infantry Regiment
Route 6, near Cisterna
48 KM south of Rome

A hint of daylight breaks over the horizon.
"Lieutenant, wake up; time to get moving."
Lieutenant Chaplain Jonathan Strauss rolls over with a groan. "What time is it?"
"Zero six hundred hours, sir. We got to sleep in late."
"We just stopped marching at one hundred hours. Ohhh, my knees are killing me!"
"My colonel talked to the big boss, General Truscott. Says there's a lot of Germans up ahead. He told me to give you a rifle."
"A rifle? I'm a chaplain. And who are you, corporal?"
"Sorry, sir. I'm Billy McClain. The colonel assigned me to you. As your aide to help you carry the oil, communion. To protect you. And you might need the gun for purely defensive purposes."
"Where are you from, Billy? You a Catholic?"
"Texas, and yes, Father I am. I went to St. Joseph's High School in Fort Worth. That's where I'm from."
"Lots of Texas boys in this regiment." Strauss has gotten up and is stomping his feet to shake off the cold and limber up his legs for whatever lies ahead.

"Sir, we're all from Texas and Oklahoma. The 36th is called the Lone Star Division. Where are you from?"

"New York City. And I wish I were there right now. Ever hear of St. Patrick's Cathedral?"

"Oh, yes! My parents took me to New York when I was twelve. Sure is a big city; too big for me."

Strauss looks hard at the young face under the too big helmet. "How old are you, Billy?"

"I'm nineteen now, sir. I enlisted a year and a half ago. I've been in Italy the whole time; landed at Salerno last September. Then we went into the mountains, captured Mount Maggiore, and fought at the Gari River. The Gari was bad! We've had lots of casualties. Two regiments, the 141st and 143rd, were almost wiped out. I guess I was pretty lucky. It's good that we got reinforcements last week."

"You enlisted at seventeen, son?" Strauss looks at the face of his new helper. It is hardened and older than it should be.

"Yes, Father. Right after I graduated from high school."

"But why?"

"When the Japs bombed Pearl Harbor, a lot of my buddies enlisted, and now we were at war. I wanted to do my part, but I was too young, so I lied about my age. I thought I'd be going to the Pacific, but I got sent here to fight Hitler. He's big buddies with the Japs, so it's okay with me."

"Aren't you scared?" Strauss begins to see his younger self in the young corporal.

"I was at first, but my sergeant told me to keep my head down and shoot back. That was good advice. Shooting back made me forget about my fear. I wasn't just being shot at, I was giving them some of their own medicine."

"Come to think of it I joined the army when I was eighteen. But I don't mind telling you, I'm scared right now."

"I suppose you get used to it. And I think I've killed at least fifteen Jerry's. I'm gonna get a lot more, maybe get a me a medal, too."

"Really? A medal. And that will make it all worthwhile?"

"Maybe. It would be nice, but I don't want a Purple Heart, that's for sure."

"Do you pray?"

"Yeah, sure. Not as much as I should, but whenever the fighting starts, I promise God that if I ever get out of this mess alive, I'll go to church every Sunday. My Mom gave me a rosary, too, but I've hardly had any time to say it. Sorry, Father."

"That's okay. I'm sure you've been pretty busy."

"Were you in the first war? Did you fight with General Pershing?"

"No. I was in the war, but I was a German soldier. I thought I was done with war, but here I am. Look, I have more for you to carry than holy oil and wafers. Carry this pack, if you will. It's heavy. We better get going. I need to get to Rome."

"What is it?"

"Bad stuff. Plastic explosives. So be very careful, Corporal Billy McClain."

"Plastic explosives. Why is a priest carrying this shit? Sorry…"

"I have no idea, Billy. I have to deliver it to someone in Rome."

The two comrades march together with their fellow soldiers, part of the 125th Battalion, 955 combat ready troops. Strauss welcomes his new charge, notwithstanding his head full of idealistic glory.

"Sir, a German soldier?"

"Let's get going, son."

Chapter Twelve

Convent of the Sisters of the Passion of Our Lord
Paris, France

The chapel is large for a convent, but there had been over 100 sisters residing there before the war. Now novices are few and the older sisters are steadily dying; they are heartsick at seeing their beloved France occupied by a hated foreign power. They no longer pray for mankind, but for an end to Nazi tyranny.

It is early evening and the last strains of daylight filter though the milky glass. The priceless stained-glass windows have been removed and stored to protect them from what the sisters know might eventually come: Allied bombs.

Colonel Claude Olivier, codenamed "Jade Amicol" by MI6, sits in the confessional waiting for an important penitent. It has been a hot day in Paris particularly for May, and the old church is warm. He wipes his brow; the confines of the small chamber are stuffy and smell of incense. A French citizen, he works for British intelligence and reports every night via transmitter to his bosses at Blenheim Palace in London. He is the vital link of the French Resistance movement to the Allies. In return, he knows almost as much as anyone about Allied plans and their internal politics and bickering.

Olivier hears the right door of the confessional open and shut. He slides open the small door exposing a grillage and semi-transparent silk screen. He says nothing.

"Bless me, Father, for I have sinned."

The "confessor" recognizes the voice immediately. The English is perfect but carries with it a noticeable German accent.

"My friend, it is so good to hear your voice again. I have been worried about you."

"I would think you would have more important things to worry about."

"There are rumors that the Black Orchestra is not long for this world."

"Is anything, or anyone, long for this world?"

"I suppose not in these times. And I'm sure your trip here was difficult. I wasn't sure if I would even see you."

"Let's leave these claustrophobic chambers and go to the convent."

"Good idea. Sister Agnes has prepared a meal for us."

"Wonderful. I'd love some French wine."

"Everything is rationed, but we do have plenty of that. I think she has roasted a hen. A rare treat, but you are a special guest."

Admiral Wilhelm Canaris gets up and opens the confessional door. Jade Amicol has done the same and the two shake hands and hug.

"It is good to see you, my friend. Now let's get some dinner."

Canaris follows Colonel Olivier from the sanctuary to a side door into a large room with high ceilings and generous windows. In the 18th century, the convent had been a military hospital where Napoleon's troops recovered. Now the space is full of beds, chairs, makeshift walls, and curtain dividers. It is crowded with people. Canaris looks at men wearing prayer shawls and black hats under which flow dark ringlets of curls. Little boys wear yarmulkes and play with pretty girls in simple sack dresses. Women tend to small stoves heating beet soup, and tables have metal plates stacked with matzoh bread.

"I see the sisters have been busy saving souls," the Admiral comments.

"Yes, God's salvation from the Nazis, my friend. At least temporarily."

The dining room is simple: whitewashed walls interspersed with three high windows open to the evening air, in the center a rustic wooden table with benches. On a pedestal in the corner of the room is a too large statue of the Blessed Mother. Two nuns serve their important guests, moving from the kitchen to the table in silence, speaking only when necessary in hushed tones. Wilhelm Canaris is finishing his last bite of apple pie.

"Sister Agnes, this meal was delicious."

"I'm a collaborator; I should burn in hell." Sister frowns clearing the empty plates from the table. The other nun quietly pours more wine into Canaris's glass, confused at the comment.

"On the contrary, Sister, I'm the collaborator." He takes a drink of the wine. "This is excellent. A Beaujolais?"

"What do you Germans know of wine? But yes, it is. I'll still burn in hell for helping you."

Canaris laughs. "Mother Superior, you've already earned your way into heaven. Look at all the people you have saved." He nods toward the great hall full of Jewish refugees.

"Yes, saved from the Nazi pigs. Saved from people like you!"

Canaris looks at Jade Amicol. "I thought you said I was a special guest?"

Amicol shrugs and laughs.

"Sister, you judge me too harshly. I have done what I can, dear woman." He takes a full swallow of the wine.

"I don't believe you." Sister picks up the last of the dishes.

The Colonel is enjoying the repartee between his friend and the nun, but realizes it is time to get down to business. "Admiral, how can I help you today?"

The nuns leave the room; they want no part of spying and intrigue. Canaris leans in toward Jade. "When is the invasion going to happen and where?"

"My friend, you know I cannot tell you that, even though you are a collaborator. The Brits have told me not to trust you; you are probably a double agent. I do not think that is true, but it is not up to me to decide such things."

Canaris passes over the veiled accusation. "We need more time. The invasion must be put off until we can assassinate the Führer."

"Unfortunately, your timetable is not even a factor in the Allies' thinking. But I can tell you this. The tides are. And as to the place, a good spy would know that nothing is obvious. It is always the opposite."

"Fine. I guess I'll just have to decipher your riddles. Tell me, has their attitude changed?"

"Not officially to be sure. The English realize they are beholden to the Americans. If it weren't for them, and with a little help from the Empire of Japan, the English would be an occupied territory right now. And Roosevelt does not want to see America back over in Europe in twenty or thirty years to settle our petty disputes again. Germany will be brought to its knees once more, I'm sorry to say."

Canaris responds in a low voice, almost hissing. "And then it will be the Treaty of Versailles all over again!"

"I am sorry, but you have brought this upon yourself."

"No, Herr Hitler has brought it upon us all. We should never have invaded Poland."

"Then you should never have elected Hitler in the first place."

"Don't the Allies realize how many lives can be saved if peace is secured before the invasion?"

"Calm yourself, Wilhelm. I am just telling you what I know. But unofficially, and I heard this from Ernest Bevin, the Labor Secretary. He's a staunch anti-Communist, and he believes that Churchill privately disagrees with Roosevelt's policy of unconditional surrender. In fact, Churchill has even reviewed several plans to kill your boss."

"Really. What plans?"

"The SOE, the Special Operations Executive, has considered a few. The first was bombing Hitler's private train. But this was dismissed because they can never pinpoint when it might run or where it might be headed. Plus there are dummy trains that are the same as the Führer's to cause confusion. The second idea was to poison the water on board his train. But that would require someone on the inside, a member of the staff. Since everyone is handpicked from the Führer's personal bodyguard unit that was not an option. The last idea, the one approved by Churchill, is to have two British commandos parachute in near the Berghof. Hitler takes a private walk every morning in an unprotected area near some woods. The Brits would be dressed as German mountain troops and would be trained snipers. They call it 'Operation Foxley.'"

"That is encouraging news. When will they attempt this shooting?"

"The plan has been set aside for now."

"But why?"

"Because the British High Command has decided that Hitler is now more beneficial to the Allies than a detriment. He is their worst general, after all."

"I am disappointed to hear that, but we are developing our own plans. It will be soon; we just need a little more time."

"The British have heard about your plans since 1939. They do not think anyone is truly serious. He's still alive, isn't he?"

"To show you how serious we are, I need four to five kilos of British-made plastic explosives and detonators. Can you get them for me?" Canaris drinks the last of his wine.

"I'll have it on the next submarine with supplies for the Resistance. I'll make sure we get it to your people in Amsterdam."

"Good. We have someone who will be in his presence frequently."

"And soon, I hope."

"Tell the Brits we can get this done. Then they have to agree to peace."

"My friend, you want guarantees from the Allies before you have done anything yourselves. Do something: kill your leader, form a new government without any true Nazis, and then sue for peace. Unconditional surrender may become a conditional surrender. What are the Allies going to say, 'No' and keep fighting?"

"I understand. Anyway, I'm going to the coast to see what the Reich has in store for the Allies."

"I can arrange one of our people to get you there."

"That will not be necessary; I have a few friends in high places. You forget we are in French Germany now."

"How can I forget? Godspeed, my friend."

From the kitchen Sister Agnes looks to the two men in earnest discussion. She looks heavenward and makes the sign of the cross.

Chapter Thirteen

142nd Infantry Regiment
Outskirts of Velletri
35 KM from Rome

Strauss and McClain continue to march, ever mindful of snipers in surrounding buildings that line Route 6. Between the hamlets are large fields on either side from which a German counterattack could come at any moment. They know what is up ahead. They hear the increasing sound of mortar rounds and gunfire. Next, the roar of 88's firing. Their commander shouts: "Flank to right. Able, Baker, and Charlie Company move it! Stay low in the ditch by the road! The town of Velletri is heavily defended."

"I need to get up there. Boys are probably dying."

"All due respect, sir, I think you'll have plenty to do right here."

"I suppose you're right..."

The noise of machine gun and mortar fire become deafening. McClain is behind Strauss who is doing his best to keep up with the troops ahead of him.

Billy yells: "Father, faster! We need to get to that ditch!"

"Sorry, I'm not twenty-one anymore!" Strauss's knees hurt and he's panting heavily. Billy sees a potato masher grenade arcing toward them. He runs up to Strauss and jumps on top of him, knocking him flat into the ground. The mortar explodes, just feet past them. McClain thinks about the plastic explosives he is carrying and shudders.

Fortunately, the backpack is harnessed across the front of his body. Strauss can barely breathe, the wind knocked out of him, and the weight of his young, fully armed bodyguard is crushing.

"Billy, please get off of me!"

"Sorry, Father. I saw the grenade coming at you."

"I guess you're my new guardian angel!"

"If you wouldn't mind carrying this, I might be able to protect you better." Billy removes the satchel and hands it to Strauss.

"Certainly. I shouldn't have asked you to carry it. You have better things to do."

"Father, up there! One of our guys is down. Take care of him. I'll cover you!"

"Right. I'll be right back."

McClain stands up and starts firing at the enemy as he moves in front of Strauss. The priest is amazed at the young man's bravery as he runs toward the dying soldier, protected by Billy's enfilade at the Nazis, who are firing from the village. He turns to look back at Billy; he is shooting off rounds like a demon. The incoming fire stops, and Strauss tends to the fallen soldier. He reaches into his pack for the sacramental oil and his hand is trembling as he makes the sign of the cross on the man's forehead. He realizes that there are tears in his eyes. "Medic! I need a medic!" Strauss wipes his face and looks back toward his young corporal. He is lying low in a ditch and reloading, then crouching making his way further down the culvert. He stands up and begins firing anew at another building, bullets flashing from its windows. Strauss runs in the same direction, finds another wounded soldier, this one breathing and holding his arm.

"Medic, man down!" Strauss cries. He makes the sign of the cross over him. "You'll be all right son, just stay still." Not five feet farther, another soldier. This time he is dead, his mid-section torn in two. "Oh God! My God!" Strauss makes the sign of the cross with the oil, not knowing what religion the young man is. It continues for what seems like an eternity. Finally, it is over. Strauss looks around for Billy

McClain. In the haze of smoke, he is nowhere to be found. Then he sees his protector, all five-foot-seven inches, walking toward him. His face is filthy from the battle, but he appears to be unhurt.

"Billy, I was worried sick. Are you okay?"

"Yeah, Father, sure. I'm good. You?"

"Yes, but so many died."

"Father, I'll tell you this, those Krauts are tough customers. But we took the town. It should be easy from here on in to Rome. I bet we get a hero's welcome; maybe I'll meet a nice Italian girl, she'll kiss me, and we'll have some wine."

"You deserve it, son, you deserve it. And I'm going to recommend you for that medal."

"Really, Father? Gee, that'd be swell!"

The 142nd Regiment and the rest of the liberating army move along toward Rome. Since Velletri, resistance has been sporadic, almost non-existent. In the small villages along the road, the Americans are cheered as liberators; Italian flags and white handkerchiefs are waved. The late afternoon sun warms the faces of the troops, who are indeed kissed by the young women. Strauss smiles and shakes hands, but his gait slows as the day wears on. His knees are on fire. Billy notices the limp.

"Father, let me see if I can flag down a jeep or a truck so you can ride. You're a chaplain; you should be riding."

"It's okay, Billy, I like walking with you. I'm sure we will be stopping soon. I saw the quartermaster trucks pulling ahead. They're going to get set up for chow. We won't be getting to Rome today, or tomorrow. The last sign I saw said we are still a way out. Look, up ahead some buildings. I'll ask someone there."

"All due respect, Father, they don't speaka da English…"

"I know but I used to speak Italian. I'm a little rusty, but you never forget."

"How come you speak Italian? And you never told me about being in the German army even though you're American."

"Well, Billy, it's like this. I was born in Germany and raised there. I was eighteen when I decided to join the army. I was of Prussian descent, from Bavaria. Ever heard of Bavaria?"

"No, sir."

"It's not important. Anyway, all Prussians join the military. All the great German generals were, or are, Prussian. My family, my father in particular, expected it of me. I hated it, but when the Great War started in 1914, I was stuck. Like you, I was lucky and made it through."

"What was it like?"

"As bad as this, I can assure you."

"So, if you're a German how come you know how to speak Italian?"

"My father was a diplomat and was assigned to the German embassy in Rome for three years, from 1910 to 1913. I learned the language."

"And now you're an American?"

"Yes, I became a citizen in 1936, once I became a priest. Now, tell me all about Fort Worth. What's it like?"

They enter the hamlet, and it is strangely quiet, but with their animated conversation and lowered rifles, they do not notice. Nor do many of the other troops, tired from a long day of fighting and marching. The main route into Rome narrows as the town closes in. The column of troops tighten to seven, eight abreast.

"Where's the welcoming committee?" Strauss jokes. Billy warily looks up at a second-floor window and freezes.

Rifles and machine guns explode like Chinese fireworks on the Fourth of July. Soldiers fall all around amongst screams and orders given too late. Strauss drops to the ground and brings his rifle around. He looks above. Gunfire is coming from the windows. He shoots like he saw Billy do earlier. He turns to the other side of the street and fires at any and all windows. Other soldiers, uninjured, use their Thompson submachine guns to rake the buildings with a barrage of firepower. Other men run into the buildings and shots can be heard along with cursed epithets of hate and death. Slowly the noise subsides; only moaning can be heard, along with pleas for God and mother. Strauss drops his rifle and begins to move to the wounded. Then he remembers Billy. He looks to his left where his guardian angel was standing. There is nothing but a bloody jacket covering the hulk of a young boy. He turns it over. Blood is oozing from Corporal McClain's mouth.

"Billy, Billy! Medic! Medic! Oh God, Billy stay with me." Strauss, hands shaking, reaches into his pocket for the holy oil blessed by a bishop, pulls the cork from the bottle and spills too much onto his hand. He applies the oil to Billy's forehead, the body quivering, in the final throes of life, and makes the sign of the cross with the oil. "Per istam sanctan unctionem, et suam piisiman misericordiam, ut venae tibi Dominus quidquid peccasti." Strauss looks around and sees a medic: "Medic, now. Hurry!"

A young man makes his way over, shoulders carrying satchels of bandages, splints and syringes of morphine. He crouches down. "Soldier, stay with me!"

Billy's eyes look over at Father Strauss and a smile breaks out. Strauss hears the words "Thank you" whispered. Then the eyes are still.

"Oh, dear God! Dear God. Billy, do not die on me!" Tears run down Strauss's cheeks and he lowers himself to Billy's face. Strauss kisses him on his anointed forehead. Then he breaks down in sobs, his body shaking.

"Come on, Father, there are others. Many others." The priest gets up and begins to follow the medic across the bodies of his fallen comrades. He suddenly stops, turns around and returns to his young friend. Strauss reaches down and begins searching through pockets. After searching in vain in innumerable hiding places, he finds it: Billy's rosary. He clutches it into his hand and moves on.

Chapter Fourteen

Hotel René Mathilde
Bayeux, France

Two BMW R-75 motorcycles with sidecars roar down the Rue Larcher, followed by a black Mercedes open-air car. There is one sole occupant in the backseat, an officer of high rank. It, in turn, is followed by another black car, occupied by four officers of lower station. The motorcade slows to a stop in front of the modest hotel's courtyard.

Standing in the small plaza of the hotel, stomach full of a breakfast of fresh farm eggs, croissants and country sausage, the immaculately dressed Admiral Wilhelm Canaris salutes toward the car. He is wearing a short-waisted green jacket today, brown riding pants, and polished brown boots. He is ready for a tour of the beaches of France.

"You make quite an entry, Field Marshal."

"It is important for the citizens to see who, my friend, is in charge." General Field Marshal Johannes Erwin Rommel touches his officer's cap with his baton of office in salute to the chief of the Abwehr. He is dressed in his full uniform, Iron Cross and other decorations adorning his neck, with gold leaves on both lapels. The German Eagle holding a swastika covers his right breast. Canaris steps onto the running board and inside to the comfortable leather seat next to Rommel.

"Herr Admiral, there is a storm coming. You'll need a topcoat."

"Yes, I see now it is quite windy. If you don't mind…"

"When we arrive at the beaches, I'll have one of my aides fetch one for you."

"I'm eager to see the progress on Fortress Europe."

"Don't get your hopes up, Wilhelm; much remains to be done. I've only been in charge since last November. The Czech and Polish laborers have been clumsy and slow; the soldiers are second-rate conscripts; the French Resistance sabotages us, and I'm woefully low on ammunition and supplies. Goebbels has told a tall tale. It is hardly Fortress Europe!"

The motorcade pulls away and heads toward the town of Vierville. Canaris slides the window closed between Rommel's driver and the backseat. The sound of the V-12 engine blocks out any discussion between the two men seated in back and the driver.

"My friend, have you given further consideration as to which side you will fight on?"

"I fight on the side of Germany, which you will be seeing shortly. I am a soldier and I do my duty. However, I can be persuaded that new leadership is necessary."

Canaris looks hard at Rommel. "Then are you with us, Erwin? We now have someone who will have access to the Führer."

"Who?"

"The less you know the better, but he is quite competent and has galvanized our group. Again, are you with us?"

"If Ludwig Beck is a part of the group and he becomes the new president, then yes, I will assist in any way."

Rommel and Canaris walk along the hillside above the beach at Vierville.

"You can see, Wilhelm, that I have placed fortifications all along the beach; I have tripled the number of mines; the beaches have barbed wire and tank barriers. Every several hundred meters, we have machine gun pillboxes for a devastating crossfire onto any troops that get to the beach, if they can even get out of their landing craft. And inland, we have steel spikes for any paratroopers."

"Impressive that you have done all this in just seven months."

"It has not been easy. But we must stop them here at the water's edge. If they gain a foothold, then I fear we are lost. I wanted all ten panzer divisions at my disposal here, close to the beaches. I got three. Von Rundstedt has three and is convinced they need to be fifty miles away. A lot of good they'll do there. The last four are in reserve and can only be released by the direct orders of the Führer. I have three tank divisions to defend over one hundred miles of coast and only one is positioned here at Normandy."

"A wise choice. All my intercepts indicate that the invasion will come at the Pas-de-Calais anyway. The Americans have massed the First Army under Patton in Kent, directly across the channel."

"I'm not so sure; it just seems too obvious to me. What else are you hearing?"

Canaris looks out to the sea and then across to the beaches. "There is much more chatter by the resistance. Most of it makes little sense, but I fear the invasion is imminent."

"Good, let them come. They will die by the thousands trying to get ashore."

"And if the Black Orchestra succeeds, we can negotiate an armistice with the Allies from a position of strength—their failed invasion and a new German leader."

"Let us only hope and pray. Now, if you do not mind, I need to get to Paris to shop for a birthday present for my wife. Then I'm headed to Stuttgart the day after tomorrow. My wife's birthday is June 6th."

"What if the invasion comes while you are away?"

"With the coming bad weather, I seriously think not."

Chapter Fifteen

U.S. Fifth Army
Via Appia Antica
Outskirts of Rome

The column made up the 36th Infantry Division, now joined by the 3rd Infantry Division, was over 20,000 troops, jamming the Via Appia Antica as they march triumphantly into Rome. It is June 4, 1944. Elsewhere in Europe, over 150,000 Allied soldiers are getting ready to board LSTs, LCVs, and every other vessel imaginable for the invasion of France at Normandy.

Lieutenant Chaplain Jonathan Strauss ignores the outstretched hands of the happy, tearful populace. Women come up and kiss him, but there is no response. All feeling, all emotion has been drained; he is not roused by the bands playing or the cheers of the Italian people, now freed from German oppression. He yearns to be home, far away from war, sitting quietly in his chambers in the rectory of St. Patrick's, reading his Breviary. But he has orders and will obey them. As his regiment moves off the road and into a small park, a faded and stained sign by the road reads: *Parco D. Scipioni*. Large tents are being set up. Strauss breaks from the ranks and pushes his way through to several officers talking. He removes his helmet.

"General Walker?"

The commander of the 36th Infantry Division looks at the interloping soldier, making note of the Lieutenant's bars on his jacket, and the backpack weighing the man down. "Lieutenant, I'm a little busy right now." Strauss lifts his helmet to the general so he can see the cross. "Oh, I'm sorry, Chaplain, what is it?"

"Sir, I'd like to be relieved of my duties."

"I'm sorry, Father…?"

"Strauss, sir, John Strauss."

"Father Strauss, we aren't done with this war yet. All of northern Italy is occupied by the Hun. Your services will be sorely needed."

Strauss reaches into his breast pocket and removes his orders and his identification as an OSS officer. General Walker peruses the papers. "I see. A priest in the OSS. Very clever."

"Sir, I'm no spy, I just have a job to do and someone to meet at the Vatican." Strauss realizes he has probably said too much.

"You didn't need to tell me that, Father, but as you have important spy business to attend to, you are relieved. And I'm very sorry about what happened back in that town. Sorry you had to shoot your rifle, but I hear you gave 'em hell. Good job."

"Thank you, sir; I lost a good friend."

"I seem to lose a good friend every day."

"I understand, sir."

"Godspeed, Father Strauss. I'll see you back in the States."

"Sir, I'm beginning to wonder just what Godspeed means." Strauss salutes and disappears into the crowd of soldiers and after a minute finds a local shopkeeper.

"Quale strada per il Vaticano, signore?"

St. Peter's Square is much bigger than how he remembered it as a young boy living in Rome for the first time. His knees burn with arthritis from the day's long march. Jonathan Strauss is stopped by Italians, clergy, and nuns who hug him and shake his hand. He has no idea where to go. Where does one find an American archbishop in Vatican City?

"Excuse me, but you look somewhat lost." A young priest in a traditional cassock stands in front of the confused cleric.

"I know where I am; I just don't know where to go from here. Are you American?"

"Yes, I sure am." He notices the cross on Strauss's helmet.

"Are you a priest also?" The young cleric cannot be more than twenty-three years old.

"Yes, I seem to be lost."

"Father, maybe I can help."

"And you're also an American. What are you doing here? Yesterday this was an occupied city." Strauss is perplexed.

"Yes, I came over here last summer for vacation and to take a few courses. I'm in the seminary. Then the Nazis occupied Rome early last September. I've been stuck here since then. Now, where do you need to go?"

"I need to see Archbishop Brendan Galloway."

"Follow me. I work for him; I'm his secretary."

Strauss shakes his head and looks heavenward. "Thank you," he whispers.

"Can I help you with that backpack?"

"No, I'd better take it the rest of the way."

Chapter Sixteen

Schneider Brauhaus
Munich, Germany

Three young recruits of the Black Orchestra are standing at a high-top table, drinking Hefeweizen. The "SB" beer hall is busy on this Friday night, and their conversations are drowned out by the Bavarian band playing on the stage. They are all students at the University of Munich. Until recently, they were members of The White Rose, a small student organization opposed to Hitler and the Nazis that distributes leaflets against the regime throughout the city, and throughout southern Germany. But these three have grown tired of the ineffectiveness of words. They have become part of the Black Orchestra, which intends to take action, and they are determined to do their part.

"It's all set. I'm going to do it tonight." The student takes a sip of his beer; his eyes are on fire.

"Jan, you're a fool. You can't go around shooting generals. It's suicide. And our superiors have not approved it." Martin can't believe what his friend is thinking.

"There's been a lot of activity at the military garrison. There is an apartment building across the road; I know a couple that live there. They said they will hide me. From the roof it will be a difficult shot, but I've been practicing. If I kill one of them, their command structure is bound to be disrupted. That makes it worthwhile: no, it makes it necessary. I'm tired of printing and distributing leaflets. And I can be hung for that just as easily as killing a Nazi officer."

"We'll all be hung, the whole cell, and tortured too!" Maria, fear written across her face, joins in the debate. She hates the Nazis but wants to live long enough to get her degree and perhaps teach. She wishes now that she had stayed in the White Rose.

"You're being overly dramatic. I'll escape across the roof down to the apartment. They have a secret room. Look, I've got to go. I'll see you in class tomorrow." Jan finishes his beer and looks at Martin. "Well?"

"Fine, I'll come along. I must be crazy, but someone has to show you how to jump across roofs!"

Maria looks at them. "I'll have none of this; I'm going to the country to visit my grandparents."

A light over the doorway is all that is necessary. Jan can see soldiers coming in and out the door to smoke cigarettes. But he is looking for an Iron Cross hanging from the collar of his prey. The evening is warm, and he wipes his face and eyes. He is having a hard time seeing through the long-range scope. His hands sweat on the wooden stock of the rifle.

"Dammit, why doesn't a general, even a major, take a break?"

"Do you have a clear shot?" Martin is crouching low beneath the parapet. He does not want to be spotted.

"Yes, as long as I can keep the sweat out of my eyes. Wait, oh yes! Finally, a general. He's under the light, it's a good shot. He's reaching for a cigarette. Get out of here, Martin. There's no use both of us getting caught."

"You don't have to twist my arm. I'll meet you at the Hofbräuhaus at 12:30 A.M. No one will notice us in a place that big."

"Got it. Now hurry! No telling how long I have this target." Jan looks into his sight and adjusts it slightly. "Now I've got you, you bastard!" he whispers as Martin runs across the roof, jumps across to the neighboring building and to the fire escape.

In a small apartment on the third floor of the building, an elderly man and woman are cleaning the supper dishes; she washes, he dries.

"It isn't safe…"

The husband replies: "We must do our part."

"Hiding Jews is one thing, but he's going to shoot a general! Why can't we just be left in peace?"

"Good. It will be one less Nazi."

"How do you know he'll be a Nazi? He might be a decorated, patriotic soldier."

"Shush, just clean the plates."

A shot rings out. The couple looks at one another. The woman goes to the window and opens it.

"Got you, you pig!" Jan gets up and hurries to catch up to Martin, barely making the leap across the buildings. He closes in on his friend as the steel ladder of the fire escape lowers to the platform below. Martin makes it down the steep flights of stairs and continues down to the alley; Jan sees the open window and in an instant is inside the tidy, comfortable apartment.

"I am sorry for the trouble. Thank you for hiding me." Jan says breathing heavily.

"Certainly, Jan. Here, help with this." The old man grabs one side of a large armoire and the boy grabs the other, moving it away from the wall. Behind there is an opening to what had been a small bedroom, its proper entrance removed years ago to provide refuge for enemies of the Reich. The boy goes through the small opening and Jan crouches down to grab the leg of the furniture. Pulling with all his might, and with the elderly couple pushing against the heavy piece, they succeed in moving it back against the wall.

The old couple looks at each other as they hear heavy footsteps of jackboots on the stairwell outside the apartment. They get louder as they proceed down the hallway. Then there is a loud banging on the door. "Open up or we will break down the door!"

The old man opens it slowly and peers out at four SS troopers. The first one, a sturmführer, pushes the door open and the old man almost falls. "What do you want? We were just finishing our meal."

"Shut up!"

"We have done nothing." The comment is ignored as the soldiers ransack the apartment, opening doors, looking in the bedrooms and bathroom. The captain looks around the room. The window is open, the curtains fluttering in the warm night air. He sees the fire escape stairs extended and smiles.

The old man looks at the captain and then at his wife in a look of admonishment and fear. "Oh, Helga…"

The sturmführer removes his Luger from its holster. No aiming is necessary; both collaborators are no more than five feet away. Four shots ring out. The captain yells an order, and the search continues. In the hiding space behind the armoire, Jan tries not to cry, or more importantly, to cry out.

Chapter Seventeen

The Papal Gardens
Vatican City

Despite the war, the grounds of Vatican City are as beautiful as ever. Each tree, every shrub, each blade of grass has been perfectly manicured and trimmed. It is as if a small piece of heaven exists within the hell that is now Europe. Even now, the German Army is massed just north of the City along the Trasimene Line, retreating but still deadly with over 60,000 soldiers. A counterattack might begin at any moment. Rome cannot be surrendered so easily.

The morning of June 6, 1944 is bright and clear, and it promises to be a beautiful day in liberated Rome. Father Strauss and Archbishop Brendan Galloway walk along the manicured, brown gravel path.

"I feel much better after that long bath and the wonderful meal, Archbishop. And I'm more at home in this new cassock than that uniform. It's beautiful; is it silk?"

"It's just very fine Italian wool with cashmere. Priests are all spoiled here in Rome. We're looked upon as minor gods, I'm afraid. We get special treatment."

"Why is there red piping, Archbishop?"

"Lieutenant, please call me Brendan, or at least major. You can dispense with the religious titles. Red piping here means the same as in the States. It's the mark of a monsignor. So I guess congratulations are in order."

"Arch...I mean, ah, Major, what do you mean?"

"It means you are a monsignor now."

"Me? I'm not even a very good priest."

"Let God be the judge of that. The Italian police, the Gestapo and the SS don't like to question or challenge priests, and the higher up you are, the more likely they'll be to just wave you through checkpoints. No one will suspect a priest is a spy, although I understand you deny that. Pardon the expression, but don't bullshit me, John."

"Maybe I did deny it to that fellow Gardner at the War Department. I was a lousy soldier, so they took me off the front lines and said I could either become a spy or be shot for desertion. Once I got into the routine, it wasn't so bad. I got to stay in nice hotels, have great meals; I even had an expense account. And because I spoke Italian, I was sent to Milan, Bologna, even a month in Venice. It was a pretty cushy job, except that..."

"Except that you had to do some pretty nasty things. I read the file."

"I'm sure a lot of it is bullshit, too. Let's just leave it that. I simply reported on Italian arms production."

"Hopefully, you remember a few of the things you learned. I must say your assignment is dicey. You have to go right into the belly of the beast if we can find a way."

"I know, and they start out by making me carry twenty pounds of plastic explosive from Anzio Beach to here. I should already be dead."

"I understand you took the fighting pretty hard. Lost your orderly. Still having a tough time with battle?"

"That young man, just nineteen, was assigned to look after me. That was all wrong. I'm forty-nine and should have been looking after him. He fought like no one I've ever seen. But now he's dead and I'm still alive."

"And you feel guilty?"

"Yes, just like I did in the last war. Why were my friends being killed and I was living? I was the crying, scared little boy, but the brave ones died."

"Son, I've long since stopped trying to figure it all out. I was in France under Pershing in the Great War. I saw a lot of wonderful boys killed, and for what? At least now we know that the enemy we fight is truly evil."

"How are they so evil? They are just angry about Versailles and Hitler capitalized on that."

"Yes, but they are in a league of their own. Example: nine months ago when the Nazis occupied Rome, the very first thing they did was enter a neighborhood called Porto d'Ottavia. It's a ghetto where all of Rome's Jewish people lived. In one day, they rounded up over 1,000 of them and shipped them off to a concentration camp."

"Concentration camps? Aren't those just rumors?"

"Most Americans aren't really paying attention to what is happening in Europe. It's not their fault really: What there is in the American papers about these things isn't on page one. I have been privy to all OSS reports for the last two years. I get to see all the classified stuff. There are camps, lots of camps and the Jews and other so-called undesirables are being killed. No, they're being exterminated."

"Exterminated?"

"Yes, systematically murdered, on purpose. Hitler wants to rid Europe of all people who are of the Jewish faith. That's why we have been hiding over 200 Jews in the Catacombs below St. Peter's. Yesterday, the Holy Father told them they were free, but they are so scared they don't want to leave. They won't even believe the Pope. And there are thousands we have hidden in churches in and around Rome, in monasteries and convents out in the countryside."

Strauss is shocked and says nothing. His head is spinning with the grim reality of the new German order. Finally, he speaks. "Why are my orders to stop Stauffenberg from killing Hitler then? Wouldn't killing him be a good thing for all concerned?"

"Jonathan, that decision is way above my pay grade. It's not a military decision, it's a political one. The way our government sees it, and the Brits have to go along, Germany can't ever be allowed to wage war again. If the plotters, Stauffenberg and friends, succeed and sue for peace, the Allies will have no choice but to accept some type of armistice. If that happens too soon, Germany is left with a sizable army and armaments that can be used again. Their factories, steel mills, their Autobahn, their cities will be intact. Just like after the Treaty of Versailles. And we now know how that turned out."

"But they can't just level Germany, even if they did start the war."

"Look at it another way. Right now, Hitler seems to be our best asset for winning the war. He was only a corporal in the first war, and now he's calling all the shots. And he's doing a pretty bad job. Look at the situation in Russia. The Germans are taking terrible losses because Hitler refuses to retreat. If he is assassinated, a competent general will take his place, and the Jerry's have lots of competent generals. And don't get me started about Hitler becoming a martyr for the Fatherland if he is murdered. Nazism would be perpetuated."

Strauss can only reply: "I still think the world would be better off to be rid of him."

"Monsignor, I can't say I disagree with you, but orders are orders. You accepted the assignment."

"No, I was blackmailed."

"Maybe persuaded is a better term."

"Right. Then what are my orders, sir?"

"Ah, your orders. First, I may not agree with them in spite of what I just said. I can't have you disobey Washington; however, I can make it a little more difficult for you to carry out your orders. Originally you were to take the train to Milan and from there on to Berlin. But I've got a small problem."

"A small problem? I don't like the sound of that."

"Indeed. Let's just say you're not done carrying those twenty pounds of plastic explosives."

"Great. Just great. That stuff scares the shit out of me!"

"Yeah, there's enough explosive there to blow up a small town."

"I don't like where this is going…"

"It's just a small detour. I'm afraid some background is required. Before the Germans left Rome, a regiment of SS police were marching down the Via Rasella, not far from here, when sixteen of my Italian associates, the Partisans, decided to push a cart full of eighteen kilos of TNT into their midst. Thirty-three of Germany's finest, most hardened soldiers were killed. The German policy of retribution is that ten Italians will die for each German. That's how they think. They executed 335 because they can't count very well, but many were Italian resistance fighters."

"That's terrible, just terrible. But what does it have to do with the explosives?"

"I have no one to take those heavy explosives to Livorno. Except you, that is."

Chapter Eighteen

Palace of the Governatorate
Vatican City

Strauss looks at his new boss in a state of amazement. Archbishop Brendan Galloway is seated at his desk smoking a cigar dressed like a civilian in a collarless white shirt with blue stripes, and black suspenders. His feet sport old brown shoes that are propped up on his desk. He is talking into the phone.

"No, you don't understand. I need you to check out what happened there. We've heard rumors. The town is Sant'Anna, uh, let's see, yes, Sant'Anna di Stazzema. Pronto, capische?" Galloway listens into the receiver intently. "No, God dammit! Not next week. Tomorrow." More silence. "Never mind, puoi andare al diavolo!" He slams the phone into its cradle and looks at Strauss and smiles.

"Oh, that's right, you speak Italian…"

"Yes, fluently," Strauss smiles.

"The Italians! They're never in a hurry to do anything. Secondly, half of them still love Mussolini, who's almost as bad as Hitler, and the rest could care less who's running the show. We're lucky to find a handful of people who want to help. So I guess I have another job for you."

"I'm beginning to think I'm indispensable."

"Just don't get caught or killed. It's too bad we didn't have time to train you in the fine art of espionage."

"I'm not planning on breaking any necks or cutting any throats. But I do have a little experience, remember? However, I'm not sure if I'll remember much of it."

"Go by your instincts; you'll be fine."

"Can I make an observation? You don't seem very much like an archbishop."

"We're in a war, Strauss; I've no time for subtleties. But if you must know, I'm not really an archbishop. Hell, I'm hardly a real bishop."

"I don't understand. You're the Papal Nuncio to the United States. You headed up St. Patrick's and the entire New York Diocese."

"Not really. It was a front made up by the OSS."

"Made up by the OSS? How can they do that?"

"Okay, here's the deal. I went to college in Buffalo, New York with Bill Donovan, the big boss of the OSS, at Niagara University. He was studying pre-law and I was thinking about the seminary. But then we had the first war. We both joined together and were a part of the 165th regiment, which he later commanded. We were a part of the Rainbow Division. I tell you, it was as bad as battle ever gets. We fought at the Marne and in the Argonne Forest. After the war, I just wanted to get as far away from war as possible. Seminary seemed like the perfect place."

"I guess we have that in common."

"Yes, I read your file. I, too, became a priest and was assigned back in Buffalo, and Bill was there running a successful law practice. Years passed. He moved to New York, and having gone to Columbia Law School with FDR, was well connected when the man became president. We always kept in touch. He was put in charge of our new spy bureau, the Office of Strategic Services, which he patterned after the British spy network, MI6. Suddenly, I was reassigned from my quiet little parish in western New York to St. Patrick's. Then I was made a monsignor, and after a brief period, promoted, you might say, to bishop. All the while I was being secretly trained as an OSS agent. Then I got assigned here. Everyone just assumes I'm the Papal Nuncio. His Holiness has approved it; he also knows that I run a good size network of priests and nuns across Europe, who are also OSS agents or in the Resistance."

"This is getting to be a lot to comprehend. A month ago, I was saying Mass at St. Patrick's; now I'm working for an archbishop, wait, excuse me, the head of the OSS in Europe."

"Not all of Europe, just Italy and all the Catholic clergy who are agents in Europe. A guy named Alan Dulles runs the whole show; he's up in Bern, Switzerland. Yes, lots of fun! One thing that I didn't find in your file, though, is how you caught such a plum assignment as St. Patrick's."

"I didn't start there. I was assigned to Little Italy first. But St. Patrick's gets a lot of international visitors, plus there are lots of wealthy Germans and Italians living in Midtown Manhattan, many who fled Hitler and Mussolini. I speak both languages and that was that. It is a pretty nice assignment. I had my own one-bedroom apartment. Imagine a free apartment in mid-town Manhattan. But now I'm here."

"I know. I didn't look forward to coming over to Rome."

"Neither did I, I must confess."

"Come on, enough of this; let's get you ready to travel. What I'm about to show you, only a select few of the hierarchy here in Vatican City know about."

Strauss follows Galloway out of his office in the Palace of the Governatorate down a flight of stairs, through a long hallway and out into a plaza. He walks at a brisk pace past the Church of St. Stephen; the Palace of the Tribunal; the Vatican Railway Station and finally the Palace of Saint Charles, a fading yellow edifice on the southern edge of the city state.

"This building houses the Vatican Information Offices. Coded messages and ciphers are sent from here every day to our bishops, priests, and foreign diplomats. It only makes sense that we have the OSS offices in here as well; they are in the basement. Follow me."

They walk down a corridor and do a sharp turn into a side alcove, missed by most. There is a locked door. Galloway finds his keys and turns two locks. He opens the door and they descend two flights of stairs broken up by a landing. Another door and they enter a large room, smelling musty, of ink on mimeograph machines, cigarette smoke, and perspiration. It is brightly lit, almost too bright, and around the perimeter are walled offices housing senior staff. It is a whirlwind of activity, augmented by the sounds of teletype machines, messages being tapped out on telegraphs and phones ringing.

"Welcome to OSS Italy."

Strauss is incredulous. "You're in charge of all this?"

"Sure. I'm an archbishop, right? Come on, let's meet Marcello." They head in the opposite direction of the big room down a corridor lined with doors, entering one.

"Marcello. Ciao. I want you to meet 'Trommler.' That's your code name, Strauss. It means…"

"The drummer, I know. Ciao, Marcello."

"Marcello, what have you prepared for my friend Herr Trommler?"

"Certainmente, signore. First I have four passports, two Italian and two are German. For Italian, you are Monsignor Pietro Raggiolo or just plain citizen Pietro Raggiolo. For the Germans, you are Monsignore Johan Becken or, you understand, Johan Becken. I took your photograph from your American passport. Next here is your luggage. See here, there is a hidden compartment, about four centimeters. The explosives fit nicely in there. Above it is the normal compartment. I have a black suit, a black shirt with Roman collar, a regular white dress shirt and tie for you to look like a businessman. Then a simple outfit of the common man, a tweed coat, wool pants with leggings, an old gray shirt and a cap. Even some old shoes." Marcello looks at the black fedora in Strauss's hand.

"Oh, yes, in Italy, all priests wear a biretta, not a fedora. So here, this is for you."

"Okay, but no underwear?" Strauss thinks the comment is funny. Marcello doesn't get it.

"No, but a plenty of a room for all other items you have."

"Marcello, aren't you forgetting a few other things?" Galloway looks at Strauss to see if he is following.

"Yes, here you are. A switchblade knife and a gun, just in case you need it. Also here is a set of picks to open locks in case you want to get into a room. And a pair of wire cutters. They always seem to come in handy."

"What, no poison capsule?" Strauss tries again to make a joke.

Galloway chuckles. "There should be, but I didn't think you would take it. Just don't get caught. The Nazis have perfected the art of interrogation."

Strauss closes the suitcase and lifts it. "Great, it's a lot heavier than the backpack. Now, tell me again what the hell I'm supposed to do?"

"Thank you, Marcello. You have done an outstanding job, as usual." Galloway takes Strauss by the arm and they exit, cross the hall, and enter a small office. "The less anyone knows about anything, the better. I've learned not to trust anyone. You might remember that, too. All right, first you're to take the train and the explosives from here to Livorno. Do you know where that is?"

"Yes, it's up the coast. It's a big seaport." Strauss's family arrived there from Germany years ago for his father's posting in Rome.

"That part of the journey should be easy once you're aboard the train. Here's your first-class ticket."

"Nice. Easy, huh?"

"Right, but just before you get there, it would be best if you change into your civilian clothes. Now, the port is heavily patrolled by the Germans. It's a major point of entry for goods, as you know. It's just merchant ships, but some of those are German ones, still off-loading supplies for the Wehrmacht. You can count on being stopped at several checkpoints. What is your name?"

"Johan Strauss. Sorry. Pietro Raggiolo."

"Good and when they ask you what you are doing, tell them you are from Lucca and looking for work. With a suitcase and dressed like a working man you'll look like someone wanting a job on a fishing boat."

"Don't tell me I have to get on a fishing boat. I get seasick."

"Just find the Vecchia Darsena marina. Look for a boat called the *Pescatore Felice*, and its captain, Guillermo Berretti. Tell him you are Trommler. Give him the explosives."

"Got it. And after I get rid of the explosives, wasn't there another assignment?"

"Yes, I want you to get back on the train and go up the coast to Forte dei Marmi. From there, make your way east about eight kilometers to a town called Sant'Anna di Stazzema. There are rumors that some SS soldiers have killed innocent civilians."

"Do I see anyone?"

"Ask around the town for a Father Menguzzo. He's the local priest."

"And if I find anything, what do I do?"

"Make your way back to Forte di Marmi and find the Ristorante Gilda. Tell Caruso the owner that I'm sorry I told him to go to hell. He's a partisan. Then ask for a phone. His is not tapped. Call me at this number. Memorize it on the train and then burn it."

"Then what?"

"There are a few hotels in Forte di Marmi but go to the Hotel Sonia. It's run by another partisan, Sonia Porchetta; I'll let her know to expect you. Rest up for a night there. Then make your way to La Spezia by train. There is a train from there to Milan. Your contact will meet you in Milan, but you have to let me know when you're getting on the train, so he can meet you at the station."

"Piece of cake."

"Now, let's go have lunch. I'm hungry."

"Do you know any good Italian restaurants?"

"A few."

Chapter Nineteen

Hotel Zurich
Luxembourg

"The Allies have successfully landed in Normandy. They already have over a half million men on the ground." General Ludwig Beck is despondent with the latest news.

"It makes little difference," Claus von Stauffenberg retorts. "We cannot abandon our mission. It's a long way from Normandy to Berlin after all. The war may be a hopeless cause, but it is not over. As long as we can put an end to Hitler, save lives on both sides, and the honor of Germany, it is worth doing."

The members of the Black Orchestra, who have made the journey to this postage stamp country, strategically located between France and Germany, are gathering again as time grows short. Luxembourg has been in Nazi hands for four years and it's full of citizens who hate the Third Reich. The Hotel Zurich is an ideal meeting place, such locations becoming harder to find for this small group of patriots. Madame Giroux, the owner of the small hotel, allows the group to meet in her dining room, connected to the hotel from the kitchen. The walls are covered in old floral wallpaper. The table is sturdy oak but the chairs light cane that seem as if they might break at any moment. There is a back entry to the hotel, off an alleyway, where the plotters have entered unseen. They are spending the night in the hotel and will leave before dawn across a friendly checkpoint where earlier that day, they crossed the border into the small country.

Beck scowls and looks hard at the new leader of the Black Orchestra. "And what about our latest attempt? Breitenbuch wasn't even allowed in the meeting with the Führer. He sat outside smoking a cigarette with a gun in his pocket. And then Busch gets sacked, so we'll have no more access to that man."

"I do have some good news. I have finally been assigned to General Fromm's staff. I will be giving regular reports on the status of the Reserve Army to our great leader."

"When?"

"I hope to make a report when the Führer, Himmler, and Göring are present. We must assassinate them all. We don't want Himmler taking over, do we?" Stauffenberg is raising the rhetorical question; everyone knows the answer.

"But when, Claus?"

"July at the earliest, at the Berghof."

"That is a month away."

"All the better. I have been revising Operation Valkyrie to suit our purposes after we assassinate him. I'll need Hitler's written approval of the document first."

Beck rubs his chin and smiles. "It will be as if Hitler is signing his own death warrant."

"Exactly."

"That is some good news." Beck picks up his glass of wine.

Wilhelm Canaris lifts his glass and toasts toward Beck. "General, I have better news. Our esteemed Field Marshal Erwin Rommel is now with us. That is, as long as you will agree to be the new leader of Germany."

"I am willing, but there will be plenty of time to determine that if we are successful. Young Stauffenberg here would also be an ideal candidate."

"Thank you, but no. I'll be busy enough. I'll have to assassinate Hitler and then fly back to Berlin to take charge of the coup. And I think that General Fromm is with us in the endeavor."

Carl Goerdeler, the presumed chancellor of a new Germany, takes command of the room. He is of Prussian descent, an aristocrat and a lawyer. He is a monarchist, and a brilliant intellectual known for his organizational and political skills. He had been the mayor of Leipzig and Price Commissioner in the Nazi government, though he never joined the National Socialists. "Gentlemen, it is not all good news. Our entire cell in Munich was arrested and hung. Most were tortured first. One of our young members, a student at the university, decided to kill a general. The foolish boy, full of idealism I am sure, shot the chief of the garrison there."

Canaris speaks. "It was a General Wolffritz; he's a minor figure, an SS pig, but it was of no help to our cause. As a result, we lost twenty-seven of our youth, our future." He looks over to Hans Speidel, Vice Mayor of Munich. "Hans, can you shed any light on this?"

Speidel takes a long drink of whiskey. He is sweating. "Very little; I just heard they rounded up a group of students and others."

"Hans, you are our contact in Munich. You have to know more." Canaris presses the case.

"What are you inferring?"

"I'm inferring that the Gestapo knew exactly where the boy might be hiding. Several buildings were in the area, but they knew which one to go to. Odd, isn't it?"

Speidel takes another draw on his whiskey. "It was a terrible, terrible thing."

"You mean the torture. They raped a girl who was a classmate. Her name was Maria Heppan. Then they shot her in the legs and arms before finishing her off with a bullet to the head. They found the boy who did it hidden in a secret room in the apartment of Helga and Joseph Luften. They were members of our group. They were lucky: The Gestapo merely shot them. It was not so easy for the young man, Jan Schoenbrün. Jan's fingers were chopped off one by one. Then they took a blowtorch to his scalp..."

"Please, I do not need to hear any more!" Speidel looks at his empty glass; he wants more liquor. Sweat is covering his face and shirt.

"Is there a problem, Hans? Oh yes, the other boy, Martin Freytag. They hung him upside down and used a surgical knife to cut off his balls. While he was screaming they poured lye in his mouth."

"Stop! Enough please! The Gestapo told me that they would kill my wife and children if I did not tell them about the Luftens and others in our group. I only wanted to save my family."

"And then they let you go so you could report back to them on where we meet, and on our activities?"

"Yes! I am so sorry."

Canaris walks over to Hans. He removes a cyanide capsule from his coat.

"Do the honorable thing, Hans. Or I will."

The meeting is over. Most have retired to bed or the small bar in the hotel. Canaris and Stauffenberg sit in Madame Giroux's parlor and speak in hushed tones.

"Claus, events are happening too quickly, and our group is at greater risk because of these stupid incidents. I am not sure we can hold together much longer."

"We must. At least now I have access to that madman. I am committing high treason with every means at my disposal and I will get this done." Stauffenberg looks at Canaris in earnest but there something in his expression. Something is not right. "Wilhelm, what is wrong?"

"I may not be able to help our group much longer."

Stauffenberg is puzzled. "Why not?"

"Because my sources in the SD tell me that the Abwehr could be dissolved and absorbed under Schellenberg."

"What will happen to you then?"

"I do not know. But it won't be good."

Chapter Twenty

The Reich Chancellery
Berlin, Germany

Brigadeführer Walter Schellenberg walks down the 500-foot-long main gallery of the Reich's Chancellery toward Adolf Hitler's office. Even for a loyal Nazi like Schellenberg, it is a bit too much. The gallery is over thirty feet wide, and just as high, adorned with rich tapestries depicting Germanic triumphs of the past. At intervals, there are groups of comfortable seating. It is said that the Führer was particularly pleased with Reich architect Albert Speer's design. After all, the gallery is longer than the Hall of Mirrors at Versailles.

Two silver-helmeted SS guards are at attention by the large double doors to what is commonly known as the Führer Study. He presents his papers to one of the sharply uniformed guards, who nods, salutes. "Heil Hitler!"

Schellenberg responds in kind and the door is opened for him. He enters not an office, but a vast reception room, over 4,000 square feet. The walls are clad in rich burled walnut and the ceiling is wood coffered, seven squares wide by fifteen in length with gold etching. At one end is an immense couch flanked by comfortable seating, around a massive fireplace. Above the hearth is a portrait of Otto von Bismarck. To one side is an enormous globe of the world, the one used frequently by the leader of the Reich to point out his conquests to admiring guests. At the other end of the almost 100-foot-long office is a ten-foot desk that is somewhat contemporary in terms of its simple lines, a lamp on one end, two upholstered guest chairs and by its side, a lounge chair in which the Führer reads his daily briefings. It is all set upon a splendid oriental rug confiscated from one of Berlin's prominent Jewish families. On the interior wall there are paintings of traditional scenes of pastoral German life, done by Hitler's favorite artist, Adolf Ziegler. The farmers represented alongside their wives and children are healthy, well fed, smiling and Aryan in their appearance.

Schellenberg walks straight into the center of the room and then makes a crisp ninety-degree turn, snaps his heels and raises his arm. "Sieg Heil!" He approaches the desk. The Führer is seated at a high-back chair looking down over a detailed isometric plan of the V-1 rocket.

"Ah, Brigadeführer. Come close. I have something I want to show you." Hitler is in a good mood. The head of the SD approaches the large desk. He was expecting to see maps of Normandy.

"My Führer, I was expecting to see you pouring over maps of the French coast. The Allies are landing troops, tanks and cannon as we speak."

Hitler waves his hand, dismissing the comment. "Von Rundstedt and Rommel have that all under control. The invasion force has not made it more than a few miles inland. Caen has not been taken, nor Cherbourg. We will eventually prevail. All ten Panzer divisions are in the fight, now that I have released the last three."

Schellenberg knows that these critical forces were sent into battle too late. Von Rundstedt tried to ask for them on the morning of the invasion, but the Führer was asleep with strict orders not to be awakened. Then he hesitated, thinking they were not needed. "Sir, my intelligence reports that those three divisions that you held in reserve, are taking serious casualties in the open country from the Allied bombers and fighters."

"I told you, Schellenberg, it is all under control. I doubt the Allies will land any more than 400,000 men anyway. It is of no concern to you."

"My Führer, they have already landed that number and many more."

Hitler points to his cut-away illustration of the V-1 rocket. "Look, I have given the order to commence firing our V-1 rockets into England in retaliation. Göring tells me that we will fire over 100 a day and we have over 9,000 of these rockets. He calls them the 'vengeance weapon'. They will bring the Allies to their knees. After a few weeks of these, the Brits will beg the Americans to sue for peace and stop the war."

"Very impressive, sir." Schellenberg shakes his head. He knows that the man is living in a fool's paradise, but he is somehow heartened; it improves his chances of holding a leading position in a soon-to-be-defeated Germany.

"Now, what is it you want?"

Schellenberg is growing tired of the abruptness and being treated as a common private. "My Führer, as you commanded me: Here is the detailed outline for merging the Abwehr into the SD. All intelligence will now be under one administrative department, and all information gathered, whether foreign or domestic, whether for the Wehrmacht or the SS, and Gestapo will be cross-referenced and come from one final source, the SD. There will be no more mishaps like the Ukraine situation. As you will see, it makes perfect sense."

"I will study it later. And who should head up this new agency?"

"My Führer, I am at your service."

"I see. I will consider it. And what do we do with Canaris?"

"Arrest him and execute him!" There is no hesitation in Schellenberg's response.

Hitler looks up from the document prepared by the Brigadeführer. He removes his glasses, hands trembling and stares hard at his subordinate. "Why?"

"I am positive he is a traitor. He is in league with the criminal organization, Black Orchestra."

"What proof do you have? The admiral has served me well; he set up the Abwehr in 1935. That is nine years."

Schellenberg is deflated. "What is your desire then, my Führer?"

"Place him under house arrest for the time being."

"But my Führer…"

"That is my decision. Find him. You will confine him to his home unless and until you can find conclusive proof. You can interrogate him in your usual manner, for all I care. Now if you will excuse me, I must read other reports before I leave for the Wolfsschanze."

Chapter Twenty-One

Stazione Termini
Rome, Italy

"Godspeed, Monsignor Jonathan. Memorize the number I gave you, call me when you can. Remember your past training, think like a spy." Bishop Brendan Galloway squeezes the arm of his charge and gives him a firm handshake.

Strauss mumbles: "Why Godspeed, again…"

"Excuse me?"

"Nothing, Eminence, nothing."

"Oh please! Brendan, or at least major."

"I'm not sure I want to do this. I'm not sure I can do this."

"You'll be fine. Your quick mind and cassock are your armor. No one likes to tangle with priests, even the Germans. They think we have supernatural powers."

"I'd like some of those powers right now. The train is boarding. I better get going." Strauss turns and heads toward the waiting train to Livorno. Then he stops suddenly and returns to Galloway.

"Major, wait."

"What, John? Did you forget something?"

"No, I mean yes. I need to confess my sins."

"Here?"

"Yes, here. I may not get another opportunity."

"Quickly then. You can't miss that train."

"I lied on my application for the seminary. I told them I had never had relations with a woman."

"That's a trick question; I lied about it, too. But you actually get points for saying 'Yes.'"

"What?"

"You are forgiven. Ego te absolvo. What else?"

"I have a son and abandoned him at birth."

"No, you didn't. You told the sister at the hospital that you couldn't take care of him. She took that to mean you were giving him up for adoption. When she came back with the papers for you to sign, you had already left. So ego te absolvo, again."

"How do you know that?"

"Seriously, Jonathan? I'm in the OSS. Don't you think I checked you out before you were assigned to me? Now hurry; get on that train. Godspeed!"

"Godspeed, indeed!" Strauss turns and runs to his waiting coach. His stride is lighter, and he smiles.

The cars are painted a gloss green with the words *Ferrovie dello Stato* emblazoned on the side. The exterior of the car is spotlessly clean. Just a week ago, the city was in German hands, but the efficiency of Mussolini's Fascist regime remains. At least the deposed dictator made many of the trains run on schedule. He turns and looks one more time at his boss and around at the large station. He imagines that he will never return to this city again. Stepping onto the outside platform of the Pullman car, he opens the main door to the right and proceeds down the corridor, locating cabin number 109. Strauss turns the handle of the wooden door with half frosted glass and enters his sanctuary. The walls are polished cherry, the seats are a dark red cloth with wide armrests. There is even a small porcelain sink. Above the seats are brass luggage racks. Strauss lifts up his heavy suitcase, having some difficulty with it. *"I'll be glad when I am done with these explosives,"* he thinks as he removes his topcoat. He drops into the seat and finds it exceedingly comfortable. As he sighs deeply, the train's whistle shatters the air. There is a sudden lurch, and then movement forward as the train slowly picks up momentum.

Strauss feels a great sense of relief. He is in his private cabin, and as the countryside passes, he feels safe, removed from the war. *"How hard can this be?"* he thinks. *"Drop off the explosives; make a report on what is most likely nothing at Sant'Anna and travel again to Milan, an overnight trip. It will be like a three-day holiday."* Civitavecchia is an hour away; after that is Grosseto, where the train will stop for an hour so the passengers can get dinner. He opens *A Farewell to Arms* and begins to read. Lulled by the movement of the train, the rural scenery and the gentle rumble of the wheels against the tracks, Strauss is soon sound asleep.

The slowing of the train and the sudden jerk from the braking wakes Strauss. Grosseto. He has slept through the stop at Civitavecchia. The daylight is fading. Strauss rubs his eyes; the city is a bustle of activity. Then he sees them: German guards walking up and down the platform. They are carrying serious weapons: submachine guns. Among them are black-uniformed troops wearing German M43 caps bearing a shiny skull and crossbones medallion, the mark of the Fascist Black Brigade. His holiday is over. He reaches up for his suitcase, no less heavy than before, opens it and retrieves one of his passports: Monsignor Pietro Raggiolo. The cabin is warm; there is no need for a topcoat as his cassock will announce him. His armor, as Galloway called it. He puts his biretta firmly on his head. Strauss then realizes he has no alibi, no reason why he is on the train. He breathes deeply. *"Think, think, Johan, what are you doing here?"* He opens the door of his compartment and gets into the queue of passengers trying to disembark, moving slowly. Everyone is being checked by a rubbery-faced Fascist guard, enjoying his brief moment of authority. "Papers, please. Now!"

Strauss complies hoping that Marcello has done a good enough job with his forged passport. The ugly soldier stares at it blankly, then makes what Strauss believes is a slight bow toward him.

"What is your business?"

"I'm a parish priest."

"Yes, that is obvious. Why are you traveling on this train?"

"I'm on my way to Livorno. I'm a vicar there."

"What church?"

Strauss looks at the guard. He doesn't know the names of the churches in Livorno. "Ah, St. Peter."

"You mean St. Peter and Paul? I'm from Livorno."

"Yes. Yes. My fellow priests just refer to it as St. Peter's. Like a joke, as if we are the same as the one in Rome."

"Yes, I get it. I go to St. John the Baptist on the south end. May I have a blessing…Monsignor?"

"Certainly, my son. May the grace of God and his divine kindness protect you in this time of trouble." Strauss makes the sign of the cross over the soldier, who hands him his passport and deeply bows to the priest. Strauss moves on with annoyed passengers behind him, hungry and thirsty. He takes a deep breath.

After two glasses of Chianti and a meal of pasta and vegetables at a trattoria off the beautiful Piazza Dante by the Palazzo Aldobrandeschi, Strauss makes his way back to the train station and his cabin. It now feels to him like his refuge away from a world of Renaissance splendor and a world at war. Sitting down in his seat, he realizes that he needs to conjure up alibis, back stories for any situations that might arise on the trip ahead. The words of Galloway resound in his head: "Rely on your past."

When he was a spy in the first war, his instincts were razor sharp. He had answers for all inquiries; he could sense someone following him; he could disappear down hidden streets and alleyways. Sometimes killing was necessary. He had to do it more times than he cared to recall. He sighs at the thought and shakes his head. Hopefully, he will not be called upon to kill again.

The train lurches forward and soon it is proceeding toward Livorno at a crisp 73 KM per hour. The dark night makes his cabin seem cozier…and safe.

Strauss looks up from *A Farewell to Arms*. He hears the brakes make a low moan and the train slows. Several hours have passed, but surely the train is not yet in Livorno. He squints out the window into the darkness and sees lights, then a sign: "Cecina - 1 KM."

"Strange. *Maybe they need coal, or there is a delay going into Livorno,*" he thinks, returning to his reading. The train slowly rolls into the station and comes to a jarring halt. He hears voices yelling outside.

"All passengers have your papers ready for inspection!" In the dim lights of the train station, Strauss can see at least fifty German soldiers.

"Sweet Jesus, are there no Italians in Italy anymore?" he mutters. "*Papers for inspection again. But why?*" He sits still, now growing anxious. His book by Hemingway will have to wait. "*Remember you are an Italian priest Johan. Do not show that you understand German,*" he thinks, rehearsing his alibi again. "*Parish priest at Saint Peter and Paul in Livorno.*" Then he thinks: "*Maybe I was duped by that ugly Black Fascist. What if there is no St. Peter and Paul Church in Livorno? What if the guard called ahead to his Nazi occupiers?*"

The wooden door to his cabin opens abruptly. Strauss looks up at a soldier, unsure of his rank. But the twin lightning bolts on his lapel and skull and crossbones on his officer's cap tell him all he needs to know.

"Get up, priest. You will come with us!"

"I do not understand you." Strauss is using his best Italian inflection, not that it makes much difference to the German scharführer. He does not want to go anywhere with him and pretends that he does not understand what the soldier is saying.

The officer switches languages to a poor Italian. "You will come with us. Get up! Understand?"

"Why? I have done nothing,"

The captain—the scharführer, stands to the side, and two heavy set soldiers enter the cabin and grab Strauss. He drops his book. They reach up for his suitcase, ignoring its weight, and force him out of the

Pullman car. Strauss trips on the last step from the train car and falls onto the wooden platform. He instantly feels the back of a rifle butt against his shoulder. It is a strong hit, but it could have been stronger. This surprises him; he gets up, wiping the dust from his new cassock. The guards motion for him to pick up his suitcase and follow them. Strauss does so without comment, but for the first time in many years, a wave of fear courses through his body. *"Keep it together, Johan, keep it together. You can outwit them."*

The scharführer is about to leave the cabin when he notices the book on the seat. He picks it up and flips through the pages. "*A Farewell to Arms*, in English!" he exclaims, smiling, leans out the door and yells for someone. In a moment, another man in uniform appears. On his sleeve is the diamond patch with the initials "SD," the Gestapo. The kriminalinspektor takes the book and nods to the scharführer. They exit the train and hasten to catch up with their newfound American espionage agent.

Strauss looks around. There is no way to escape. Four soldiers are in front and two are behind him. One continually jabs his back with the barrel of his rifle, laughing. He doesn't know why; he is walking as fast as they are. They bypass the station building and go directly to a parking area, there is a waiting VW Kübelwagen. It is running, a driver ready to pull away. A soldier opens the rear door and Strauss gets in, pretending that his suitcase is lighter than it really is. The other two seats are taken by soldiers, one pointing a gun right at Strauss, fear still embracing him. Strauss reaches into his pocket and grabs Billy McClain's rosary. He begins to say the "Our Father" silently. As the lorry drives away, the scharführer and his Gestapo kriminalinspektor reach the station, they see another waiting vehicle and wave to it.

"Follow them!" Climbing in, the Kübelwagen goes into gear and speeds toward Strauss.

Once out of the small town of Cecina, the road is unpaved. It is dark on this cloudy June 9th night. The headlights of the vehicle provide an eerie illumination of the terrain. Strauss keeps his eyes on the road and the surroundings in case he is lucky enough to make it back to the train station on foot. As the road twists and turns and rises, he can see small fields of crops, then orchards of olive trees, and even a cow or two, startled by the bright beams of light. He smells lilacs and cedar.

After ten minutes, he sees a fire, a small farmhouse, and tents. And more soldiers. His guards all bear the SS insignia. He assumes there are more up ahead. He is being driven into a wasp's nest. The lorry comes to a stop and the car door is opened. The hard butt of a rifle in his back tells him which way to go. In the camp, he sees more tents, men eating by the fire or standing around smoking; most are dirty, bandaged, in a kind of trance. He stops, but the guard in charge motions him to one of the larger tents and holding the flap, he enters. There are over two dozen cots occupied by men bleeding and crying, badly bandaged, blood seeping through the dressings, hanging plasma bottles, and an officer dressed in a white gown.

"Do you speak German?" he asks Strauss.

The priest cannot let on that he does. But before he realizes it, he says: "No." He takes a deep breath.

"Italian then?" The doctor seems fluent in both languages and ignores Strauss's knowing reply.

Strauss is relieved. "Yes, Italian. I am Italian."

"These men are dying. Perform your Catholic ritual; what do you call it, the Last Rites? They have cried for a priest. It is the least I can do for them." The words are spoken in fractured Italian.

Strauss nods in sudden understanding, a thin smile breaks across his face. He sets his suitcase down, opens it and retrieves his scapula and holy oil. He removes his biretta, lifts the scapula over his head onto his shoulders, and makes his way to each man. One is holding a rosary, another a small Bible, one more clutches the cross around his neck with the only hand he has left. After thirty minutes or so, he is done. The doctor bows and shakes his hand, and motions to the waiting soldiers to take him back to the German jeep. Strauss turns to leave. The scharführer and the kriminalinspektor are standing in his way, both of them smiling.

Chapter Twenty-Two

Amsterdam
Occupied Netherlands

A blackout is in effect throughout the city. The Allies have landed in France and the local German authorities feel that it is just a matter of time before more bombs fall on the city. In 1941, the Wehrmacht constructed numerous bases after the occupation of this small, but important country. It was, after all, well positioned as a staging point for the planned invasion of England.

There are few, if any, cars driving on the narrow roadway alongside the canals. Fuel is almost impossible to secure. It has all been taken to supply the German Panzer divisions fighting in the south. They are doing their best to stop the advancing Americans and British, soon to be an army of over one million men. And every day, it increases through the Mulberry ports at Arromanches and Omaha Beach. Only a great storm on June 19, disabling the port at Omaha, will slow the procession of what will eventually be 2,500,000 men, 500,000 vehicles, and 4,000,000 tons of supplies.

Wessel von Loringhoven walks down Elandsgracht toward Prinsengracht, which runs alongside the canal by the same name. It is very dark, but he knows this route by heart. He has been here many times before. He stops, listens. There are no other footsteps. No one is out. Most of the populace is saving their strength, sustained from what little food is available. Conditions in Amsterdam have been steadily deteriorating all year. So much for being integrated into the greater Germanic Reich.

He turns right and walks alongside the canal. His steps resonate on the cobblestones, which concern him. He can make out the protective railings alongside and the outline of barges and houseboats. The interiors of most of them are darkened by curtains.

Loringhoven tried to make this pickup earlier in the day, during broad daylight, when the streets would have been full of people. His tall, lean frame fits in with the genetic Dutch makeup of the country and he would go unnoticed. But then the Gestapo arrived in force and entered the house across the canal at 587 Prinsengracht. At gunpoint, they took away twenty or so Jews who had been hiding in an upper floor apartment. Even in the deteriorating situation, the Nazis' focus on arresting and transporting the Jewish population to their deaths continues unabated and with great determination. Before it is all over, more than 100,000 people from Holland will be sent to their deaths in concentration camps.

The ranking member of the Black Orchestra, and close friend of Claus von Stauffenberg and Wilhelm Canaris, turns right again down an alley, down a block and left again to another alley, running parallel with the canal. He crosses another canal, a wide one. At that point, he turns left once more until he is back at the Prinsengracht Canal. Now he is sure he has not been followed. He finds the barge, steps across a small gangplank and onto its deck. Loringhoven knocks on the door.

"Who is it?"

"The Black Orchestra makes a beautiful sound." The door opens and he quickly enters a small dark cabin.

The owner of the barge lights several oil lamps inside the small area. He checks the curtains, and satisfied that they are doing their job, offers his visitor a Heineken beer. It is gratefully accepted. It is one of the few food items not rationed and is manufactured no more than a kilometer away.

"Were you successful on your run?"

"Yes. I returned yesterday at daybreak. I was able to rendezvous with the British submarine, but the waves were very heavy, even though it was right off the coast. The old barge took a beating, but she is strong. I picked up ten cases of small arms, grenades, and explosives. Here is what you asked for." The man hands over a satchel containing the two blocks of plastic explosives. They are made in England, and the Black Orchestra hopes that their plot will be construed as an MI6 operation. Each weighs just over two kilograms. It is enough to easily blow up two tanks.

"Are the detonators in here as well?"

"Yes, everything you need. May I ask what it is for?"

"No, you may not, my friend. But you will know soon enough. I will toast to the future, however." Loringhoven raises his mug. "To a free Germany."

"And to a free Holland!"

Chapter Twenty-Three

SS Camp
On the Trasimene Line
Cecina, Italy

The ancient farmhouse built of stone and tile is four rooms divided by a center hallway. There is a steep flight of wooden steps that leads up to two sleeping areas; they are not bedrooms, only lofts where you cannot even stand. Off the main hall is the living room, now used as the commandant's office. Directly across is a dining room connected by a doorway to the rear kitchen. It is being used as a bedroom for three senior officers. The last room, the sole bedroom, has been turned into an interview room. Father Strauss sits quietly in a chair. No one has bound his hands; if he wants to, he can make a run for it, probably to be shot as he tries carrying his heavy suitcase. If he leaves it, the Germans will discover his multiple identities, the plastic explosives, and other proof that he is not merely a traveling priest.

"This is a walk in the park, Johan. Remember that," he runs the thought over and over in his mind. *"You are Father Pietro Raggiolo."* He feels the rosary beads from Billy McClain in his pocket. Billy the Fearless. He draws solace from them.

The scharführer and the kriminalinspektor enter the room. The plain clothes SD man looks Italian: dark hair, brown skin, and brown eyes. He speaks Italian.

"Father…"

"Raggiolo."

"Do you have your papers?"

Strauss reaches under his cassock to an interior pocket and produces his passport, handing it without words to the man. It is scrutinized and Strauss thinks he sees a slight indication of disappointment in the kriminalinspektor's face.

"Where were you born?"

"Bologna, 1895."

"Why did you become a priest?"

"To serve God of course. Why are you questioning me? I was on my way to Livorno after visiting Rome. I'm a parish priest there."

"What happened in Rome?"

"They kicked out your kind for starters."

"Such impudence. Be careful, priest." The inspector shakes his head.

The SS officer standing off to the side, about to open the suitcase, understands. He moves toward Strauss with his hand raised. He is held back by the inspector.

"I mean, what were you doing in Rome?

"Visiting my sister; she is ill."

The scharführer understands Italian, but will not condescend to speak it, says nothing, and hands *A Farewell to Arms* to the interrogator.

"Then why are you carrying this book?"

Strauss feels his face begin to flush. He takes a deep breath realizing the stupid mistake he has made. If he had been reading his Breviary, he would be in a warm bed at a hotel in Cecina right now. "When I was in Rome, an American priest gave it to me. I told the priest I hope to visit America someday and was trying to learn English. So he gave me the book as a gift."

"You are an excellent liar, Father Raggiolo. You are an American spy. Admit it."

Strauss looks over at the SS officer. He is searching his suitcase, fortunately having been set on a table by a low-ranking soldier. His clothes are being thrown out, tossed on the floor. The white shirt is pulled out and examined, a quizzical look on the face of the Nazi.

"I'm not a spy, and as for that shirt, priests don't wear cassocks all the time. Leave my things alone. That is almost all of what I possess."

The scharführer has heard enough impudence from this man of God. Deviating from the good guy, bad guy approach agreed to earlier by the two, he slaps Strauss hard across the face.

"Sie werden mit respekt Kleriker sprechen!"

Strauss thinks: *"I have no respect for SS goons like you,"* but feigns ignorance of the remark. The kriminalinspektor moves directly in front of him.

"Do not lie, priest. We know that many of your kind are working for the Partisans. You are one of them." The Gestapo agent slaps Strauss across the other cheek.

"No, I am not a Partisan, and how dare you touch a man of God! It is a grave sin!"

Goon number two slaps Strauss again, this time harder. "Your people, the partisans, ambushed my friend's unit. We took heavy casualties. There will be reprisals. We will teach you and yours a lesson. You will be the first to die!"

"I was on a train! I had nothing to do with what happened to these men. I'm going to my parish in Livorno, St. Peter and Paul. I am telling the truth!"

Goon number one clenches his fist. "Then who is your superior there?"

Strauss's eyes widen. He hesitates, but only for a second. "Monsignor Eugenio Pacelli." Strauss remembers Pope Pius XII's given name; it seems like a reasonable answer. Hopefully, neither of these pagans will recognize the ruse.

"Why don't I call him then and we can straighten out this whole situation, Father Raggiolo?"

"Please do that." The blood drains from Strauss's face. He feels his legs weaken. The SD officer leaves the room for the office and

Strauss hears the dialing of a phone. At that moment, the scharführer turns to his captive, holding up the cleric's gun; he smiles broadly. Strauss lowers his head. His mission is over before it has even started. Then he feels the cold steel of the handle crash into his head. He winces, slumps in his chair seeing a night sky of stars on his eyelids but does not cry out. He feels warm liquid running down his face into his mouth.

"Connect me with a church in Livorno, please, St. Peter and Paul. Thank you...Yes, I'll wait."

Strauss shakes his head trying to recover from the blow and decides he will have to make a run for it. Perhaps he can get lost in the rural darkness outside. *"To hell with the suitcase; I need to save my own ass,"* he thinks. Then he hears footsteps and looks up.

The doctor, clad in the blood stained frock, his stethoscope around his neck, enters the room. The surgeon points his Luger at the scharführer. He yells: "Put down the phone, Inspektor, and get in here." In a second the SD officer enters, and the doctor points the Luger at him.

The two salute. "What is the meaning of this, Herr Doktor?"

It is apparent that the oberarzt, the officer doctor, outranks the two. "This man was brought here to give the last blessing to our brave German soldiers who are dying, and you treat him like a common criminal! Explain yourselves."

"He is a spy. We found this book."

"So? It is just a book."

"But it is written in English..."

"And that is your proof?"

"He also had this." The officer holds out the gun.

"If I were traveling in Italy now, I'd carry a gun too. You will let him go. He is under my protection. You are both fools!" The doctor lifts a woozy Strauss from his chair. He takes a clean cloth from his pocket and wipes the blood from the face of the cleric. Before anyone can assist, the priest is at his suitcase, repacking it. He grabs the gun from the Nazi and throws it on top, then the book, staring at the man who pistol whipped him. The suitcase is shut, and Strauss lifts it as effortlessly as possible. He follows the doctor outside.

"I am afraid you will have to walk. To give you a ride back to town would raise too much suspicion. I am a Polish conscript. Fortunately, as a doctor, I outrank those two baboons. Now hurry, before they check with..."

"Monsignor Pacelli?"

"Yes, Monsignor Pacelli." The doctor winks, shakes Strauss's hand, and smiles. "Pacelli indeed. Godspeed, Monsignor."

"And Godspeed to you, Doctor."

Strauss turns and heads into the darkness, following the gravel road away from the wasp's nest. The suitcase seems heavier than ever.

Chapter Twenty-Four

Cecina, Italy

Father Strauss feels nothing but the burning pain of arthritis in his knees. Years of jogging in Berlin, hiking in the mountains of Bavaria, playing soccer, and walking around New York have worn them out. He has walked most of the night down a rutted, rock-strewn country road. He has tripped and stumbled, fallen twice, and almost been attacked by a wild boar. "Some holiday this has turned out to be," he mutters as he sees the quaint stone houses of Cecina ahead. Hopefully, there will be a train this morning to Livorno, and he can get rid of the hated twenty pounds of explosives. At one point on the journey from the SS camp, he seriously thought of jettisoning them into the woods. Let the fisherman find another bomb elsewhere. But his background as a soldier and an obedient priest would not allow it. Maybe it is because he is just a stubborn German.

The sun begins to silhouette the rooftops of the buildings ahead. He makes his way into town and to the station at the far west end of the small city. He can see the Gulf of Genoa across the train tracks. Strauss enters and drops his precious cargo. He looks around for a schedule board. There is none, so he walks up to the only open ticket window. The man on the other side has a thin jumble of unkempt gray hair, an unshaved face accented by pince-nez glasses and arm garters about his upper sleeves. He looks up to the priest with uncaring eyes.

"When's the next train to Livorno?"

"Soon. Any minute, no later than 8:00 A.M." Strauss smiles and hands the man his original ticket.

"Is this ticket still good?"

The ticket man nods.

"Thank you," Strauss walks away, eager to sit down. *"Things might be looking up for me today. Thank you for delivering me from the Nazis, Lord,"* he thinks. He goes back to his suitcase and literally drags it to a wooden bench. He has no more strength left to lift it. Strauss is famished, but he dares not leave the station and risk missing the train, though he can see a small trattoria beyond the open doors of the station across the street.

A half-hour passes. There is no train. His stomach is aching. Strauss gets up and goes to the window. "I thought you said the train was coming. I'll be right back."

"I won't be able to hold the train for you."

"But I'm the only one in the damn station. Like I said, I'll be right back," he says out loud as he leaves and crosses the street. He can smell pork frying and coffee.

"Madam, can I get a sandwich with an egg and some fried meat. And a coffee?"

'Oh Monsignor, certainly. Right away."

"Thank you, I am in a bit of a hurry. The train is expected any minute and I cannot miss it."

The old, rather large woman rushes into the kitchen. He sees her rustling about and hears the distant whistle of the eight o'clock train.

"Please hurry. My train is arriving."

"Yes, I am going as fast as I can."

Strauss walks into the cucina and the woman is nowhere to be found. There's a door leading to a small backyard. She is coming back from a chicken coop in the back. Her apron is turned up, and she carries some eggs.

"Father, I want you to have the freshest eggs."

He hears the chugging of the train getting closer and the whistle of the air brakes. "Mother, it is not necessary. The train is almost here."

"It will only take a minute. Do not worry. The train will be stopped for some time, I assure you."

The priest looks upward to heaven. *"Really, is this necessary, God?"* He watches her prepare everything in slow motion. Now the train has come to a complete stop; a few passengers are getting off as soon as the stepstool is placed on the station platform by the conductor. Looking back at the cook he sees that she is just starting to fry some pork.

"Mother, hurry up! The train will be leaving." Strauss gets out 200 liras so he can pay her immediately upon receiving his long-awaited breakfast. He would have left already but he is famished, and the aromas are increasing his hunger. The train's whistle blows. The stepstool is gone. Strauss hears the hiss of the steam releasing the brakes.

"Mother…!"

"Here you are, Monsignor, perfecto!"

"Thank you!" Strauss grabs the sandwich wrapped in brown paper, tucks it in a pocket and runs across the street, hot coffee spilling onto his hand; the train is slowly beginning to move. He grabs the vertical handrail and lifts himself onto the first step of the moving coach.

"My suitcase! Dammit!" Strauss looks down at the station platform as the train slowly picks up speed. He throws the coffee away and leaping, almost falls, and manages to keep his balance, feet stumbling one in front of the other. He regains his footing and runs to the bench where his bag is and grabs the handle. The suitcase feels heavier than ever. He turns and gallops to the now steadily moving train. The conductor appears at the back of the last coach and climbs down the steps with his hand outstretched.

"Hurry, faster!" the conductor shouts.

Strauss is running hard now, his knees feel the pounding of every footstep. With all his might, he launches the bag that comes to a hard landing on the coach platform, just missing the conductor. Running with every ounce of energy, he can see the end of the station platform coming. His lunging hand connects with the conductor's, who pulls Strauss onto the train as it leaves Cecina. He falls to the floor exhausted and reaches into his pocket. The breakfast sandwich is gone. Looking back at the platform, Strauss sees it lying on the station floor.

Chapter Twenty-Five

Vecchia Parsena Dock
Livorno, Italy

"I am Trommler." Monsignor Jonathan Strauss drops his heavy bag at the feet of the hulk of a man in front of him. Hopefully, this will be his contact. He can read the name on the boat, painted in red, chipped and faded: ***Pescatore Felice***. "Ah, si. Yes, I am Guillermo. Guillermo Berretti. Here, let me carry your bag. Come on board."

"I won't be staying. But there is something in there that you want." Strauss stands on the dock.

"Yes, I know. We have been expecting you. You were delayed…"

"You might say that." Strauss thinks back to his journey so far. A holiday indeed! Taken by the SS; interrogated by the Gestapo; a three mile walk with a heavy suitcase to Cecina; no sleep; and then the breakfast sandwich. He had forced himself to stay awake on the short journey to Livorno, lest he miss the stop, like Civitavecchia. On the short trip, he changed and now looks like an everyday citizen of Italy, perhaps a fisherman, and it worked. There were at least three checkpoints at the large port, and he got through each one with ease. Of course, Vecchia Darsena was the last marina, located in the most remote and inconvenient part of the seaport. That only meant an extra kilometer to lug the bag.

He is exhausted and starving. There was always plenty of food at St. Patrick's. Two wonderful cooks; three squares a day, plus cakes, pies, and cookies. He yearns to be back there. His knees are throbbing. His mouth is dry.

"I'm very hungry. Do you have anything to eat?"

"Of course, my friend. Please come on board. I will have Filippo serve you something. You can rest too. We will not leave until nightfall."

"I will not be going with you."

"No? But aren't you going to help us?"

"I'm just a courier and I have another assignment."

"Certainamente. No problem. You won't want to go anyway, I can assure you. It will be very dangerous. Filippo, get our friend some lunch."

Strauss climbs on board. On the port and starboard sides are great nets hung high to catch the bounty of the sea: prawns, red and yellow snapper, and mussels. Entering the cabin of the shrimp boat he drops down onto a built-in wooden bench next to a polished wood table, anchored to the floor. Filippo sets out tableware and a large bowl. Fresh Italian bread and butter appear, then a glass of Chianti, and a steaming pot. With a wooden ladle the first mate serves up a fish soup, heavy with chunks of fish and shrimp, lobster, mussels, potatoes, carrots, celery and peas in a rich, white broth. In an instant there is a side of angel hair pasta set by the soup bowl. Strauss eats ravenously.

"Slowly, Father. Enjoy the food, but slowly."

Strauss nods. "Excuse me. I am sorry, but I am so hungry. It is delicious."

After a slice of Siena cake, the priest is stuffed. Across from the table is a small couch with some pillows. He moves over to it. In a moment he is fast asleep.

Berretti looks up from trying to untangle some small nets toward the guardhouse at the end of the dock. The gate is locked, as usual. The old man who checks everyone coming through is arguing with two people. One is dressed in a military uniform, the other in plainclothes. On the narrow road by the dock, a Kübelwagen is parked. The guard shakes his head. There is arguing. The old man shakes his head waving away the identification badges of his two visitors. Shots ring out. The old man slumps over his table.

"Filippo, Mario, Stefano, we are leaving! Cast the lines! Hurry!"

Accustomed to making quick getaways from their Nazi occupiers, the crew jumps to action. Guillermo runs to the bridge past the sleeping priest. He looks toward the front and rear of the boat. Mario and Stefano have loosed the ropes and are onboard. He starts the engine and looks back at the two Germans. Another shot rings out. The gate's lock has been blown off and the scharführer and the kriminalinspektor are running toward the boat. Turning the wheel hard right he guns the engines. The boat responds but the rudder does not turn the boat sufficiently; Berretti hits the starboard rear of the shrimp boat in front of him. Fortunately, doing so causes the *Pescatore Felice* to move well into the wake zone of the marina; its propellers churn the water. In a moment they are over one hundred feet from the dock heading out to the Gulf of Genoa. The two pursuers reach the now empty birth and fire their Lugers.

The shattering of broken glass wakes Strauss. "Mother of God!" He tries to get up, but the small boat is moving at such speed that the floor is at a twelve-degree angle; he cannot stand and he is covered in glass shards. Strauss looks out the rear window and sees the two Nazis.

"You don't understand, Guillermo, I can't be on this trip with you."

"Perhaps I should have turned you over to your two friends? They will report our little boat and soon we'll have company; our mission is compromised." Guillermo is not happy.

"I am sorry about that. I thought I was done with them."

"Why are they after you?"

"They think I'm a partisan spy."

"Are you?"

"No, of course not. I told you I'm a courier. But I can't stay on this boat. I have to get to Forte dei Marmi."

"Then you're in luck. When we get done with our mission tonight we're going there. I can't go back to Livorno. At least not for a couple of days, or even a week. But no one pays attention to fishing boats in Forte dei Marmi. We'll be safe there. For now, you come with us. You can probably be of some help."

"What are you planning?"

"We're going to blow up the German patrol boats at the naval base at La Spezia."

"What! Are you crazy?"

Stefano speaks up. "Boss, he's right. I don't think that's too good an idea. With what just happened, everyone will be searching for us."

"And that's why we're going to do it. No one will expect us at the docks tonight, so we'll go in at midnight. Mario, take the wheel and head north northwest. Go slow. When we're five miles out, we'll stop and eat."

"Are you sure, boss?" Filippo says in a low voice.

"Yes, I am sure. Screw the Nazi occupiers."

Chapter Twenty-Six

Hotel Lutetia
Paris, France

Wilhelm Canaris strolls down the Boulevard Raspail just like any other Frenchman on this popular thoroughfare. He is wearing a tan trench coat and brown fedora to ward off a rain that seems imminent from the darkening, putty gray clouds above. Despite the dreary day, the street is alive with Parisians who appear upbeat. Is it because the Allies are making their way out of the Normandy peninsula and will soon be liberating their beloved city from the hated German occupiers?

He reaches number 45 Boulevard Raspail, an imposing building in the Art Nouveau style. The façade is richly decorated in garlands of stone flowers and cherubs, interspersed with that most Parisian feature known as Juliette balconies. Before the war, it was a luxury hotel, hosting the likes of painter Pablo Picasso, jazz singer Josephine Baker, and novelist James Joyce. Now it is the headquarters of the Abwehr.

Canaris walks through the formerly grand lobby and up two flights of worn marble stairs. The building is strangely quiet. Down a well-appointed hallway, he proceeds to a door marked "Import/Export Office," and enters. He looks around and seeing no one, calls, "Alfred, are you here?"

"In the back office. Who is it?" Alfred Toepfer walks to the reception area. He is one of Canaris's top assistants in Paris, having the rank of captain. He is in charge of controlling the black market and selling Nazi contraband, particularly art and treasure taken from the Jews; he also procures valuable foreign exchange by selling occupied France's goods to Spain and Portugal, and the Nazis reap the profits. From these efforts, he has skimmed off a fortune, and Canaris has received a handsome cut. "Wilhelm, what are you doing here? I am surprised, but very happy to see you. I wanted to contact you but didn't even know where you were."

"It is good to see you, my friend. I was in Luxembourg on other Abwehr business. Why is everything so quiet around here?" Canaris takes off his hat and shakes Toepfer's hand.

"Have you not heard? The Führer has eliminated the Abwehr."

Canaris stares at his friend and nods in understanding. "Schellenberg, that son-of-a-bitch."

"You suspected this? It's become a part of the SD."

"I knew he might try something. He is power hungry."

"They've placed you under house arrest. You need to leave from here immediately. The SD has been in and out all day, arresting people, taking files; they even shot a few of the workers. They were suspected of being double agents. I was just destroying files that neither you nor I need them to see." Toepfer's voice sounds urgent.

"We only needed a little more time."

"Time for what?"

"Never mind; what about you?"

"They told me to report to SD headquarters on Avenue Foch tomorrow. But I think I will just slip out of the city tonight and then resign my commission. My term of service is nearly up anyway."

"Lucky you. Listen, can you give me some of that money you keep in the big safe of yours?"

"Certainly. How much?"

"At least 5,000 Reichsmarks."

The captain whistles. "Planning a round-the-world trip?"

"No, but there may be a lot of people to pay off."

"I'll get it from the safe." Toepfer leaves the reception area and heads back to the rear office. Canaris reaches into the pocket of his topcoat for his Luger; at this point he can trust no one. Toepfer returns with a briefcase.

"You can't carry that much money in your pockets. You'll need this; I put some papers and a shirt on top of the money in case you are stopped. Where will you go?"

"I could go to my house in Berlin since I'm under house arrest. It's quite pleasant there and they probably won't expect that, but I have unfinished work to do. I'll get there eventually. And I could use a holiday from this war."

"Be careful and let me know where you go if possible. I can get you to Spain or Portugal. I've sold a lot of French goods there, and I know many people."

"I'm sure you do, but I'm afraid the less we contact one another, the better off you'll be."

"I'll be fine. There is more money back there, a lot more. I may take a pleasure cruise."

"I'm sure there is. I should have asked for 10,000 marks!"

"Then you would need a wheelbarrow. Now go, before the SD comes back for more files…and people. I would go down the fire stairs to the rear door."

"My thought exactly. Goodbye, my friend, and thanks for the money."

"Good luck, Wilhelm; be careful."

"Thank you, Alfred. Enjoy your cruise." Canaris lets go of the gun in his pocket and takes the briefcase. He is out the door and heads to the staircase. Toepfer watches him until he is inside the stairwell. He returns to his office and looks out the window. He watches Canaris cross the alley and into the rear door of a restaurant that the two have both enjoyed together. He turns to his desk and lifts up the receiver of the phone and dials five numbers.

"Yes, connect me with Standartenführer Knochen. It is urgent." He waits.

"Hello. Yes, I have information. Canaris was just here."

Chapter Twenty-Seven

The Gulf of Genoa
7 Nautical Miles from the Italian Naval Base
La Spezia, Italy

The *Pescatore Felice* rocks gently in the calm water. It is nine o'clock and the quarter moon is beginning to illuminate the water. The captain, crew, and priest have just finished what might be their last meal. But it was a good one. Filippo is an excellent cook, even given the constraints of the small galley. There was broiled snapper and shrimp, fresh pesto pasta, vegetables, bread, and lots of wine, this time from Tuscany.

"This is turning out to be quite a nice boat-ride, Guillermo. And Filippo, that was an excellent meal. Now, Captain, why don't you just take me to Forte dei Marmi and I can get onto my next assignment? Spend the night in port and do what you have to do tomorrow night. There will almost be no moon then." Strauss is trying his best to be persuasive.

Filippo speaks: "It's a good idea boss and I'm a little drunk anyway. Plus, I just opened another bottle of Brunello."

Guillermo looks at the group and finishes his last bite of cake. He slowly nods his head. Strauss looks at him in anticipation. *"Please agree,"* he thinks. The captain's face is brown and ruddy, with deep lines from squinting at the sun; his black hair pasted onto his scalp. His hands are thick and look like old leather. Berretti's eyes are dark with bags under them from sleepless nights.

"Okay, maybe that would be for the best. What's another day? Mario, take the wheel and head toward Forte. Go slow. We don't want to arouse any other boats."

"Si, si captain, right away!" Mario smiles and heads to the bridge.

Berretti reaches for Strauss's wine glass and pours him a generous amount; he does the same for himself. "Salute, Trommler. Now how about you tell me your real name, Signore Spy?"

"Raggiolo. Pietro Raggiolo."

"That's your real name?"

"The less we know about each other the better, especially with those two Nazis back at the pier still wanting to find me. I don't think I've seen the last of those two."

"Agreed. But why were you late?"

"It was strongly suggested that I accompany them to their camp so I could render services to some of their dying soldiers."

"Are you a doctor?"

"In a way. Did your partisans have anything to do with the condition of those men?"

"They did. It was a good ambush. But it was only in retaliation for something the Nazis and Fascists did to my people."

"What did they do?"

"I don't want to talk about it. It was in a town not far from Forte dei Marmi."

Strauss is intrigued. "What town?"

"Sant'Anna di Stazzema. Now, I need to get revenge for what they did."

"Sant'Anna? Tell me what happened, please?" Strauss pleads.

As Berretti chokes on his first words, the boat speeds up.

Mario yells from the bridge: "We have company!"

Berretti takes a gulp of his wine and rushes out to the back deck. A boat is speeding toward them. "Full speed, Mario, full speed! It's a German patrol boat!"

The shrimp boat increases speed, but it is no match against the faster naval vessel designed to go over twenty-five knots.

"Raggiolo, get me a block of the plastic explosives, quickly."

"Right." Strauss shakes his head to clear the effects of the multiple glasses of wine. The sudden rush of adrenalin helps too.

"And get me a flare from that cabinet," he yells above the roaring engine, pointing to a small door alongside the stair to the bridge.

"Got it!" Strauss makes his way down the steps to the bunk area and finds his suitcase on top of one of the beds. He opens it and realizes that accessing the plastic explosives will not be easy. It is in the hidden compartment. He tosses his clothes on the bed and stares at the seamless fabric bottom of the suitcase. He runs back to the galley and retrieves a long knife. Back to the sleeping quarters in an instant, he cuts the satin lining revealing a wooden panel; he tries to pry it with the edge of the knife. The knife slips: it hits sharply on his finger and cuts it. "Shit!"

He inserts the knife into the case again and he bends the implement upward toward himself. This time it catches hold, and the panel pops up, but the ragged wooden edge cuts into his other hand. *"I'm way too old for this foolishness,"* Strauss thinks. With a block of the explosive in his bleeding hand he stops. He turns and goes back to the pile of clothes on the bed, fumbles around and finds his gun. He leaves the confines of the small cabin and stumbles up the stairs, hitting his knees when the boat bounces up and down. Pain reverberates through his legs. Opening the cabinet, he finds a flare and makes his way out to the rear of the boat.

Berretti has a life ring and is cutting some cord. Strauss looks out into the darkness. He can see the running lights of the pursuing craft; it is gaining on them, firing from its bow gun. Bullets pierce the night sky like flaming arrows. He drops below the gunwale just in time. Bullets whiz by, but they are high. Mario is heading into the west, and the waves are increasing in the wide-open gulf. The small boat pounds on every wave, creating a huge wake. The German patrol boat cuts through the rough sea, and fortunately, the wake of the fishing boat and the waves of the gulf slow it down a little.

The captain grabs the explosives and ties them securely to the life ring; he does the same with the flare. He attaches a long rope, lights the flare and throws the flotation device overboard letting out the line so that it drifts out within the confines of the wake, moving toward the enemy patrol boat.

"Grab this line and let it out carefully!" Berretti hands the rope to the courier priest. Strauss does so and tries his best to guide the ring toward the Nazi boat as he crouches down, bullets whizzing by him. He looks around for Berretti.

As quickly as he left, the captain is back on deck with two rifles. Ignoring the movement and swaying of the fishing boat, he loads the rifle.

"Here...take this and load it. Then start shooting!"

Strauss stares at Berretti with a slight hesitation. "I'm not a very good shot."

"Just shoot at the explosives! Tonight, you may get lucky!" The lifeline fully extended, Berretti ties it to a cleat on the rear gunwale and begins to shoot at the life ring. Strauss loads the rifle. He stands on the opposite side from Berretti. He looks at the captain shooting at the explosives.

The Germans are still firing, and their aim is improving. Bullets ping off the mast, outriggers and bridge. Mario is ducking down and steering blindly. Bullets pierce the superstructure of the boat. From the access hatch below, white smoke appears.

"We're overheating! Keep firing!"

Strauss braces his legs against the gunwale; his knees are throbbing with pain. He fires several times. He is wide right and hits the patrol boat. Berretti is firing, but he is wide left. The flare illuminates the flotation device and the cargo of explosives, but the round ring keeps disappearing beneath the waves, only to pop up again.

The German boat is now within 100 feet and gaining. The life ring is alongside its hull. Bullets continue unabated from the German boat.

Mario screams. "I've been hit!"

Strauss and Berretti feel the boat start to turn. Mario is no longer at the wheel. But now they can see the ring more clearly, the flare illuminating the hull of the speeding boat...and the explosives. The boat is about to ram them as the *Pescatore Felice* swerves hard to starboard on its own. Berretti fires, misses. He is out of bullets. He looks at Strauss; his life is now in the hands of the courier. Strauss fires one more time as the patrol boat sweeps pass them.

The explosion is deafening and accompanied by a bright orange ball of flames. In a second, the deck of the small boat is littered with twisted metal, wood, glass and human body parts.

Berretti puts down his rifle, breathing hard. "We have to get to La Spezia. We have to finish this."

"Guillermo, listen to me. That would be suicide. And Mario probably needs a doctor." Strauss is staring hard at the captain.

"No, we go and do this tonight. When that patrol boat does not return, they will be on full alert. If Mario dies, it will be for the cause!"

"You can't mean that?"

"I do. And you'll come with us, Raggiolo."

"No. I have a much more important job to do than blowing up some boats. I need to get to Forte dei Marmi, and so does Mario."

"You don't know my pain! I lost my family because of the Nazis. Why should I take orders from you?"

"Fine. My name is Jonathan Strauss and I'm a lieutenant in the OSS. Yes, I'm an agent. Your revenge can wait. You'll take me to Forte dei Marmi tonight and we'll get medical help for Mario. That's an order, partisan." Strauss takes his pistol out of his pocket and aims it at the stubborn captain.

Berretti stares at Strauss in surprise. "You're in the OSS? You said you were just a courier..." He stares at the gun and then out to the black night and the hard, rough waves, pondering. "All right then; seeing as how you saved us from that Nazi boat, and because Mario is my cousin, I'll take you there first. But then I must get revenge for what happened to my brother and his family."

Strauss is relieved, but wonders. What possibly could have happened in Sant'Anna di Stazzema?

Chapter Twenty-Eight

Piazza Navona
Rome, Italy

Brendan Galloway, in civilian clothes, is sitting at a busy café on an already too warm June morning. Summer is coming quickly in the Mediterranean in 1944. He stirs his cappuccino and looks around at the crowd passing through; a few American soldiers stop to take photos of the *Fountain of the Four Rivers*. The day is bright, sunny; the nine-month occupation of Rome by the Nazis seems like a distant bad memory. He checks his watch: 9:30 A.M. His guest is late. He looks toward the interior of the restaurant for a waiter to order another cappuccino. When he turns back to look out to the crowd again, Jack Lawrence is sitting in the other chair.

"Good morning, Archbishop. Did you forget your priestly attire?"

"Lawrence, how are you? You snuck up on me." Galloway has only met Jack Lawrence a few times. Each time, he has not enjoyed the encounter.

"Just like a good OSS officer should."

"I hate wearing my cassock and Roman collar. When I do all the little old ladies come up to me wanting a blessing, or worse, to kiss my hand."

"I completely understand. I, too, prefer to just blend in."

The waiter arrives and looks quizzically at the two men. Galloway orders two cappuccinos and a plate of Italian pastries in passable Italian. The waiter hustles off.

"How's our boy?" Lawrence is not much for pleasantries.

"I haven't heard from Strauss. He's two days late. You guys in the States needed to train him before turning him loose. He's just a priest, for God's sake."

"He was a spy in the first war. It's like riding a bicycle. You never forget. From his file, there wasn't much we could teach him anyway."

"Nazi Europe is not a bicycle. The SS and the Gestapo are worse than anything I ever saw in 1918. Back then, there was at least a code of honor of sorts. He may have numerous passports and his monsignor robes, but it may not do any good."

"You made him a monsignor?" Lawrence frowns.

"They made me a bishop…"

"I'm glad you're into the OSS but there are too many clerics in it for my taste."

"And why is that?"

"Your religious beliefs and what we do are in conflict, wouldn't you agree?"

"Sometimes, but evil is evil, and last time I checked I'm playing on the good guys' team. I must admit, sometimes it's more than I bargained for. I hate to lose good people like Strauss."

"Do you know where he is?"

"I sent him on some errands to season him a little; maybe hoping new orders would come along. But they haven't and here we are."

"New orders? He has orders. He's to stop the Black Orchestra from assassinating dear Adolf." Lawrence is confused and mildly annoyed.

"Look, Jack, I kind of agree with Strauss. I think the world would be better off without the S.O.B. But as I told him, that decision is above my pay grade."

"Where is he? You, more than anybody should know that time's running out to get this done. You need to stay with the game plan."

"Lawrence, I don't report to you. I report to Alan Dulles. Relax; he's on his way to Milan. I just sent him by the scenic route. But I should have gotten a call from him by now." Galloway looks toward the interior of the restaurant. He wants his coffee and pastry.

"I'm well aware you outrank me. But I'm responsible for the mission," Lawrence says with offense.

"And I'm responsible for Strauss." Galloway is getting annoyed with this bureaucrat.

"The mission trumps everything. The goddamn army found him by searching immigration records, put him in the OSS and now I'm stuck with him. Hell, he doesn't even want to be in Europe. He just wants to be praying at St. Patrick's."

"I can't say I blame him."

"You know, sometimes you're no fucking help." Lawrence grows more frustrated with the cleric spy.

"Well, I'm sure he'll turn up. From the little I've seen he has pretty good instincts. Since he grew up in Europe and spent plenty of time in Italy, let's give him the benefit of the doubt."

The cappuccinos and the pastries arrive. Lawrence quickly grabs two. Galloway stares at Lawrence. "I haven't had breakfast." Lawrence bites into his almond filled cannoli, and then takes a drink of the cappuccino. "I have a problem," the worried archbishop says, taking a sip of his frothy coffee.

"Oh, what is that?"

"I don't know how to get Strauss into the Black Orchestra."

"That is a problem. Who was his contact in Milan?"

"The head of another anti-Nazi organization called the Kreisau Circle. His name is Helmuth von Moltke. But the Gestapo threw him in prison for thinking impure thoughts about the National Socialists."

"Strauss has no one to meet in Milan? No wonder the Brits think we're amateurs at this spy game. Jesus, Galloway!"

"Hey, watch it. That's only part of my problem. For years, we've told the Black Orchestra that they're on their own, that the Allies won't help them with their assassination plans. Now, I must tell them we want to help. I'm not sure they'll believe us."

"I see the predicament. Don't we have any German contacts in Rome? Someone who is in the diplomatic corps? An ambassador to the Vatican...someone like that?"

Galloway pauses to think. "Wait. There is someone I think we can talk to. His name is Josef Müller." He takes another sip of the coffee. He wishes they had Coca-Cola in Rome, like they did before the occupation.

"I've heard of him. Isn't he known as Agent X?" Lawrence looks for a waiter so he can order more pastries.

"Right. He's in both the Abwehr and the Black Orchestra. He was the Vatican's intermediary to both the German government and, secretly, to the German Resistance, that is until last year. I can't believe I didn't think about him earlier."

"The Abwehr? That's not good. My sources tell me that it's been taken over by the SD. You know Canaris, the head of the whole deal? He's one of our key sources of intelligence and now he's missing." Lawrence takes a last bite. A waiter appears. "Two more pastries, por favor."

Galloway shakes his head and looks up at the waiter. "Un altro pasticcio, per favore." He looks at Lawrence. "We can't do anything about the Abwehr, but I know that Müller's here in Rome now. I can arrange a meeting."

"Which takes us back to your original problem. Why would he help us in stopping the plot against the Führer?"

Galloway finishes his cannoli, sips on the cappuccino. He says nothing. A sly smile finally breaks across his face. "I know...yes, it could work."

"Pray, tell me, Archbishop." The single pastry appears, and Lawrence grabs it, looking at Galloway, who shakes his head.

"Easy. We tell him that the Americans have had a change of heart."

"And why would we?" Lawrence is confused, and bites into the soft flakey crème filled dessert.

"Because of the invasion." Galloway is smiling broadly as he considers his idea.

"The invasion has been a success, though."

"Yes and no. So far, the Allies have suffered over 50,000 dead, and many more wounded. Caen has not been taken. Sure, we may be close to taking Cherbourg, but we haven't, and our casualties across the board have been much greater than expected."

"Okay, 50,000 men is bad, really bad, but we are going to land over two and a half million men by August." The handler looks at Galloway.

"But the Germans don't know that. We tell Müller that the Allies have come to the realization that the Krauts are going to fight until the bitter end. We might not be willing to lose the men it will take to defeat Germany. We want to help in their plot, and we can offer one of our best men to be at their disposal."

"Right, an old priest who hasn't even bought into the mission," Lawrence smirks.

"Maybe not that, but we can tell him that Strauss was a German espionage agent in the first war. Tell him that Strauss is a stone-cold killer. Sort of."

Lawrence laughs. "I guess it's worth a try." He gets up with the remainder of the cannoli in his hand.

"I'll let you know when I hear from Monsignor Strauss and I'll ask the Holy Father's secretary to get in touch with Herr Müller. I know they are in constant communication."

"I'm at the Hotel Giulio Cesare. Room 815. Call me."

"I just hope Strauss is all right."

"If he's not, we're in big trouble all the way around, Galloway."

Chapter Twenty-Nine

Hotel Sonia
Forte dei Marmi, Italy

Sonia Porchetta is making a big fuss over her lodger. Hearing his code name, "Trommler," she knows he has been sent by the American archbishop in Rome. That makes him important. Strauss pushes himself away from the table. He has had three pieces of chicken; lasagna; Caesar salad; three glasses of wine, and a dish of mascarpone with fresh berries. He is stuffed. Sonia comes into the dining room from the kitchen and sees unfinished food. Her face turns into an expression of pain.

"Mangiare, mangiare! You are way too thin, Signore Trommler."

"Signora, I cannot eat any more lest I commit the sin of gluttony. I didn't even expect a meal. I just wanted to get a room so I could put my suitcase down. But thank you; it was delicious."

"Stasera ti preparo gli spaghetti e le polpette," Porchetta says, smiling at the thought of being able to make another big meal.

"Spaghetti and meatballs! All right, but first I have to go to Sant'Anna di Stazzema. What is the best way to get there?"

Porchetta's look becomes truly anguished. She puts her hands to her face. "No! No, no, do not go there!" She quickly leaves the room to the safety of the kitchen and her sink full of dirty dishes. Strauss gets up and decides not to press the subject.

"I'll see you tonight, dear lady."

Outside, the afternoon is hot. He takes off his tweed coat and looks around for a car. Maybe he can pay someone to take him to the tainted place. After he sees for himself what happened, he'll head back to the Restaurante Gilda, see Caruso and call Galloway in Rome. After that, more eating with Sonia.

There are no cars on the street where the Hotel Sonia is located, even though it is the main thoroughfare. He notices signs at the corner: Massa - 8 KM; Pietrasanta - 5 KM; and Stazzema - 7 KM. The last sign points to the east. Perhaps he will have better luck on a side street heading in that direction, out of town. He might see a car in front of a house; he is willing to offer 500 lira for the trip. That should interest someone.

He walks through several streets. The town is quiet; at the two houses where automobiles are parked, no one is home to bargain with. Strauss has no interest in walking seven kilometers; his gait is slow, the legs still sore from the adventure on the boat. In the distance, he hears the sound of hoofs on the cobblestone road. He looks back from where he came, and rounding the corner is a large chestnut draft horse pulling an empty wagon. An old man is on the buckboard seat with a whip that he doesn't have to use. The horse knows his job. Strauss watches as it gets closer to him; he waves at the old man, who tips his wool cap. Strauss wishes he had changed back into his cassock as it would ensure a free lift. He is in luck; the hunched over figure pulls back on the reins and stops in front of the priest.

Strauss smiles and puts his hands together in prayer. "Good afternoon, signore, where might you be headed?"

"To my farm in Foce di Porchette. I have to load up this wagon with hay and come back to town. I sell it to the cattle farmers north of here. Where are you going?"

"Sant'Anna di Stazzema." Strauss looks at the old man for a reaction. He gets one. The man looks heavenward and makes the sign of the cross.

"I go by that town. From this road, it is just a kilometer further. Get up; I'll take you."

"Thank you, thank you." Strauss grabs the armrest of the buckboard and puts his foot on an iron rail below it and lifts himself up. "I am Raggiolo, call me Pietro."

"I am Tommaso. Having company will be nice. The road outside of town is slow; there are lots of twists and turns all uphill. But Simon here is a strong horse. Un cavallo cosi bravo. He will get us there." Then the man is quiet. This suits Strauss just fine; the less asked about his reason for going to the town the better.

The respite is momentary. After fifteen minutes, the old man speaks, perhaps tired of the awkward silence. "Why do you want to go to that town? No one lives there now."

"No one lives there?"

"No. Not since the Germans and Black Brigade came through. Did you have family there?"

"No. I have business in the town with the priest, Father Menguzzo."

The old man blesses himself again and says in a flat voice with no emotion: "He is dead."

Strauss crosses himself and says in a low voice: "Dio reposi la sui anima."

The horse continues to pull the wagon up another switchback. The smooth gravel road out of Forte dei Marmi has become two deep ruts up into the Tuscan hills. After a quiet hour, the narrow road levels out and they reach a plateau where there is a fork in the road. Tommaso nods in the direction of a dirt road on the left. "Down there. It is not far. You will find there what no one should find."

"Thank you. Here are some liras for your trouble." Strauss hopes the money may give the old man a thought. It does. "Thank you. I will be back here in the morning, very early. The wagon will be full of hay, and if you are here, I will take you back."

"You are very kind. I'm sure I can find a house to stay in tonight."

"No, you won't. But there is a cave ahead with a place to get out from the weather. You will see it." The man snaps the reins and Simon slowly starts moving down the road to the right.

After walking for about fifteen minutes, Strauss sees the large rock outcropping with an opening hewn into it. The only sounds are birds calling to each other, and the air rustling through the branches of olive and cypress trees. But the air is not fresh. It smells of smoke and something foul. The road bends sharply to the right. Strauss continues walking, rounds the corner and stops in horror. The village of Sant'Anna di Stazzema is a smoldering ruin, burned to the ground. Wisps of smoke still rise from some of the remains. In the town square, surrounded by the burnt-out shells of buildings is a large pyre, gray vaporous clouds rising upward to the sky like sacrilegious incense. He walks toward the mound consisting of hulking piles and shapes that he cannot fathom. He notices what looks like the end of a church pew, with ornate scrollwork and a carved cross in the center. There are many pews piled on top of the mound. There are other timbers as well, smoldering now, previously a raging fire. Under it are black forms. His eyes focus through the haze of smoke. He puts his hand to his mouth as he gags. They are charred bodies; he can make out human skulls with burnt hair, limbs missing flesh, and charred bodies. The wind shifts and the acrid smell of burned human beings invades his nostrils. Strauss staggers away from the monument of hate. A woman is sitting on the ground crying, swaying back and forth.

"Mother, tell me what happened?"

She continues to cry in deep wails of sorrow, unable to talk. He looks toward the remains of the church and heads in that direction. He arrives at the shell of what must have been a simple but beautiful sanctuary, goes in and finds another heap of dead bodies, all burned. He can still make out the anguished faces of the victims. He runs back out, turns a corner and vomits Porchetta's great feast. When he is done, he looks up. A boy about ten years old is staring at him.

"Hello. Don't be afraid. What is your name? I'm Father Strauss." There is no reason for a charade and Strauss thinks that perhaps the young boy will speak to a priest. The boy says nothing. "Let's see if we can find you some food, then maybe you will tell me what happened?" The boy nods and takes the priest's hand leading him toward a house, partially destroyed but still standing.

They climb through the doorway and step gingerly to the back where the cucina is. There is a large cupboard, seared by the fire but unscathed. The boy points. Strauss opens the doors and sees some old bread, cheese and hard salami. There are also a few bottles of wine. He takes the food and the boy leads him out to the grassy backyard behind the house. They sit on a log. In the late afternoon, the sun has begun to set. In the distance are rolling hills, lavender and Judas trees, vineyards with their fruit and orchards of olive trees, the green and blue sea far off on the horizon. It is as beautiful a view as Strauss has ever seen. It is a world apart from the horror he has just witnessed on the other side of the house. The boy grabs the food, tears the stale bread off and eats it. He motions to Strauss to open the bottle of wine. Strauss has no appetite, but it looks like his new friend has not eaten in days. He speaks at last.

"I hid in the hills, like the partisans did after the SS and the Fascist Brigade came into the village. I only came back today for food. I am hungry."

"How long ago?"

"I don't know, maybe two days. Or a little longer."

"Where are your mother and father?"

The boy nods in the direction of the town square. "There."

"I am so sorry." Strauss hugs the boy who is now biting into the slab of cheese.

"My younger brother and sister were killed too. When the soldiers came, my brother pushed me into the goat pen on other side of the village. The soldiers didn't see me. I hid there until they made other people go into the barn, including my brother and sister. They shot them and then set it on fire. I crawled under the fence and ran into the woods."

"How many soldiers?"

"Many, many. So many, I don't know, maybe 500."

"What is your name?"

"Enrico."

"Is this your house?"

"Yes. It used to be." Tears run down his cheeks and Strauss hands him the bottle of wine; the boy takes a drink, then another.

They hear footsteps from the front of the house. In a moment, a strapping young man is standing above them. Strauss reaches for his knife but sees that the man is unarmed. Enrico looks up.

"Uncle Alberto!" Enrico jumps up. He hugs his relative.

Strauss and Alberto walk along a path leading to an orchard, beyond earshot of young Enrico. The orange Italian sun is lower in the sky; Strauss can clearly make out the anguish on the young man's face.

"Father Strauss, I am a partisan and was hiding in the woods north of here with my unit. Reprisals on the part of the Nazis are expected; but in this case, we had done nothing to warrant what took place here. People from the south had fled to the village to escape the Nazis, but as those animals are pushed back by the Allies, they simply exact revenge because they are losing the war."

"How many people lived here at Sant'Anna?

"About 400 but with the refugees, it was over 600."

"Do you know how many were killed by the SS?"

"It was SS and Italian Fascists, too, dressed as German soldiers." Alberto spits on the ground. "They are worse than vermin and they have betrayed their country. How can they kill their own countrymen?"

Strauss presses the question. "Do you know how many?"

"Everyone! There are maybe twenty or thirty people left. They are hiding out there." He points out to the countryside.

Strauss hangs his shaking head. "Sweet Jesus, the entire village?"

"Yes. Most of the men had fled into the hills because they did not want to become slave labor for the Germans. But they did not think their mothers, wives, or daughters would be harmed. They were wrong! They made people go into basements and then threw in grenades. The SS lined the people up along walls and started shooting at one end, slowly, down to the other. If you were the last to be shot, you knew that you would soon die. They machine gunned the women and children who were trying to run away. People who did manage to escape into the hills told me they killed babies and pregnant women. And…" Alberto breaks down and begins to sob violently.

"I am so sorry. Please…so I can tell others." Tears are welling up in Strauss and he puts his arm around Alberto, who buries his face into the priest's shirt.

"There's one woman, Evelina Berretti…she was eight months pregnant. They shot her first and then cut out the baby from her womb and shot it separately!"

"Dear God in heaven!" Strauss makes the sign of the cross. He remembers the name of the fishing boat captain: Guillermo…Berretti!

Alberto continues between sobs, "Do you know what the soldiers did when they were done with their killing? They sat down by the village square, watching the bonfire they had set to cover up their evil work, and they ate lunch!"

Strauss is nauseous; he feels lightheaded and flush. He finds a tree stump and drops down to sit, his legs shaking. *Why God, do you allow these things to happen?* he wonders. "I am so sorry, Alberto. But come; we need to get back to Enrico. He needs you."

The floor of the cave is hard and rocky. Strauss has tried to smooth a covered area large enough to sleep. He looked in the remains of the houses and finally found a partially burned blanket. Under it was a body, probably dead from smoke inhalation. He returned to Enrico's house and took the last of the three-day-old bread, a wedge of cheese and small cacciatore salami. He found another bottle of wine and in a drawer, some candles and matches.

Strauss has no desire to share his modest quarters with another wild boar or worse, a snake. The candles are lit and placed around the perimeter. He forces himself to eat a little, though he is still not hungry after what he has seen in the town. Alberto has taken Enrico into the hills to hide until the war is over in this part of the world. After that the boy will have to create a new, different life. It will be devoid of the warm embrace of his mother, the tussling of his hair by his father in the midst of important life lessons, or the welcome annoyance of teasing brothers and sisters. Strauss's eyes water up again. He takes a deep drink of the wine. It is all he wants. *"Why, God? Why do so many have to suffer?"* He knows it is not the fault of God, but what he has seen shakes his faith in all he believes in, just as it did in the last war. Strauss prays, then lies down and falls into a troubling sleep.

Chapter Thirty

Von Stauffenberg Estate
Schloss Lautlingen, Bavaria

Claus von Stauffenberg is enjoying this week in late June, a brief leave from the rigors of war, and particularly from planning the assassination of Adolf Hitler. His large house outside the pretty city of Albstadt, tucked into the Swabian Alps, is as removed from the war as a town can be. And his family's handsome, rambling home, his refuge, seems more distant yet. He walks with his wife, Nina, to a small lake, while Uncle Nux, a Prussian general in the Great War, tends to a passel of children. There are Claus and Nina's four children plus two other cousins, all at mischievous ages. Nikolaus von Üxküll-Gyllenband is telling them vivid stories of when as a young man, he was a big game hunter in Africa on great safaris. He wants to give Claus and Nina some privacy. Uncle Nux knows time is short.

Only Nina, Uncle Nux and Claus's brother, Berthold, know the details of the plan that von Stauffenberg is going to attempt in the coming weeks. Nina shares her husband's hatred of the criminal Nazi regime. Yet her friends and her children are not aware of her views. In Germany listening to a far-off foreign radio station, speaking ill of the Führer, even expressing a defeatist attitude, can result in arrest and maybe death.

"Why, my darling, must it be you? Think of the children if not of me." Nina looks lovingly at her husband. Even with a missing hand and a patch over his eye, he is exceedingly handsome.

"I think of you and them all the time. Don't you think I am torn apart by this? One part of me struggles with performing this deed against Germany. The other side sees how many innocent lives can be saved." Stauffenberg squeezes Nina's hand.

"Claus, you will save Germany. Hitler is a monster. And God will thank you. But if you do not succeed, you will lose your life and your family."

"Yes and this peaceful life. I knew I should have been a philosopher. No, a poet...that's right, a poet!"

Nina kisses him on the cheek. "I think of you as a general or better, the president of a new Germany, but not a philosopher or much less, a poet."

Claus smiles at his wife. "Well, there we are..."

"You've already decided, haven't you? This pleasant walk has just been to inform me that you are going to do something soon."

"Nina, my love, I have been struggling with this for many months. But I have finally concluded that as a Christian, I have no other choice."

"I just wish it could be someone else."

"No one else has been able to organize it properly. And they have sent von Tresckow to the front in Russia. Now that I am chief of staff of the Replacement Army, I am the only one with direct access to him."

"How much longer will I have you?" Tears are welling up in Nina's blue eyes.

"Forever. I have planned everything down to the last detail. Do not fret any longer." He takes her face in his hand and kisses her on the lips.

The two sit on a bench at the lake and look out into the distance, to the Alps. The day is picture perfect. The children run up to their father and he kisses each one of them.

"Father, Uncle Nux is going to let us go fishing!"

"Wonderful! We need something to eat for dinner!"

"I am sorry for the interruption, nephew. They are quite a horde!" Uncle Nux's bearing is as regal and charismatic as his nephew's. The Stauffenberg family has a fine gene pool, far superior to the current ruler of Germany. It is a close knit, loving family, strong in their faith and in their love of their country. "Come, children. Let's go to the barn and get some fishing poles."

The children scamper off and their favorite uncle tries to keep up. Nina laughs, and then she is quiet.

"What else is on your mind, my love?" Stauffenberg knows his wife of eleven years is holding something back.

"I am pregnant again, my dear husband."

Chapter Thirty-One

A cave
Outside Sant'Anna de Stazzema

The vehicle slowly makes its way up the narrow-rutted road and turns toward Sant'Anna de Stazzema. Before long, the Kübelwagen is in front of the cave. It stops; it is still dark out. The scharführer and the kriminalinspektor get out of the vehicle with two hostages, hands bound behind their backs.

The scharführer shines a flashlight into the eyes of Father Jonathan Strauss. He stirs. The other kicks his shoe. Strauss opens his eyes. Enrico and Alberto are standing in front of him, fear consuming their faces. The goons are holding them tightly from behind. Both Nazis have twisted, evil smiles. Simultaneously, Strauss sees the glint of bright metal blades on the necks of his two new acquaintances. In one choreographed motion he watches as the boy and his uncle have their throats slit, blood spurting out all over him.

"Nooooo!!!" Strauss screams and sits up. His face is covered with perspiration, his body shakes. He looks around. Only one candle is still lit, flickering in the last minutes of the waning night. He rubs his eyes. There is no one in front of him. All he can see is the first rays of sun creeping above the rolling hills in the east. He rubs his eyes, looks again. No one is there. Simply a nightmare. No worse than those that he had after the killings he carried out the first war. Killing that was necessary for the Fatherland, and more importantly, so that he would live. It took years, but finally the dark dreams subsided and mercifully ended. Now, were they to come back?

Strauss gets up. He is thirsty; he could drink a bucketful of water. He bends down and picks up the blanket and gathers up what is left of his food, blows out the last candle and gathers the other four that have gone out, and places everything into the old blanket that had been his sleeping bag. Rolling it up, he places it in a small recess so it may be found by the next visitor to this corner of hell. Shaking himself, rubbing his stiff knees, he walks back to the fork in the road. He cannot afford to miss his ride back to Forte dei Marmi with Tommaso. Soon he hears the sounds of Simon's hooves on the rocks and gravel.

"Buongiorno, signore."

"Good morning, Tommaso. Thank you for taking me back to town." Strauss is relieved to see a kind face and a warm welcome, a small testament to a better humanity in the world.

"This early, I like company. Simon does not say very much."

"No, but I can tell he is a good horse." This morning, after his dream, Strauss is happy for conversation.

"Did you see what you wanted to see?"

"No one should see what I saw. It was terrible. Thank you for warning me, but I had to go." Strauss looks at the face of the old man; it is sad and tired.

Tommaso looks ahead as the wagon lumbers down a steep hill. "I have been fortunate. I was too old to be in the Great War, which was fought in the mountains a long way from here. Not long ago, this part of Italy was free of this new war. But then the Germans came; came into my country. Why? It is not their land. They have their own land, but they are greedy. And so, God brings war to us."

"Not God. It was other men that brought it. Bad men." Strauss looks at Tommaso's hard, wrinkled face for his reaction.

"Yes, they are bad men. But He lets all this happen. I guess He did not create us in His own image as the Bible says. I think He made some mistakes. You saw it yesterday in the town. This hill country has known war, but not like this. Who kills like that? Women, children, babies. They were not soldiers; they are the innocent. But they were slaughtered like pigs."

Strauss has no good response, only "I understand, Tommaso, I understand."

The old man continues: "I just want to carry my hay to the ranchers, but God has put war here to hurt us and to confuse me. I am too old for war."

"We are all too old for war, my friend."

It is close to 8:00 A.M. when Tommaso and the priest enter the small city of Forte dei Marmi. A truck passes by carrying blocks of Carrara marble from the great stone caverns north of the city. It is said that Michelangelo would go to the quarry caves to personally choose the marble blocks that would become masterpieces like *David* and the *Pieta*. Now the caves are being used by the Germans to store ammunition and supplies.

Strauss looks toward the train station. He hopes there is a train this morning back to Rome. First, he must call Brendan Galloway from the Ristorante Gilda and tell him what he saw and other bad news. News Galloway will not be happy about.

"I am turning here, Signore Pietro. You can come along if you like to pitch hay to cows. I have enjoyed your company." Tommaso puts out his hand to Father Strauss who shakes it with appreciation.

"And I have enjoyed traveling with you, my new friend. May the peace of God be with you and with this country." Strauss gets down from the wagon and blesses Tommaso who looks surprised. "Si, Tommaso, I am a priest."

The farmer doffs his worn cap, blesses himself, and snaps the reins, and Simon turns the corner. Once the wagon passes, Father Strauss looks toward the restaurant. Parked in front of it is a Kübelwagen.

"Damn, here we go again!" Strauss mutters. He changes direction and heads in the opposite direction to the Hotel Sonia. As he walks briskly, he can hear the distant sound of a train whistle. He breaks into a trot and is at the hotel momentarily.

"Signore Trommler, where have you been? I made a nice meal last night."

"Madam, I am sure you did. I was delayed. I am sorry but here are two thousand liras for the room and the wonderful food. I will just be a minute; I need to get my suitcase." Before Sonia can speak Strauss has bound up the stairs two steps at a time, and with the turn of the old-fashioned key, is in the room. He opens his suitcase and takes out the gun. For the first time, he checks to make sure that it has bullets. He hears the train whistle again.

Caruso is serving the two Nazis breakfast. His restaurant does not open until noon, but his guests have insisted that he make an exception. As he cooked the scrambled eggs he spat into them. "Vai a l'inferno, Nazis!"

He is standing at the bar, cleaning glasses. Every so often, he looks over at his two unwanted visitors. They make him nervous, constantly looking at him. Across the road, he hears the train come to a stop. Perhaps they will leave to search the passengers, but they do not seem concerned with its pending arrival. The phone rings.

'Ciao, Ristorante Gilda…"

"Caruso, my friend. It's me, Galloway. Let me apologize for telling you to go to hell."

"No, I do not need any tomatoes today."

"What? Caruso, have you seen Trommler? He has not called me."

"I said, 'No' I don't need any tomatoes, but I, ah, need lettuce."

"Oh, I understand now. Are you in any danger?"

"No, I don't need carrots, either." Caruso is trying hard to keep a calm voice. The two Nazis are looking at him, trying to hear the conversation. "I do need some pole beans."

"All right. Then please tell him to report in when you see him."

"Okay. Yes, I will. Ciao." Caruso hangs up and looks out to the train and passengers getting off at the station. He heads to the kitchen passing by the table of his diners. *"My God, they eat slowly,"* he thinks. As he writes up a check he is sure they will not pay, he thinks about the phone call. Perhaps he should ask around town if anyone on his side of the war has seen the man named "Trommler." He looks out into the dining room from the small opening where food is passed. Goon One and Goon Two are now lighting cigarettes, still drinking their coffee. He should be a good host and refill the cups. As he goes to fetch the coffee pot, he hears chairs moving, one turning over and hitting the floor.

"It's him!"

Caruso hurries back into the dining room as the two men run out the restaurant. He goes to the front door; they are heading toward the train pulling away from the station. Climbing onto one of the passenger cars is a tall man dressed like a peasant, hauling a suitcase. He disappears into the railway car. Realizing they cannot get to the now rapidly moving train, the two pursuers stop and head back toward the restaurant. They reach the Kübelwagen and get in, turn on the engine and head in the same direction: toward Rome.

"Just as I thought. They didn't pay for breakfast!" Caruso says to no one in particular.

Strauss falls into a seat in the Pullman coach. He shakes his head. He looks to heaven but says nothing. Presently, a conductor appears.

"Where is this train headed?" Strauss inquires.

"Most people know where a train is going before they get on it, my friend. It goes to Rome."

"Perfect. One ticket please. Do you have a first-class cabin?"

"Certainly. In the next coach up ahead. Take cabin four. It's on the opposite side. That will be 1,200 lira."

"Is there a dining car?"

"Yes, you are in luck. This is non-stop to Rome. We have lunch and snacks. Three cars back. If you hurry, they are probably still serving breakfast."

"Wonderful." Strauss pays the man and gets up and heads to what he hopes will be his sanctuary for the day. He'll get rid of his suitcase and head to the dining car; he is suddenly famished.

Cabin four is all his. Strauss puts up his suitcase after opening it and taking out *A Farewell to Arms* and his black suit, shirt and roman collar. "*Time to be a priest again.*" He looks out the window to the road, which parallels the train tracks. Running along at the same speed is the Kübelwagen and his two friends.

"God almighty, is there no peace?!" Strauss sees that the scharführer is trying to get the attention of the engineer to make the train stop. That cannot happen; he has to get to Rome, quit and then go to America; enough of this war. He lowers the window and the air rushes into the small space as he pulls out his pistol. He aims and shoots just as the train hits an uneven joint in the rails. The scharführer appears to have heard something but he goes back to flailing his arms at the engineer. Strauss puts one knee onto the seat and against the wall for more stability; he presses his arm holding the gun against the jamb of the window to steady his aim. He fires again. The bullet hits the hood of the utilitarian vehicle, but it keeps moving. Another shot. Nothing. One more. The tire explodes. The Nazi is trying to maintain control, but to no avail. The Kübelwagen and its two passengers swerve off the road and slam into a telephone pole. Strauss lets out a yell of joy and sticks his head out the window. The vehicle is engulfed in flames.

The priest sits down and lets out a deep sigh. "Maybe now I can get some breakfast!" He reaches for his book and heads to the dining car.

Chapter Thirty-Two

Paris, France

He is not as familiar with the backstreets of Paris as he is with those of Berlin or Madrid. After walking into the back of his favorite restaurant, shaking the hand of the owner, and making him swear that he was never there, Wilhelm Canaris leaves through the front door. He can hear the distinctive sirens of the police and assumes it is not the French Gendarmes but the SD. Strange. They can't be following him, but for now he has to assume the worse. Canaris crosses the street, walks to the end of the block and turns right onto the Rue du Cherche-Midi, and after a short distance, left onto the Rue Dupin. There he finds a small restaurant with a bar. He decides that it is a safe place to wait out the manhunt that is going on.

"Beaujolais, s'il vous plait…"

The owner/bartender looks at his guest. White hair, well dressed, looking a little distracted. He tries to remember all of his new customers in the event he is interrogated by the Carlingue, the French Gestapo, a bunch of thugs and common criminals. Failure to cooperate would mean his establishment would be closed down, or worse, he would receive a vicious beating.

He decides that the man can afford one of his better vintages and selects a Domaine Calot Morgon 1937. He pours the glass and sets it in front of the man. It is two o'clock. Canaris is the only customer.

The owner goes back to drying freshly washed wine glasses. He is hoping for a busy evening. "Est-ci bien?"

"Oui. C'est trés bien!" Canaris smiles and nods. Outside a Wehrmacht Stabswagen speeds by as its siren blares. He takes a deep gulp. This is the first time he is the hunted, not the hunter. Canaris realizes that he will need new papers if his life on the run can succeed. He will have to make his way to the Convent of the Sisters and find Jade Amicol. Surely he can provide them, and if Canaris has to pay, he now has plenty of money. Additionally, he needs help getting to his next destination, wherever that might be.

The former head of the Abwehr finishes his glass, having enjoyed it thoroughly, and leaves a 20 Reichsmark note on the bar. A stupid thing, but he has no francs. Hopefully, it will not come back to haunt him.

"Merci beaucoup." Canaris gets up, puts his hat on low over his forehead, and leaves. The owner finishes his chore and goes over to the empty glass. He raises his eyebrows as he stares at the German note. A few minutes later he has company, but they do not want a glass of wine.

Canaris walks quickly to the Rue de Sèvres, a wide boulevard where he hails a cab. Finally, one of the few left in the city stops and he gets in. As he looks back, he sees several suspicious automobiles in front of the establishment he just left. He shakes his head.

"Convent of the Sisters of the Passion. It is in Montreuil, 64 Rue de la Santé. And please hurry!"

"Oui, monsieur, provided I am not stopped at a checkpoint. I've already been stopped at two. The police must be looking for a bad criminal!"

"Indeed…" Canaris looks out the window. He begins to think that he might enjoy house arrest. The cab makes a quick U turn and heads back in the direction of the Hotel Lutetia. He slumps low in his seat; as they pass Abwehr headquarters, he sees his friend, Toepfer, walking out of the building with two men in black leather coats, deep in conversation.

The cab crosses over the Seine and there are no checkpoints. Soon, it is making its way east on a wide boulevard, speeding. There are no police to stop him. The cabbie turns down several narrow side streets and reaches the convent that is located on the west side of this industrial neighborhood. The building complex surrounds a large courtyard, full of peach trees. It is a sanctuary used by the nuns for prayer and meditation. Canaris gets out and again has no option but to give the driver a 10-mark note. The driver shakes his head and drives on.

"I have come to pray." Canaris speaks past the door that has been barely opened by the Mother Superior, Sister Agnes.

"You! What do you want?"

"I need a place of refuge, dear mother. I am a wanted man."

Sister Agnes opens the door. "Justice at last. Well, come in. I have some soup warming."

"Thank you. I knew you would not turn me away."

"It is only because Colonel Olivier vouches for you. You may be a good Nazi, but you are still a Nazi!"

"Has he been here? I must get in contact with him."

Sister Agnes is in a sour mood, as she is most days. She wants to be an abbess to nuns again, not a member of the Resistance, helping Germans. "He does not check in with me, Admiral, and he does not keep regular office hours. I'll show you to the phone. Maybe you can reach him. Come this way to the kitchen."

The two unlikely companions make their way down a long arcade with openings to the great room full of Jewish refugees. Canaris stops and goes inside. He looks around; the place looks more crowded than during his last visit. He returns to the areaway.

"The business of saving poor souls is good?" Canaris notes.

"There is no shortage of these unfortunate people needing shelter. They make their way here at night or they are brought by the Resistance. Even now, with Paris about to be liberated, the SS hunts them down like dogs. These are your people!"

Canaris says nothing. The two walk on and reach the large kitchen. Sister points to an alcove where there is a phone on the wall. Canaris dials a number.

"Yes…"

"Jade, it is me. Please come to church tonight."

"I'll be there shortly."

The admiral puts down the phone and returns to the kitchen. There is a large center counter topped with butcher block and four stools wait at one end. Sitting before one of them is a steaming bowl of vegetable soup, some bread and a glass of wine.

"You spoil me, Mother, in spite of the fact that I'm a German."

"No, a Nazi."

"I admit that at first, I was a Nazi, in thought if not in actual affiliation. I believed in a strong country under strong leadership. And I wanted the wrongs of the Versailles Treaty reversed. And the Nazis were against Communism. That itself would be enough to get my support. Then I realized that all Hitler wanted was war against Europe and that his hatred of the Jewish race would become a stain on our national conscience." Canaris sips at the hot soup and decides on a drink of the wine instead. It is not as good as the vintage he had at the café, but it is still palatable.

"What have you done to stop him?"

"What I can. I have allowed the Abwehr to become inefficient and that hinders the Reich. I pass information along to the British and so do my agents. Most of them in England have been captured and now are on the Allie's side. It's fine by me."

"But the Gestapo still rounds up the Jewish people…"

"I have no control of that. It might be of interest to you to know that I saved over 500 Dutch Jews back in 1941. Some of them were made spies for the Abwehr just so they could escape to unoccupied countries."

"Are you Catholic?" Sister Agnes is intrigued by her guest.

"Lutheran, but not a good one. Faith in God goes by the wayside in war for those of us who are involved in it. We have to choose between a god on earth, and the one in heaven. I made my choice, so I guess if there is a hell, there is a place assigned for me."

"It is not too late for you, Admiral. I think you are not such a bad man after all. You are, I think, a work in progress."

"There has not been much progress, I'm afraid."

"Why have you returned here?"

"You'll be happy to know that I am wanted by my people."

"Well, there you are: progress." Sister refills his glass of wine.

The small parlor is lit with a single lamp. There are two comfortable chairs beside it. The thick convent walls provide natural insulation to the warm night outside and the room is comfortable. On one wall is a crucifix; the figure of Jesus in more agony than usual and there is an abundance of blood flowing from his wounds. Canaris does his best to avoid looking at the cross, staring instead at Jade Amicol.

"I have 5,000 Reichsmarks. That is a sure giveaway in free France. Can I exchange a few of them for francs? And I'll need a car and a new set of identification papers. Maybe I can be Louis Bourbon or Napoleon Bonaparte?"

"I think the resistance can come up with better aliases than that, my friend. You look tired."

"I guess I'm not used to being on the other side of the hunt. I must say, I've enjoyed getting away from them. I hate the violence but enjoy the cat and mouse. And I still have some gas in the tank." He looks up at the crucifix.

"What troubles you, my friend?" Olivier picks up on his friend's sudden silence.

"It may not have turned out so well for a bartender." He looks again to the crucifix and he silently asks God to spare the innocent man from the wrath of the Carlingue.

"The war goes on. But now we have to get you out of here to wherever you are going."

"I'm going to go to Strasbourg, my friend. The perfect combination of France and Germany."

"Indeed. Both countries have fought over that city for centuries."

Chapter Thirty-Three

Vatican City
Rome, Italy

"Attentzione! Attentzione! Prossima fermata Roma." The announcement from the speaker in the cabin is harsh, piercing Strauss's eardrums. "Mother of God, we're here already. *It's time to have that talk with Galloway.*" The reluctant spy frowns as he pulls down his suitcase. This meeting won't be pleasant. He is quitting the OSS. With luck, he is sure he can get out of his assignment and be on a troop ship to the USA within the week. Back to the comfort and refuge of St. Patrick's. It is 8:00 P.M. and a pleasant late June summer evening, so Strauss decides to walk to the Vatican. There is a small hotel for visiting priests; if he is lucky there will be a room. In the morning he will go and visit the boss and deliver the news to Galloway.

"Jonathan, what in the hell are you doing here? You should be in Milan by now."

"I quit! I've seen all of this war that I need to. I'm going home to America. Let the OSS court martial me. I don't care! I think one war is enough for anyone to endure." Strauss is trying hard to be firm. He wants no argument.

"Sit down. I'll get you some coffee. Let me go to the kitchen…I think there might even be a few pastries."

"I don't want a pastry." In deference to his superior he decides it is best to sit down. After all he can't just walk in, quit, and book the first trip back to America. He needs Galloway's help.

"Sit. I'll be right back." The Archbishop leaves the room and returns quickly with a coffeepot.

"Sorry, no pastries. Tell me, what happened? Why this change of heart? I've heard reports, and I wasn't sure if you were okay." Galloway is trying to be as soothing as possible; he needs this American priest and time is running short.

"Where do I begin?" Strauss prepares his cup of coffee practically emptying the sugar bowl.

There is a knock on the closed door. It opens; Jack Lawrence is standing there.

"Brendan, have you gotten hold of Strauss? Strauss! You're supposed to be in Milan meeting your contact."

"The train I got on to get away from two Nazis happened to be headed in the opposite direction. That is fine with me because I'm done with this little European holiday!"

Lawrence goes over to the coffee pot and pours a cup of black. "Father…"

"It's Monsignor now, Lawrence."

"Oh yeah, I heard about that. I'm surprised Galloway didn't name you Pope."

"It wouldn't make any difference. Get me on the first troop ship to the States! I'm done!"

Galloway realizes that this discussion will take some time. He needs to talk his errant priest off the ledge. "Jonathan, tell us what happened."

"First, a Gestapo and an SD thug pistol whipped me. Then they followed me all over central Italy."

"What happened to them?"

"I shot at the tires on their vehicle and it hit a pole and they were killed."

"Well, there you go! Good work. I understand you also got the explosives to Berretti."

"Yes, and I hope he blew up the entire Italian Navy with them. A German patrol boat came after us and we were nearly rammed!"

"But you weren't. You blew it up. Good shooting."

"Oh, you know that too?"

"It is my job after all…but I don't know anything about Sant'Anna di Stazzema."

"I don't think I can tell you."

"Why not?"

"It's too horrible."

"I figured it would be bad. The preliminary reports were…discouraging. But we have to know."

"Okay. An SS Brigade and some Black Fascists, over 500 of them came into the village and systematically killed everyone. And it wasn't a reprisal. Almost 600 people were slaughtered, most of whom were women and children. The men had gone into the forest because they did not want to be conscripted for slave labor. I found a small boy. His mother, father, and siblings were murdered."

Galloway looks heavenward and makes the sign of the cross. Lawrence puts down his coffee.

"Then they tried to hide their deed by piling the bodies in the town square, took all the pews from the church, put them on top and started a bonfire. While it raged, they ate their lunch and laughed. They even cut babies out of their mothers' wombs!"

"Oh, dear God!" is all that Galloway can say.

Lawrence gets up and goes to the window to look out to the beauty of the Vatican Gardens. "Sounds like an ugly sight, Monsignor."

"That's why I want out. This isn't an honorable war, if such a thing exists: its sadism! And you want me to stop the Black Orchestra from killing Hitler? Where do I sign up to personally cut his throat? Otherwise, I'm going back to the States."

"Strauss, your feelings don't matter. Your job, your mission, the one you accepted, is to stop the Black Orchestra from killing Hitler. Don't you understand that?" Lawrence is growing frustrated with his charge.

"Didn't you hear me, Lawrence? I'm done. Finito. Get me on a ship back to New York!"

Galloway speaks in a calm voice. "Jonathan, I understand how you feel, but no one said it would be easy. I even told you it would be difficult. It's probably best you came back. We may have a better contact for you here."

"Didn't you hear me, Major? I'm not doing this anymore! Find someone else!" Strauss gets up to leave.

Lawrence turns away from the idyllic view. "Michael Wagner's father died last week."

"What? Who?"

"Your son, remember? His father, his adopted father, died last week of a massive heart attack. There is no money to send him to that fine upper west side Jesuit high school. Hell, he won't even be able to go to high school. He'll have to get a job. He's the breadwinner for the family now. Did you know he has two sisters and a baby brother?"

"Thank you for enlightening me, Lawrence." Strauss glares at his handler. He turns to Galloway. "Surely, I've done enough to warrant my being discharged from this insanity! I went to Sant'Anna and I got the explosives to Berretti."

Galloway looks back at Strauss. "Yes, you did, John. And the next night, the night you were seeing the horrors in Sant'Anna, Berretti went back to La Spezia. His boat was caught in a trap by three German patrol boats. They were boarded. The Nazis found the explosives and detonating devices. After taking the supplies, they set the boat on fire, with Guillermo, Mario, Filippo, and Stefano tied up on board, bound up in the fishing nets. They burned to death. Partisan fishermen found the burned-out hull of the boat two days later."

Chapter Thirty-Four

Galloway's Office
Vatican City

"I don't think any of that cheered him up." Lawrence is lighting a cigarette and looking out the window to the Vatican Gardens. "We need to decide what to do with him. He's not reliable. Josef Müller will be here shortly."

"I believe a week off in Rome will help his disposition. He's been through a lot, some R&R and he'll be fine. Once you told him about his son's adopted father and my news about Berretti, I think he's willing to get the job done and even the score. At least get back at what they did to the fisherman. You know revenge is a powerful motivator. I can't believe that Berretti's brother and entire family were murdered at Sant'Anna."

"This war isn't getting any more pleasant, is it?"

"No, but it never was. The Nazis exist on a whole different plane of evil. And now we are trying to stop the Black Orchestra. As I told Strauss before he started his journey, that decision is above my pay grade. I think I agree with him. Why are we trying to stop the killing of Hitler? It makes no sense."

"It makes plenty of sense to President Roosevelt and Prime Minister Churchill and that's all that matters. But you've wasted several days, making him an errand boy. It didn't help his outlook either. It's almost July now." Lawrence pours another cup of coffee and goes back to looking at the manicured gardens below. "I'm not sure we can trust Strauss to get the job done."

"He's all we have. Look, he's German; I'm sure he'll follow orders. They're very good at that." Galloway tries to be re-assuring.

"I wouldn't bet on it." Lawrence says without turning to Galloway.

There is a knock on the door. Lawrence puts down his coffee, goes over and opens it to find their guest, Josef Müller.

Galloway takes his feet off the desk and puts the unlit cigar in the ashtray. He makes sure his red cap is on correctly and stands, brushing off his silk robes. In a moment, he goes from OSS operative to a prince of the Roman Catholic Church.

"Herr Muller, thank you for coming. Please come in. I'm Jack Lawrence. I'm from Washington and I'm with the OSS. I believe you know Archbishop Brendan Galloway?"

"A pleasure to meet you, Mr. Lawrence. Your Eminence, so good to see you again."

"Josef, you look well. Would you like some coffee? Come and sit." Galloway motions the diplomat turned liaison between the Vatican and the German Resistance to a comfortable seating area with a leather couch and two upholstered chairs. A coffee table is in the center and all of it is anchored by a deep blue Persian area rug. Intense late morning light radiates through the several large windows of the handsome office. Instead of religious paintings, the American prelate has hung high quality reproductions by Winslow Homer.

"Just water will be fine." Müller sits down while Lawrence goes to a carafe and pours a glass.

The liaison is a short, stocky man with a broad round face, double chin, and a full head of hair. He is a lawyer and looks it. "The Pope's secretary said you want to speak to me. My curiosity is piqued."

"Indeed, Herr Müller, what we are about to tell you is top secret. Only the president, General Eisenhower and his immediate staff, and a few others in the OSS know about this decision."

"Well, then, perhaps I will have that coffee. I hope it is strong."

Archbishop Galloway tries to paint as depressing picture as he can about the Normandy Invasion for Black Orchestra's de facto liaison to the Vatican. High casualties and lives lost, little ground gained, low morale among the Allied troops. Müller listens first in disbelief, then because of ingrained Germanic pride, comes to realize that perhaps the German army is comporting themselves with strength and resolve. The thought both pleases and saddens him. Since 1939, he has worked as a secret intermediary to the Vatican, simply known as "X," passing along plans made by the German resistance to remove Hitler. Pope Pius XII reviewed the documents and passed them along to MI6. But after quick Nazi triumphs over France and the Low Countries, most resistance to Hitler and his plans for total domination of Europe died as he became idolized by the masses. Those in the opposition could do little. Müller continued in the underground, trying to defend Nazi opponents in the National Socialist kangaroo courts. His past double dealings have now been discovered. He dare not return to Germany. He is a marked man.

Slowly Galloway and Lawrence introduce the idea of an American agent to assist the Black Orchestra. Müller is skeptical, incredulous.

"And you are offering us the services of one of your best men now? At this late moment?"

"Yes, we think 'Trommler' can be of great help. As I said, he is a German-American. He was even an agent for German intelligence in the first war. Our problem is that we have no way to get him safely into Germany."

"I can't help you there. I dare not return to Germany; but I think I can do better than that." Müller finishes his coffee and looks at Galloway.

"Yes. How so?"

"Let's just say that your agent and I will need to get to Strasbourg. There is an important meeting I need to attend. With some luck, perhaps I can get him into it."

Monsignor Jonathan Strauss is following a newly re-instituted tour of the Villa Borghese Gardens but his mind is not on the historical facts being rattled off by the guide, or by the beauty of the gardens themselves. He rehashes his discussion with Galloway and Lawrence over and over in his mind. More to the point, the fact that he agreed to continue with the mission. With every day that passes, he sees himself less as a priest, a man of God, and more as the man he despised long ago: an espionage agent, a person who dealt in deceit, and worse, a killer. He tried to change his life by attending college and becoming a teacher, but he was still tied to his military past, and that tied him to his job as a spy. Then the Nazis came to power and all they preached was unreasoning nationalism and re-armament. The United States seemed to shun war and it was thousands of miles away. And from there, the seminary and becoming a man of God was an easy step, a further escape from a world that he had begun to hate. Now it is all back in his face: the hatred, the inordinate killing, and the madness of the world.

But none of that matters now. He wants to get revenge for what happened to the people of Sant'Anna and to his friends on the fishing boat. And then there is his son, Michael. That is the greatest reason of all. He had abandoned him once before. He cannot do so again and live with himself.

The tour ends. For Strauss, the tour is just beginning.

"How did you like the Villa Borghese?"

"Lawrence, what are you doing here?" Strauss returns to reality. He looks around at the beautiful gardens.

"Galloway told me you were coming here today. I thought we might need to have a little chat. Clear up any concerns you might have about your job." Lawrence lights up a cigarette.

"Such as?" Strauss is growing annoyed with his handler, and having the pleasant day ruined by some kind of pep talk.

"Such as, how do you plan on stopping Stauffenberg from assassinating Hitler?"

"I don't know at this point. I'm kind of making it up as I go along."

"Exactly. I think we need to be a little more specific than that."

"At this point, all I can figure is that I need to make sure the bomb he plans on using doesn't work."

"And if that fails?" Lawrence is looking hard at Strauss, waiting for some reaction.

"I guess we're out of luck, then." Strauss starts walking; he is done with this useless conversation.

Lawrence trots up to his reluctant agent. "No, we're not. If you can't diffuse the bomb, you'll need to kill Stauffenberg."

"Are you out of your mind? Go to hell!" Strauss walks on toward the Spanish steps.

Lawrence sighs, throws his smoke to the ground and steps on it. He watches Strauss, shaking his head.

PART III

GERMANY

Chapter Thirty-Five

JULY 7, 1944
Outskirts of Milan, Italy

Müller and Strauss have been together all day; Strauss is driving the two-passenger Fiat Topolino. With his six-foot, two-inch frame and Müller's wide girth, the Italian compact car, having a top speed of fifty-three miles per hour, has made for a long trip. The journey from Rome to Strasbourg is over 1,000 KM, and though the two Germans share much in common, especially their Catholic faith, Strauss has had to watch every word he says so he doesn't give away his true mission.

Müller, in turn, is still skeptical of Galloway's story about the Allies now wanting to find alternatives to war in the face of a little adversity. But he can see the logic of the Americans wanting to help. After a successful assassination of the Führer, it makes sense that they would only trust an American to relay the news of such an unlikely coup. With the advancing Allied armies, the thought of a cease fire, temporary or permanent, is most appealing. But a report about Hitler's demise could easily be a Nazi trick. He just hopes he can convince the other members of the Black Orchestra to see the usefulness of American help.

"Watch the road ahead. There is debris everywhere from the bombings. Where in God's name did you learn to drive?"

"I don't know where I'm going. It's been years since I was here, and it looked a lot better then. And you have been on my back all day about my driving. You're worse than a nagging wife." Strauss's legs are cramping up in the tight confines of the small car. When he got into it, he tried to push the seat back, only to find out it was already fully extended. And the little fat German never offered to drive.

"Someone has to advise you. And you're still a terrible driver."

"I'm from New York City. No one drives there except the cabbies, and I always took the subway. What do you expect? Tomorrow, you can drive the entire way."

"I am not licensed to drive in Italy." Müller's excuse rings hollow.

"We'll be in Switzerland tomorrow. And what difference does it make; if we're stopped, they're not going to give us a speeding ticket. We're spies, for God sakes! We'll be shot."

"You're probably right, but I have a confession. I don't know how to drive. I'm quite embarrassed about it." Josef looks out the window at all the hollowed-out buildings in the early evening light.

"Then you'll just have to put up with my driving. Look, we are getting into the center of the city. What is that large building up ahead?"

"I don't know. But maybe there will be a hotel shortly."

The road is wider now and appears to have been cleared of the Allies' frequent and devastating bombing of this major industrial city. As a result, Milan is a former shell of itself, and 400,000 residents are now homeless. To the right as they drive down the boulevard, they can see at least a dozen railway tracks leading toward the immense building that caught the priest's attention.

"That's the main railway station. Look at all the people unloading from trucks. The plaza is full of German soldiers. What is going on?" Strauss cranes his neck; the large front windshield provides ample view of the scene ahead.

"I don't care. Go faster so we won't be seen by those soldiers." Müller crouches down into his seat, but his bulky frame is still readily visible. Strauss does just the opposite. As he approaches the station building, he sees a long line of freight cars stopped at the station. He slows down even more. The Star of David is on the coats of simply dressed people who are carrying suitcases, shoulders hunched; husbands and wives cling to each other; scared, crying children are getting down from the backs of the trucks. Rifle butts jab and hit the men and even some women. Children hold tight to their mothers. They are all, hundreds of them, being directed into the station through one of the large double doors, of which there are many. Above the door, a sign indicates the platform it leads to, the case with all of the doors. This sign reads "Platform 21." Beyond it are the freight cars. Strauss has come to a complete stop in the road. It doesn't matter; there are few cars out anyway.

"Why did you stop? Are you crazy? We'll be arrested!" The fat lawyer's face is turning red and he is beginning to panic.

"No. I don't think so. Those Nazis are enjoying their work too much. Those are Jews. They're being loaded onto the trains to go to concentration camps. Dear God!"

"Welcome to the morality of the Third Reich, Trommler. I suggest, if you've done enough sightseeing, that we get the hell out of here. I'm tired and I'd like to find a hotel before dark. And I'm hungry."

Unloading the trucks continues and Strauss looks in horror at the scene. There are gunshots. The crowd disperses; in the center of the plaza outside of the great railway station lie three dead bodies. A German soldier stands over them; he's smiling.

"I think I just lost my appetite." Strauss puts his foot on the gas and heads down the road looking for a hotel.

"We were very fortunate to find this hotel. And the food is quite good." Josef Müller takes a bite of his veal risotto. Father Strauss has no plate in front of him, just a glass half filled with a light brown liquid.

"And more fortunate that they have scotch. After what I saw I'm not sure I can ever eat again. How can you eat?"

"Trommler, I've been an eye-witness to the madness for over four years now. My eating isn't going to change anything. But perhaps the Black Orchestra can. Oh, thanks for noticing the sign for this place."

"Lucky. I try to be observant. Yes, this is a very lovely hotel: The Petit Palais. We are in a small palace while hundreds of Jews are packed like animals in cattle cars on their way to their deaths."

"From the intelligence I have, I believe all Italian Jews are being sent to Auschwitz in Poland."

"Poland. All the way from Italy to Poland?" Strauss is incredulous.

"It's a seven-day trip. The camp was built for the express purpose of killing Jews and others, such as the Roma and Russians. It is so large there are three camps at Auschwitz. And of course, Germany has built it and many other camps in Poland. They don't want the German people to see what they are doing."

"How many are being sent there?"

"Thousands, many thousands. By the time those poor people arrive, they will be living in their own excrement or be dead. That's fine with the people who put them in the freight cars."

Strauss takes a deep pull on his scotch. He looks to the bar to ensure the bartender is still there. He's sure that he'll want another. "Herr Müller, we are both Christians. Back in Forte dei Marmi a farmer blamed all this on God. I told him that God was not responsible for what men did; that we have our own free will. But the more I see of this war, the more atrocities, the more I think he is right. Why does God allow such things? It shakes my faith. I don't even have a proper word for it."

"The word is evil, Trommler, if you believe that there is good in the world, then there has to be an opposite of that. Evil, immorality, call it what you like, it is the side of the darkness. If good exists, the other naturally has to exist. Otherwise we would not understand what good means. I cannot understand it in any other way. In Germany today, Satan rules. The good people are frightened beyond belief, for their own lives, and they dare not say anything against the Reich."

"But still..."

"You know that God is allowing these things because he gave us a free will. He created us, and then left us to our own instincts, good or bad. Sometimes that free will turns to evil and God looks on in pain. There is no other way to explain it."

"And so we have our mission...to kill the Satan of Germany."

"It is your mission. If I return to Germany, I will be arrested and sent to a camp for sure. So I'll do my best from France to help the Resistance. But remember, and you saw it today, we are still in a very dangerous place. The Italian Social Republic is a puppet state of the Nazis and anyone affiliated with it are thugs who love lording power over others. They enjoy terror."

"I hope we are safe here..."

"It would seem so, and we have falsified papers, but I'd rather not be checked."

"I'll be glad when we are in Switzerland." Strauss finishes his scotch and realizes that he is very hungry. "I suppose I should probably eat something." Strauss looks around the small dining room for a waiter. The occupants engage conversations filled with laughter; cigarette smoke swirls in the air, and people lift glasses of wine with their substantial meals. All of them seem to be very wealthy and above the scarcity and want of the war.

"Since I have been back here, all I see is the contrast between those who are affected by war, and those who seem to be immune to it. To look at this gathering, you wouldn't know that Milan has been bombed incessantly for the last year. The city is practically in ruins. Even the Milan Cathedral and the La Scala Opera House have been damaged."

"My friend, if you are in the right place at the right time, and have connections, war can be very profitable. Look at Switzerland; why do you think they have been allowed to remain neutral? Because the Nazis need them to exchange their stolen gold into Swiss francs. Gold that has been looted from the treasuries of the Reich's conquered countries, from the aristocracy, and the Jews." Josef finishes his last bite of risotto.

By the main entrance to the hotel Strauss notices some activity. A group of soldiers dressed in black, shouldering Carcano rifles, is filling the lobby. They begin to argue with the desk clerk, ignore him and enter the richly appointed dining room. One of the soldiers shouts: "You can't hide, you filthy Juden! Stand up and show your papers. There is still one more train leaving tomorrow and many of you can be on it!"

"This is not good, Müller. It's the Black Brigade." Strauss recognizes the uniform from his stop in Grosseto.

"Indeed. What does your passport say about you?"

"I am Father Pietro Raggiolo."

"Really? A priest. But you are not dressed as a priest?"

"I didn't think I'd need a…such a disguise. But I am told that the authorities are scared of giving priests trouble. You?"

"I am Vernazzo Capelli, an Italian lawyer."

"I hope you speak good Italian."

The rough looking soldiers check from table to table. They stop at one where a man and a woman were enjoying a meal. The man begins to plead. His voice is growing louder, more desperate. "I am not a Jew! I swear it!"

"Strauss, they think those people are Jews." Müller is getting nervous; he has never had much of a stomach for confrontation or lying. "What if they question us?"

"Not if, when. Stay calm. Think of something legalistic to say."

"Like what? You have no grounds to question me?"

"Well, that's a start."

"Let's make a run for it…"

"That's a great way for us to get arrested."

The two soldiers grab the couple and two other thugs surround them. They are hustled out of the dining room. All of the patrons look concerned, fearful. The previous din of voices is now punctuated by silence; then one of the diners stands and yells: "You're just a bunch of Fascist animals! Get the hell out of here and leave us alone!"

The soldiers move quickly to get to the well-dressed Italian man. One hits him in the stomach with his rifle butt and the man doubles over in pain. The soldiers demand to see the papers from everyone at the table. The manager of the hotel enters the room. "Please leave my customers alone! They are all loyal Italians."

Another soldier unholsters his pistol and aims it at the manager. "Shut up!"

Strauss stands up and goes over to the soldier with the gun. He reaches into his pocket for his gun. "Get out of here!" Strauss points the revolver at the Fascist's head right beneath his helmet.

Müller looks at the scene in horror. "Trommler, no!"

The group of diners stands motionless. The hotel manager is frozen, and the soldier is deciding the next step. "Who the hell do you think you are? I am the authority here."

"And I'm from a higher authority. Now leave us alone and get out!" Strauss's words linger in the air.

The wail of an air raid siren pierces the room. It grows louder and shriller. In an instinctive reaction, the diners look toward the windows. In the distance, bombs are exploding. People get up and walk quickly toward interior spaces, ignoring the interrogators. Some get under the tables. The soldier looks at Strauss in fear and turns, entourage in tow, toward the main lobby and exit. The sound of the bombing grows louder. Strauss lowers his gun and returns to his table. He finishes his glass of scotch and turns to leave.

"Where are you going?" the lawyer wants to know.

"To my room; I'm going to bed. If we're lucky, and I think we are, the bombs won't hit us. I would be grateful if you'd have them send some food up to my room. Enjoy your dessert."

Strauss, his dinner finished, the bombing stopped, has read his nightly prayers in his Breviary. He returns to his book, *A Farewell to*

Arms. Soon a peaceful sleep comes to the priest; he has finally done something to stop the madness. And tonight there will be no ugly dreams of his past war, Black Fascist thugs, condemned Jews, or extermination camps.

Chapter Thirty-Six

JULY 8, 1944
The Bendlerblock
Reserve Army Headquarters
Berlin, Germany

Claus von Stauffenberg reviews the modified plan for Operation Valkyrie. It was originally drafted by his friend and confidant, Major General Henning von Tresckow, a year earlier. But von Tresckow is now on the Russian Front. The job of finishing revisions to the document and getting the written signature of approval from his superior, General Fromm, and from the Führer, rests on the shoulders of the colonel. His new adjutant, Oberleutnant Werner von Haeften, looks on from a guest chair as he reads:

> *"The Führer Adolf Hitler is dead! A treacherous group of party leaders has attempted to exploit the situation by attacking our embattled soldiers from the rear in order to seize power for themselves."*

"Sounds fine...but only if the populace buys it, my Colonel." Von Haeften is skeptical.

"If the country, and more importantly, the Reserve Army, doesn't buy it, I'll see you at the firing squad, or worse."

"I am with you in this to the end, Colonel. I'll be happy to put an end to that madman before Germany is totally destroyed."

"Listen now, there is more:

> *In this hour of greatest danger, the government of the Reich has declared a state of military emergency for the maintenance of law and order, and at the same time has transferred the executive power, with the supreme command of the Wehrmacht, to me.*"

"Nicely written, sir. Now, what is the real plan?"

"Once we return from the Wolf's Lair, the Reserve Army will be immediately mobilized and will occupy all the government ministries in Berlin, Himmler's headquarters, all radio stations and telephone offices. We will arrest Goebbels and Göring as well. Goerdeler will then be named chancellor and Beck president."

"That is all well and good, but how do we implement a cease fire with the Allies and eventually sue for peace, an honorable peace?"

"I don't know. According to Canaris, the Allies do not trust us to accomplish this. They will think it is just a ruse. I will think on it. Some solution will present itself."

"Do you think General Fromm will sign your amended Valkyrie Plan?"

"I believe he is with us in this venture. After all, he would gain prestige by seeing the Reserve Army in such a major role in a new government. In my conversations with him, though brief, I feel he is unhappy with the current state of the war. I will press him further but must be careful. If I have misread his words, mine will be clear to him and he will see me for the traitor that I am."

"A traitor for Germany, my Colonel."

"But a traitor nonetheless."

Von Stauffenberg stands in rigid attention before his boss. He is nervous but cannot show it.

"Why is this revision necessary, Colonel?"

"My General, it is unlikely that we will have a breakdown in civil order due to the Allied bombings, because of an uprising of the Jews, or conscripted labor. But there is danger from within, if you understand my meaning?"

"Indeed, I have heard rumors." General Fromm sits at his desk fiddling with a letter opener that looks like a dagger. He seems only mildly interested.

"Sir, if there is an attempted coup and the Reserve Army ruthlessly deals with it, your prestige with the Führer will be increased ten-fold. But if the coup is successful with the Reserve Army doing its part, you will earn a place of high honor in any new government that will be formed." Von Stauffenberg chooses his words carefully.

"I see your point, Stauffenberg."

"Understand, sir, that only you, as head of the Reserve Army, or Herr Hitler, can authorize Operation Valkyrie. So, at that moment, will you be willing to do what is right for the Fatherland?"

"What you really mean is: Will I stand by those that have set a different path into motion?" Fromm studies the document in front of him, letter opener set aside. He takes the document in his hands and swivels his chair, his back to his chief of staff. He looks up at the tapestry of Tristan and Isolde. The palace intrigue is becoming like a Wagnerian opera.

"What I mean, sir, is will you do what is best for Germany?"

"Colonel von Stauffenberg, I know exactly what you infer. I assure you that when that moment presents itself, you can count on me to do so. Now let me study your revisions, but you will have this document back with my signature by the end of the day. That is all."

Stauffenberg stands at attention, clicks the heels of his boots and gives the Nazi salute with his right arm. However, he does not say anything. He turns crisply and leaves the office. He is smiling.

Chapter Thirty-Seven

JULY 8, 1944
Convent of the Sisters of the
Passion of Our Lord
Paris, France

Admiral Wilhelm Canaris and Colonel Claude Olivier, aka Jade Amicol, walk around the courtyard of the convent; the scent of peach blossoms fills the air. The nuns will have a good crop of the fruit this year. The acidic soil in this part of the city has made peach trees a prominent feature throughout the Montreuil neighborhood.

"I was dead wrong about the Pas de Calais, wasn't I?"

"Perhaps it is best that the Abwehr was disbanded; their chief couldn't even see the Allied ruse of Patton's fake army. I told you that the answer was in the tides."

"Yes, I am getting too old for all this. I heard that the Allies went so far as to have inflatable tanks, trucks and jeeps made, along with hundreds of tents so it would look like a real army in waiting. It certainly fooled my agents in England, but most of them have been turned by the Brits anyway. So, what progress have they made at Normandy since we last talked?"

"They have captured the entire Cotentin peninsula, including Cherbourg on June 26. They are rebuilding the port there as we speak, and it will be operational soon. The storm on June 19 knocked out one of their Mulberry harbors, so supplies have been slow in arriving. Once Cherbourg is back in business, it won't be good for your side."

"I'm not sure which side I'm on anymore...but go on."

"To the south they have advanced as far as Caumont, about thirty-two kilometers inland. Progress has been very slow due to the French hedgerows; additionally the Nazis flooded all of the farmland. They are just small, individual patches of land, so once the Allies get through one, another is waiting for them, with the German defenders exacting a serious toll. On the east, Caen is surrounded on three sides. But the Germans have been putting up a tremendous fight for a month now."

"It does not sound very encouraging for the Allies. All the more reason I have to get to Strasbourg."

"I have an old Peugeot for you; it has a wood pellet engine. There is no gasoline to be had. In the trunk are 1,000 French francs. You can keep the 5,000 Reichsmarks for your stay in Germany. And here are new identification papers. How do you like the name Jacques Brunel?"

"I would have preferred Napoleon Bonaparte, but Jacques it will be. I don't know what will happen when I get to Germany. I suppose I'll still be Wilhelm Canaris."

"I'm sure you know some people who can turn you into Otto von Bismarck or someone else."

"I think I'll stay with Canaris. Not many know about the Abwehr. I had better go."

"What is so important in Strasbourg? I would have thought you'd head to Nice or Marseille where you can get on a steamer to North Africa."

"My people are meeting, perhaps for the last time. We are running out of time and I have to get there. From what you tell me, if we can succeed with our plan, we may be in a good position to negotiate peace with the Allies, given their current difficulties in Normandy."

"I hope you are right. What route do you plan to take?"

"I don't know. Any suggestions?"

"They're all bad. You could be stopped on any road by the Gestapo, the SD, the Carlingue or even the Milice."

"The Milice? I've heard of them; who are they exactly?"

"Vichy's version of the Gestapo. Now that all of France is occupied by the Reich, they feel free to roam anywhere they want. They are just criminals and punks, like the Carlingue."

"I'm beginning to think I'd rather be on the run in Germany. I know the bad guys there."

Chapter Thirty-Eight

JULY 9, 1944
Berlin, Germany

It is a hard, late afternoon thunderstorm. The imposing frame of von Stauffenberg hustles through the back streets. Though he is getting drenched, he does not mind. There are few, if any, other pedestrians to notice him. He is dressed in civilian clothes: a dark brown suit that is getting more soaked by the minute, white shirt and deep red tie. Covering his head is a brown fedora that is doing little to stop the rain from hitting his face. He is not wearing an eye patch; he has had a prosthetic eyeball made and it is inserted into the void in his skull. He is too unique a figure with his eye patch and today he dares not be seen or recognized.

Stauffenberg turns onto Livländische Strasse, a narrow street containing non-descript warehouses, many of them bombed out shells from the over 350 Allied air raids that were a part of daily life in Berlin until late March. The rain heightens the residue odor of thermite, magnesium, and amatol, along with charred wood, mortar dust, and the stench of human remains. The city is literally a mere shell of the grand metropolis it was meant to be, a symbol of the Thousand Year Reich envisioned by the Führer in 1935.

Fortunately, for the wet colonel, there is a small metal awning providing protection to the entry to the building. Von Stauffenberg knocks hard on the door. The back of his suit is still subject to the incessant rain, although as he turns to check for unwanted pedestrians, he can see blue sky to the west. The door opens a crack.

"The Black Orchestra makes a beautiful sound." The door opens fully.

"Herr Colonel, good to see you." Wessel von Loringhoven is wearing a lab coat and ushers his visitor inside, onto a metal platform and then down a short flight of steps into the warehouse.

"It is good to see you as well, my friend. You look well." Stauffenberg removes his suit coat and shakes it but all it does is raise the aroma of wet wool into the air.

"Where is your patch? Did you grow another eye?" Loringhoven has known his friend a long time and such jokes are taken in stride by Stauffenberg.

"No, I had a fake one made. See" He puts his good hand to his face and squeezes around the eyeball; it pops out. "Pretty impressive, wouldn't you say?"

"Yes, I see. Please put it back. I hope you will be as dexterous with the detonator charge. Follow me this way."

The two friends pass by several workers working on Maschinengewehr 42s, Panzerfausts, and other specialized bombs to be used against the Gestapo. It will not stop the madness, but it is better than doing nothing. They arrive at a small worktable with two plastic explosives and several detonator sticks.

Loringhoven looks at the remnants of Stauffenberg's left hand. "If I remember, you are right-handed?"

"I decided I liked being left-handed better. Why do you ask?"

"You'll see. First, I do not think that a bomb armed with a timer and a battery, plus the explosives will fit into your briefcase without creating a severe bulge. It would be noticed."

"That's the same type of bomb Tresckow and Hellmuth Stieff put into the gift-box of Cointreau liquor last year. The one that didn't go off on Hitler's plane as planned."

"Correct. The fuse was defective, plus the whole apparatus takes thirty minutes to detonate."

"The meeting may well be over by then."

"Which gets us to the alternate method. We will have to use a copper tube containing an acid called cupric chloride. We got them from the British."

"All right. Fine; we'll do that then." Stauffenberg is confused; what could be the problem?

"The copper tube needs to be constricted with a pair of pliers. When it breaks it will release the chloride liquid acid, and it will then drop onto the wire that is holding back the firing pin inserted into the explosives. It will slowly eat through the wire in about ten minutes, releasing the firing pin. Then bang! The bomb goes off."

"And you are worried I won't be able to squeeze the copper tube."

"You have only a thumb and two fingers. And it is not your dominant hand. That hand is, unfortunately, gone."

"I am well aware of that, Wessel. I am reminded of that fact every day when I try to button my shirt."

"I meant no offense. No one should lose what you have lost for this stupid, unnecessary war."

Stauffenberg is growing annoyed with all the reminders of his past battles. "Give me the pliers."

Loringhoven does as requested. He tries to put them into Stauffenberg's hand, who fumbles as he tries to grasp them, and they fall to the table. Loringhoven says nothing and this time lets his friend pick them up. With difficulty, he does; with greater difficulty, he positions them to work. "What now?"

"Now you pick up the copper tube and squeeze it until it breaks over the wire. Simple."

"Yes, if you have your ring and pinky finger." Stauffenberg moves his hand slowly down to the pencil sized copper tube. He opens the pliers to grab the tube and as he does so, loses his grip on the tool. It falls onto the worktable. "Damn! Let me try again."

The process is repeated two more times without success.

Loringhoven sees his friend's frustration. "Perhaps we should use the timer and the battery."

"No! It has failed us twice. Don't you have some other kind of pliers? These handles are too smooth. There are no grips."

"Let me see what we have back in the tool shop."

Stauffenberg takes out his handkerchief and wipes his brow, now covered in perspiration, both because of the summer heat and the effort entailed by the simple job of crushing a pencil-sized tube. He shakes his head, wishing he still had all his digits. He looks up to heaven and silently asks God for the agility he needs to kill an evil human being.

His friend returns. "Here, try these. The handles are bound with rough cloth taping, and the tongs are longer and slimmer. It should make it easier to pick up the copper tube."

The German assassin in training takes a deep breath and resumes practicing. This time he picks up the pliers on the first try. A smile appears on his face. He lifts the pliers while opening them simultaneously, and then moves them down toward the tube. The long needle nose head is more efficient than the previous diagonal pliers. He grasps the copper tube then moves it onto the main section of the shaft and starts squeezing. The tube rotates and turns almost parallel to the shaft. It slips loose and drops to the table.

"Damn!"

"Claus, let me work on the battery and timer. I am sure I can make it smaller for your briefcase."

"I almost had it. Let me do this again." Stauffenberg picks up the pliers. "We don't have time for creating a smaller bomb."

The effort continues. Failure is always the result. The remaining middle finger does not have the strength of four to crush the copper tube, even after Stauffenberg successfully cradles the tube of acid in the shaft of the pliers.

"My friend, what do you want to do?" Wessel Loringhoven feels for his friend. He wishes he could be there with him and set off the bomb.

"I don't know. Can you make a tube with thinner copper?"

"No. We didn't make these. They are the ones that have to be used."

"Fine, I'll work on making my hand stronger."

Chapter Thirty-Nine

JULY 9, 1944
The Episcopal Palace
Strasbourg, France

Müller and Strauss have arrived in Strasbourg after a long, two-day drive across the Alps in their cramped Fiat Topolino with its inadequate 569 CC, four-cylinder engine. The word Topolino aptly means "Little Mouse" and there were uphill moments when Trommler was ready to tell his new German friend to get out and push.

"These are some pretty nice lodgings for a bishop, don't you think, Josef?" Strauss looks around the office of His Eminence Charles Joseph Ruch, Bishop of Strasbourg. There are three pairs of great French doors with large glass transoms that let in a generous amount of the golden, late afternoon sunlight. The bishop's desk is an ornate Louis XIV affair with gold trim, set with a brass lamp, gold inkwells and a leather desk pad. Behind the desk is a fine reproduction of Michelangelo's "Holy Family". It is almost as good as the real painting hanging at the Uffizi in Florence, Italy.

"Right now, I would be happy to be in a barn. I think we should have taken the train from Rome. You really are a horrible driver, my friend."

Bishop Ruch hears the conversation of his two guests as he quietly enters from a rear door that leads to his private study. He is a totally ordinary looking man in height, weight, and appearance. Undistinguished, one would never pick him out in a crowd, yet there is an open kindness in his face.

"That would have been difficult, Herr Müller. You would have made it through Switzerland, but all the rail lines from Basel to Strasbourg have been bombed by the Allies. Welcome! I am glad you are here, whether you drove or came by a wagon pulled by mules."

"My dear bishop, I assure you the wagon would have been preferable than the drive by car."

Ruch turns to look at his other visitor, one he does not know. "I am sure our grumpy German friend does you a disservice. I have driven that route myself. It would make anyone nauseous. I am Charles Ruch, and you are…?"

Strauss rises and is ready to say "Jonathan Strauss" as he opens his mouth. "Eminence, you may…call me Trommler. I am an American with the OSS."

"Indeed! You came all the way from Rome? How is my good friend, Brendan Galloway?"

"He is well and sends his regards. Herr Josef has criticized my driving, but I am from New York. No one drives in New York, and he unfortunately does not drive at all. So here we are."

"Indeed. Well, I do have pleasant accommodations for you. This Palace is way too grand for my tastes, but it has been the Church's home since 1855. It used to be a hotel, so we have plenty of room for you and for the other guests coming to the meeting tomorrow evening. I understand it is one of great importance. My dear friend, Hans Oster, wanted to hold the meeting in the crypt of the Cathedral, but I thought it would be unseemly, if not sacrilegious, to discuss killing someone there, even if that someone is Adolf Hitler. So, the meeting will be here. We have a basement wine cellar that is large enough for your group. During and afterward, you can drink wine. We have an excellent collection of both French and German vintages."

"You are most kind, Eminence."

"Please, Trommler, call me Charles. I feel like I am almost a member of the OSS, too. But tell me, as I am curious. The Black Orchestra is going to allow an American to attend their meeting?" Müller looks at Strauss. "I hope to get approval for his attendance, Charles. I must say I am surprised that after their lack of interest, the Americans now want to help in our little plot. Trommler could be a spy, but since he has been recommended by Archbishop Galloway, I have no choice but to trust him."

"Eminence, I beg your pardon, Charles." Strauss now warming to his espionage role interjects, "the Allies are having a bit of trouble west of here. There are a lot more casualties than they would like to admit. Perhaps a brokered peace versus unconditional surrender would not be so bad. And if they succeed and I can help in some way, and then confirm the death of Herr Hitler, then the Brits and Americans will agree to a cease fire."

"I would welcome it. This disease called Nazism must be stopped in any way possible. Just yesterday, I heard very disturbing news. Right here in this beautiful city of Strasbourg."

"What news Bishop?" Müller queries, and then turns his gaze out the French doors past the well-maintained garden to the busy Rue Brûlée. There are few cars, but many people are out for a late afternoon walk on the pleasantly warm summer day.

"Since Germany took over our fair city in 1936, the University of Strasbourg has been supplanted by a new university, the Reich University. Just like the former school, they have a Department of Anthropology. Its chairman is in the SS, if you can imagine that. He petitioned Himmler, and was given permission, to prove that Jews are a sub-human species by studying their skeletal make-up, particularly the form, shape and size of their skulls."

Strauss stares at the bishop, almost lost for words. "I don't think I want to hear anymore."

"I am sorry, my new friend."

Müller turns away from the lovely view and looks at Ruch. "Go on, Eminence."

"About 100 Jews were hand-selected at Auschwitz as superior "specimens" and have been brought to a concentration camp near here; about thirty kilometers away. Natzweiler-Struthof."

"I've heard of it. It's the only camp of its kind in France." The German lawyer has stayed abreast of all things involving the Nazi killing machine.

"Correct. At this very moment, they are being well fed and fattened up, so to speak. Then they will be gassed, embalmed, and finally decapitated. The preserved heads will be brought to the university so that plaster casts can be made, and then stripped of their bodily flesh. Their skeletal heads will be measured and studied, their brains dissected, and finally the skulls put on display to show that they are an inferior race to the Aryan's."

Strauss drops his head. "Dear God in heaven. Why?"

"Yes. Why? So have your meeting tomorrow night. And for the love of all that is good and decent in the world, kill that maniac." The bishop goes to his desk and pulls some keys out of his desk drawer. "Now, if you'd like, I can show you to your rooms. I'm sure you are tired after your journey. Rest up and come to the lounge at 6:00 P.M. We'll have some wine before dinner, or liquor if you like."

"I think I could use a scotch," Strauss responds quickly.

"We just so happen to have scotch, Trommler. How very American." The bishop smiles at his visitor.

"A nap would be good. I am tired," Müller says, slowly lifting his portly frame from the chair. "Thank you, Bishop, for your hospitality. It seems that even in a beautiful city such as Strasbourg there is much ugliness."

"Indeed, Herr Müller, indeed."

Chapter Forty

JULY 10, 1944
The Brandenburg
Hitler's Personal Train
Leaving Berlin, Germany

Adolf Hitler sits in the barber chair of his private bath coach. His personal barber is trimming his hair as he does whenever the Führer travels on the sixteen-car train, which is pulled by two giant DR-52 steam locomotives. Two specially constructed Flakwagen cars at the front and rear of the train carry 20mm anti-aircraft guns that can deliver their deadly payloads over three miles away.

The leader of Germany looks out without emotion at the many ruins of the once great city of Berlin. It does not matter. After final victory is achieved, he will rebuild it, with the help of his personal architect, Albert Speer. It will be more grand than ever and renamed Germania. The centerpiece will be the Volkshalle, its great dome reaching almost 1,000 feet high, with room inside for 180,000 loyal Germans to adore their leader. From this "People's Hall," a grand boulevard flanked on either side by huge cannons will extend to the Triumphal Arch. The Arc de Triomphe in Paris could be placed under the interior arch of Hitler's planned victory monument.

The haircut completed, Hitler goes to the adjacent bathroom with its solid marble tub and gold-plated fixtures. His personal valet helps him remove his brown uniform, bullet-proof vest, and then leaves him to soak in the large tub. For a few minutes, the hot water soothes his body, afflicted by Parkinson's and eczema, and purges some of the many drugs he takes, including barbiturates and opiates. His mind wanders, recalling his triumphal victory parade upon his return to Germany, after the annexation of Austria into the Third Reich in 1938.

Later, as the train hurtles through the dark night at 95 KPH, he sits at a table in the largest room of his own personal train car, the Führerwagen, dining on a bland supper of noodles, peas, cauliflower and brown bread. He hunches over, slowly eating his vegetarian meal. His hand trembles with each bite. He spills food on the table and does not bother to wipe it up.

The room is well-appointed in veined linden wood paneling, but it is surprisingly austere. It is meant for constant work and planning, not for relaxation or parties. A young, blond-haired adjutant in starched white tunic enters the room. "My Führer, Brigadeführer Schellenberg is waiting to see you."

"Very well, send him in." Hitler does not look up from his food.

The head of the SD enters the room, salutes, and clicks his heels while eyeing his superior. He is shocked. The Führer is wearing a flannel bathrobe under which is a pair of faded white pajamas, the look finished with a pair of old, brown leather slippers. His face is ashen: deep drooping circles gather under his eyes. His freshly cut hair has not been re-combed since the bath.

"My apologies, my loyal general, I was not expecting company this evening, but I have made an exception for you. Make your report, please." The voice is tired, and not terribly interested.

"My Führer, we have shuttered all of the Abwehr's offices and have absorbed their people, at least those who are loyal to the Reich, into the SD. The others have been dealt with. I must sadly report to you that the Abwehr was a den of traitors for the most part. Their work was sloppy at best, and totally false at worst. Many of their spies were turned into double agents by the British."

"And what about Canaris?"

"All the evidence supports my belief that he is a traitor to the Reich, and worse, a member of the Black Orchestra. Not just a member, but one of its leaders."

"Have you put him under house arrest?" Hitler looks up at Schellenberg with vapid eyes.

"My Führer, he has disappeared. We almost arrested him in Paris, but he escaped with the help of one of his colleagues in the Abwehr. We have reason to believe this individual gave Canaris a large amount of money to escape."

"You have dealt with that person in the harshest of ways?"

"He was an informer. He called us as soon as Canaris left the Abwehr headquarters. He has been stripped of his rank. Charges are pending."

"And Canaris?"

"He was last seen at a restaurant having a glass of wine. Rest assured, we will track him down."

"Good. When you do, you are to interrogate him thoroughly. I want him to confess his disloyalty to the Reich."

"Yes, my Führer!" Schellenberg smiles. "Will there be anything else?"

"Find all the members of this so-called Black Orchestra and kill them! I want them hung. Every one of them."

"I will, and it will be filmed so you may see the traitors die." Schellenberg salutes and departs, disappointed that there was no further mention of his assuming full command of the new organization.

A moment later, the door that leads directly to the Reich Leader's bedroom opens.

"Are you coming to bed, my Adolf? I am lonely." Eva Braun is dressed in a thin negligee and pumps with pink pom-poms adorning the top of her high heels. Her legs are shapely but a little fleshy.

"Yes, I will be there momentarily. But I am tired."

"I know, lately you are always tired."

Chapter Forty-One

July 10, 1944
The Episcopal Palace
Strasbourg, France

The wine cellar of the Episcopal Palace is a series of brick-vaulted rooms beneath the massive edifice, making up the foundation for the structure above. The vaults repeat themselves in long, regular rows and are interconnected by short narrow passageways, between the four-foot thick walls that support the building. Wine racks line the walls and contain over 5,000 bottles of the best French and German wines available. Lighting is provided by a few bare bulbs and is augmented by candles set on sturdy oak tables with benches. The temperature is a perfect fifty-eight degrees; it is chilly enough that some of the Black Orchestra collaborators leave on their coats, and a few, even their gloves. Wine is poured from brass carafes carried by friars who walk around the room making sure each glass is filled.

Up two flights of stone steps in a small sitting area, Jonathan Strauss paces like a defendant waiting to hear the verdict of his case. He is eager to gain access to the meeting. If he is denied, his mission will be a failure; part of him is not unhappy about that possibility.

"Herr Müller, what you are telling us is shocking news. Unbelievable news." General Beck stares at their infrequent guest.

"I know. I was skeptical at first." Müller surveys the room. Heads are shaking.

"I think it is a trap," Hans Oster says in his high-pitched voice. "Why even now, with this so-called American agent upstairs, our entire organization is in danger. Why did you bring him here?"

"I assure you, Hans, he is not a spy. He is in the OSS."

"And he is called 'Trommler'? Silly name, the drummer. For all we know, you are now working for the SD."

Müller is quick to retort. "I resent that, my friend. I have hated the Nazis since the start. Some of you were fooled with Hitler's talk of German honor and getting even with Europe for the disgrace of the Versailles Treaty. I saw it as getting our just due for beginning such a terrible war."

"No true German would look at it as such!" Oster's temper rises.

"Gentlemen, stop! This does us no good. We don't have time for argument. Admiral Canaris, what do you think?" Von Stauffenberg is tired of the bickering. But he cannot let on that his partial left hand can't even crush a thin, acid-filled tube. Until he does, there will be no assassination. Even as he speaks he fiddles with the pliers, slowly squeezing and repeating the motion to build up the strength in his middle finger. At this moment he wants to raise the digit up to all of them and leave the room. Let the madman live for all he cares. He can go home to his four children and his pregnant wife.

Canaris gets up to speak; he wants everyone to pay attention to what he is about to say. "My friends, my latest intelligence from the French Resistance, from just yesterday, support what our lawyer friend has reported." The room is now silent as the words sink in. Can the enemy possibly be losing?

"Yes, the Allies have taken Cherbourg, but the city is in shambles. They have surrounded Caen on three sides, but have not taken it, which they planned to do just one day after the invasion. Progress inland has been slow due to the flooded hedgerow country. It is now one month since they landed, and they are having a much tougher time than expected. As casualties mount, and there are many, their resolve diminishes."

"So, now they want a negotiated peace?" Carl Goerdeler, the future chancellor of a new German Republic, is already running possible terms of an armistice through his head.

Müller speaks. "I didn't say that. What I said is that they are willing to help in our effort, and if successful, they would have a verifiable source to confirm that Herr Hitler is dead. After that, I hope that the fighting would stop, at least temporarily."

Beck interrupts in an angry voice. "They have never believed in our cause. They have never been willing to assist. Müller, you know this. As far back as 1939, when you were our intermediary to the Pope and he passed along our plans to the British, they were skeptical. We had planned a coup in March of 1940, but they gave us no help. And now because our side is winning, they finally want to get involved?"

The heavy wood door to the wine cellar opens. Agent Trommler, dressed in his black suit, white shirt and tie, with his distinguished, lean six-foot-two frame, enters the room. There are gasps. An American has entered the conspirators' nest.

"Yes, that is correct. My adopted country has had a change of heart. And if I can, I am willing to help you in your sacred mission. Do you want our help or not?" Strauss commands the room.

"Get out of here! You were not invited to this meeting!" Beck is furious.

"Trommler, you were to wait until I came for you. I almost had them convinced." Josef Müller is annoyed.

"Let me see if I can help you. Gentlemen, I am a fellow German. I fought in the Great War. I was also an intelligence officer. Then I taught at the Kriegsakademie…"

"Is it you?" Claus von Stauffenberg is looking hard at this interloper. Pages of his past are turning quickly in his mind.

"Yes Claus, it's me. It is good to see you again after all these years. I hope your family is well." Strauss smiles. The connection he needs to make has been made.

"You two know each other? Galloway said nothing about this…" Müller is incredulous. He had not given the American OSS organization much credit; he thinks they are a bunch of amateurs, not like the seasoned MI6.

"Yes, Johan Strauss!" Stauffenberg stands and walks toward his old teacher and friend. "Gentlemen, I know this man. Our families knew each other. He was my teacher at the Kriegsakademie. But more, he was like an uncle to me."

Beck is skeptical. "He can still be a spy. Even more so. He's a German, probably a Nazi."

"Herr General Beck, I will thank you to never call me a Nazi. Ever." Strauss looks hard at his accuser. Though they have never met, Strauss has done his homework, reviewing files on all of the key members of the Black Orchestra. He walks to Stauffenberg. They hug in a warm embrace. "Claus, I heard that you have suffered much for your country. Let me help you now."

"Johan, I am surp…you are in the OSS? You are an American?"

"Yes, all those things and many more. I am told that you are the de facto leader of this little band of plotters, so I hope you will both vouch for me and allow me to help you. The time is now. If the Americans break out of the French farmland and the Brits take Caen, they might not be in such a good mood to agree to a peace."

"That is correct." Canaris, still standing, and amazed at the coincidence of two souls being re-connected, walks toward Strauss. "My friends, I do not think we have any choice but to trust this friend of Stauffenberg."

"Thank you, Admiral Canaris. It is a pleasure to make your acquaintance." Strauss holds out his hand, and Canaris takes it.

"Herr Strauss, it is a pleasure to meet you."

"Please, my papers say Johan Becken. Call me that."

"Now we just have to get you into Germany," Canaris continues to shake the hand of their newest recruit.

Stauffenberg stands back to look at his old mentor. "Germany will not be the problem. Getting into the Wolf's Lair, now that will be the trick."

Chapter Forty-Two

July 10, 1944
The Bishop's Study
Episcopal Palace

"Well, Herr Trommler, I am told that you certainly know how to make an entrance," Bishop Ruch is sipping on a glass of Grand Marnier in his comfortable, wood paneled study. There is an entire wall of rare books and a large desk. To one side are four easy chairs, each with its own side table for drinks or books.

"I got tired of pacing around waiting for my personal invitation. The war continues after all."

"Eminence, did you know that Strauss and I are old family friends?" Claus von Stauffenberg has replaced his pliers with a glass of Beaujolais.

"Ah, so you do have a name. A good German name too: Strauss. And shall I now call you that?"

"Please call me Jonathan, or Johan. Claus here knows me as Johan, but I Americanized it. When I arrived in America in 1932, I wanted to become all things American." Strauss has afforded himself a generous pour of Johnny Walker Scotch compliments of the Bishop's stocked bar.

Wilhelm Canaris is smoking a cigarette and has joined the bishop in a glass of brandy. "I would say becoming an American spy is as Yankee Doodle as one can get. You said you were a German agent in the last war. Did we perhaps meet each other? I was in Madrid for a short time."

"No, I do not think so; I was stationed in Milan and then Bologna. My job was to determine the amount of war material and armaments being made by Italy. It was pretty boring stuff."

"Indeed, spying can be quite tedious. It's a lot like being a U-boat commander: hours of boredom interspersed with a few minutes of high excitement." Canaris takes a sip of the brandy, savors it in his mouth and then swallows. It warms him. He looks around the paneled study and imagines that he might be in an exclusive men's club. Such moments are enjoyable, as long as the company is educated and interesting.

Ruch steers the discussion to the matters at hand, bringing Canaris back to the current reality of their situation. "So, gentlemen, what role do you envision for your new associate?"

"First, we need to get him into Germany. Did you say you have papers, Johan?" Stauffenberg reaches to the table for his glass of wine. With just three fingers he is surprisingly dexterous picking up the stemware.

"Yes, I am Johan Becken. I'm in the import-export business."

"That is a problem. I fly back to Berlin tomorrow. I cannot bring a civilian back with me. I came here on official Reserve Army business to purportedly check on the strength of our garrison in Strasbourg. Göring and what few pilots he has left are extremely loyal to Hitler. It was hell even commandeering a plane with fuel resources being so scarce. I'm sure my trip will be reported, and questions will be asked."

Canaris frowns. "Pity. I was hoping we could join you. It's a long drive to Berlin; over 700 kilometers. And my Peugeot will never make it; it uses wood pellets. It broke down on my way here from Paris."

"What about taking the train?" Strauss sips on the scotch without ice. His Americanization includes a new love of "on the rocks" but he understands this is not possible or common in Europe.

"Johan, train travel has become very unreliable between here and Berlin. The north line goes through Frankfurt, which has been heavily bombed. The south line through Stuttgart and then Nuremberg, has been bombed as well. All these cities are centers of German industry." Bishop Ruch sets down his empty snifter of Grand Marnier.

"Claus, if we secured a uniform for Herr Strauss, could we accompany you? I am the head of the Abwehr after all. That must carry some weight with the Luftwaffe."

"A uniform? What kind of uniform?" Strauss practically spits out his liquid comfort.

"Why a German soldier's uniform, Johan. Not to worry, we will make you an officer." Canaris smiles.

"I didn't sign up to wear a Nazi uniform. I'm an American."

Stauffenberg responds: "You wore a German uniform in the Great War. What's the problem, old friend? Anyway, it would not be an SS uniform, but one of the Wehrmacht."

"Oh, well, that's so much better."

Stauffenberg looks at the admiral. "Wilhelm it wouldn't matter anyway. I cannot bring two unregistered guests on board that plane. It will arouse too much suspicion, and our plans could be discovered."

Canaris shakes his head. "I guess Strauss and I will just have to hitch-hike to Berlin. I still like the uniform idea though. I don't think Herr Becken, the importer, will carry any weight if we travel together. I prefer traveling with a German officer."

Bishop Ruch pours himself another brandy and walks to the window, though it is dark outside. "I am hesitant to do this, but this mission is of the greatest importance. I have a car, and I have gasoline. It is stored in the coach building. It was to be my means of escape if the Gestapo ever found out what I have been doing. I would end up in the camp I told you about earlier, Johan. But you two need to get to Berlin, and this automobile will get you there. I bought it before the war, a 1938 Citroën Reine de la Route, six-cylinder engine with rack and pinion steering, and it has only 22,000 kilometers on it. It is even black in color, so you will look very official. And I can get you that uniform, Herr Strauss, I mean, Hauptman Strauss, and new papers. We have a very dedicated underground here, mostly French Resistance."

"Captain Strauss. I must say it has a nice ring to it. I was only a lieutenant in the American army and a private in the German one."

"See, then you've been promoted, Johan!"

"The only thing that happens on this journey is that I keep getting promoted when I'm just happy to be a pri...a private." Strauss finishes his scotch and heads for the door. Then he turns and looks back on his fellow plotters. "By the way, what happens when I get to Berlin? And how do I rendezvous with you, Claus?"

"I'll meet you at a warehouse in the city in three days. The address is 8414 Livländische Strasse. Write the address down, Bishop, for our friend. By then, I'll have a plan in place. We have to get you to Rastenburg. I will find a train to take from Berlin. They are leaving everyday with more troops to stop the advancing Red horde."

Canaris goes over to the bottle of Grand Marnier and pours himself another generous snifter. "Thank you so much for the automobile, Bishop. I promise to take good care of both your car and this American. We'll leave in the morning."

Strauss opens the door. "I'll see you tomorrow, Admiral. And Bishop, thank you as well for the car. By the way, might you have breakfast for us in the morning?"

"Certainly, my son. You have a long journey ahead. And I'm sure it will be full of adventures."

"Wonderful. I do love breakfast." The American spy leaves the room.

―――⋅―――⋅―――⋅―――

His eyes heavy, Strauss puts down his book. The intense day, the scotch, and the late hour make him ready for sleep. *Three more days to Berlin. I'm now in the Black Orchestra, and only beginning to get into trouble..."*

Chapter Forty-Three

July 11, 1944
September 1935
Nuremberg, Germany

It is a late afternoon in 1935. The warm autumn day is turning into a cool fall night. Below the massive structure named the Tribune, columns of more than 150,000 Wehrmacht and SS troops goosestep into the Zeppelinfield in what seems a never-ending procession. They slowly fill the center of the vast interior plaza joined by 25,000 elite Luftwaffe and 20,000 Kriegsmarine officers and enlisted men. They, in turn, are joined by 25,000 Hitler Youth; 15,000 girls of the BDM, the Band of German Maidens, and other military and paramilitary organizations. In the stands of the horseshoe perimeter are over 70,000 loyal German citizens, full of National Socialist pride.

Admiral Wilhelm Canaris looks out at the mass of humanity, all standing in perfect formation and at strict attention. He is attending his first party rally and is on the huge grandstand, the Tribune, with other high-ranking officials. At last, the stadium is filled by the 400,000 faithful Germans who have sworn loyalty to Adolf Hitler, Führer of the Third Reich, a Reich that surely will last a thousand years. They eagerly await their leader.

Finally, walking down the wide central boulevard, he enters the stadium to frenzied cheers, all arms outstretched in the Nazi salute. He is accompanied by Rudolph Hess, Deputy Führer; Herman Göring, head of the Luftwaffe; Heinrich Himmler, head of the SS; and Reinhard Heydrich, chief of the Gestapo. Their walk to the podium takes a full ten minutes, accompanied by the martial music of Richard Wagner. Time does not matter; the masses continue their cries of adulation. In the blue sky above, a squadron of Messerschmitt fighter planes flies over in a precise swastika formation, followed by hundreds of Stuka dive bombers. Führer Adolf Hitler ascends the stairs to the top of the podium. Looming above him at the top of the Tribune is an enormous stone swastika, over twenty feet in diameter. Great swastika banners are everywhere and hang from each of the thirty-seven rectangular portals in a grand colonnade that extends 370 feet in each direction. It culminates in two huge stone pillars topped by urns that bookend the monumental Tribune structure. As night descends on the gathering, 152 giant searchlights pointing straight up to the sky are turned on. The Zeppelinfield has been turned into the "Cathedral of Light." The mass of humanity erupts into a chorus of cheers that slowly turn into the chant of "Sieg Heil" repeated again and again by the 400,000, now of one voice.

It goes on for more than five minutes. Wilhelm Canaris feels the hairs rise on the back of his neck. This is a spectacle he has never seen, a power unleashed, both thrilling and ominous. He is happy that he has supported Adolf Hitler, and now, installed as head of its fledgling spy organization, the Abwehr, feels a great sense of pride. But there is also a feeling of terrible foreboding. How long before this formidable military machine will be unleashed on the world? No matter. The genie is already out of the bottle.

He thinks back to earlier that same day, in the morning. He was present at the Luitpoldarena with 150,000 Herrenvolk, the Master Race, to see the Führer, Himmler, and Hess perform the Blood Flag Consecration ceremony, where new Nazi flags are touched to the sacred relic, the "Blood Flag" carried by NSP rebels during the abortive Beer Hall Putsch in 1923. That flag was soaked in the blood of those nineteen loyal National Socialists killed in the attempted coup.

As the crowd quiets, the Führer begins to speak...

"Watch where you are going!"

Wilhelm Canaris jerks the black sedan back onto the road. "And you call me a bad driver! What were those buildings back there?" Jonathan Strauss is happy to reprimand his new friend's driving ability. All he has heard was criticism of his driving earlier in the day.

Canaris returns to the present from his memory of glorious days past. He shakes his head. "Sorry, that, my friend, is the Nuremberg Rally Grounds, site of our Führer's famous orgies of adulation for all things Nazi. It was like nothing I have ever seen or ever will see. The rallies to celebrate the new world order ended in 1939, once Germany invaded Poland. I was just thinking back to the time I was there. I think it was in 1935. I had just been installed as head of the Abwehr, so my presence was required. The theme that year was the 'Congress of Freedom.' Ironic; the Nuremberg Laws had just been passed denying the Jewish people most of their freedoms."

"I'm glad I left in 1932. I could see where the leaning and the curriculum of the Kriegsakademie were heading. We were no longer studying the horrors of war but celebrating them."

"I'm getting tired of driving, although this is a truly fine automobile. I believe if necessary, it could fly."

"You should have been in the Fiat Topolino with Müller and me; but that would not have been possible. It only fits two and not well. Indeed, we are in the Bishop's debt. I will return the car to him when this adventure is done."

"I'm sure I won't be able to. I fear I'm driving toward a death sentence."

"Then why are you going back? You were in Paris. You could have made your way southwest to the Allied front lines and surrendered. I'm sure British intelligence would have loved to have you as a 'turned' spy."

"To be honest, if I'm going to be arrested, I want it to be in my house, around my friends and staff. They can come in and take me after I finish a martini in my study. I want to see Valkenburg once again. Tomorrow, we'll arrive there. It will be good to be home."

"Wonderful, but what about tonight? This city has been bombed back into the Stone Age."

"It is the geographical center of Germany, which is why the Führer picked it for the rallies, not to mention there is a lot of military industry here. I guess the Americans and Brits wanted to send us a message for those numerous reasons. Last March, if I remember the reports correctly, the city was hit by 700 British bombers."

"700 bombers?"

"Yes, but look on the bright side. We shot down over 100 of those planes, so they suffered heavy casualties."

"Hello, I'm an American. How can that be the bright side?"

"Oh yes, I forgot. I was starting to think of you as a German captain."

"Yes, I hate this uniform. And it is a size too small." Strauss pulls at the tight collar.

"It shows off your Aryan physique." Canaris lets out a hearty laugh.

"Slow down. Look at that sign by the handsome house up ahead. What does it say?"

"Touristenheim. Wonderful, I don't think there are many tourists of late. I'm sure that they will be happy to take in a Wehrmacht captain and a government official for the night. I'll pull over."

"Please do, I need to stretch my legs and take a leak."

Chapter Forty-Four

JULY 11, 1944
Valkenburg Estate
Wannsee, outside Berlin

The shiny gray Mercedes slowly motors down the cobblestone street lined with linden trees. The fashionable and expensive residential neighborhood in the far southwest corner of the city has escaped the Allied bombings other than a few errant bombs that were prematurely dropped by a rookie bombardier, spooked by the heavy flak from anti-aircraft guns. Interspersed every so often between the trees are ornate cast iron gas lights that suffuse a warm yellow glow on the sidewalk below. The passenger in the backseat of the elegant automobile looks out the window and sees pedestrians hand in hand, out for an early evening stroll; people riding bicycles; and others reading the evening paper while waiting at a bench for the bus. What war?

"Turn here. Then at the corner, turn left." Brigadeführer Walter Schellenberg knows his old friend Wilhelm Canaris well. It would not surprise him if the old man was at his comfortable estate at this very instant, imbibing a cocktail. After all, house arrest means what it says. "There, the third house on the right. Pull in at the gate." Schellenberg has been here many times before, but under more pleasant circumstances. This time he intends to interrogate his old friend and, once he has confessed that he is a traitor, arrest him. Then his takeover of the Abwehr will be complete.

The car turns onto a smoothly raked, pea gravel driveway, confined by granite curbing. Even in his absence, the grounds of Canaris's estate, Valkenburg, are well cared for. There are maple and chestnut trees, and garden beds brimming with seasonal dahlias in all colors. A row of gas lights lines the inside of the drive up to the front door of this classical limestone-clad home. Large steel windows are capped with ornate scrollwork lintels. As the car slows to a stop at the pair of ornate oak doors, the maid and manservant come out to the front steps. They are husband and wife of forty-two years; Otto and Karla Rampling have served Canaris faithfully for over fifteen years.

"Otto, can it be that the admiral has finally come home?"

"I'm not so sure, wife. He usually calls before he comes so we can prepare the house for him."

Schellenberg opens the car door and gets out. He can see the disappointment on the faces of Otto and Karla. "Good evening."

"And good evening to you as well, Herr Schellenberg. To what do we owe the pleasure?" Otto, in traditional fashion, does all the talking.

"I came to call on the admiral. Is he in?"

"No, we have not seen him for several weeks now. And he has not called. I am sorry you drove all the way out here. I do wish you had phoned us first."

"No matter. If you do not mind, I'd like to look in his study. He asked me to find a document for him."

"Sir, I'm afraid that is most irregular, particularly given his duties for the Reich." Otto looks at Karla with a questioning stare.

"Ah yes, his duties for the Reich. Well, you needn't concern yourself with that." Schellenberg walks up the steps, past the servants, and into the house without gaining further permission. He knows the house well. It has been the scene of many parties, elegant dinners, and even a New Year's Eve party for over 150 guests. He heads directly to the wood-paneled study. Arriving there, he wastes no time. At first, he shuffles papers on the desk, giving a cursory glance to some of them. Then he opens drawers and digs through their contents. As his search yields nothing, his anger rises; he begins to throw drawers, correspondence and letters onto the floor.

"Generalmajor, this is unacceptable!" Otto and Karla have rushed into the study only to see their boss's desk being tossed as if he were a common criminal. Schellenberg looks at the two with eyes of disdain.

"If Canaris comes home, you will let me know. Understood?"

"Yes, Generalmajor. Now, I beg you to stop."

Schellenberg continues his search without looking at the two servants. "And do not try to leave. I have posted two of my soldiers at the gate. Are we clear?"

Karla begins to cry, and Otto puts his arm around her. "Yes, you are quite clear. Good evening. Come Karla, let's go to the kitchen."

Schellenberg looks around the room and focuses on the bookcase. "I won't be long. Go and have your supper."

Chapter Forty-Five

July 11, 1944
Lautermilch Tourist Home
Nuremberg, Germany

Strauss steps out of the Citroën and stretches his legs. They are stiff from three hours of sitting, leg room notwithstanding. He slowly climbs up a serious flight of steps to an immense wood door and lifts the brass knocker at the center. After a moment, the door opens to a tall, thin woman with mussed, light brown hair streaked with gray, and held tight in a babushka; thick stockings with runs; and a faded printed dress. She shows evidence of former great beauty, resembling Marlene Dietrich; now she looks old, worn down and slightly confused. "Good day, Frau…"

"Frau Lautermilch…I am Marta Lautermilch."

"Thank you, frau, would you have two rooms for my associate and me? He is a high government official, and me, well, you see what I am."

"Ja, ja. Of course! We have plenty of room. And I will serve you dinner, as well."

"Wonderful. We will happily pay you whatever the nightly tariff is."

"No, please you will be our guests. It will be good to have company."

"No. We will pay. I insist. I am Hauptman Johan Becken. My associate is Mr. Canaris. Let me get our bags. And thank you in advance for your hospitality."

"Karl, we have guests! They must be here for this year's Congress Party Rally!"

The bedroom is quite comfortable and next door, there is a small bath with a tub. In an adjoining suite, Wilhelm Canaris is taking a nap. Dinner will be at 7:00 P.M.; Marta Lautermilch quickly rushed to the butcher shop to get a pork roast. Hopefully, there is going to be one available for this is going to be a special dinner for her special guests.

Strauss has cleaned up and sits on his bed, reading. He feels a great kinship toward Frederic Henry, the American in Hemingway's novel, who volunteers as an ambulance driver during the war in Italy. The priest reads, his eyes close, and he dozes, and wakes again. Repeat. Through the door, he hears a dinner bell ring. Getting up, he inhales as he buttons his tunic. It is like wearing a corset. For a moment, he thinks that he could change into his black suit but disposes of the idea. Too chancy. He buttons the snug collar of the jacket, hoping that a nice German wine will be served. He opens the door, thinks he hears some noise down the hall; he ignores it and turns to see Canaris.

"Ah, Admiral. Well, it isn't the Petit Palais where I stayed in Milan, but it will do nicely."

"They seem like a lovely couple. I'm sure they did quite well in the thirties. In 1935, I stayed at the Hotel Deutscher Hof, the same hotel where the Führer stayed. He took an entire floor, and I had a tiny room with the bath down the hallway! Anyway, we must leave a generous gratuity for these people."

The two proceed down a wide staircase with a thick handrail and carved balusters. A faded oriental runner is held in place with brass rods. Arriving at the central foyer, they see the parlor to the left of them; they turn right into the dining room. The room is large and accommodates a heavy, polished mahogany dining table that seats sixteen in large, richly upholstered chairs, fit for an Austrian archduke. The table is set with the finest Schlaggenwald bone china, Spiegelau crystal water and wine glasses, and Koch & Bergfeld sterling silverware. All of it is set on beautiful lace placemats. Though there is still an infusion of the day's reddish light into the room, twin candelabra, each holding eight long tapers are already lit, and the flames skip off the glistening crystal.

"I believe this might be better than your Petit Palais, my friend," Canaris says, grinning widely.

"Once again, there is beauty and wealth amongst all the ugliness." Strauss notices a carafe on the immense, ornate sideboard, the wood etched in great detail with garlands and cherubs. The pitcher is filled with red wine. "Do you suppose our hosts will mind?"

"I don't think so; I believe we are honored guests." Canaris reaches for an etched piece of crystal stemware.

Karl Lautermilch hurriedly enters the room from the kitchen. "Here, please allow me, although I do not think it has breathed enough. No matter, I'm sure you are thirsty after your trip. From where did you travel?"

Strauss glances at Canaris. It is time to role play. "Ah, from Basel. Yes, Basel. We are traveling from northern Italy."

"I see, Herr Captain. And where are you headed?"

Marta comes in and sets bread and butter plates down to complete the table. "Karl, do not be so inquisitive; it is not polite. I am sure they are here for this year's Party Congress. It should be greater than ever this year."

Strauss glances at Canaris quizzically. Karl looks at both of them embarrassed. "Marta, the rallies ended years ago."

"Oh no, Rolf told me they would be starting again as soon as we win the war. I am sure they will be held this year." She walks ramrod straight back to the kitchen.

"I am so sorry. She is not herself. My dear wife gets confused these days, ever since the bombings. They took a terrible toll on her, almost every night, for weeks on end. How this house survived, I can only thank God."

Strauss nods. "And who is Rolf?"

"Our grandson. He is fourteen. Let me call him as it is time for dinner anyway. He steps into the hallway and calls up the stairs. "Rolf, dinner. Come and meet our guests!"

The sound of stomping, adolescent footsteps can be heard in the upstairs hallway followed by quick thuds down the stairs, and a sharp, military turn into the dining room.

"Sieg Heil!" Rolf exclaims, his arm raised sharp and straight in the National Socialist salute. He clicks the heels of his high-top brown shoes, spit polished to a military shine. Tan knee socks rolled at the top cover coltish legs, and are followed by rugged black, khaki shorts and a black, leather belt with silver swastika-embossed belt buckle. His long-sleeved shirt is khaki brown with two buttoned pockets. On the left pocket is a medal he has earned at one of many summer camps. A lanyard runs from his buttoned shirt into the right pocket that holds a whistle, signifying that young Rolf is a Youth Leader. A black scarf, held tight with a leather woggle, is draped under the collar. It flows down to the wide belt, secured by a black leather shoulder strap that crosses his chest. Completing the ensemble is the red and white armband emblazoned with a black swastika. The uniform bears a striking resemblance to those of the SA, the original Nazi Storm Troopers, disbanded after the Night of the Long Knives in 1934, when the SS and Gestapo murdered hundreds of people to consolidate Hitler's power over Germany.

Rolf surveys the room, and his sky-blue eyes brighten at Strauss's gray Wehrmacht uniform. A true German soldier is dining with them! Rolf's hair is as blond as yellow flaxseed. His skin is pure white but tanned from summer activities. His face is square, handsome and Aryan. He is the perfect embodiment of the Master Race.

"Gentlemen, this is our grandson, Rolf von Heflin. His father is away fighting on the Russian front. His mother sadly died last year during the bombings. Rolf, this is Captain Becken and Mr. Canaris, who works for the government. They are on their way to…?"

"Ah, yes. You had asked that. We are going to Dresden. It is my hometown and Mr. Canaris has business there for the Reich." Strauss is enjoying getting back into the role of double agent; perhaps the wine is also having its intended effect.

Rolf walks ramrod straight up to the two men and salutes again, then shakes their hands, hard and firm. "It is a pleasure to meet you. I am Rolf, Group Leader of the 5th Nuremberg Brigade of the Hitler Jugen. Soon I will be old enough to join the Schutzstaffel and serve my Führer in the war."

Canaris looks at the boy. If he is fourteen, his birthday might have been a week ago. "The SS? Why not the Wehrmacht, like Captain Becken here? The Wehrmacht has a proud Prussian military history."

"Please, let us sit down. You can discuss military branches during dinner. And Rolf, you should listen to Mr. Canaris. He is very wise." Karl, uneasy, wipes his forehead with a handkerchief, and heads into the kitchen.

Rolf speaks with a sense of authority: "The SS belong body and soul to Adolf Hitler. They have sworn total allegiance to him, to the death, and so do I. It would be an honor to die for him."

"I see." Canaris gives Strauss a glance imbued with sadness.

Strauss speaks. "Young man, there is only one being that you should give that kind of allegiance to, and that is God." Strauss hopes his words do not betray him. He is a German soldier after all.

"Do you not serve the Führer? Are you a traitor?" Rolf sneers at the captain.

"I serve the Fatherland, my Germany. There lies my loyalty. By doing so, I serve the leader of the country." Strauss places his napkin on his lap as Marta brings in bowls of steaming noodle soup.

"Rolf, is your brigade attending the Rally this year?"

"If they have it, Grandmamma. But I think it will be next year after we achieve victory over those that want to destroy the Reich."

Canaris tries to lighten the conversation a bit. "Have you ever attended the Party Congress, Rolf?"

"Yes sir, in 1938 when I was eight years old and a member of the Jungvolk. I actually saw the Führer then. At that moment I knew I was born to serve him. I received this medal after I wrote an essay in camp on his great leadership."

Strauss looks at the boy. He reminds him of young Billy McClain. Can there be that much difference between their idealism and their dreams? Both want to win medals, but Billy never got his. He decides to tread into deep water as Karl, head down, works on his soup. "Rolf, do you have any Jewish friends?"

"I did when I was six. But he went away. I was just a little boy then. I didn't know about them then."

"And what about them?"

"They are vermin. They want to destroy the Reich. All they care about is themselves and money. They aren't even of Aryan blood. They all deserve to die!"

"Rolf, we are all God's children, even the Jews." Strauss catches a glimpse from Canaris that says: "Don't push it, Johan."

"God did not make them. The devil made them. I hate them and will kill them myself if I see one!"

"Stop it, Rolf!" Karl cannot take it any longer. "The Nazis have filled your head with hate! And what has it gotten us? Your mother is dead from the bombings. Your grandmother is confused and sad; your father is fighting a losing battle against the Russians, and my beautiful city has been destroyed all because of that madman you worship!" Karl gets up and begins to clear the table.

"You stupid old man! I will report your disloyalty again to my Stammführer." Rolf stands and is about to leave.

"It is all right. Rolf, I'm sure your grandfather doesn't mean it. He is upset about the war, that's all." Canaris tries to calm the room. He does not want the dinner spoiled with discontented talk.

Rolf sits down again. "He is a traitor, Mr. Canaris. He is always saying bad things, lies, terrible lies about the Führer! I have told my Stammführer. Soon they will come and take him away."

"You shouldn't wish that, Rolf. This is his house, and you live here. He is your protector and loves you." Strauss reaches for the carafe of wine and pours another ample glass thinking, *"First the dinner at the Petit Palais, now this. Can't people eat in peace?"*

Rolf says nothing, leers at his grandfather, and Marta brings in a steaming pork roast surrounded by vegetables and potatoes. "Soon this house will be filled with visitors to this year's Congress Party rally! I am so happy!"

Strauss looks to heaven thinking, *"I think we just had the rally, compliments of young Rolf."*

Chapter Forty-Six

July 12, 1944
A Local Road
Near Leipzig, Germany

The two-lane road runs parallel to the *Reichsautobahn*, now closed to all traffic except military convoys and trucks carrying parts for the war. By early evening, Strauss and Canaris should reach Valkenburg if there are no unforeseen problems. Strauss drives, enjoying the warm July day. The windows are down in the fine automobile and a breeze cools his face.

"Young Rolf is certainly a true believer. It's very sad. Are all the children like him?"

"All boys are required to be in the Hitler Youth. Other groups, such as the Boy Scouts, have been banned. There are over eight million boys in it. If you do not join, you are ostracized. Your parents are interrogated. As the war wears on, it has become more and more of a quasi-military organization. It is the training ground for future soldiers."

"Yes. It seems Youth Leader Rolf is ready to fight for his hero and he is barely fourteen."

"They are getting younger and younger. There's already a division made up entirely of Hitler Youth, the 12th Panzer Division, 20,000 boys. While their leaders are experienced SS men, the troops are boys; some are as young as fourteen. It is currently defending

Caen in France. I have heard those boys are fierce fighters with their zeal for the Führer. Nonetheless, I heard the division is suffering heavy losses."

"My God, children fighting in the war?"

"It illustrates the desperation of the Reich."

"You're a good German. Don't you feel disappointment that you're going to lose the war?"

"No, I feel relief. If you think Stuttgart and Nuremberg are bad due to the bombings, wait until you see Berlin. The country is in ruin."

"But you are head of the Abwehr. Aren't you a traitor in the eyes of your countrymen?"

"Was head of the Abwehr. And yes, I am a traitor to Nazi Germany, but not the true Germany."

"But at the beginning? Back in 1932?"

"I was a true believer then. I even hated the Jews. And I did my job. I was involved with getting Austria to capitulate to Germany in the Anschluss. They are mostly Germans anyway and not a shot was fired. But I opposed the invasion of Poland; I knew it would be the beginning of a war we could not win. Then I saw the atrocities we committed against the Poles and the mass murder of the Jews by the Einsatzgruppen."

"The Einsatzgruppen? What are they?"

"Deployment Groups. They are special squads of SS whose only job was to murder Jews, Polish nobility, clergy, Communists, homosexuals, political dissidents, and on and on."

"Did you try to stop it?"

"Yes, I went to see Hitler to protest, but Keitel stopped me and told me it was none of my business. The matter had already been decided by the Führer. Later I saw the same atrocities on the Russian Front. This time Keitel told me this was not a chivalrous war but a matter of destroying a world ideology. It was no use. So, I began to put a group together to rid us of this maniac."

"The Black Orchestra?"

"Yes, the Gestapo's name for our group, but we liked it and have adopted it. What about you? Why did you become an OSS agent? Loyalty to your adopted country or a desire to change your old one?"

"Let's just say the U.S. government can be very persuasive. I thought I was done with war, and I have seen more in the last five weeks than I care to. And yet they want me to stop…" Strauss catches himself.

"Stop?"

"Stop…the madness. You know put an end to the man, just as you want to. What do you think our chances are of accomplishing this mission?"

"Not good, I'm afraid. But we have to try. Our collective conscience requires it. We are not all Nazis."

"I believe you. I think you are a good man at heart."

"A nun told me that, too. Maybe there is hope. Look, something is going on up ahead."

Strauss slows the car. "I think it is a checkpoint, a roadblock. Who will you pretend to be today?"

"Myself. You are my captor and are taking me to Berlin to place me under house arrest. I think that makes a plausible story, don't you? If not, well, we'll see. I'd be flattered if there were wanted posters for me."

The line of cars moves slowly toward a group of four soldiers, two posted on each side of the vehicles to be checked. Strauss is nervous; he reaches for Billy McClain's rosary in his pocket and rubs it as if it were a good luck charm. The line moves slowly; it seems that each car is being thoroughly vetted. He looks up ahead and a passenger and driver are being taken out of their little Volkswagen and taken away. One of the guards gets in the car and moves it off to the side. "I don't like the look of this at all," Strauss says as he pulls on his tight collar.

"Keep calm, my American friend. You are a German officer so you should have no trouble. It's me we need to worry about."

"You, who didn't want to get a new set of papers. Are we regretting that decision now?"

"No, I am German and I'm in Germany. I have nothing to be ashamed of."

"Other than Der Führer wants your head on a pike!"

The Citroën finally arrives at the checkpoint. The automobile's infrequent presence in Germany raises suspicion on its own.

"Papers, please, Hauptman. Where are you traveling to?"

"Berlin, Master Sergeant," Strauss's voice is military as he hands his passenger's papers to the guard.

"Why are you traveling to Berlin, and who is this man with you?"

"My brother-in-law. We are visiting family." Strauss looks at Canaris who is in disbelief. This was not the script agreed upon. The guard goes into a small shed, not much bigger than a phone booth and looks through some papers on a clipboard. He picks up the phone on the wall and begins to dial.

"I don't like where this is going," mutters Canaris. "You should have told them I was your prisoner. All the bases would have been covered."

"I couldn't. They might have decided to take you themselves. You're a big catch, you know." Strauss turns the beads of Billy's rosary over and over in his hands. The stupid collar is insufferably tight. His tunic prevents him from breathing heavily; a good thing since he is trying to look nonchalant. He looks toward the sergeant and smiles wanly. The guard looks passively at the captain in the car, listening to the voice on the other end of the phone. Another guard walks around the beautiful automobile, admiring it and running his hand alongside the hood. Canaris sits still, looking into the distance, ramrod straight.

"Ja dankeschön." The sergeant hangs up the receiver and walks back to Strauss and leans over and puts his elbows on the windowsill.

"What family?" he says with a smirk.

"Normal family. Wives, children, my mother, cousins, fathers, you know…"

"Get out of the car, now!"

Strauss looks at Canaris. "Caught!"

He slams his foot on the accelerator and the Reine de la Route roars to life. First gear goes to second, and second to third, as Strauss does his best imitation of a Grand Prix driver. The car is doing 97 KMH in an instant and is eager for more.

Two of the soldiers at the checkpoint run to their BMW motorcycle; one jumps into the sidecar and the other guns the 750 CC engine as they give chase.

"They have our papers, Strauss!"

"So, we can get new ones! Hold tight...there's the entrance to the Autobahn up ahead. I'll have to go through the barrier. The bishop won't be happy!"

Canaris sticks his head out the window and sees the motorcycle in pursuit. "We have company!" Though distant, the BMW is gaining fast.

The ramp is upon Strauss in an instant, the car slams the wood barricade to pieces, and the car descends down to the four-lane masterpiece of engineering, recessed into the landscape. Strauss steps on the clutch and throws the stick into its final fourth gear. The black stallion surges ahead, as if it dreamt of cruising one day on this highway of the future. It is going 140 KMH. The motorcycle fades in the distance.

"After lunch, it will be your turn to drive." Strauss smiles at his new friend.

"I'll be happy to."

Strauss is dozing as the car smoothly motors on.

"Johan, wake up. Look, we're almost to Berlin. Just ten more kilometers. Fortunately, my home is in the far southwest part of the city, so it won't be long now. It's really its own town next to Potsdam; the village is Wannsee."

Rubbing his face and adjusting his eyes to the view, Strauss sits up. "Good, I'm very hungry. Breakfast was a long time ago."

"I'm sure Otto and Karla will be quite surprised to see me. She is a wonderful cook, and Otto makes an excellent martini."

"I believe this race car driver will join you in that martini."

"Don't let it go to your head. That driving was the exception. Your motoring skills still leave a lot to be desired."

"I got us away from the Nazis, didn't I?"

Chapter Forty-Seven

July 12, 1944
Valkenburg Estate
Wannsee, Germany

Strauss gazes out at the picturesque town of Potsdam. Memories of his childhood flood back as he remembers visiting his wealthy grandparent's home during carefree boyhood summers. There was swimming in Lake Wannsee, picnics in the park and evening band concerts. There was peace, and it permeated the air and the lives of its inhabitants.

Canaris drives over Glienicke Bridge into the suburb of Wannsee. The homes are smaller than the priest remembers; back then they were like castles to him. They are still impressive, fronting the lake. They pass the yacht club and Strauss's mind turns back to sailing, with his Grandpapa at the tiller. They pass the palace of the Great Elector, Frederick William of Brandenburg, the Jagdschloss and then Glienicke Palace. The late afternoon sun filters through the leaves of the linden trees, standing like so many German soldiers in strict symmetry, along the streets. Strauss thinks: *"Once again, beauty in the midst of horror."* Canaris drives slowly into the wealthy village of Wannsee, savoring his return and the beauty of the neighborhood. As he approaches the gates of Valkenburg, he speeds up. There are two German SS soldiers guarding the entry drive.

"Well, this is a problem of sorts."

"What do you mean? Those guards?" Strauss is confused.

"That's my house."

"House? It makes the Episcopal Palace look like a hovel."

"Rank does have its privileges. Why do you think I stayed on as long as I did in the Abwehr? It was very lucrative. Not as lucrative as it's been for Göring and Goebbels, or Bormann, but I've done quite well. Right now, however, we have a situation."

"What are you going to do?"

"Visit my neighbor. They have a tunnel to my house. I haven't used it in years, but I'm sure it is still intact."

"You're full of surprises, Wilhelm."

"As are you, Johan."

Canaris speeds up and proceeds down the boulevard, then slows to turn right and after a short block turns right again, now on a street that runs parallel to his. "I hope we'll be able to get into my friend's compound. She doesn't live there anymore."

"She?" Strauss's interest is piqued as he gets out of the car and follows Canaris to the gate with its bronze rose escutcheon, substantial lever, and keyhole.

"Her name is Halina Szymanska. She's Polish, Polish nobility actually. And quite beautiful. I know what you're thinking, 'Did they have an affair?' The answer is yes. Quite a sordid one, too, as she was married at the time. Hence, the tunnel I had built so she could discreetly visit me. And the Reich paid for it."

"Why doesn't she live here anymore?"

"Her wealth could only buy her so much time. The Gestapo finally arrested her in 1939, after we invaded Poland. She was a Jewess."

"Couldn't you save her?"

"I tried, but to do too much would have aroused suspicion and I couldn't risk compromising the Black Orchestra. They sent her to Treblinka; she died there last year." He speaks in a very matter-of-fact voice as he reaches for the lever. It doesn't move.

"I am sorry for your loss."

"We've all suffered for Hitler's war." Canaris works the handle, and it starts to move. "Ah, we're in luck, now the gate is opening." The two men push the iron gates back.

Canaris turns onto a rare, poured concrete drive. Just ahead is a modern Bauhaus residence, stark white walls with glass block expanses, square windows arranged in a strict geometric pattern, capped by a flat roof. It looks out of place in this neighborhood of Baroque chateaus and neo-Classical extravagance. He pulls up to a four-car garage that has a full second story comprised of servant's quarters.

"Halina built this house in 1932 and it caused quite the commotion. But she was very independent, and no one could tell her what to do. The famous architect, Walter Gropius, designed it."

"I rather like it; it is simple but strong. All these other homes are full of too much gingerbread and history."

"You'll probably detest mine, but I got a good deal on it."

"Don't tell me, you bought it from a Jewish family?"

"They wanted to emigrate to England. It was a win-win for all concerned in 1934."

"You mean needed to emigrate…"

The two get out of the Citroën, its front grille showing minor damage from the barricade earlier in the day. Strauss opens the hood and works to knock the grille back into place.

"Let's go find the tunnel. It's been a while since I used it."

"It must have been quite the affair…and a long lasting one."

"Seven years. The best years of my life."

"Why didn't she get a divorce and marry you?"

"A Jew and a Protestant? By 1935, the Nuremberg Laws forbade it. And especially in my position, it could never have happened."

"Did her husband ever suspect?"

"He traveled a lot and preferred their castle in Poland. I'm sure he put two and two together, but he really didn't care. He had his boyfriends."

"My, the company the Nazi keeps, Jews and homosexuals."

"Like you say, I am full of surprises. Tonight, I'll try to discover yours over those martinis."

"We all have our secrets."

They reach an eight-foot-high white concrete wall that surrounds the property and Canaris starts kicking about the leaves and loose dirt, pounding on the ground as he steps. The ground finally resonates with a hollow sound. "There we are!" He gets down on his hands and knees and pushes away the leaves and debris revealing a round hatch. He cleans dirt off a recessed handle and attempts to pull it up without success. "Help me. There's another handle on the opposite side."

Strauss gets down and with some effort they lift the heavy cast iron lid. "She must have really been in love with you," he says.

"Herr Strauss, you may not believe it, but I was pretty dashing back then, and she was very beautiful."

"That's not quite what I meant."

"Oh, you mean the lid. There is a pneumatic piston opener. It doesn't seem to work anymore." Canaris reaches in and searches the perimeter of the wall with his hand, finding a switch. Turning it on, a single bulb reveals a steep set of stairs, like a ship's ladder. He gingerly descends the stairs, Strauss following with difficulty.

At the bottom, Strauss sees a long concrete corridor with no end in sight. Strauss is amazed. "And Germany paid for this?"

"Well, yes, one way or the other. Come on, I need a drink."

As they proceed down the corridor, Strauss sees paintings lined up along the wall. There must be over fifty of them, all modern art. He is about to speak but Canaris senses the question.

"Halina loved modern anything, especially art. She was a prolific collector."

Strauss continues to be amazed. "I recognize some of these. There's a Picasso, look a George Braque; that's Paul Klee. Oh my God, there's even American art. This one is by Georgia O'Keefe!"

"You seem to know your art, Johan. See, you too are full of surprises."

"It might interest you to know we studied more than just God in the seminary…"

"What?"

"A…in a seminar. I took an art class at the Metropolitan Museum in New York. What else do you do when you can't have affairs with wealthy women?"

Canaris looks at his friend, decides for the moment to ignore what he heard. "When she knew the Gestapo was coming, she hid her 'children', as she called them, down here. So, our little secret tunnel served more than one purpose."

The long walk ends, and they ascend another set of stairs; Canaris opens the door into the bright light of a handsome kitchen, blue and white Delft tiles covering the walls. Karla Rampling lets out a scream.

"I am so sorry, Karla. It's me…Wilhelm. I'm home at last."

"I would have preferred to have our cocktails in my study, but you saw how Schellenberg left it; I think I know what he was looking for."

"What?"

"It's not important."

Strauss peruses the large, comfortable space. "This room is lovely, beautiful really. Is there a war on somewhere?" He is refreshed from a hot shower, a great luxury, and is wearing his black suit. It's almost like the first war when he stayed at the Cipriani in Venice or the Grand Hotel in Rome. He looks around the great lounge, which runs the width of the first floor, imposing windows at either end.

"Indeed. Now you understand why I wanted to come home. What is keeping Otto? I need a martini."

"It has been an exciting and illuminating day, I must say." Strauss admires the landscape painting over the huge marble fireplace. A small light above it brings the colors and textures to life. It looks like a real Cézanne. He shakes his head and smiles.

Otto enters the room with two martini glasses and two small silver shakers on a sterling silver tray. He proceeds to shake one of the vessels, firmly, but not too hard.

"I taught Otto to make the best martinis. I prefer old English gin. I think it is known as Old Tom. Sweeter, but it suits my German taste buds."

"I'm a scotch man myself. Americans like scotch more than the Scots, I think."

"I have noticed. Yes, very American."

Otto hands a martini to his boss and bends down to whisper in his ear. Canaris shows no emotion, and then merely nods. The houseman proceeds to Strauss and hands him a stemmed glass, full of the cold, clear liquid with two olives on a sterling cocktail stick. He departs as quietly as he entered, leaving the shakers sitting on the tray.

"To the success of your mission, Johan. I have enjoyed our time together." He raises his glass in a toast.

Strauss returns the gesture. "Yes, to the mission indeed."

"My friend, do you know what an interesting little town this is?"

"I only remember it as a summer resort. My grandparents lived in Potsdam."

"My, they must have been wealthy."

"No, but they were…comfortable. They certainly didn't live in a house this grand. But their home felt warm and welcoming. I spent many wonderful summers there. So, what else is there to know about Wannsee? Have the Nazis tainted this place, too?"

"In fact, they have. In early 1942, the key ministers of the Reich, the SS and the Gestapo met at a house no more than a half kilometer from here and decided the fate of Europe's Jewish population."

"I don't understand."

"The Nazis refer to it as the 'Final Solution.' They decided that all German, Polish and Russian Jews should be sent to special camps in Poland, Lithuania, and East Prussia as slave labor, to be starved or immediately exterminated. That meeting planned the elimination of an entire race of people."

"My God! Thank you for ruining this perfectly fine cocktail hour!"

"I'm sorry. Indeed, we should change the subject to more pleasant conversation."

"Like what will you do now that you are home and under house arrest."

"I would have liked to walk outside, but Otto just informed me that I have a new gardener, thanks to the Gestapo. The soldiers outside on the street wouldn't have seen me in the backyard, and I could enjoy the lake while I puttered around, but now that won't be possible. This gardener is living in the coach house and will let Schellenberg know I'm here as soon as he sees me. So, I'm stuck in the house if I don't want to be discovered."

"Damn Nazis. You shouldn't put up with it."

"Well, what would you have me do?"

"Sorry. I don't know. I'm just fed up with them, and I don't even live in this country."

"I'll put my study back in order, and there are plenty of books to read. I'll survive."

"It's not right. After all you have done one way or the other for Germany…now to be a hunted man."

"Forget about the gardener. You haven't told me anything new to surprise me."

"All right then, how's this?" Strauss pauses, thinks, and decides, *"What harm can it do?"*

"I'm a Catholic priest in my spare time."

"A priest? What are you talking about?"

"Before I became an OSS agent, I was a Catholic priest in New York. Well, I suppose I continue to be a priest wherever I am."

"A priest? I can't believe it."

"You wanted me to reveal a secret. By the way, this is an excellent martini. I may have several."

Chapter Forty-Eight

July 13, 1944
Valkenburg Estate
Wannsee, Germany

"I wish you would have told us that you were coming home, Herr Admiral. I would have done some grocery shopping, although it is getting harder and harder to find basic food like sugar and bacon. My apologies, Captain Becken; I hope eggs, some sausage and toast will do?" Karla places four thick links into a cast iron skillet with melted lard.

Wilhelm Canaris sits in the kitchen enjoying a cup of tea, while Strauss sips at his plain, dark coffee, a luxury. The morning sun streams through the high windows above the three-section copper sink set in sturdy cream-colored cabinetry and tiled counters. The kitchen is comfortable and inviting, as it should be in a country estate.

"I am just happy to be home and to see you and Otto again. Have you seen him?"

"He went off early this morning, I don't know where."

"Hmmm. Do you know our guest told me last night that he is a Catholic priest?"

"I thought you're an army officer. Are you a chaplain? They are rare in the Wehrmacht."

"No, my dear lady, I am not. It is just a disguise."

"A good one, too; you fooled me. More Abwehr intrigue, Admiral. I wish you would retire."

"I have, my dear woman. Didn't Schellenberg tell you?"

"No, but he didn't seem happy about you not being home."

"He'll catch me soon enough."

The door opens and slams from the rear mudroom, beyond the kitchen, with the sound of heavy feet. Canaris looks up and Karla goes to the doorway. Otto is prodding the gardener into the kitchen with a large, spade shovel. His hands are tied, and his mouth bound. He knocks him down onto the floor. Karla puts her hand to her mouth in shock.

Canaris is wide-eyed. "What have you done, Otto?"

"I didn't like the way he was taking care of the dahlias. I don't think he's a very good gardener." Otto stands over the pseudo-caretaker, ready to hit him with the shovel. "Yah, he is a Gestapo pig stooge. I'm going to kill him. Then you can walk around your gardens."

Strauss looks at Otto, smiling. He wishes he had helped the butler.

"Well, now we have a new situation." Canaris finishes his tea.

"Indeed, you do, my friend," Strauss drinks his coffee, and winces from the bitter taste of the unsweetened beverage.

"Otto, you have caused me a great deal of trouble. You cannot kill him, and I really do not want to. When he doesn't report to Schellenberg, the Gestapo will be all over this place."

"Wilhelm, I hate to add to your predicament, but you need to take me to Berlin today. I need to rendezvous with our friend, remember." Karla shakes her head and serves their breakfasts. "Thank you, Karla, it looks wonderful."

"That's right, I totally forgot; I thought it was tomorrow. I was so looking forward to your company tonight. I was hoping I'd find out more secrets."

"I wish I could stay. I admit I'm not looking forward to the week ahead." Strauss cuts into his thick pork sausage link. The gardener squirms on the floor but is ignored.

"Otto, take him down to the wine cellar and lock him in there. Make sure you take all the corkscrews. I don't want him getting into my Lafite Rothschild '24 Bordeaux. I'll deal with him when I get back from Berlin."

—•••— —•••— —•••—

"And I thought the Citröen was a fine automobile. You spoil me, Admiral." Strauss, dressed in his black suit, white shirt and black tie has his arm on the door of the cream and blue Mercedes convertible as it goes through Wannsee, top down.

"I bought this in 1937 to impress Halina. Then the Gestapo came for her, so this is my consolation prize. It's the 320 Cabriolet A model. The brochure said it was for those who had arrived in the world of commerce but were still careful with their money. Neither applied to me, I'm afraid."

"It purrs like a kitten."

"Yes, that's a 3.4-liter six-cylinder engine."

"Where is the Citröen? I meant it when I said I want to return it to the bishop."

"That automobile would stand out in Berlin like one of Hitler's limousines."

"And this automobile won't?"

"I don't really care. I wanted to take this beauty out one more time. Listen, I parked the Reine de la Route in Halina's Bauhaus wonder of a garage. You'll find it there when you return."

"If I return."

"Don't be so pessimistic. Although I don't understand why you are not wearing your uniform."

"Because it is insufferably tight."

"Not to worry. You look like the Gestapo in your black suit. And it's unlikely we'll be stopped. The police force has been decimated as more and more of them have been conscripted for the war effort."

"And what about you? And the gardener?"

"I'm sure by the time you return to Wannsee, I'll be in some prison somewhere. As for the gardener, I haven't decided."

"Please do not kill him. Don't lower yourself to the level of this war."

"Don't be so smug. You may lower yourself, too, before you are done."

"I pray I won't, I'm a priest, remember? Please, just let the gardener go."

"I may have him join me for a martini since you won't be there to keep me company." Canaris looks at Strauss, a big smile on his face. The cabriolet speeds toward Berlin.

Chapter Forty-Nine

July 13, 1944
The Tiergarten
Berlin, Germany

Strauss is close to tears as Canaris maneuvers through the bombed-out streets of Berlin. Hardly any district has escaped the incessant Allied bombing raids. On the streets, brigades of old men, young women and children pass bricks from one person to another, creating useless stacks of stone. It is work ordered by the municipal government to keep Berliners focused on the war effort, and not on the hunger in their bellies.

"I cannot believe what I am seeing. This was such a beautiful city. Now it is a pile of rubble."

"And Göring said that the British would never be able to touch Germany with her bombs. Well, that was a lie. The Brits bombed us for the first time in August of 1940. They have been coming back ever since. Since 1943, there have been almost thirty bombing raids. And every time they covered the sky with 400 to over 500 planes."

"I lived just a few blocks from here when I taught at the Kriegsakademie. My favorite pastime was going out for a run in the Tiergarten, and afterward meeting friends at some café for a few beers. The city was so vibrant and alive then. Now, look at it."

"You said you were not looking forward to your journey. I am sorry you had to see this."

"Visiting Berlin is not what I was thinking, in spite of how it looks."

"Let's head toward the park. It may not have been too badly bombed." Canaris turns onto the Charlottenburger Chaussee, toward the Victory Column in the distance, the geographical center of the 520-acre urban oasis. There are few cars on the grand boulevard widened by Hitler and Albert Speer. Most are military vehicles, Volkswagens, the people's car, and an occasional Mercedes or BMW of ranking Nazi officials. As they approach the monument, crowds of people are heading toward its wide plaza at the base. Nazi flags and regimental banners crowd the large, round, grassy area divided into four quadrants, surrounding the two-hundred-foot-high Victory Column, capped by a gold statue of the Roman goddess, Victoria. Canaris parks the car.

"Are we sightseeing?" Strauss is perplexed as he exits Canaris's luxury statement.

"Perhaps. Sometimes they have rallies here. It won't be like Nuremberg, but it might give you a flavor. Even in 1944, there is still a lot of fervor for the Reich."

Strauss and Canaris cross the wide expanse of boulevard and move into a deep crowd of Berliners. Some are stoic, others crying, especially the women. Old men with medals stand at attention. The two sightseers make their way through the throng with polite expressions of "Excuse me," "Pardon me," "So sorry." They finally exit the mass of people. A makeshift stage has been created by four Wehrmacht flatbed trucks. The platform has been covered with a black tarpaulin. Nazi flags line the rear of the trucks. Hanging from the front of the temporary platform is red bunting, adorned with swastikas. Makeshift steps have been constructed at each end. It bears little resemblance to the grand, limestone Tribune of the Nuremberg Rally grounds.

Young boys in dirty field-gray uniforms, bearing the SS insignia on the right collar, rank on the left, slowly make their way up to the stage. On their heads are old, dented helmets that are too large. Many walk with a limp, others with the aid of a crutch. Still more have bandaged heads, hands, slings and eye-patches. Some have no hands or arms at all. A few are carried by their comrades on stretchers. It appears to be a graduation ceremony from an upper school field hospital, the wounded ready to receive their diplomas. But it is medals they will get today: Iron Crosses of the first and second-class order; wound badges; and Merit Crosses for valor on the battlefield. A military band plays martial music and the procession to the stage is endless.

Canaris nudges Strauss. "Remember I told you about the 12th Panzer Division; the division made up of boys. It looks like they have returned from the front, from Caen. Or at least the lucky ones."

"They're no more than fifteen years old, if that." Strauss is shaking his head. Then he peers beyond the dais, one way, and then the other. "My God, those are coffins stacked two high as far as you can see."

"Yes, that is how these boys will be buried. You remember that from the first war. We always bury our soldiers with a comrade, or someone you died with in battle, so you have a friend with you in the afterlife."

"These boys should be in their mother's arms, and alive. And there are so many…and they are all just children."

"Once the war is over, I'm afraid this will be a country only of women. Come, we have to get you to Stauffenberg."

The Mercedes coupe pulls up to the warehouse at 8414 Livländische Strasse, stops, then moves on. Canaris turns the corner and finds an alley cleared by the Resistance workers so they can load trucks at night. The afternoon sun is in retreat, but it is hot.

"At the doorway I pointed out to you, around at the front, the one with the awning, knock on that door. When it opens, you will say: 'The Black Orchestra makes a beautiful sound.' Then you will be admitted."

"Are you serious? We never said such things in the first war."

"What did you do then?"

"I said, 'I'm Agent Strauss, let me in.'"

"We Nazis are all about pomp and circumstance. Good luck, Father Strauss, and may your mission be a success."

"Wilhelm, it's actually Monsignor Strauss." Strauss smiles. "There, another secret about me."

"My, my. We're both full of surprises. Here's my last one. When you get back to Wannsee to get the Citroën, you'll find 5,000 Reichsmarks in the trunk. Take them, they're yours."

"Why?"

"Consider it a gift from a grateful Germany for your service. I would, however, make my way to Switzerland and exchange the funds there for gold. Those notes won't be worth the paper they're printed on in a few months."

"Thank you, Wilhelm. You are a good man."

"As are you, Jonathan 'the American' Strauss, as are you."

Strauss climbs out of the convertible, suitcase pulled from the rear seat, and heads for the street and the warehouse. As he turns the corner he stops and looks back at the Cabriolet.

"Beauty amidst destruction," he thinks, shaking his head as he walks to an assignment he now barely believes in.

Chapter Fifty

July 14, 1944
The Resistance Warehouse
8414 Livländische Strasse

Strauss sits up in the small tool room, reading to pass the time, until his accomplice arrives. After meeting with Stauffenberg and sharing a simple meal of soup, boiled beef and potatoes, he was shown his sleeping quarters. Unlike the four-poster bed and goose down pillows at Canaris's estate, this bed is burlap sacks stuffed with newspapers and rags. The room smells of machine oil, gasoline, and dust. He looks at his watch. It is now 9:00 A.M. Where is his host?

The door moves with a simultaneous knock. "Johan, good morning. How were your accommodations? My, you look like a peasant."

Strauss is dressed in his workingman's disguise, not wanting to wrinkle his suit or uniform, and he can't let on that he is a priest by donning his cassock. "Claus, good morning. It wasn't as pleasant as Valkenburg, I must say."

"I'm sorry. It would not have been safe for you anywhere else. You are an American agent after all. And this place is most likely being watched. In fact, we're closing it down after today. What are you reading?"

"*A Farewell to Arms*. It's quite American, and the hero, Frederic Henry, and I seem to have a lot in common; we're both Americans fighting in foreign countries. He's joined the Italians in the Great

War. Me, I'm headed into hell." Strauss tries to stand but his body is sore. He slowly rises but the muscles in his legs are stiff and burn as he stands. "I'm too old to be doing this."

"It would seem so. Why are you here, really? Do you expect me to believe that the United States sent you to help us kill Hitler, after they went to all the time and trouble to land at Normandy?"

"Claus, just trust me on this; we go back a long way. The Allies want to cover all their bases. You may be successful in your plan and if you are, the whole dynamic of the war changes. If I can be of some assistance, then all the better."

"I still don't believe you, but I know you wouldn't double-cross me. At least I don't think so. Anyway, I'm in a good mood. I have mastered squeezing the detonator to release the acid. Now I just have to get the bombs into the Wolfsschanze. After that, the rest should be easy."

"And what about me? How do I get to the Wolf's Lair?"

"Tomorrow, I'll take you to the train station. There are trains leaving every day for the northern front in Russia. Our army has taken serious casualties, and replacements are desperately needed. I've found a troop train that leaves tomorrow at 3:30 that stops at Rastenburg. Get off there and make your way to St. John's Church. It's a small parish, but Father Cletus is one of us. I'll meet you at the church on July 19."

"Today is July 14. What do I do for five days?"

"Trust me; it will take you several days to get there. Nothing runs on schedule now. I will meet you at the church before I go to the Wolf's Lair. July 19 is the next meeting with the Führer. If I'm successful, you'll know immediately afterwards."

"I suppose I'll have to put the uniform back on to ride the train."

"No, I have a different one for you. You've been demoted to sergeant. You'll blend in better with less expected of you."

"Can you get one in my size this time?"

"I think that can be arranged. We don't only make guns and bombs here."

Strauss is quiet and looks at the handsome young colonel. "Claus, did you marry?"

"Yes, to Nina von Lerchenfeld; it's been eleven years. We have four children and another on the way."

"I remember her family, nice people. I remember her as a little girl. She always fancied you. But my God, why can't they find someone else to kill the man?"

"Henning von Tresckow was going to do it, but they sent him to the Russian front. Last week, Hellmuth Stieff was going to kill him at a presentation of new uniforms for the Russian front, which is humorous because soon there will be no Russian front. At the last minute, the meeting was cancelled. So, it's up to me. We've tried to kill him ten times now. My children and Germany deserve this act. We are not all murderers."

"But still, Claus…" Strauss's feelings come back for the boy who he considers a cousin, a nephew, a younger brother. His heart aches for Stauffenberg's family.

"What about you? Did you marry a nice, American girl?"

"No, but I loved a German girl in New York. Unfortunately, she died. I have a son I need to help, and the pay for being an American spy is pretty good."

"If I remember the stories, back in the day, you were a pretty dangerous German spy. You were one of the best."

"The stories are exaggerated, my friend. I regret many of the things I did. Why do you think I left Germany in 1932? To escape this insanity around us. And now I'm back to stop it."

"I'm the one that has to stop it, not you."

"You may need my help yet."

"Perhaps. Let's get you fitted for that uniform, Sergeant Trommler."

"I don't suppose there's breakfast?"

"What do you think this is, Valkenburg?" Stauffenberg laughs. "I'm sure we can find something." Stauffenberg puts his arm around his friend and leads him out of the tool room.

Chapter Fifty-One

July 14, 1944
8414 Livländische Strasse
Berlin, Germany

Strauss stands at a mirror in a back room of the warehouse. It is surprisingly well-appointed with floral papered walls and some comfortable furniture. Before the war, it was the office of the owner of the tool and die works, now used by the Black Orchestra for all manner of activities against the Third Reich. He is wearing a sergeant's uniform. A tailor is chalking the too-long sleeves.

"Johan, you look impressive in that uniform, and it fits so well. Just a little generous in the sleeves, but Fredric will have that remedied shortly." Stauffenberg looks at his watch: 11 A.M. Plenty of time to get Strauss on the 3:30 P.M. train to the front.

"It's a damn Waffen SS uniform. After what I've seen them do, I detest having to wear it. Don't you have something else?"

"This isn't the Wertheim Department Store." Stauffenberg says referring to what was Berlin's largest department store. It was confiscated by the Nazis because Georg Wertheim was a Jew. "Calm yourself. You only need to wear it until you get to Rastenburg. Then you can go back to being a Wehrmacht lieutenant."

Loud banging comes from the front of the building, at the main entrance. Unintelligible shouts can be heard. More banging. Strauss looks at Fredric and then Stauffenberg, wide-eyed.

"We need to get out of here! Quick, follow me," Stauffenberg opens what Strauss assumed was a small door to a lavatory.

"Wait. I need the gun from my suitcase," Strauss insists.

More banging. Stauffenberg can make out the shouts now. "Open up! Security Service!"

"It's the SD. They are the worst. Dammit, hurry Strauss!"

Newly created SS Sergeant Fritz Mercht retrieves his pistol from the suitcase, closes it and follows the colonel. Fredric is behind them. The hallway is long and narrow, then ends at the opening to the large factory floor. Stauffenberg stops. Machine gun fire pierces the metal front door beyond. "We need to get across the factory to the rear loading dock. Run!"

The younger Stauffenberg sprints like a 1936 Olympic athlete, grabbing the satchel that carries the critical plastic explosives and detonators from a table. Strauss summons every bit of strength in his arthritic knees to move faster than at any time throughout his entire odyssey. He is not far behind his surrogate nephew. Fredric, an old man, follows at a disappointing shuffle. The SD invaders flood into the warehouse, shooting workers who were assembling guns, potato mashers and makeshift bombs, trying hopelessly to defend themselves. At the far end of the large assembly room, the two runners and the old man are practically at the door leading to the shipping room. Machine gun fire continues; Fredric falls, shredded by a multitude of bullets. Strauss goes through the door as errant projectiles explode around him in sparks against metal and concrete.

"They killed Fredric!" Stauffenberg moans.

"I'm sorry, but what do we do now?" Strauss is breathing heavily; Stauffenberg is barely panting. The shipping area has a large overhead garage door and a man door.

"We need to get lost in the back alleys and ruins."

The two men stand by the man door. On the other side of it, he can clearly hear desperate attempts to open the locked barrier.

Stauffenberg shouts: "Stand behind me!" Strauss complies, gun in hand. Flashes of gunpowder surround the doorknob and two SD thugs enter.

Stauffenberg lifts his leg like a road crossing barrier. The soldier trips and falls to the ground and turns with his gun aiming at the colonel.

Shots ring out. Strauss shoots the soldier on the floor, then instantaneously the other, who drops on top of the first. "Lead the way, Colonel."

Stauffenberg stands in amazement, motionless. Strauss shakes him. "I think I had better get on a train straight away."

The two men exit the building, hearing boots in the distance. Adrenaline flowing, Strauss, suitcase in tow, keeps up with the younger colonel as they make their way through the ruins of Berlin: piles of bricks, streets with craters the size of a car and foyers and corridors of bombed-out structures. Running, tripping, there are more back alleys, more buildings, and teetering walls ready to collapse. Strauss stumbles, falls, and is helped up. He can barely run anymore but knows he must. After fifteen minutes, they reach a building that is in fairly good condition. Entering, they pass through a warren of rooms to a staircase leading down to a basement. At the bottom is a closed door. Stauffenberg, now breathing hard, knocks. The door opens a crack.

"The Black Orchestra makes a beautiful sound." The door opens. Strauss shakes his head, smiles and exhales.

Part IV

East Prussia

Chapter Fifty-Two

July 15, 1944
The Wolf's Lair
Near Rastenburg
East Prussia

Since arriving at the Wolfsschanze, Adolf Hitler, Führer of the Third Reich, rises each day at eight o'clock after a night of restless, sporadic sleep. An insomniac, what sleep he has is induced by a strong tranquilizer, Pyramidon, given to him each evening around midnight by his personal physician, Dr. Theodor Morell.

As he shaves in his underwear, the hand trembles trying to trim the iconic square moustache. There is no running water or sink. In front of him is a basic ceramic bowl, a pitcher of water and a white towel embroidered with a small black swastika. The walls of the windowless room are a pale gray-white concrete, six feet thick. Narrow corridors lead to the cluster of small rooms. The leader of Germany has made himself a prisoner in his own world.

His hair has grown since the train trip on the *Brandenburg*. It is disheveled and goes off in several directions. "Set aside time later today for my barber; I need a haircut. And where is Morell?"

"Yes, my Führer. Will three o'clock be suitable?" Hitler's personal valet, Heinz Linge, tries to anticipate his boss's every command.

"Three is fine. Where is Morell? I need him." His face droops, eyes bloodshot from the hated restless nights. If he dreams, only he knows if they are sweet dreams of victory, or nightmares of defeat.

There is a soft knock on the door. A pudgy man with bad grooming habits slowly enters. He carries with him a scent of sulfa drugs and body odor. "My Führer, good morning."

"Ah, Morell, there you are. Do you have my shot?"

"Of course." Hitler's personal physician, grown rich from selling quack concoctions that he administers daily to his boss, places his leather kit on a table and opens it, pulling out a syringe. He wipes the Führer's arm with alcohol and slowly inserts the needle. Hitler looks stoically at his visage in the mirror; he is used to this, and many other daily dosages of drugs. Over forty different prescriptions during the last years: stomach cramps, leg pain, migraine headaches, depression, and more. This morning's shot is 500mg of Pervitin, the same powerful and addictive methamphetamine that has been given to German troops throughout the war. It is what has allowed them to go days on end during the famous Blitzkrieg into France, Belgium, and Russia. Now it is being given to the young boys in the 12th Panzer Division. It causes hallucinations and violent behavior in their growing bodies. Some go crazy after taking it, killing their fellow soldiers.

Hitler sighs, feeling the drug course through his veins. He begins to feel energized, and slowly thoughts of defeat fade away. It is a new morning, a new day. The Reich will be victorious. He manages a slight smile as he turns to his aide.

"Heinz, the vest, please. And today I will wear my dark gray uniform with black boots."

Linge has already been at the wardrobe by the bed, and has pulled out both the gray military uniform, and the less used dark brown. He has the bulletproof vest at the ready; it is heavy. He does his best to place it gently onto the weakening frame of his master. As he lets it fall on the shoulders, he sees it weigh him down, as if the weight of the entire German nation is on the man.

"Thank you, Herr Doktor, for your ministrations. You are the only one I trust to maintain my health and vigor. Will you join me for breakfast? I'll have it as soon as I finish walking Blondi."

"I would be honored, sir. Enjoy your walk and I'll see you in the Tea Room, say in an hour?"

"That will be fine. Heinz, I'll have oatmeal today and some fruit with stewed prunes. Fix the doctor eggs and cold meats and lots of toast."

"You read my mind, my Führer." Morell packs his kit and leaves. Linge waves his hand in front of his face.

"Sir, you need to discuss the good doctor's personal hygiene with him."

"Fetch Blondi for me. I'll see you in the Tea Room with the schedule." He ignores his valet's pleading about Morell's poor grooming habits.

Margot Wölk sobs after tasting each bite of oatmeal and fruit, fearful that she will be consumed with some kind of poison meant for the paranoid leader of Germany. She is one of three food tasters, all women, who, an hour before the Führer's meals, taste it, hoping they will survive. She travels with the Führer on the *Brandenburg* to this large complex deep in the godforsaken woods of East Prussia, about five miles from the town of Rastenburg. It was commissioned by Hitler in 1941 just before Operation Barbarossa, the invasion of Russia. The leader of the Third Reich believes that Napoleon's defeat in Russia was because he was never close to the front lines. He will not repeat that critical mistake. The complex is heavily fortified and top secret. There are three security rings, each more inaccessible than the previous one, extending outward from the complex of over thirty buildings, the largest being Hitler's lodgings and personal air raid shelter, the Führerbunker. Even now, in 1944, work continues to increase the size of the facilities.

Margot has lost weight in a despicable job she never wanted. With her husband away at war, she moved in with her parents to a small hamlet near Rastenburg. The Nazi mayor, part of the Gestapo, chose her and several other women personally to taste the Führer's food. Later, at the end of the war, she will be captured by Russian troops and raped so often that she will never be able to bear children.

As Hitler picks at his food, he reads reports, his mail and the morning newspapers. Dr. Morell eats; he does not expect breakfast to include conversation with his boss. Being in his presence is honor enough. Linge enters the small dining room full of windows with the day's schedule. A slight breeze dissipates Morell's noxious body odor.

"Mein Führer, here are today's meetings. As usual, there is the general staff meeting at noon. At five, Croatia's Armed Forces Minister, Slavko Kvaternik is paying a visit, with a state dinner to follow at seven."

"And my haircut?"

"At three, sir. And you will also note an important meeting at one o'clock with Generaloberst Friessner."

"Regarding..."

"My Führer, I am sorry, it is regarding approval of a strategic retreat of our forces from Estonia and Latvia to the Daugava River."

Adolf Hitler slams the table with his hand. Then in a great sweep of his arm, the breakfast dishes fly across the room. Morell is glad that he has finished his food, although he was going to request a second helping.

"Friessner has lost his nerve. He's a weak-kneed old woman! How many times do I have to order it: There will be no retreat!"

Chapter Fifty-Three

July 15, 1944
Valkenburg
Wannsee, Germany

Karla picks up the crystal pieces that had once been Admiral Canaris's Baccarat ashtray, a treasured possession since 1917, a gift from the Kaiser, honoring him for sinking several enemy ships as a U-boat commander. When she is done, she will use a hand sweeper to clean the dark blue Persian rug, left by the former owner of the estate. Set upon it is an English cherry wood desk, also a gift from the previous owners, purportedly once belonging to the Prince of Wales.

"The man just marched right in here and began going through your private papers. Like a common thief."

"You mean, like the Gestapo, don't you Karla? It is fine. Everything is almost back in order. Although I was very fond of that ashtray. I placed many fine Cuban cigars on it." Canaris looks at the spine of one of his many rare volumes and locates its proper home on the shelves that hold rare and new books, from *The Rights of Man* by Thomas Paine to *Mein Kampf* by Adolf Hitler. "There, almost done. Now to my next project. Do you know where Otto is?"

"He is in the butler's pantry, polishing the silver. I am sorry but, in your absence it has become tarnished."

"I should fire you both." Canaris puts his arm around his faithful cook and gives a squeeze, polite but comforting.

"Well, it should always be clean. And tonight, I have a very special meal for you. I bought a leg of veal at the market. We will have it with all the trimmings."

"Veal. Such an extravagance!"

"It cost dearly. I hope you don't mind, but I wanted to celebrate your return."

"It's fine. I'll look forward to another fine meal, but first, Otto and I have some unfinished business to attend to."

"That man in the basement?"

"You just worry about the roast. It would be a shame to burn it." The former head of German intelligence heads to the wine cellar.

"I am sorry, my friend, I had forgotten all about you. Are you hungry?"

"What do you think, you shit? I've been locked down here for two days. Release me immediately..."

"And then what? Nothing more will be said to Schellenberg?"

The Gestapo gardener says nothing but glares at Canaris. Otto has no patience; he pulls out a pistol and wants to be finished with this interloper. Canaris has more subtle plans and raises his hand to Otto.

"Otto, please escort our guest. We are going for a ride." Canaris leads the way through the basement leading to a door and the tunnel. He walks at a brisk pace. As soon as he is done, he can enjoy a martini in his study.

The gardener looks in confusion and fright down the long tunnel. He does not want to be put in some crypt and die of starvation. They reach the end, ascend the stairs and are immediately outside. The late afternoon light dapples the white Bauhaus home beyond in a yellow tint. The gardener struggles: It is a chance to escape, but Otto punches him in the stomach, doubling the man over. Now he can't walk but it doesn't matter; Otto drags him. They reach the garage.

"Put him in the car. Make sure the bindings are tight and cover his mouth. We don't need him crying out for his mother."

"Or his swine of a boss." Otto does as his employer instructs, adding a punch to the ribcage. Canaris turns the ignition and in a moment, they are slowly cruising down one of the beautiful boulevards of Wannsee toward a small park with a dock. He parks the car, and Otto drags the Gestapo informer out of the car.

"My friend, I'm going to let you go. Put him in the boat, Otto. Let me get this life ring."

While Otto forces the reluctant boater into the skiff, Canaris goes up to the life preserver hanging on the boat house wall. He takes out his fountain pen. He writes "Juden" in big letters at several places on the life preserver, blows on the indelible ink, lifts the ring off the wall, and throws it into the boat. "Damn, I ruined the nib of my Mont Blanc. And all because I want to be nice and save your life." He climbs into the boat and sits beside his captive. "Otto, if you would do the honors, let's go boating out to the middle of the lake."

Otto unties the boat and picks up the oars. Momentarily, they are gliding out into the green-blue waters of Lake Wannsee. Canaris removes the gag.

"I can't fucking swim!" The Gestapo officer's eyes are wide in fear. With Otto's strong arms, the boat is making good progress. The orange sun reflects on the lake, and a light breeze cools his face.

"Otto, it's a pity we have no wine and cheese."

"Didn't you hear me, asshole? I can't swim!"

"That's why I brought the life ring. You can either learn to swim quickly, or you can hold onto that." He points to the round preserver, the words he has written now fully dry.

"Otto, you have outdone yourself again. This is the best martini." Canaris takes another sip of the cold liquid. He reaches for a cracker topped with bleu cheese.

"I'm glad we got rid of that gardener. He needed to die." Otto stands erect after setting down the silver shaker.

"Otto, we didn't kill him. My friend, Father Strauss, implored me not to. We merely gave the man a choice. Swim or become a Jew. It was entirely his decision." Canaris smiles slightly and takes another sip of the martini. "Excellent, Otto, excellent."

Chapter Fifty-Four

July 15, 1944
Lehrter Bahnhof Train Station
Berlin, Germany

SS Sergeant Fritz Mercht, aka Johan Strauss, looks in amazement as thousands of soldiers, Wehrmacht and SS, queue in line to board old trains for the long trip to the Russian front. The soldiers are either old, forty years plus, or young, teenagers. At forty-nine years, he fits in nicely with the first group.

Stauffenberg leads Strauss through the mass of soldiers. The air is dense and hot this afternoon. The vast, steel-arched train hall is draped in swastika banners, showing signs of age and smoke. The great vault is constructed with iron box trusses that sit on stone pediments, part of the heavy stone walls of the station constructed in 1870. It has a few gaping holes in the roof, the result of Allied bombings. Only three tracks are operational.

"The train on Track E leaves next. It's the best I could do. It goes to Vilnius, but it gets you out of here before the SD can find you. A lot of fighting is going on in Lithuania, too, and it should make a stop somewhere near Rastenburg."

"Somewhere near Rastenburg? Why don't you come along with me? I could use some help."

"I'd love to, but I have to get back to Reserve Army headquarters. Help? I really don't think you need any. Nice work back at the warehouse. Your reputation is intact."

"Yes, my reputation; I just killed two men."

"They deserved it. Fredric was an old friend of my family. He was a tailor in Albstadt, and I convinced him to help with our cause. Now his blood is on my hands."

"I'm sorry for your loss. There are so many good people dying."

"Yes, and it isn't nearly over. Look over there, get in line with those regular troops. They won't question an SS soldier. I've got to go. I'll see you at the church."

"All right. I'll see you on the 19th by the grace of God."

"Godspeed, my friend."

"A little more speed from God would be nice."

Strauss and Stauffenberg hug and Strauss moves into the crowd, sliding in between a Wehrmacht sergeant and a young private. The sergeant eyes him with interest and confusion. Strauss says nothing, turns, and looks back for his old friend, but Claus von Stauffenberg is gone.

The train car is nothing like the first-class Italian coaches he enjoyed in Italy. The seats are hard wood slats with little leg room. To secure an outside seat to stretch his legs, he nudges the private to a window seat, and before the boy can react, slides onto the bench beside the young soldier, no more than seventeen. Outranked and fearful of anyone in the SS, the boy says nothing. Strauss throws his suitcase onto the luggage rack above. He sees that his traveling companion is confused. Why is a soldier carrying a suitcase?

"I lost my backpack in France…I'm sure I'll find another soon."

"I see." The young man offers his hand to Strauss. "Private Lukas Drockler."

"Where are you from, Lukas?"

"Stuttgart."

"I see…good." Strauss sits and says nothing more.

After several minutes of awkward silence, Lukas speaks: "You haven't told me your name?" He hopes he will have someone to converse with on the long trip.

"Yes, I'm sorry. I'm Jo…I'm sorry, Fritz Mercht. I'm from Munich. How old are you, Lukas?"

"Almost eighteen."

"Have you ever been in battle?"

"No, Herr Sergeant, I graduated from upper school last April. It was supposed to be June, but with the war I immediately went into training, and here I am. I'm a little nervous. This is probably easy for you."

"War is never easy. A good friend once told me, if you are scared, just start shooting back. It will make you forget your fear and you might even kill some of the enemy."

"I'll remember that, sir."

"Private, let's switch places. I think I'd like to take a nap."

"Certainly, sir."

The two exchange places, and Strauss tries hard to get comfortable with his head against the window and legs confined. The train begins to move and with its gentle rocking sound, he is soon asleep.

Sergeant Mercht shifts in the tight confines of his seat. "No, I can't do that. I'm just an agent. Don't make me kill. No! Leave me be…" His voice rises, head shaking, hands begin to flail. Fortunately for Strauss, his words are in German.

"Private, wake up the sergeant."

"Yes, sir!" Lukas jabs Strauss in the ribs. He awakens, startled, hands moving for the neck of the young private. He remembers himself and looks up at a stern-faced Wehrmacht Hauptman standing in the aisle.

"Sergeant, your papers, please."

Strauss does as commanded, not knowing why. "What is the problem, Captain?"

The senior officer peruses the military identification papers that had been prepared for Strauss at the factory. The priest clutches Billy McClain's rosary. Surely Stauffenberg's group have created an acceptable forgery.

"Why aren't you with your brigade? They left hours ago."

Strauss is still groggy from his nightmare infused sleep. He tries to think. *"What is a good excuse? What will this rigid commander accept?"* He doesn't want to be suspected of being absent without leave.

"I had a forty-eight-hour pass to visit my sick father. He was dying and I couldn't leave his side. I just missed the last train. I'll find my division once we get to the front."

"Where is your pass?"

"I am sorry. I left it at home. My father died. I was upset."

The captain stares at Strauss, who stares stone-faced right back. He slaps at the paperwork, looks up at the ceiling. Shaking his head, he stares at the papers, rubbing the ink with his gloved hand. Strauss clutches at the rosary beads in his pocket.

The captain hands the papers back. He is in no mood for a confrontation with the hated SS; they are all zealots and killers. "I'm sorry for your loss. Good luck, Sergeant." The officer moves on, checking identifications when necessary. Strauss lets out a sigh of relief and looks at Private Drockler.

"You had a bad dream, Sergeant. Maybe you shouldn't sleep anymore."

"Lukas, wake me when we stop for food."

The troop train chugs on into the deepening night.

Chapter Fifty-Five

July 16, 1944
Soldau Concentration Camp
Ilowo-Osada, Poland

The early morning air is thick and humid. Even though it has been dark for more than six hours, the temperature has dropped by only a few degrees. The stationmaster raises the signal post arm, changing it from green to red. The oncoming train will have to be moved off to a siding, where the soldiers destined for the northern front will get off for an hour to eat miserable food. In the weeks to come, most will die by the thousands fighting the enraged Russians.

The stationmaster hears the horn from far away. What an unfortunate coincidence; two trains in his small yard at the same time. He looks over to the left. The freight train, full of Jews, Communists, gypsies and other undesirables, arrived only a half-hour ago from the east. The SS guards are trying to move them as fast as possible, but even with their German shepherd dogs, the disembarkation is slow. The human cargo is weak, their legs unsteady, the people cough and stagger out of the cars, many falling. There are no steps with a railing for these passengers. Only the yelling of orders, the fearsome growling of dogs, and hard rifle butts to the back.

"Herr Sergeant, please wake. We are coming to the station."

Strauss jerks up. "No! I'm not an assassin!"

"Wake up. You had another bad dream."

Strauss stares at Lukas. "Where are we?"

"I don't know, but we are stopping; it's almost morning. Maybe this is where there will be food."

"I am sorry for my dreams, son. I have seen too much war."

"Do you think I will have bad dreams when this is over?"

"You can only pray that you will. It will mean that you are still alive."

The train slows and jerks across the switch track to its temporary home. Strauss cannot see through the windows; they are dirty and there is condensation from all the soldiers crammed into the poorly ventilated space. He stands and tries to open the window; the top portion should slide down, but it is jammed. He bangs each side to no result. He fiddles with the latches, banging again. Finally, it gives way and slides down. He can hear the yelling and the barking. This is not a welcoming committee for the troops.

Strauss sticks his head out the window. Floodlights from the top of a two-story brick building beside the main track provide ample illumination of the horror. He knows exactly what he is looking at. It is the same as Milan, except this time the passengers are not getting into cars but getting off. It is the end of the line for them. Shots ring out, an old man falls. Two men with armbands pick up the body and take it away. Children cling to their mothers, but then are pulled away, and put into their own caged area. The men are lined up as one and slowly shuffle off under the snarls of the dogs, lunging at the queue of prisoners.

"My God, please help them," Strauss mutters under his breath. He begins to make the sign of the cross but stops at the instinctive priest-like gesture. SS soldiers do not bless themselves or pray.

A loudspeaker blares: "There will be a one-hour stop for rest and food. Exit to the building in front of you. Heil Hitler."

"Come on, Private, let's get some food. I haven't eaten since yesterday and that wasn't enough. Listen, empty your backpack and bring it. Maybe we can help ourselves to some extras for the rest of the trip."

"Yes, sir; that's a good idea."

"Stay with me I'll show you the ropes, son." Slowly, Sergeant Mercht and Private Drockler make their way out of the train with the other troops and into the commissary building. The stone structure is adjacent to the track sidings, separated by the main track and the two spurs from the central processing building of the Soldau Camp. Beyond that building, fencing with barbed wire extends in either direction. The air is full of ash and smells of burning flesh and rotting death.

Inside the commissary, four lines of hungry soldiers make their way toward two serving areas. Everyone is pushing and shoving to be first. Strauss holds Lukas back, surveys the layout, and then moves him toward the far line, less used. At the end of the hot food is bread. There are rolls, plain slices of white bread, entire loaves. He looks out through the large dirty windows of the building toward the camp.

"Would you like to see what you are fighting for, Lukas?"

"What do you mean?"

"Just do as I say. First, get behind me. Go slowly in choosing your food. There will be a commotion when you get to the bread. People will be distracted. Then fill up your pockets and the satchel with all the bread you can. After you eat, meet me by the doorway."

"I don't understand."

"Just do what I say. We'll have an adventure."

"Well, all right." Private Drockler is wishing he were still in upper school. Who is this SS sergeant?

Strauss moves through the line. There is no meat, just sardines, cold fish, boiled potatoes, fat tasteless carrots and a thin soup. He reaches the bread, which is plentiful, but takes none. He walks over to a table with four soldiers. A large heavy-set man, in his twenties, is shoving food into his mouth, eating like a pig. He has three pieces of uneaten bread. Strauss reaches across the table and takes two pieces.

"Hey, that's my bread. Get your own." The large soldier glares at the SS sergeant but is wary.

"I was in a hurry and forgot bread. You'll share yours, won't you?"

"No, I won't. Go back and get your own fucking food. I'm hungry; we've traveled all night."

"Look at the line. I'm not going back there. You can share with your fellow soldier..."

"Not with an SS pig!"

Strauss stands and continues to argue; Lukas looks back as others stand and join in the altercation. Fortunately for Strauss, SS guards from the camp are also eating and come to his assistance. Everyone is enjoying this yelling match between the SS and the Wehrmacht. The boy soldier arrives at the bread line and fills up his pockets with slices of bread and puts two loaves of bread and many rolls in his satchel. Filled to the top, he covers the treasure with the flap of the backpack.

Sergeant Mercht looks back and sees that Lukas is through the line.

"Fine, keep your bread. I'll get some when I'm done eating. I'll see you on the battlefield, so you better watch your back." Strauss gets up and heads toward the table full of guards and silently eats his food.

"Did you eat, Lukas?"

"Yes, but it wasn't very good. I'm glad we have a lot of bread. We can eat it on the train." The two soldiers are standing outside the troop train.

"Now for our adventure, Private. Give me the backpack and go get my suitcase on the train and hand it to me out the window. I'll meet you at the end of the car, but on the other side."

Lukas does as instructed. In a few minutes, they are alongside the freight train that brought its sad humanity to Soldau. There are no steps onto a Pullman platform and down the other side. They will need to crawl under the coupling mechanism.

"Lukas, crawl under there; I'll pass you the satchel and suitcase."

"Sir, I'm not sure we should be doing this. Maybe I'd better wait for you back on the train."

"Son, what you'll see is more important than your basic training. Come on, do as I say."

Drockler shakes his head and having practiced the alligator crawl countless times in the past two months, is quickly on the other side. Strauss hands him the case and backpack, then slowly lowers his long body to the ground and makes his way under the coupler, knees stiff from the long trip. In a minute, they are part of the madness of frightened people, SS guards and barking dogs.

"Follow me. Hurry." Strauss heads down the wooden walkway until it turns into a dirt path. The crowd thins. The sun is rising, improving his view, and he looks for an opening in the stout fence but there is none. In the distance he sees a sentry, walking slowly away from them. It is only a matter of time until he turns and heads their way. "Come on; stay behind me." Now the two break into a jog heading toward the sentry. He is just fifty feet away. Strauss reaches into his pocket for his knife. It is out in an instant, button pressed, blade unfurled. They reach the soldier as he turns.

"Hey, you can't be…" The knife plunges into the gut, then it comes out as the sentry falls into Strauss's arms; he thrusts it deep into the throat.

Strauss directs his charge: "Help me. Let's put him under the freight car." Lukas is frozen; he has never witnessed a man being killed before. He does as he is instructed; he fears that he might also be killed by his new companion, who is certainly crazy.

Strauss kneels down, opens his suitcase and finds the wire cutters, heavy affairs that during his journey through Italy, he wished he had tossed. Now, he feels differently. As Lukas watches, Strauss cuts the fence from the bottom up, three feet and more, pulling back the fence so they can enter into hell. Lukas is shaking, still in shock from the dead sentry and all the blood. "You killed a fellow countryman, Sergeant."

"You'll see why in a minute, boy. Believe me when I tell you that I'm saving your life. Now go through the fence. We're going to that barrack building over there. Run and stay low. Is your sidearm loaded?"

Tears are beginning to fall from the young soldier's face. "No, they didn't have any bullets to give us."

"Of course...well, it's probably for the best. I don't want you shooting anyone." Strauss covers his suitcase with dirt and leaves it hidden by the fence. They run across twenty meters of open area; a searchlight sweeps past them just as they arrive at the back of a crude wooden building.

"Help me pull off these boards." Using the wire cutters as a prybar and with the boy's strong arms, the boards peel off like the outer layer of an onion. Strauss pushes the boy inside with his backpack and follows. With a couple of dim bulbs and the help of the breaking day, the priest and the private see rows of wooden bunks, stacked three high. The place reeks of excrement, disease, and malnutrition. From the bunks, heads slowly rise and stare out at the two unwanted intruders.

One prisoner notices the SS uniform. "Achtung! Out of your beds!" Those that can, mostly young women, straddle the outside of their bunk and stand at attention; others are helped up; some cannot leave their three-by-five deathbeds. Strauss sees the fear on their faces.

"No, no, I'm a friend."

Lukas does not know what he is seeing. "Sergeant, what is this? Who are these people?"

"My son, they are the detritus of humanity. Judged by Hitler and the Nazis as inferior, and therefore, needing to be killed. This is what your country is doing; this is why they make you fight. Give me your backpack." Shaking, Drockler hands the important canvas bag to Strauss. He pulls out two pieces of bread, one in each hand. Strauss looks at Lukas and nods; Lukas reaches in and does the same. In seconds, they are surrounded by grateful faces and trembling hands.

"Please, slowly, there is so little. Take only what you must." Strauss looks at his young friend. Tears are streaming down his face onto a great beaming smile. Strauss smiles, too. Pulled down by the grateful and ravenous inmates the two Samaritans are on their knees as if in prayer.

From the other end of the barracks, the sound of jackboots reaches them. More lights are turned on. An SS Hauptman and two soldiers march down the long aisle.

"What is going on here? What is all this commotion?" Seeing the huddled masses, the guards start pulling them away, one by one. Reaching the straw bed, there is nothing but breadcrumbs on the ragged blanket.

"I see. Someone has stolen bread. You people never learn; you force me to do unpleasant things. The scum responsible for this will come forward and take your punishment."

Strauss and Lukas are on their stomachs under a bottom bunk just off to the right. Strauss has one hand on Billy McClain's rosary, the other over the mouth of his terrified partner-in-crime. No one steps forward.

"Very well. If the guilty does not come forward this…" the captain looks around the area for a suitable hostage. He sees a young girl, maybe twelve years old. "If you do not admit your thievery, this Jewess bitch will atone. I will count to three." The young girl wails in terror as she is held tight by her hair.

Strauss cannot believe what he has done; must another innocent die because of his deeds? He clutches Billy's rosary and feels the trembling body of young Lukas next to him.

"One…two…three." Without saying a word, the Luger is drawn from its sheath and a shot is fired. Blood and gray matter spray prisoners and straw mattresses; the captain lets go of the girl's hair. She drops in a heap at his feet. "Ten will die the next time bread is stolen." He turns and marches out, his murderous retinue following.

"Lukas, get out of here. I'll meet you three hundred meters east alongside the tracks in fifteen minutes. I need to take care of unfinished business."

Chapter Fifty-Six

July 16, 1944
Soldau Concentration Camp
Ilowo-Osada, Poland

Strauss walks out at the far end of the barrack building. Grateful prisoners reach out to touch him and kiss his hands. But he feels no happiness; a young girl has just been killed. He goes through the door, blinded by the morning light. His eyes adjust to a landscape of hate and horror. At least twenty long barrack buildings go off into the distance. Prisoners file out and head to the central courtyard, where men in dirty striped garb are counting off, ready to march to a munitions factory to work an eleven-hour shift. Gunshots ring out through the compound. Those who are too weak to work are simply shot in their beds.

Gallows stand at the edge of the courtyard and at least twenty bodies hang motionless, except for blackbirds picking at their flesh, causing the corpses to swing back and forth. Several inmates with wheelbarrows and ladders head in their direction. Beyond is a large brick building with six tall chimneys, emanating thick gray smoke and ash that falls around the camp like human snow.

Strauss can only shake his head as he looks for the Hauptman. He sees him heading away from the courtyard toward the commandant's house. He is about fifty feet away, talking to the two soldiers, strolling and chatting as if in a park on an afternoon stroll. Strauss pulls his gun out of his pocket and walks briskly up to the back of the captain. He taps him on the shoulder; the officer turns around.

"Yes, sergeant? Wait. I don't know you..."

Strauss raises the gun and fires. The bullet enters the forehead, and blood sprays the two soldiers. "I have been sent from God. It's Judgment Day." As the two witnesses fumble for their holsters, Strauss fires into each of them. They drop to the ground and as he walks past them, picking up one of their guns, he fires again into their heads. The sound of gunshot blends in with the noise and the horror. Then Strauss breaks into a run, heading for the hole in the barbed wire fence.

As the priest climbs through the opening, he hears sirens. The suitcase is quickly retrieved, and he trots along the tracks, estimating the 300-meter distance, one-hundred long steps. The fence of Soldau has made a right turn in the other direction, heading south.

"Lukas, Lukas, where are you?" Strauss keeps walking, moving off from the tracks and into some underbrush that partially hides him. "Lukas, Lukas," now in a louder voice. He thinks, *"Dear God, don't let him be caught for my indiscretions."* Strauss stops and opens his suitcase. He reaches for his cassock, the 'Armor of God.' He despises the SS uniform and pulls it violently off his body, tossing it into the woods. The sirens continue and then he hears dogs barking. But he also makes out a human voice. "Sergeant, I'm coming. Wait for me."

Strauss looks back at the cattle cars, and the black locomotive next to it, steaming and hissing. Out of the white vapor he sees a human form coming toward him, running. Eyes focus on the boy; no one is following him. "Sergeant, it's me, Lukas!" Panting, the young soldier reaches Strauss. "Sergeant, why are you dressed like a priest?"

"Because I am one." Father Strauss hugs the young boy. "I'm so glad to see you. Where did you go? I said wait for me 300 meters down the tracks."

"I went back to the train car to get my things. They are precious to me. I have a picture of my mother and father and sisters. Plus my Bible."

"Of course; I understand. Here, get out of that uniform. Put these clothes on. They might be a little big, but it will help with your disguise." Strauss reaches into his case and takes out the peasant clothes.

"But I'm a soldier sir, I mean, Father…"

"Not any longer. I'm saving you. What you just saw; didn't that convince you?"

"It was awful. Germany is doing that?"

"Nazi Germany. Hurry, the uniform."

Lukas Drockler takes the simple tunic, unbuttons the collar and pulls it over his head, the gray Wehrmacht coat discarded. He pulls off his striped trousers and quickly steps into the wool pants. He hides the shiny boots under the wool pants. Strauss puts on the cap and helps with the too-large coat.

"When I was fourteen, two of my best friends were taken away late at night. I watched from my window. They were loaded onto trucks. I didn't understand what was happening. I guess I do now. Did they get sent here?" Lukas is confused.

"Maybe, or to a place like it. They were killed because they were Jewish. Now, you look just like a regular peasant. Head north toward Lithuania. They're not fond of Germans, but they hate the Russians even more. Find a family that will hide you for a while. This war will be over soon."

"How do you know?"

"I'm a priest. Trust me. By the way, what faith are you?"

"Lutheran."

Strauss reaches into his pocket and finds Billy McClain's rosary. "I'm not sure Lutherans say this anymore but take this rosary. It belonged to a good friend. It will protect you, even if you don't recite it."

"Thank you. Father, I'm scared."

"Trust me, if you had stayed a soldier you will be dead in a week. This is the better choice."

"What if I get caught?"

"Move fast, stay hidden. Get at least 100 kilometers from here. Find a farm and ask for shelter. Here's some bread that I have left. And take this gun; this one is loaded. Good luck and Godspeed, Lukas Drockler."

"Why can't I stay with you?"

"Because I have other business. Now go. Stay in any woods that follow alongside a road. I'll pray for you."

Tears stream down the boy's face. He turns and runs into the nearby forest.

"Godspeed again," Strauss mutters as he closes his suitcase, picks it up and heads east toward Rastenburg, leaving the road for the safety of the woods.

Chapter Fifty-Seven

July 17, 1944
A country road
75 KM from Rastenburg
East Prussia

Strauss has been walking for a full day with his suitcase. He has no idea where Rastenburg is, or how far he must walk until he arrives there. And the suitcase is not getting any lighter. If it was filled with canned meats and vegetables it might be different. He is famished. Late yesterday, he picked some berries and devoured them, only to get painful cramps an hour later.

There were canteens he checked alongside the rotting bodies of dead soldiers, but they were empty; he takes them anyway. Then he found a small stream. He prostrated himself on his aching knees and was about to drink. But the water didn't smell right. He looked upstream; a dead cow lies alongside it, its innards opened to the running water.

The priest comes to a large rock; a good place to sit for a few minutes. He lays down his suitcase and opens it. The wire cutters are jettisoned into the woods. His two books, *A Farewell to Arms* and *A Tale of Two Cities* will have to wait for more peaceful times. He sets them down by the rock after wrapping them in his white shirt. They are precious, and perhaps someone who reads might eventually find them. He looks at his Wehrmacht uniform. It probably will fit him now, and he had better keep it for Rastenburg. Closing the case, Strauss hopes a small hamlet might be up ahead. He knows he cannot go much farther. Sleep the previous night was momentary; he had tried to rest, sitting against the trunk of a tree, but any noise startled him awake. Now, he rises slowly, lifts the lightened case, and continues down the road.

"Hail Mary, full of grace, blessed art thou amongst women..." Strauss has said the rosary in his mind several times to keep his mind off his thirst and the pain in his legs. He looks down. When did the rural dirt road turn to macadam? And it is wider. He looks ahead; on either side of the road, there appears to be railings, and the grass shoulder slopes down into a gully. Instinctively, he quickens his pace. For hours there has been no change to the unrelenting grass-covered plains other than an occasional dead horse, or worse, a dead body. Strauss hears a slight bubbling sound. Faster, he reaches a low bridge. Beneath it runs a free-flowing stream. To him, the thin creek looks like a torrent of water.

He runs down the bank and drops to his knees scooping up a handful of water, then stops. *"Damn, be careful, Strauss,"* he thinks. Getting up he heads up stream for at least eighty meters. He sees no dead bodies, no cows, no flies or maggots. But he sees little minnows. He falls down now, looks to heaven and says: "Bless this water, Lord," takes a deep breath and drinks. It is cool, sweet, fresh. He scoops up handfuls of water until he feels like his stomach will explode. He takes the two canteens he found next to the dead soldiers, rinses them out, and then fills them to the brim, closing them tight. Then he lets himself fall backward onto the grassy bank, looks up at blue sky, closes his eyes, and falls asleep.

It is four o'clock and there is no sign of a village. Strauss's stomach cramps from drinking so much water after having had so little. But his stomach aches from lack of food. The last meal he had was in the commissary at the railroad station. It tasted bland and tired, but right now, it seems like a feast.

He looks up and stops. He hadn't noticed the telephone poles before. But there they are, regularly spaced every thirty meters or so. Bodies hang from the poles, ropes thrown over the thick power wires and fastened around the necks of German soldiers. Strauss walks, but does not change his stride. He will see death soon enough. At that moment, another fear strikes him. He walks up to the first soldier. The fat, red-veined bootless feet are about two feet above his head, the rope tied lower around the pole. Around his neck, a sign reads:

Desertur / Verrätur

"Deserter / Traitor." Strauss looks at the face of the soldier above. The man is at least thirty years old. Now he quickens his pace to the next pole. *"Please God, for all that is still good in this world, don't let me find Lukas."* He reaches the next pole. The dead soldier has no helmet on and Strauss sees that it is a young boy. But the hair is blond. When he placed the peasant cap on Lukas, he remembers dark brown hair underneath. "Thank you, God."

Quickly he moves down the road, now lowering the dead bodies to the ground. Their only crime is that they simply did not want to fight in a losing war any longer. Strauss reaches the last one. He can tell from the condition of the body that this is the most recent example made to dissuade the German Army from deserting their posts. It is another young man, but he is dressed in civilian clothes. With the late sun in his eyes, he cannot tell if they are the clothes he gave to the young private. "Please God, no." With his knife he cuts the rope and lets it down slowly with his free hand, the other joining in after dropping the knife to the ground. Strauss lowers the body slowly, as is if an honor guard was lowering a flag at dusk. The body drops in his arms. He looks at the face, with all of the pity of Mary looking at Jesus in *The Pieta*. It is a handsome young man, dark brown hair, who looks as if he were sleeping. Tears well up in Strauss's eyes. It is not Lukas. He looks to heaven. "Thank you, God."

Chapter Fifty-Eight

JULY 17, 1944
Near Olsztyn
East Prussia (Formerly Poland)

The road sign says Olsztyn 5 KM. It is almost eight and the sun is setting hard on this mid-summer afternoon. Strauss looks at the sign: Five kilometers, over three miles. The suitcase that felt lighter after his house-cleaning is heavy again. The pain in his knees is unbearable, and he is weak from hunger.

A fallen tree lies alongside what he hopes is the eventual road to Rastenburg. Five kilometers or not, he has to rest. If it is midnight when he gets into Olsztyn, so be it. He sets down the case and takes a deep drink of water. One canteen is already empty. He forces himself to put the cap back on. As he wipes his face with a well-used handkerchief, he recalls the last three days.

He killed two soldiers at the loading dock in Berlin; worse, he did not hesitate. He hangs his head regretting this act. He realizes that he has, once again, become the person he escaped from in 1932. He visualizes the concentration camp, where, he stabbed a soldier to death. Then, he shot three more human beings. Yes, they were flawed, evil people, but he isn't God and had no right to kill them. He rendered a judgment that was not his to render. His head aches, and his soul feels empty and cold with the acts he has committed.

"This is war, and they were the enemy. But you are a priest and to follow Christ, you must forgive your enemies. Yet, if they had found me and young Lukas, we would be dead now. Innocent people are being exterminated; soldiers are strung up like sides of meat in the road. Surely, God, you will forgive my sins, if they are sins at all."

Strauss sucks in a deep breath of fresh air. He holds his head in his hands, shoulders slumped; tears well up in his eyes. He begins to sob great, anguished sobs of contrition and confusion. The deep hidden thought, the reality of what he did, rises up in his conscience like molten lava. Strauss knows what troubles him so. He enjoyed killing all those men. He liked it! The tears and cries of "Forgive me" pour forth. "Oh, my God, I am heartily sorry for having offended Thee and I detest all my sins, because I fear the loss of Heaven and the pains of Hell…"

He finishes the Act of Contrition. Minutes pass. The tears subside. Strauss takes another drink of water. Better get to the town. There has to be a church and food. Then he will feel better; make a confession, if he can find a priest. He turns and looks back. Great sweeping plains interspersed with heavy stands of trees, the narrow road in a straight line west.

There is a wagon coming. A wagon! All he has seen in his journey have been military vehicles heading east, or trucks full of wounded men heading west. There was an old man with a cart and donkey who ignored him, and straggling, hungry people in a daze. But now, there is a small wagon pulled by miniature horses. Strauss stands and waves. As the wagon draws nearer, he sees a nun holding loosely on the reins. As she approaches this unlikely priest standing in the road, she stops.

"Good evening. Who are you?"

"I am, oh let's see, I'm Father Johan Becken, I think."

"You look tired, Father Becken."

"I am."

"And hungry."

"That, too. Can I ride with you to town?"

"Certainly, Father. Climb up. I am Sister Paulina of the Order of St. Catherine."

Strauss looks at the back of the wagon. It is stacked two high with cages of chickens. He shakes his head. "That is quite a cargo you have. Do they lay eggs?"

"Indeed, they do. I give a few dozen to the grocer in the town, but the chickens go with me to the front. The soldiers must be fed."

"German soldiers?"

"Yes, I leave the chickens and bring back the wounded. But I'll tell you a secret, if you promise to keep it to yourself."

The wagon moves toward Olsztyn and Strauss feels his legs lighten. "If you like, but I might be an informer."

"You have a good face; I don't think so. I collect guns at the camp when no one is looking. Some of the wounded give me theirs. They want nothing to do with fighting anymore. I bring them back to the Polish Resistance."

"I see. And where do you get the chickens?"

"We raise them at the convent. I'm afraid this is almost the last of the lot."

"Sister, are you going to Rastenburg by any chance?"

"No, but close to it. Why?"

"That is where I need to go. I'm to relieve Father Cletus at St. John's Church."

"I know him. He's with the Resistance. He told me nothing of being relieved."

"It's a secret."

"I see. Everyone has lots of secrets these days. Well, I don't suppose a small detour would matter. We'll go to Rastenburg first. It will take us another day. We should get there by noon the day after tomorrow. But now, we stop at the rectory in Olsztyn. Father Jerzy is expecting me." Sister Paulina looks closely at Strauss's soiled cassock, noticing the red piping. "I'm sure they will be happy to set another plate for an honored guest…Monsignor."

"I was hoping you wouldn't notice."

"You have to pay attention in wartime."

"Will we be having chicken?"

"I would count on it." The nun whistles, and the two Konik ponies do their best to quicken the pace.

Strauss smiles at the thought of dinner, looks up to heaven and makes the sign of the cross.

Chapter Fifty-Nine

July 17, 1944
Valkenburg
Wannsee, Germany

Wilhelm Canaris is in the potting shed. He wears an old, brown, collarless shirt, and wool knickers. His wool stockings are rolled down to a pair of Dutch wooden shoes. A sturdy canvas apron covers the ensemble. The shed is part greenhouse, part work room with well-used pine tables holding pots, potting soil, and small rakes and trowels. He whistles tunes from his childhood as he works on re-potting a fern. Otto enters with a bucket of manure. He places it at the feet of his employer.

"Where did you get that? It stinks to high heaven."

"The estate across the road. The Henekels keep chickens. It is also where Karla gets eggs. It will make your fern grow nicely."

"And what about the 'chickens' guarding my driveway?"

"I bring them coffee and pastry every morning. I tell them that you are still not home; they shrug, and that's that. The Gestapo is so stupid."

"Not all of them. Be careful, my friend."

"If you were smart, we would take those two out into the lake and let them drown."

"I'm surprised that Schellenberg has not paid me a visit. It's been two days now. He must have bigger things on his mind."

"Maybe his man was not only a bad gardener, but a terrible informer." Otto laughs at his joke, and Canaris joins in.

"These last five days have been everything I have yearned for during the last year. Working in the garden; reading my books in the study; Karla's cooking; and your martinis. If this is house arrest, I'll take it any day. I might have to write the Führer a thank you note." The Admiral goes back to his fern, scooping up some manure and placing it in the bottom of the pot. Otto looks on with a furrowed brow.

"Sir, I hate to tell you this, but we're out of gin. You finished the last bottle and there is no more in the cellar. And gin hasn't been available for years. It's British, after all."

"I guess I'll just have to rough it tonight. Do we have American bourbon or rye?"

"Yes sir, everything but gin and scotch."

"Fine, I'll have a Manhattan tonight."

"I don't believe we have any cherries. Karla said she's going to the market in Potsdam this morning. I'll tell her to buy some."

"Wonderful. And what's for dinner?'

"It's getting very hard to find anything. She'll have to surprise you."

"I love surprises." Canaris looks out in the direction of Berlin and thinks about his friend, Monsignor Strauss. "Yes, surprises."

Karla Rampling drives her small Volkswagen, the People's Car, to the market in Potsdam. The car a gift to Canaris from the Führer in 1935. Northeast, in the city of Berlin, there are food shortages of everything. Even potatoes are scarce. But in Potsdam, Wannsee and other wealthy towns on the southwest edge of the city, where wealthy industrialists live next to high-ranking Nazis, anything can be had for a price.

She parks the small car on a side street and with her basket and satchel, makes her way to the open-air market that runs parallel to grocery stores, butcher shops and bakeries. On this warm and sunny day, the market is full of domestic help buying whatever they can so they can prepare rich meals for their employers. Some are even buying provisions for merry dinner parties. The war is far away.

"Hello, Gunter, how are you today?" Karla enters the butcher shop. She knows everyone at the market.

"As well as can be expected, Frau Rampling. What can I get for you today?"

"I was hoping for beef for a stew."

"You're in luck. I have a side of beef that came in yesterday. I cut it this morning. How much?"

"About one kilo should be fine."

"You're cooking a lot lately."

"Yes, a…my niece has been visiting."

The purchase made, Karla heads to the greengrocer. As she enters, she sees a fellow domestic and they engage in a lively conversation.

"Ladies, how can I help you today?"

Karla is distracted by the question and does not want to be rude by ignoring the clerk. And it is important that she does not forget cherries for her boss. Otto reminded her twice before she left for town.

"Please, Hans, I need cherries for the admiral. He wants them for his Manhattan."

"Ah, the admiral is back! Please send him my good wishes."

"I'm sorry, he's not back. I mean, we expect him soon. Maybe not soon, but sometime."

"Of course. Sometime. That will be two Reichsmarks. Cherries are very hard to find. And thank you, Frau."

Karla leaves the small shop. She covers her mouth. She prays Hans is not an informer. The shopkeeper waits on Karla's acquaintance, and the transaction complete, she leaves the shop with some apples. Hans goes into the back room, to an old desk with a hand-crank phone. He is connected with an operator, telling her the number.

"Hello, let me speak with the kriminalkommissar, please." Hans looks forward to the fine reward for the information he is about to reveal to the Gestapo.

Chapter Sixty

July 18, 1944
Sistine Chapel
Vatican City

Archbishop Brendan Galloway and OSS Special Agent Jack Lawrence crane their heads upward at Michelangelo's masterpiece on the ceiling. They have the famous chapel all to themselves. Visitors are not allowed in during the war.

"Lawrence, did you know it took four years for Michelangelo to paint this ceiling? Four years! And he didn't even want the commission. He thought of himself as a sculptor, not a painter. Not bad for a man that didn't like to paint."

"It's beautiful, but what does it all mean?"

"It would take hours to explain all of it, my friend. In a few words, these are scenes from the Book of Genesis, frescoes of Old Testament prophets, and episodes depicting the salvation of the Israelites, just to name the major paintings. It is one of the major accomplishments in all of civilization."

"Yes, a civilization that others want to destroy. I confess I'm not a religious man, but this does stir my soul, such as it is."

"Civilization, yes, but you might find it interesting that my sources, priests and nuns throughout Europe, have reported that the Nazis are stealing all kinds of religious art from our churches. They're even taking out stained glass from the churches and altar pieces. And they haven't stopped there. They've confiscated private collections, particularly from the Jews, but have also sacked museums in France, the Netherlands, Belgium, and Czechoslovakia. Hitler was a failed painter in Vienna after World War I. The Academy of Art there rejected him two times for admission. Perhaps if they had admitted him, we wouldn't be in the mess we're in right now."

"Perhaps not. I did hear about a group the Brits assembled to find those works of art; the Americans are assisting. It's called the Monuments, Fine Arts & Archives Program. We're trying to fight a war, and these guys are looking for a few inconsequential paintings."

"They're not inconsequential, Lawrence. They are the heart and soul of Western civilization. They are really what we are fighting for; to keep Western civilization intact and not have it perverted by some twisted ideology."

"I see your point, but we have a war to finish."

"If the Nazis had stayed in Rome for any length of time, they would have found a way to take this ceiling back to Germany. The Führer has built an enormous museum in Linz, Austria, his hometown, to house the looted art, and he is personally picking the artworks to go into it."

The two sit in silence for a time absorbing the great mural of *The Last Judgment* on the wall behind the altar. "I assume there is another reason you brought me here besides an art history lesson?" Lawrence takes out a cigarette. Galloway frowns and points to a sign on a stand.

Vietato fumare!

"Can't you read English? It says, 'No smoking.'"

Lawrence puts the cigarette back into the package. "Sorry, it's pretty unusual English."

Galloway looks at his cohort. "I'm worried about Strauss. We know he made it to Strasbourg on July 9 because I received a letter from Bishop Ruch. The Black Orchestra bought into our little ruse, thanks to his very convincing argument."

"So, why are you worried? He seems to be doing fine."

"It's July 18," Galloway frowns.

"Yes, and it's a long way from Strasbourg to the Wolf's Lair," Lawrence says as he looks wistfully at the pack of Lucky Strikes.

"I'm still worried. It's a long way, indeed. Through Berlin, Poland, and God knows where else." Galloway goes back to looking at Michelangelo's masterpiece. Lawrence has lost interest in great art and stares down at the floor.

"You said he has good instincts. Anyway, we can only wait and see what happens. Personally, I still don't think he's up to it. He even told me to go to hell when I gave him a little pep talk." Lawrence puts the pack of cigarettes into his coat pocket.

"What did you tell him?" Galloway's interest is piqued.

"I told him that if he didn't figure out how to disarm a bomb, he needed to eliminate Stauffenberg."

"You mean kill him?" The archbishop is incredulous.

"Please, Galloway, that's so harsh."

"No wonder he told you to go to hell. So would I."

"Like I've said before, there are too many damn clerics in the OSS." Lawrence gets up and heads for the exit. "Strauss is our only inadequate hope to stop the Black Orchestra, and if we're too late and they succeed, we'll have to deal with a bunch of Prussian generals who think they should be allowed to keep their army, Czechoslovakia and the Rhineland."

Chapter Sixty-One

JULY 18, 1944
A road to Rastenburg
East Prussia

The cart rumbles along the road, once again dirt, gravel and rocks. The ponies, only four and a half feet high and uniquely Polish, do their best to pull the cart with the added weight of Monsignor Strauss. It is a slow, bumpy trip, but Strauss appreciates that it is far better than walking.

"You know, Monsignor, I think I would fancy you had I not become a nun."

Strauss flushes in embarrassment. "You forget your vows, Sister. And I'm way too old for you."

"I think not, I'll be forty-two next month."

"I'm forty-nine, but lately my legs tell me I'm much older. I forgot to tell you, thank you for the delicious meal last night. You are a wonderful cook."

"I did very little. Father Jerzy did most of the work."

"I think it was the other way around. He is fond of his Krupnik. I've never had it, and it was quite good, except my head doesn't agree this morning."

"Did you know Krupnik was invented by Benedictine monks?"

"Catholics...drinking is not only permitted, it is encouraged." Strauss chuckles.

"Johan, what are you really doing here? I don't often find priests walking along the road, especially in the middle of nowhere. And don't lie to me with that story about replacing Father Cletus. I just met with him last week. He said something was up and I expect you are involved."

"All right, but if you are a member of the Polish Resistance, explain why you bring back German soldiers from the front."

"Wounded soldiers. I am doing God's work because they are still God's children. In return, I help out the Polish Resistance. We do not intend to be a part of the Nazi Empire forever. Very soon, we will rise up against the Nazis in Warsaw. We intend to take it back, and the Russians will help us. So yes, I am in the Resistance. But I have a confession to make. I take as long as I can to get back to the field hospital. If in the process some of the soldiers die, well so be it. Then I get the guns. Now, about you?"

"I am to meet a German officer in Rastenburg. The rest is very complicated."

"War seems to create many complicated situations for humanity. To live, or die…to kill, or be killed."

"Can I tell you something? This weighs on me heavily every day of my life."

Sister Paulina places her hand gently on Father Strauss's knee. He reaches down and takes her hand in his. The softness and warmth of it brings back old memories of Anna. He has not touched a woman's hand since he held hers, as she lay dying in the hospital.

"I'm a good listener and we have all day." The nun gently squeezes his hand.

"I was in the German Army in the Great War, but I was a poor soldier. I almost went mad in the trenches from the constant shelling, the stench of death, and seeing all my friends get killed. One night, I was ordered over the top in another useless attack. I couldn't move; I sat there in the mud, frozen with fear. I was going to be court-martialed but my father, who had powerful connections, intervened. I was put into military intelligence, the Abteilung, as it was known."

"What if you had refused?"

"A firing squad awaited me."

"It sounds as if you made the practical choice."

"Once I got into it, it was not so bad. Intelligence gathering was much better than being in the trenches. Since I spoke Italian, I was sent to Italy. My assignment was to get war production data on Italian arms manufacturers, three in particular. I posed as an Italian government official visiting factories and making reports on what was being manufactured and in what quantities."

"Sounds simple enough. Were you ever suspected or caught?"

"No. In fact I became good friends with the executives of these companies. I wined and dined them, and they came to trust me. I got all the information my superiors required."

"And you feel guilty about that?"

"No. But I was given new instructions. I was told to kill those same executives who had become my friends."

"Why? They were giving you the information you needed."

"The thinking was that their deaths would disrupt the companies' operations and therefore, the production of the arms. Beretta made rifles and sub-machine guns. Fiocchi Munizioni produced ammunition, and Ansaldo & Company made planes and even battleships. I was told to assassinate the heads of three of the biggest companies in Italy."

"Did you do it?"

"It was against ever fiber in my being. Hell, I couldn't even shoot a soldier in the trenches from 300 meters away."

"And..."

"To disobey orders in the Abteilung was impossible. It was a death sentence. I shot the first one in the back of the head. His name was Fiocchi. Then I poisoned the food of one of the members of the renowned Beretta family. And don't ask me what I did to Mario Perrone. He was a young man, my age, and we were great friends."

"Tell me."

"I cut his throat! Then I went back to Germany and said I was done, that I'd had enough. They said no, and they sent me back. I had become too skilled at being a hired killer. I did more assignments, so many I can't remember, but finally the Americans entered the war, and it was all over."

"You were doing your duty. It was war." Sister Paulina pulls her hand away and pulls Strauss to her in an embrace. Strauss hangs his head.

"They were civilians, non-combatants. And what is worse…" Strauss hesitates for a minute.

"Yes, go on." The nun looks with compassion at her new friend.

"After the first killing, the rest became easier and easier. I think I liked it."

"You did your job. God has bigger arms in times of war. He forgives more. Did you confess these regrettable sins?"

"Yes, but absolution in a confessional from a priest does not take away what I did, or how I felt, and who I still am."

"You are a man forgiven by God, Johan. Leave it at that."

"Don't you understand? I liked what I had become. I was no longer the scared little coward in the trenches of France. I came home a man, a dangerous man, and my father finally respected me… the assassin!"

"You trouble yourself too much. If it helps, I've killed a few Germans, too. When you get to Rastenburg you'll do the right thing. So tell me, what is your complicated job?"

"I have to stop some people from killing Adolf Hitler."

"Really? Are you going to do it?"

"I don't know. It's a decision I wish I didn't have to make."

Chapter Sixty-Two

JULY 18, 1944
Valkenburg
Wannsee, Germany

Wilhelm Canaris sips on a cup of tea, looking out to the large, manicured backyard, full of linden, black poplar and maple trees, and curving beds of ferns and flowers. He wonders who will care for these grounds now that he has no gardener. It doesn't really matter though, as he is living on borrowed time. He is surprised at his good fortune; six days of peace to enjoy his treasured estate.

Karla comes out from the kitchen to the rear patio with breakfast. Fresh eggs from the Henekels' chickens, scrambled with Gouda cheese, and several pieces of toast and the last of the plum jam.

"Karla, the eggs are so yellow. You spoil me."

"The Henekels have very fine chickens. However, I hate having to go there, passing those two guards at the gate."

"Otto says they are harmless. Look, I've been home six days and they do not even suspect."

The cook shakes as she sets down the food tray. She wrings her hands and then puts them to her face, and a towel wipes her eyes.

"My dear woman, what is wrong?" Canaris looks up at his faithful servant of fifteen years.

"Admiral, I told someone in town that you were back. It was an accident; I said it without thinking and I have tried to be so careful."

"Who did you tell?" Canaris's voice displays worry.

"Hans, the greengrocer. I had to get the cherries for your cocktail."

"Hans? I have known him since I bought this house. Remember I used to have to do the shopping before I hired you. I can't believe that Hans is an informer."

"I hope you are right. In these times people will do anything for money. All the shops are struggling."

"Dry your eyes. I would not give it another thought."

Karla curtsies, picks up the tray and leaves for her kitchen domain. Canaris returns his gaze to the rear yard. He would have preferred to be directly on Lake Wannsee, but in his position, as head of the Abwehr, such a location was deemed too vulnerable. He thinks about Hans and can recall nothing in the man's past that would cause alarm. *"I wish Father Strauss could be here to enjoy these eggs,"* he thinks as he shovels a good size bite onto the fork. He recalls Strauss's love of a hearty breakfast and is positive that he is not enjoying one on this day.

Otto trots out of breath onto the patio. "We have visitors!"

"Who is it Otto?" though Canaris knows what the man is going to tell him.

"Gestapo…several cars. We must get out of here."

Canaris takes a last bite of his eggs. "Get Karla and go to the tunnel. Did you prepare Halina's coach house as I told you?"

"Yes sir, we have stored plenty of provisions."

"Good. Now go…"

"You must come too."

"I have to get something. I'll be along, I assure you." Over the last few days, Canaris has pondered the types of interrogation and pain that await him for the gardener's disappearance and his membership in the Black Orchestra. Any thoughts of standing up to Schellenberg have vanished from his mind. The thought of torture does not intrigue him.

Canaris heads to the study; once there he goes to the window and looks through the curtains. Four cars are speeding up the long drive.

He turns and hurries to the opposite wall and to the Impressionist landscape painting that hangs there. The painting is hinged, and when opened reveals a safe. A turn left, a turn right, a full turn one-and-a-half times left again. He pulls out several bound stacks of Reichsmark notes, and a worn, black leather book. He throws the heavy door shut, quickly proceeding out to the main hallway toward the door to the basement.

"Halt, hör auf!" A shot is fired into the ceiling.

Canaris stops, tosses the book into a potted palm. His house arrest is over.

Chapter Sixty-Three

July 18, 1944
A forest clearing
10 KM from Rastenburg

Strauss and Sister Paulina can hear the distant booming of artillery, cannon, and howitzers. The sky in the north flashes from the explosions like a lightning storm. The duo is happy they are heading east.

"We are close to Rastenburg, but it has become too dangerous to travel at night. Some deserters travel together as bands of thieves. We should camp here, and we'll get up early to be at St. John's just in time to welcome your German friend. And we'll have some more eggs, too, for breakfast," the nun nods toward the back of the wagon.

"Perhaps one of those chickens can make a sacrifice tonight, rather than a contribution?"

"I think so. If you build a fire, I also have a can of beans and a potato. And under the seat are blankets and two bottles of wine I've saved."

The fire is blazing, and the OSS agent and the Polish Resistance fighter have made a comfortable campsite. Strauss wishes he had the loose-fitting peasant clothes, which he gave to Lukas, rather than his heavy, unwieldy cassock. He won't complain. Sister Paulina's habit looks confining.

"Is your name really Paulina?"
"Is Johan Becken your real name?"

"No, it's Johan Strauss. We're all somebody else in wartime."

"Strauss. Very strong. Mary Paulina is the name I took when I became a nun. After St. Paul. He was a man who first persecuted Christians and then turned to God, while I, on the other hand, was a good Catholic girl who has been forced to do unpleasant work because of the war."

"You told me not to be too hard on myself; I might offer that same advice to you. What was your baptized name?"

"Very simple. Anna Marie."

"Your order should have let you keep Anna Marie. It is very beautiful. Where are you from?"

"Warsaw. And you?"

"Augsberg in Bavaria."

The nun removes her belt and large rosary and then pulls over her tunic revealing a white petticoat undergarment. She removes her coif, wimple, and veil exposing short, light brown hair, and revealing a finely-boned face. She is beautiful without makeup. She stares at Strauss through deep green eyes. "You don't expect me to sleep in that do you?"

Strauss looks at Sister Paulina. In the waning fire, the light displays a woman with wisdom, but with the presence of youthful innocence. His body stirs with old emotion, an emotion hidden for so many years. "Why did you become a nun?"

"To serve God. What about you, why did you become a priest?"

"Honestly?"

"Johan, we're out here in the middle of the woods. I think this is a good time for honesty."

"To escape the world and what it had turned me into. A killer. A killer who became good at killing."

"Quite an about-face…killer to priest. And why did they pick a priest to send on this mission? Who sent you?"

"It's complicated like I told you. Perhaps all you need to know is that now, I'm hopefully a better priest than a secret agent."

There is a crack of dead wood breaking, branches rustling, and noises from a short distance away. Strauss stands and pulls out his gun. Paulina is still, listening for the direction of the sound. There is more rustling of branches followed by heavy steps on the forest undergrowth. Strauss tries to adjust his eyes as he looks out into the darkness. The flashes of artillery have subsided, providing no help. Eyes focused, he makes out two figures coming from the woods into the clearing. Their uniforms are beyond dirty, but he can make out the SS on their collars. They seem to be staggering along, and they both have guns.

"That's far enough. Turn around and go back to the pit of Hades you came from."

"A priest. Oh, and look, a woman. This will be fun."

"I told you to leave us."

"Do you have whiskey? We're thirsty."

"We have nothing for you. Now leave." Strauss's firm voice rises, without much conviction.

"If there is no whiskey, this bitch will do. And your wagon would be very nice."

Sister Paulina looks at Strauss, fear in her eyes. To hesitate is to die in this country. She puts her hand into her petticoat, pulling out a Nagant .38 caliber revolver. With wide eyes, Strauss looks at the large handgun.

"You heard the man. Leave us."

"Oh, come now, we just want to sit by your fire…"

Two shots ring out. The drunken SS visitors drop like felled trees.

"Shit. You killed them."

"That was the idea. I'm in no mood for the SS tonight. Is there any more wine?"

"Yes, another bottle. Do you want to celebrate?"

"Let's drag these two into the woods. Let the wild boars have them."

Strauss throws the last of the wood he has scavenged onto the fire. He lies down propped up on one arm. A simple metal cup holds the rest of the wine that the two have passed back and forth. Paulina gets up from the opposite side of the fire and sits down next to him, takes his cup and drinks from it. "I want to sleep beside you. I'm a little scared."

Strauss looks at her face, the passions of the man he once was, now fully stirring. "We make a good pair, Anna Marie."

As the fire dies, they fall asleep, Strauss's arm around the nun.

Chapter Sixty-Four

July 18, 1944
Valkenburg
Wannsee, Germany

Brigadeführer Schellenberg stands over his captive, strapped to a large armchair in the study; he has a sick smile on his face, an easy, sinister glare. Wilhelm Canaris has been hit repeatedly with a leather and metal truncheon by one of Schellenberg's goons. He remains unbowed. He can only hope they don't find the black book he tossed into the potted palm.

"Walter, if you weren't behaving so rudely, I'd offer you a beer."

"We are way past pleasantries and 'for old times' sake,' Wilhelm. I know you have been an active participant in the Black Orchestra. One of its leaders. What are they planning?"

"A protest march at the Tiergarten, nothing more." Schellenberg nods; the goon swings the truncheon again, hitting Canaris in the jaw. His mouth bloodies, and he spits out a tooth.

"You were seen with a Wehrmacht captain at a roadblock between here and Nuremberg. There is no Captain Johan Becken. Who is he?"

"Schellenberg, I'm getting tired of doing your work for you. You're the head of the SD. Figure it out."

Schellenberg looks about the room. He goes over to a side table with a lamp and yanks the plug out of the socket. As he walks toward Canaris, he removes the bulb. There is an outlet in the floor. Schellenberg motions to his assistant who bends down and plugs in the lamp. The Brigadeführer holds the lamp in front of the Admiral. "Please, Wilhelm, help me. Illuminate us. Who was that captain?"

Canaris stares at the lamp without a bulb, its socket exposed. The goon has grabbed his hand holding it like a vise. The interrogation is everything he expected, and worse. His mind goes back to his time as a submariner. He was almost electrocuted by a bad wire attached to one of the many batteries that powered the boat. The pain was beyond excruciating. "It is not my fault that you do not know a Captain Becken. He is a loyal soldier in the Wehrmacht. He was my traveling companion."

Schellenberg looks at his helper and nods. A finger is forced into the socket. Canaris screams as he twitches from the jolt of electricity.

"Who is he?"

Canaris says nothing. The finger is inserted again.

"He's a priest!"

"A priest? That makes no sense." Schellenberg holds the lamp, and the assistant forces a finger into the lamp socket again. He holds it in for five seconds. To Canaris, it is an eternity.

"An American!"

"You expect me to believe you? You're talking bullshit!" Schellenberg nods. This time the electricity starts to burn Canaris's white hair.

"He's going to Rastenburg. To a church!"

"This is all bullshit! An American priest. Perhaps a few days in Spandau Prison will improve your memory. Get him out of here."

The thug unties the bindings and motions toward the doorway for more help. Canaris is dragged out of the room to a waiting car.

———

Otto and Karla dare not move a curtain or look out the window toward Valkenburg.

"He said he would come…"

"They have him. We are on our own. We must stay here, as he instructed us. In time, we can leave."

"When?"

"I do not know, wife. I do not know."

"Mayor, this is Brigadeführer Walter Schellenberg. You are to send a couple of our agents to the St. John's Catholic Church in Rastenburg. Arrest the priest there. If he resists, kill him."

Chapter Sixty-Five

July 19, 1944
Rastenburg, East Prussia
German Territory

The little wagon lumbers into the sizable town of Rastenburg. Sister Paulina guides the ponies through the cobblestone streets toward St. John's Church.

"I think I like you in that uniform, Johan, perhaps more than your cassock."

"It doesn't fit very well, but after the last few days, it's better. I've lost weight with all the walking."

"Thank you for comforting me last night. I'm not used to killing people."

Strauss looks at his new friend, "I was happy to be there. You know, without your coif hiding your head, you are a most beautiful woman."

"Now who's forgetting their vows?" Paulina smiles.

"Have you ever thought of leaving your order?"

"At first, but now I've been a little too busy with a war going on. I suppose I am content to be married to God."

Face flushed, Strauss says, "Perhaps I chose my vocation too hastily."

"Or for the wrong reasons. Have you decided what you're going to do about your hard decision?"

"No, not yet."

Tucked into a small square with a fountain in the center, is the old, yellow stucco church She guides the wagon around it to the front of the building, its wooden doors three steps above the street.

"Here we are. We can enjoy breakfast with Father Cletus. Ah, here he is now."

Father Cletus, a small, old man walks out of the church, fear on his face. "Sister, please move on. You cannot stay here."

"What do you mean, Father?" As the words come out, the old priest breaks into a trot toward the wagon. Two SD agents exit through the same door. Gunshots reverberate through the square. The priest falls as he reaches the wagon.

Without hesitation, Sister Paulina pulls her Nagant revolver out from her robe. "Johan, take the one on the right," she barks. Strauss is ready, his gun drawn.

"Got it." Two more shots ring out. The Nazi agents fall.

Strauss and Sister Paulina jump out of the wagon and go to the body of the priest. He is still breathing. Sister holds his head, stroking his forehead. "Father, be strong."

"They were looking for a priest…an American," the words coming forth in his last breath. His head goes limp in Sister's hands.

"They were looking for me?" Strauss is confused. He looks down at a man he has never met and is overcome with sadness.

"I think your cover has been blown, Agent Strauss."

Strauss walks into the small kitchen of the rectory. He is shirtless and sweating, though he still has on his military trousers and polished boots. "I buried them in the garden out back. It was the least I could do."

"We should have strung them up in the square; shooting an old, defenseless priest in the back!" Paulina slams a cast iron pan on the wood-burning stove. "Breakfast is almost ready."

"At least we were able to lay out Father Cletus in the sanctuary, close to God. Do you know an undertaker in town?"

"I'll tend to it. Where is your German soldier contact?"

"I don't know. He said he has a meeting today at the Wolf's Lair."

"Father Cletus has said Mass there for some of the troops every Sunday. I think tomorrow is Sunday, correct?"

"I'm not sure anymore. Yes, you are right; it will be Sunday. If he doesn't show up, they may be suspicious. They might send some soldiers to find out where he is."

"He told me that he was always searched and then watched closely. Hitler despises religion and the church but allows services as long as it is well away from his compound. He realizes most of the soldiers consider themselves Christians."

"I'm sure he doesn't want disgruntled troops guarding him. Despite his efforts to become their 'god', some cling to the religion of their youth and believe in the true God."

"Come and sit. It's ready."

"I'll eat, and then I need some time to pray."

"Feed the body, and then the soul, I always say."

Strauss kneels in a pew beside the dead priest, hands clasped in prayer. Father Cletus is laid out on a catafalque in the center aisle adorned in his best vestments. *"The man tried to warn me. Now, he's dead. How did they know an American priest was coming?"* He looks at the altar, rich white and gray marble with a white linen mantle cloth. The tabernacle is at the center, its gold door enclosing the consecrated bread and wine, the body and blood of the Savior. A red lantern with a candle glows off to the side, indicating the presence of God in the small sanctuary. Above the altar is an ornate crucifix, showing Christ in agony; Strauss looks at it, empathetic with His suffering.

"Dear God, my mind is a muddle of confusion. I was safe once I gave my life to you. So why did you send me on this journey? Is it because you knew I wasn't sincere in my vocation, but just escaping my terrible past? You

sent me back to confront the man I was, with the man that I should be? And now, you have put before me the ultimate test. And where is your answer? Answer me, my God, please answer me."

Claus von Stauffenberg enters the church and sees the body of Father Cletus in repose. Then he notices the hunched-over figure of Father Strauss. He walks up to the pew behind him, slides onto the kneeler, and whispers: "Hauptman Becken, what has happened?"

Strauss is startled; he was praying so fervently that he did not hear the footsteps of his old friend. "Claus, you are here. The Gestapo shot him while he was trying to warn me. Somehow, they knew I was coming here."

"Then we need to go immediately. My meeting with the Führer is in one hour, at one o'clock."

"We?"

"Yes, you will come along as my aide. In case I have trouble with the detonator, you can squeeze the pins for me. This time, we cannot fail. I'll be out front by the car." Stauffenberg gets up, blesses himself, turns, and goes out of the church.

Strauss looks at the altar and then looks up at the cross. *"Now is the time. Thy will be done, Lord."*

Chapter Sixty-Six

July 19, 1944
Wolfsschanze
The Wolf's Lair
East Prussia

Strauss walks outside into the bright morning sun. As his eyes adjust, he sees another soldier at the wheel of the Einheits-PKW, a standard-issue military staff car. Oberleutnant Werner von Haeften, smoking a cigarette, nods in the direction of Strauss. Strauss sighs. Now he has to contend with two people dedicated to assassinating Hitler. And he has to figure a way to dismantle a bomb. He knows one thing for certain: He won't kill his friend Claus von Stauffenberg.

"Werner, meet my American friend, Hauptman Johan Becken. He has volunteered to assist me today. Johan, this is my aide, Oberleutnant Werner von Haeften."

"In that uniform, he looks very German. Nice to meet an American. John Wayne?"

Strauss smiles. "Yes, John Wayne…"

"Exactly. We'll all be John Wayne today. Let's get going. No one keeps the Führer waiting."

Strauss gets into the back seat and Stauffenberg hands him his briefcase.

"Two bombs made of plastic explosives are in there and the detonators. When we get to the Führer's bunker, I will ask to use a bathroom. In the bathroom, I will insert the detonators and arm them. If I have difficulty, I'll open the door and bring you in. Otherwise, wait outside and do not let anyone enter. After the bomb is armed, we have only ten to fifteen minutes. I've arranged to be called away for a phone call. You will not be allowed in the meeting, so you'll leave and wait with Werner."

"Understood." Strauss can think of no way to stop the attempt other than shooting von Haeften while he is driving. Then there will be a wreck. He looks down the long road with heavy forest on both sides. Such a plan does not seem very practical.

"Johan, I did not have an opportunity to tell you. I mentioned our reunion to my wife. She was delighted to know that you would be looking after me again after so many years. She sends her regards." Stauffenberg is almost lighthearted a half-hour before he is going to kill the leader of the Reich.

"I am very pleased that she considers me your protector." Strauss shakes his head. Protector indeed.

The dull gray automobile reaches the first checkpoint. Haeften slows to a stop. From the top down, the guard peruses the armored military vehicle and its inhabitants.

"Ihre papiere, bitte."

The occupants of the car produce their identification papers. The review of the three documents is perfunctory, and the gate lifts.

"There are three checkpoints. That was the easy one. But so far, they are buying into Hauptman Becken," Stauffenberg looks at Strauss.

"What about the next two?"

"I never thought about it much before, but I never had a bomb with me. I assure you, the next two stops will be more difficult."

Another road to the left merges into the main road; a black Mercedes is moving fast and gets in front of von Haeften.

"What's his hurry?" Strauss asks, curious.

"They look more important than we do. Give them plenty of room. I don't want any problem with other senior officers today."

They arrive at the second checkpoint, slowly pulling up behind the Mercedes. There seems to be some discussion and the high-ranking officer is throwing his hands in the air. Then the vehicle moves on as the gate arm is raised. Von Haeften pulls up to the SS guard.

"Ich werde ihre papiere inspizieren."

This time, von Haeften has collected all the official documents and passes the stack to the SS soldier.

He frowns and admonishes von Haeften. "Next time you will hand me your papers individually. I have no time to sort through these. Are you here for the one o'clock general staff meeting?"

"Yes, sir, we are." Von Haeften's response is short, to the point.

"All attaché cases, bags, or cases of any kind will be searched at the next checkpoint and at the Lagebaracke, by order of the Führer. All right, you may pass."

"Dammit!" Stauffenberg looks at Strauss, who turns away, looking to heaven. He says a silent prayer of thanks.

"Here Strauss, help me. Take out the bombs and the detonators before we get to the last checkpoint."

Strauss takes the briefcase. The straps on each side are tied. He fumbles with the first one; he can see that this is a new case that Stauffenberg has purchased for this very purpose. The buckle and the clasp keep engaging into each hole. He looks up; the checkpoint is approaching. One strap is undone. The next one gives the same trouble. The leather and buckle are stiff and unwieldy.

"Hurry, we are almost there!"

"I'm doing my best; the leather is stiff." Strauss is fumbling with the clasp; it keeps reinserting itself back into the holes. Finally, it is free. He reaches in, searching without seeing, and pulls out one soft block of plastic explosive, then the other. He reaches down and slides them under the empty seat in front of him. He throws the flap of the briefcase over but has no time to buckle the straps. Von Stauffenberg takes the bag and realizes it is not closed as von Haeften slows the car. It is too late to close the case.

"Wir werden ihre aktentaschen durchsuchen." The SS corporal is large and menacing.

"Yes, I understand that this is a new regulation. And why this new regulation?" Stauffenberg hands over his case.

"Because, the Führer has said so. And why are these straps loose?"

Stauffenberg lifts up his arm, showing that he has no hand. Then he lifts up his left hand showing that there are only three fingers. The guard stares, shrugs and then nods. He searches the contents—papers, folders, a map, and the two detonators! He removes them and holds them up. The thin copper tubes do not look like fuses. It's hard to discern what they might be.

"Oh, those are parts for a radio transmitter. I was told to bring them from Berlin to the telegraph office." Stauffenberg hopes the soldier will buy it. Strauss silently prays that his stupid mistake will not give them away.

"Ihre papiere, bitte." Von Haeften hands over the papers of the three conspirators as the guard hands the briefcase back to Stauffenberg, with the detonators dropped back into the briefcase. The SS guard studies the papers with great intent. He goes into a small booth and retrieves a clip board, flipping through sheets.

"Colonel von Stauffenberg, my admiration for your service to the Reich. As Chief of Staff of the Reserve Army you are permitted one guest to accompany you to the meeting, an Oberleutnant von Haeften. That is your driver, I see. Who is this man, Hauptman Becken? He is not on the list."

"General Fromm requested that he accompany me today. He has reports that I have not been fully briefed upon. This was only decided this morning. My apologies." Strauss is impressed with the quick thinking of his old friend.

"All right, what reports, Hauptman?"

Strauss stares wide-eyed at Stauffenberg. *"Yes, what fucking reports, Claus?"* he thinks.

Strauss blurts out: "I am sorry, Corporal, but that information is highly classified. It is for the Führer alone. I can only tell you that it has to do with the internal security of Berlin." Strauss sighs, satisfied with the fabrication, and his quick thinking.

The SS guard looks down at the papers. He hands them back. "Fine, you may pass. Again, Colonel, my thanks for your sacrifice."

Haeften presses his foot on the gas and the Opel staff car moves on. Strauss looks ahead and can now see an assembly of buildings. As they approach a parking area, he sees Wolf's Lair is full of activity. Officers of high rank stand and talk, smoking cigarettes. Men in suits walk by with folders under their arms. Each building is guarded by a black-uniformed SS guard sporting a shiny black helmet with white lightning bolts on the side. He takes a deep breath. Three months ago, he was having a piece of apple pie in the rectory. Now he is in the belly of the beast.

"What about the explosives?"

"It's too risky. Here, take these detonators too."

"Come, old friend. Let me introduce you to the Führer. You'll see what a charming person he is. Werner, we will be back soon." Stauffenberg exits the utilitarian vehicle; Strauss follows.

"Now what will you do?"

"I do not know, Johan, I do not know."

Chapter Sixty-Seven

JULY 19, 1944
Valkenburg
Wannsee, Germany

Brigadeführer Walter Schellenberg puts down the lamp. He cannot understand why Canaris didn't confess everything. How could he endure such pain? The man is tougher than he thought, even making up fantastic stories. An American priest? Well, that base is covered; he should receive a report from the mayor of Rastenburg by tomorrow.

He looks around the study. The landscape painting on the wall looks strangely out of kilter; it is hanging at an angle. He walks over to it and realizes that it is hinged on one side. He swings it and nods; a safe. The vault's door is closed, but it is not locked. He opens it. There are bundles of Reich's notes similar to the two that were found in the pockets of the admiral. *"He took out money and left some. Perhaps he took something else…"*

Schellenberg goes out to the long hallway that is the foyer to the enormous house; he looks to the front door where his SD agents came in, then turns and looks down the loggia toward the rear windows and door leading to the garden. He walks slowly, looking under chairs, behind paintings, and in the potted palms. The dirt is black, and he can discern nothing. He bends down again and then sees it under a low frond. A black book. He reaches down, picks it up, and goes into the living room. On a sideboard is a set of Baccarat crystal glasses and decanters. He picks one that has a brown liquid, removes the stopper, and takes a whiff of the contents, and smiles. He pours a generous amount and goes over to the couch. Sitting down, he takes a sip, savoring the fifteen-year-old American bourbon. He opens the book.

Personal Diary
Of
Admiral Wilhelm Canaris

"Well, my dear Admiral, we may finally learn something about the Black Orchestra," the Brigadeführer smiles, taking another taste of his drink. He turns the page and begins to read.

Spandau Prison
Berlin, Germany

Exhaustion and hours of torture have overcome Canaris. Despite the pain, he is finally asleep. The SD has pulled out all of his molars; they have pounded his fingers with a mallet, breaking several knuckles, and injected him with a truth serum called sodium pentothal. He would only mutter "American priest" or "American spy." The interrogators will wait until Schellenberg arrives with further orders.

Schellenberg stands at the door to the cell, smiling. It is now around midnight, but he needs to confront Canaris. The little black book has been very informative. So informative that he has no further need to interrogate his old friend. Just a few clarifications and then he can send the man to the gallows. He has all the confession he needs. "Wake him."

The guard opens the door and is quickly at the bed; he kicks the small, broken man. He groans and rolls over. As he does so, the thin sheet covering his body, falls off and reveals his nakedness. His face is puffed and bloody, the glorious head of white hair now a disheveled, bloody mess. Schellenberg looks down at the bruised body.

"Wilhelm, I am sorry for such harsh treatment. If you had just given this to me to begin with, then none of my interrogation would have been necessary." He waves the book in front of his prisoner's face. "I only have few questions, clarifications really."

"Fuck you, Walter, go to hell."

"We will both be going to hell, but you will be first. Who is Johan Becken?"

"He is a Catholic priest, that's all."

"An American Catholic priest? He is dead. I had him shot in Rastenburg."

Canaris shuts his eyes at the news. It is worse than the pain he feels all over his body.

"Is he a part of the Black Orchestra?" Schellenberg presses.

"There is no Black Orchestra…"

"Your little book says otherwise. Lie again and your kneecaps will be smashed."

"We're a fraternity, that's all," the admiral speaks in a whisper.

"A fraternity that is planning to kill the Führer."

"We have no illusions. No one can get to him. It's all a little game. We talk, and dream about it and then we get drunk."

"Where is von Stauffenberg? Your black book says he's the leader."

"How should I know? He just thinks he's the leader. I was comfortable under house arrest and was done with the whole lot of them."

Schellenberg looks toward the door to the guard. "Get in here. Smash his knees." The guard follows orders without hesitation. The truncheon is raised. Canaris screams: "No! Please don't."

Schellenberg nods anyway. The iron pipe wrapped in leather comes down on the first knee. Canaris's anguished scream is heard down the corridor over the cracking of bone. "Stop! I'll tell you!"

The Brigadeführer raises his hand. "Leave us. He bends down close to the admiral's mouth. "Then tell me. I'm paying rapt attention."

"He's at a meeting at the Wolfsschanze. He's making a report."

"Is he going to try to kill the Führer?"

"What do you think?" Canaris looks at his nemesis and passes out.

Chapter Sixty-Eight

July 19, 1944
St. John's Rectory
Rastenburg

"Anna Marie, the man walked right past me. You know he is not as tall as I thought. And he certainly didn't look invincible. His hand was shaking, and he was hunched over." Strauss sits at the table drinking a dark beer in the rectory kitchen. Sister Paulina works on dinner. A single light bulb hangs above them and illuminates the space, the poor light augmented with several candles.

"You should have killed him right then and there," she says sternly.

"I had no gun. Everyone has their weapons checked at the door. And then he didn't even have the meeting. More pressing business, we were told. If we had the bombs, it would have all been for naught."

"Why are you supposed to stop Claus from killing Hitler? Claus is one of us; I won't let you do it." Her voice rises.

Strauss puts a finger to his lips. "Speak softly. He's asleep in the next room."

"Yes, he's exhausted traveling from Berlin to put an end to that madman. And you want to stop it?"

"Those are my orders."

"You make no sense. After all that you have seen since you came from America, you want to keep Hitler alive?"

"It doesn't matter now. After the fiasco with the bombs, we had to leave them in the car, thank God. I guess without lifting a finger, I've succeeded in my mission."

"To keep Hitler alive?"

"Yes. That's my job."

"It's a fool's errand."

"It doesn't matter. There is no way to get a bomb into Wolf's Lair."

"Does Claus know you are a priest?"

"No, it has never come up. He just thinks of me as an American OSS agent."

"I'll be right back." The nun leaves the kitchen.

"Where are you going?" Strauss lifts his stein to his mouth. He waits. He looks at the pot on the stove; he gets up and stirs the chicken stew.

The nun returns holding a square case with a handle. It looks like a miniature suitcase.

"What is that?" There is a small silver cross on the front of the case.

"I have an idea. Tomorrow is Sunday. I told you that Father Cletus went to Wolf's Lair to say Mass for the soldiers. You can take his place."

"What are you talking about?"

"You can say the Mass! Father Cletus told me there's an open assembly area within walking distance to the main compound. Father Cletus showed me his chaplain's case."

"What of it?"

Sister Paulina opens the box. There is a gold chalice, a plate for communion wafers, a small pitcher for wine, and other implements for the consecration of the host.

"Wonderful. I'll say Mass for the troops, God will be pleased, and everything will be all right. Only Stauffenberg will be unhappy." Strauss shakes his head.

"Johan, look." The nun removes the items in the case, then reaches down to the felt bottom and two small ribbons. She lifts the felt board, revealing a hidden compartment. "I would think there is enough room in here for your bombs."

Strauss stares at the hidden compartment. He frowns. The moral conflict, his hard decision that he thought was behind him, is back. "What did he use that for?"

"He kept a gun in there. He hoped he might get close enough to Hitler one day."

"And you want me to carry the explosives into the Wolf's Lair, say Mass for the soldiers, and then what, switch suitcases with Claus?"

"Something like that." Sister Paulina smiles and looks at Strauss hoping he might agree.

"It's not possible! Every guard saw me today at all the checkpoints."

"Father Cletus bicycled to the Wolf's Lair on a back lane that ends at a service road and then onto the compound. The road is used for deliveries and troop rotations. There will be different sentries. Plus, you'll be dressed as a priest, not as a captain."

"You try me, woman. I told you that my mission is to stop anyone and everyone from killing Adolf Hitler." Strauss gets up and goes over to a small keg and refills his stein of beer.

"Johan, all your life you have tried to escape your past because you made wrong choices. Why not do what is right for once, and then you can embrace your life and be proud of it?"

"I have my orders."

"To hell with your orders! Bad orders are meant to be disobeyed!"

"Orders are still orders. Don't you think I'd love to see the man dead? And I have other reasons."

The nun puts the liturgical paraphernalia back in place, closes the case, and takes it to the doorway, setting it down. She shakes her head in sadness. "I'm very disappointed in you, Johan."

"I'm going to my room. I'm not hungry. When Stauffenberg gets up, say nothing of this crazy scheme of yours."

"As you wish, Monsignor Strauss, as you wish."

The late-night rainstorm lashes the window of Strauss's small bedroom. He can feel cool air rush through the leaky panes of glass. He kneels at his bed, tears run down his face. He looks up at a small crucifix on the wall. *"Answer me, God, please answer me."* On the bed is the chaplain's case. He looks away from the cross on the wall and stares at his destiny. "Thy will be done, Lord. Let him be killed." Strauss makes the sign of the cross.

Chapter Sixty-Nine

JULY 20, 1944
Reich Chancellery
Berlin, 8:30 A.M.

The phone connection between Berlin and East Prussia is poor. "Yes, this is Brigadeführer Schellenberg. It is imperative that I speak to the Führer immediately." He strains to hear the voice on the line. "Did you not hear me? Again, I need to speak to the Führer... Yes, I'll wait."

The head of the SD would prefer to be riding his Holsteiner stallion this morning in Grunewald Forest, albeit without his favorite riding companion, but he must warn the leader of the Third Reich about the plot of the Black Orchestra. It is a call that may decide his fate, and the Führer's. All he can hear is static on the line. Then he hears clicking, a buzz, then a voice.

"Generalmajor, please hold one moment for the Führer." Schellenberg's pulse quickens at the announcement. He holds for longer than he cares to.

"Schellenberg, is that you?"

"My Führer, thank you for taking my call. I know you are always very busy."

"What do you want? Have you found that traitor, Canaris?" The head of Germany has no time for small talk. The abruptness catches Schellenberg off guard.

"We have, sir, we have. He is in custody at Spandau Prison."

"Good. What has he told you? Has he confessed disloyalty to me?"

"He has. He will be executed shortly."

"Good. Now, if there is nothing else…"

"May I ask, my Führer, is Reichsführer Himmler there at the Wolfsschanze?"

"No, he rarely comes here. He says that the air does not agree with him. Why?"

"May I ask, sir, is Reichsmarschall Göring in attendance at the compound?"

"No, Schellenberg, he is not. He was called back to Berlin on urgent business. Why all these inquiries? The schedules of those men are of no concern to you. What did Canaris tell you about the Black Orchestra? That is all I care about. Now, tell me."

The Brigadeführer seethes at the admonishment. He pauses, thinks. "My Führer, you need not concern yourself with the Black Orchestra. They are minor functionaries, being arrested as we speak. Canaris called them a little fraternity of drinkers. You have nothing to fear. I am afraid the Gestapo has over-estimated their importance."

"And what about a plot to kill me?"

"It's pure fabrication, a fantasy. As I said, they are a poorly organized group of discontented rabble."

"Very well. I knew I was safe here at Wolf's Lair. Speer and I planned the complex well. Let me know when Canaris has been executed, that ungrateful traitor. Make sure it is filmed. Others may need to see it and be reminded of what disloyalty means, yourself included."

"Yes, my Führer. Have a pleasant and productive Sunday. Good day."

"Good day, Schellenberg." The phone goes dead. Schellenberg muses, a wry smile forming on his mouth. *"Fine. Let Stauffenberg kill that pompous ass. Then Himmler, Göring and I will take over Germany and form the Fourth Reich. Perhaps I'll go for a ride after all. Tonight, we may have a new Führer."*

Chapter Seventy

July 20, 1944
St. John's Rectory
9:30 A.M.

Von Stauffenberg and von Haeften drink dark coffee around the table in the kitchen. Sister Paulina cooks German pancakes and sausage. She has said little to the two men, and the irritation in her mood permeates the room.

"Sister, you are not yourself this morning. Is something wrong?"

"I am just tired of the war, all the killing, and all the failures." She opens the heavy oven door and peeks in at the heavy skillet and its rising contents.

"As am I. I have racked my mind all night. There must be a way to get our bomb into Wolf's Lair. Perhaps I could hide it under my jacket?"

Von Haeften looks at his superior. "I would not recommend that. There would be a bulge, and besides, everyone is searched before we enter the Führerbunker. Worst of all, it might explode from the heat of your body. It is very unstable around heat."

"There is a way, but it requires a priest." Sister Paulina says as she looks toward the doorway where she put the small case. It is not there.

"The only priest we had is dead." Stauffenberg blows on his coffee to warm it.

Strauss enters the room. He is wearing his cassock. "No, you have another priest, Claus. Me." He is carrying the chaplain's case.

"Strauss, what are you doing dressed up like that?"

"I told you, Claus, that I was many things. A Catholic priest is one of them."

"You're a priest?"

"Yes, and an OSS agent."

"Are you going to say Mass today? I need a Wehrmacht captain, not a priest." Stauffenberg is perplexed.

"Sister Paulina has concocted an implausible scheme. It might work, or it might get us all killed. But if we can succeed in killing that lunatic, it will be worth it."

Sister Paulina looks at Strauss and goes to him. She hugs him, smiling. "Johan, good morning!"

Strauss is taken aback at the affection. "You forget your vows, Anna Marie, but for once, I am glad." He smiles at her, beaming. Sister Paulina kisses Strauss on the cheek.

Von Stauffenberg and von Haeften look at each other. They shake their heads and laugh. "So, tell us about this scheme that you two have conjured up."

Chapter Seventy-One

July 20, 1944
Service Road to Wolf's Lair
10:30 A.M.

The rain the night before has brought cooler temperatures. Strauss pedals hard up-hill. For the most part, the road is hard-packed gravel, but in other places it is mud. The suitcase rests in a basket that is too small; hitting a bump in the road could cause it to fall out. In the bottom of the basket are the vestments for Mass, wrapped in old newspaper.

The priest hits a rock in the road that almost causes him to lose control of the bicycle, a form of transportation he has not ridden since childhood. He pedals on, wondering if he will ever get to the first checkpoint. As his aching legs pump up and down, he goes over the plan, for the umpteenth time, in his head.

> *"First, get through all three checkpoints. You are Monsignor Johan Becken. You are visiting Rastenburg where your elderly parents live. Father Cletus has come down with bronchitis and you have volunteered to take his place today. You need to ask them where to go to perform the service.*
>
> *"Stauffenberg arrives just before Mass begins, and he will find you. He comes to the open area and asks to make his*

confession. As you bend over to hear his sins, he places his briefcase under your chasuble. Have the chaplain's case, with the bombs in the hidden compartment, on the ground next to you. As he recites his sins, he switches cases. He then departs for the meeting. You, in turn, begin Mass. Dispense with the sermon. Work quickly. Once he comes out from the Führerbunker, you must be done with Mass. Head for von Haeften and the car. Leave everything behind. Do not delay. If everything goes according to plan, you'll see the bomb explode."

Strauss sees the first checkpoint up ahead. He pedals harder. He thinks, *"This will be a walk in the park, Johan..."*

Wolf's Lair
Troop Assembly Area
11:30 A.M.

Strauss is winded but works quickly to set up the makeshift altar on a wooden table. He barely made it through the last checkpoint. The guards perused his papers thoroughly and searched every square inch of his chaplain's case. It was a miracle they did not find the hidden compartment. He believes he must have held his breath for two minutes.

There are a handful of rustic benches and some old chairs in a circle around the table. Some of the soldiers are beginning to arrive for the noon service. An SS corporal, Strauss's assigned host, stands under a tree, watching him. Under the scrutiny of this soldier, the switching of the two cases will be difficult, if not impossible.

Strauss puts on the chasuble directly over his cassock. He opens the chaplain's box and places the chalice, communion plate, wafers, a pitcher for water, and the small beaker for the wine on the altar. He closes the case, its deadly contents hidden under the felt panel, and sets it near the altar. He looks toward the walkway that goes over to the parking area. Stauffenberg is exiting the staff car. He approaches the open area, eyed by the SS guard. The soldier notices the right sleeve of the tunic, then the partial hand carrying the briefcase. The man also has a patch over his left eye. He shakes his head, perhaps feeling sorry for him. He watches von Stauffenberg until he reaches the priest. They greet each other and von Stauffenberg nods and then gets down on his knees.

"Hey, my friend. Yes, you. Over here, do you have a light?" Von Haeften is seated in the car, behind the steering wheel, waving a cigarette. The soldier sees that the lieutenant is calling him. The corporal leaves the shady spot under the tree and goes over to von Haeften.

The corporal salutes, and asks, "What's your boss doing?"

"Catholics call it confession. The colonel is a very pious man, but last night he got a little drunk and took liberties with a girl in town. I think he shtupped her."

"And now he has to tell the priest. That's stupid."

"I know. It makes little sense to me, but it will improve his mood. I'm sorry, want a smoke?"

The SS soldier nods and takes a cigarette, lighting it. "Thanks. This happens to be my brand too. So your boss got lucky last night?"

"Yes, it would seem so."

"I wish I could get lucky. I'd like to get out of this place for a night."

Conversation begins and the lonely soldier forgets about the penitent and the confessor in the clearing.

"Bless me, Father, for I have sinned."

"Lieutenant von Haeften is doing a good job diverting my host's attention. They seem to be having a nice chat. Claus, open your bag. You need to get out some documents to put into the case."

"Good thinking. I forgot that."

"Hand them to me."

Strauss puts the suitcase on the table. He opens it, and quickly places the papers inside, his wide vestments hiding his subterfuge. He turns back to Stauffenberg. The priest makes the sign of the cross over the colonel.

"Where is the meeting?" Strauss asks.

"With the cool weather, it will be in Hitler's bunker, not the wooden barrack where it was yesterday. The concrete bunker will contain the blast better."

The bunker's six-foot-thick walls will do more than contain the blast; they will cause a reverberating concussion. No one will survive. If the wood-framed Lagebaracke had been the meeting's location, as on the previous day due to the summer heat, the blast would have blown outwards, destroying the structure. Some of the meeting's occupants might have lived, including the Führer.

Strauss looks at his friend. "Now you have the explosives. The meeting will be in a concrete tomb. You just need to set the fuses. I think God is smiling on you today."

"Don't delay with the service. When I come out of the building, you must be finished."

"I will. Godspeed, Claus von Stauffenberg. Now go and sin no more." Strauss looks down at his old friend, smiles, and squeezes him on the shoulder.

The Führerbunker
12:15 P.M.

Thick concrete walls create a spider web of corridors and small rooms in Adolf Hitler's headquarters building. Officers stand and chat in the narrow hallways, as others try to pass, trying to subtly eavesdrop on privileged conversations. There are offices, small meeting rooms, stairs to an upper floor, a pair of bathrooms, but no single gathering point, except for where the general staff meeting will be held: the Briefing Room. It contains three small exterior windows. A few officers wait there, but because there is no smoking allowed, few take advantage of its commodious size.

Claus von Stauffenberg has instructed von Haeften to remain in the car. He wants a quick getaway, and his lieutenant has been instructed to do what he can to see that Father Strauss does not tarry at the altar.

Stauffenberg walks quickly to the Führerbunker, a ten-minute walk. Hitler wants no superstitious religious rituals anywhere near the main buildings. The trek gives him a chance to review his plan and to calm his nerves. The Black Orchestra finally has an opportunity to succeed in its dangerous mission. If it were not for his American friend, a priest, it would not be possible. All he has to do is arm the bombs.

Stauffenberg enters the massive concrete fortress, shows his credentials to an SS secretary, and is patted down in a perfunctory manner. His square case is searched; nothing but papers and files. An eyebrow is raised at the small cross on the front of it, but it is handed back to Stauffenberg without comment. He exhales and goes to the telephone/telegraph center, where he informs the switchboard operator that he is expecting a call after the meeting starts. He must be informed. Stauffenberg had called his co-conspirator in Berlin, General Olbricht, to tell him another meeting was planned, and to make the call at 12:35 P.M. The task done, he heads to the restroom, enters, and locks the door. He looks at his watch: 12:23 P.M. The meeting begins in seven minutes. He opens the case, takes out the papers, and uses his one hand to lift the felt ribbons. It is tedious work.

Stauffenberg removes the panel, gently lifts out the bombs wrapped in brown paper, tears off a small section revealing the white plastic explosive, and slowly inserts the thin copper tube that contains the cupric chloride acid and the firing pin. He takes the pliers. He has added additional electrical tape to the handles to improve their friction on his three fingers. His hand trembles, though he has practiced the procedure innumerable times. He takes a deep breath, steadies his hand, and squeezes. The tube bulges outward but is not crushed. He squeezes again. This time he hears the snapping sound. It is 12:28 P.M. There is a knock on the door. "The meeting is about to begin. Please report to the Briefing Room."

Stauffenberg unlocks the door and opens it a crack. He holds up his arm showing nothing but the stitched sleeve of his coat. "Thank you, I'll be there momentarily. I am having a little difficulty."

"I see; well, be quick. The Führer does not appreciate tardiness."

"Yes, thank you." Stauffenberg shuts the door. The conversation has just cost him another precious minute, and one bomb is already armed. He repeats the procedure with the second explosive. This time, with all his strength directed into every digit of his remaining fingers, it crushes immediately. Beads of sweat cover his forehead and dampen his collar. He lets out a sigh of relief, reaches for a hand towel, and wipes his brow. He places the two devices back into the briefcase, swaddling them at the sides with his papers, and snaps the case closed. He unlocks the door, and as he heads down the corridor, places his officer's cap on his head. The moment has come. It is 12:31 P.M. He hurries down the corridor to the Briefing Room.

Troop Assembly Area
Mass, 12:25 P.M.

"Take this bread all of you, and eat of it, for this is my body which will be given up for you." Father Strauss raises the host on high, and the thirty or so kneeling soldiers bow their heads and make the sign of the cross.

He lowers the round, thin wafer, and takes up the gold chalice that Sister Paulina has polished to a bright luster. "Take this and drink from it; for this is the chalice of my blood, the blood of the new and eternal covenant, which will be poured out for you, and for many, for the forgiveness of sins. Do this in memory of me."

Strauss sets the chalice on the table and looks toward the Führerbunker. He does not see Stauffenberg. He looks to the car. Von Haeften is in animated conversation with the SS guard who seems glad to have someone to keep him company. Strauss knows he must hurry. Today, there will be no time to recite the Nicene Creed before distributing communion.

Von Haeften offers another cigarette to his new friend. "Are you Lutheran? I am. It's Catholicism without all the statues."

"No, I'm nothing. I don't believe in God. I believe in Germany and the Führer. Do you know I have seen him several times?"

"It must be an honor to be assigned to this post."

"Indeed it is." The SS guard begins to tell von Haeften about his luck in securing this assignment to Wolf's Lair. He could easily be at the Russian Front.

Strauss lets out a sigh. He can finally begin to dispense Communion. The soldiers form in line. One by one they bow, cross themselves, and come up to the American OSS priest.

"Der leib Christi."
"Amen."
"Der leib Christi."
"Amen."
"Der leib Christi."
"Amen."

The Briefing Room
12:33 P.M.

Von Stauffenberg enters the conference room. He is the last to arrive, the twenty-fourth attendee. Chief of Staff Wilhelm Keitel looks at

Stauffenberg and frowns. He will have a chat with General Fromm about his assistant's tardiness. Hitler, distracted by the newest guest, looks up at von Stauffenberg, nods, and returns to the map on the table.

The colonel assesses the situation. There is a spot under the conference table to the right of the Führer, who is only one of eight people seated around the long rectangular table, the rest are standing. The table is supported by three-inch slabs of oak. The ends of the table cantilever a meter beyond the solid legs.

Stauffenberg politely makes his way up to the table, and sets the briefcase under it, on the inside of the leg. The case is no more than one and a half meters from the leader of the Third Reich, who nods toward General Heusinger.

"You may continue, Field Marshal."

"Führer, the Russians are advancing with strong forces west of the Duna, toward the north."

Stauffenberg backs up toward the door. *"Where is the phone call?"* He pulls out his handkerchief and wipes his forehead. There is an inordinate amount of sweat pouring from it. A major standing next to him leans over and whispers; "It's hot in here, no?" The assassin nods.

Heusinger continues. "The Russian spearheads are already southwest of Dunaberg. If the army group around Lake Peipus is permitted to…"

The door to the Briefing Room opens. It is the switchboard operator. He sees Stauffenberg immediately, and whispers in his ear. Stauffenberg nods. The courier exits. Stauffenberg stays, not wanting to appear too anxious to leave. He counts to ten, opens the door, and heads quickly for the main entrance walking to the communications office. Inside, he takes the call, talks, but not too long. "Danke dir, General Olbricht." He hangs up the receiver and leaves, headed for the main entrance.

Outside, he looks toward the car. The walk from the Führerbunker now looks like a long kilometer. His pace is quick.

Keitel notes Stauffenberg's hasty exit. He will definitely have a talk with Fromm about this new chief of staff, war wounds notwithstanding. At the table, General Brandt is seated next to the briefcase. It was rude of Stauffenberg to place it by his feet. Now he has no room to stretch his legs. He has already kicked the case twice.

He thinks about moving it to the other side of the solid table leg but does not want to cause a disruption to the meeting, especially now. Heusinger is at a critical point of his presentation; he is about to utter the word "retreat." Things should get interesting from here on. "Sir, I am sorry, but with the breakdown in our defenses, and the continued advances of the Soviets, I fear that…"

Assembly Area
The Outside Chapel
12:38 P.M.

"Der leib Christi."
"Amen."
"Der leib Christi."
"Amen."
"Der leib Christi."
"Amen."

Strauss turns and looks toward the Führer's building. Stauffenberg is walking at a brisk pace. He looks back at the line of soldiers. There are still at least fifteen in line.

"Der leib Christi."
"Amen."

Stauffenberg is waving at him. Strauss continues to give the Body of the Christ to the soldiers.

Von Haeften sees his boss coming. He looks at his new friend.

"Well, it has been delightful talking with you. Ah, I see my colonel is coming. He must have to leave on urgent business."

He looks toward Strauss. Soldiers continue to step forward.

"Der leib Christi."

"Amen."

"Der leib Christi."

"Amen."

Stauffenberg reaches the automobile and gets in. The SS private studies the colonel and his eye patch. He sees that the man is transfixed on the priest giving communion about fifty meters away. Strange.

"Der leib Christi."

"Amen."

"Der leib Christi."

"Amen."

Stauffenberg looks at his watch. 12:40 P.M. *"Why hasn't the first bomb gone off? I set the fuse at 12:28. That's twelve minutes. Any second now..."*

"Der leib Christi."

"Amen."

The Briefing Room
12:41 P.M.

"My Führer, I apologize, but if we do not withdraw our troops immediately and retreat, there will be a catastrophe. All of our divisions are seriously out-numbered and out-gunned." Heusinger wipes his forehead with the back of his hand; he is sweating profusely.

Adolf Hitler reaches up to his glasses with a slight tremble in his hand and removes them. His dark black eyes look directly at the apologetic general. He is beyond fury. In a barely audible voice, he says, "No retreat. All the cowardly troops deserve to die."

Stauffenberg's Automobile
Near the Assembly Area
12:42 P.M.

"Der leib Christi."

"Amen."

The last soldier receives communion. Strauss puts the silver serving plate on the table and blesses the troops. Then he turns and runs toward the automobile, throwing off his chasuble as he makes the fifty-meter dash. Stauffenberg and von Haeften look at each other, and then at Strauss. They want to yell out but cannot. The SS guard is confused.

The ground shakes violently. Can it be an earthquake? Then an immense roar...a great explosion. Flames shoot out of the three windows of the Briefing Room. Mixed in the flames, smoke and debris billows in great volumes from the small orifices. Another explosion follows this one greater than the first. The concrete of the Führerbunker breaks apart and large boulders of cement and stone fly in multiple directions. The ground continues to tremble. Great cracks in the formidable walls of the building can be seen through the smoke.

The SS private is stunned. Then he understands what is happening. He takes out his gun and aims it at von Haeften. He shoots, hitting the lieutenant in the arm. At that moment, Strauss reaches the automobile. He grabs the guard's shoulder, turns him around, and kicks him in the groin. The soldier doubles over in pain, allowing Strauss to spin him around. The shiny black helmet falls away; Strauss slams the man's head into the armored car. Unconscious, the soldier drops to the ground. Strauss opens the car door and pushes von Haeften across the front seat.

"Get us out of here!" von Stauffenberg says as he looks behind seeing people running from the inferno that was the Führerbunker.

"I'm trying!" The gears stick; he is not familiar with the gearbox and the high shift rod. Finally, the vehicle lurches forward. He grinds through the stubborn gears, zigzagging toward the service road where he cycled earlier that day.

"Watch the road! You're all over the place."

"Quit bitching! Werner, are you okay?"

"I'll live unless you wreck us."

"Everyone is a critic. Claus, I think you have succeeded in your mission."

"You mean our mission, Agent Strauss."

Strauss has the tank-like vehicle speeding at 88 KM. He has no intention of stopping at any checkpoint for inspection. A plane to Berlin waits.

"Haeften, give me your gun."

The lieutenant obliges with great difficulty. The first checkpoint approaches rapidly. The wooden gate will be easily broken, but the checkpoint is heavily guarded. Strauss begins to fire the Luger. The guards scatter.

"Werner, please reload this. Two more to go."

The Einheits-PKW speeds on to the next checkpoint.

"You amaze me, Father Strauss." With difficulty, von Haeften reloads the pistol and hands it to the priest.

"We're not out of the woods yet, gentlemen."

Chapter Seventy-Two

July 20, 1944
Rastenburg
Luftwaffe Airfield
1:10 P.M.

The armor-plated staff car bounces on the grass runway to the waiting Junkers JU-52 twin-engine plane. As soon as the pilot sees the car racing toward it, he starts the engines. They kick-off slowly and then roar to life. The oval door is open, and three steps are extended. By the plane is a little wagon with two small horses. Sister Paulina waves to the approaching vehicle.

"Look, Sister Paulina is waiting for us."

"Strauss, you are a terrible driver! Thank God, we're here. You hit a guard and side-swiped several trees."

"Collateral damage," Strauss says, waving to the nun.

Von Stauffenberg reaches forward and touches the unhurt arm of his adjutant. "Werner, stay strong. There is a first aid kit on the plane. As soon as we're aloft, we'll tend to that arm."

The automobile comes to a stop beside the wing of the plane. Strauss jumps out and runs to his friend. "Anna Marie, we were successful. Hitler is dead!"

The sister makes the sign of the cross and looks up to heaven, mouthing "Thank you, God." She hugs Strauss. "You made the right decision, Johan."

"I know, for once. Now, I need to face the consequences, but I don't care. Killing that monster was the moral thing to do."

"What can they do? Put you in front of a firing squad?"

"You have a point. But what will you do now?"

"I think I'll just take the chickens and the guns and head to Warsaw. I told you we were going to take back the city from the Germans."

"Anna Marie, come with me. Come back to America and become Mrs. Johan Strauss. Marry me."

"Johan, I'm very touched, but I am married to God, and you are his priest. But I already knew you are a much better priest than a spy or an assassin. It's what you were meant to do. And I'm needed in Warsaw."

"I had to ask."

"I understand."

Von Stauffenberg has helped von Haeften onto the plane. He sticks his head out the door and yells, "Let's go, Strauss. I have to get back to Berlin!"

Strauss looks at Sister Paulina, kisses her on the lips, and goes up into the plane. He shuts the door, and the plane moves down to the runway. She blows a kiss at the Junker as it rolls away.

"What's next?" Strauss works on the bullet wound in von Haeften's arm, as von Stauffenberg holds it as best he can.

"Operation Valkyrie goes into effect as soon as I get back to Berlin. The Reserve Army is mobilized, we arrest all of Hitler's cronies, and we announce his death. Goerdeler will become chancellor and Beck president. You will let the Americans and the Brits know that we killed the Führer and ask for an immediate cease-fire."

"You have to contend with the Russians, as well. They are part of the Allies, and Germany has really pissed them off." Strauss looks at his friend.

"I never said running a country would be easy, Johan."

"One other thing. Canaris knew he was going to be arrested; it was only a matter of time. Father Cletus said that the soldiers who shot him were looking for an American priest. There's only one way they would know that. They have Canaris and tortured him. He must have told Schellenberg about me."

"I'll check Spandau Prison when I can, but there will be a lot to do. The most important task is to find and arrest Himmler, Göring, and Schellenberg. They will oppose us."

Strauss finishes wrapping a bandage around von Haeften's arm. "There, Werner, you'll be fine. Claus, promise me you'll find Wilhelm. He and I became close during our time together. He's a good man."

"Johan, I hate to say this, but he is probably dead. Schellenberg is a ruthless man; as soon as he got what he wanted from Canaris, he probably shot him."

"Then I need to get to Wannsee and find out what happened. Plus I borrowed a car; it's there. I need to get it back to Strasbourg."

Von Stauffenberg looks hard at Strauss: "Do your many travel plans include telling the Allies what we accomplished at some point?"

"How can I get to Rome from Strasburg?"

"Rome? You need to get to Bern, Switzerland."

"Why, what's there?"

"Good God, Strauss! The OSS Europe headquarters is there. You need to make your report to Allen Dulles."

Chapter Seventy-Three

Sonderzug Asien
Göring's Private Train
En Route to the Wolf's Lair

The fifteen-car train of Reichsmarschall Herman Göring heads at full throttle toward Rastenburg. Reichsführer Heinrich Himmler and Generalmajor Walter Schellenberg are sitting in Göring's lounge. The head of the now outmanned and outgunned Luftwaffe has appointed his private train with every luxury imaginable, in contrast to the Führer's train, *Brandenburg*, which is more ascetic. The walls are an exotic, book-matched paneling, on which is hung the finest French art; the wood furniture is rare mahogany from Burma; the couches, supple red leather.

There is a temperature- and humidity-controlled freight car to carry art treasures that the Reichsmarschall has appropriated from all over Europe. Today, upon the news of the terrible death of the Führer, it was hastily loaded with Göring's favorite pieces, removed during the night from his country estate Carinhall. He knows he will never return to his home, complete with a museum full of vintage first war aircraft, a zoo for his pet lions, and several model railroads.

Himmler looks at his two potential adversaries. He thinks of himself as the rightful heir to their deceased leader. Göring secretly disagrees, but there will be ample time to work out the details of leadership once the three men establish the Fourth Reich in Bavaria.

"Gentlemen, this is how I propose we proceed. The body of our beloved Führer, at least those parts we could identify, will be placed in the next car, in the conference room, for the trip to Munich. I secured the finest casket that could be found in Rastenburg. It is too modest, but it is the best we could find. Once we arrive in Munich, I have arranged for one made of black ebony wood that is more befitting of his stature."

"The traitors, von Stauffenberg, Goerdeler, and Beck, have already proclaimed the New Republic of Germany. They should be drawn and quartered in front of the Chancellery." Schellenberg does not hold back his contempt for the assassins, though he is pleased about the outcome. But he is unsure whether this new venture will succeed. "Do you believe we can take over Bavaria?"

Himmler responds quickly, "I have ordered all my best SS Divisions to retreat from their fields of battle and depart immediately for the south. Each commander has been given one of the seven districts to commandeer."

Göring is curious, "How many men is that?"

"About 250,000, maybe 300,000 at most. But they are the best in Germany."

"It's not very many men for such a large territory. Bavaria is one-fifth the size of all Germany."

"Then why don't you contribute some planes, Reichsmarschall?"

"There is an airfield near Munich. We have perhaps 100 planes left there after the Allied bombings."

"Perfect! The Luftwaffe of the new Fourth Reich." Himmler's sarcasm permeates the room.

"From Bavaria, we can rebuild the air force. Why don't you get us a bigger army, Himmler?"

Schellenberg interjects to stop the petty squabbling. "My friends, Bavaria with its mountains and natural boundaries will be much easier to defend against any outside aggression than our leader's vision of Lebensraum. Why he thought we needed the lands of Russia, I'll never understand. He was living in a fantasy world. It's probably best he is dead. But I'm not at all sure the people will embrace us. Munich has been badly bombed. They are tired of war."

"Walter, you worry too much. Rest assured, once we arrive in Munich with the body of our leader, the populace will clamor for the New Reich. We will establish a new government and defend our borders against the Americans and British on the west, and from the pig Bolsheviks to the north if they get that far. Austria and Czechoslovakia will never become a part of the conspirators' new regime in Berlin. They will reclaim their independence, and I am confident they will welcome our new nation and help us defend it." Göring pats his stomach and smiles.

The Bendlerblock
Berlin

Claus von Stauffenberg is issuing directives for the new Democratic Republic of Germany as quickly as he can think of them. He has not slept since he arrived in Berlin, greeted as a hero by his fellow Black Orchestra conspirators. They have finally achieved success. Hitler, along with Field Marshal Keitel, Field Marshal Heusinger, and other high-ranking Nazi and SS officers were killed in the two blasts. The bodies, including some principled and decent Wehrmacht officers, were torn to shreds by the immense explosions.

"What do you mean, you can't find Himmler, Göring, or Schellenberg? We have Goebbels and Bormann in custody. Keep looking!" Stauffenberg slams down the phone, and sees Carl Goerdeler at his desk. "Yes, Herr Chancellor?"

The chancellor of the New Republic of Germany looks at his new state secretary to the minister of war. "I spoke with Dulles. He will not order a cease-fire until his American agent verifies that he saw the blast and confirms that Hitler is dead."

Stauffenberg shakes his head. "Meanwhile, the Allies are still attacking our soldiers on all fronts."

Goerdeler looks at his friend and conspirator. "When will your friend get to Bern? For some reason, all the SS divisions have retreated to the south. We are fighting with one hand tied behind our back."

"He's expected there tomorrow. He had to go to Strasburg. I've arranged for a plane to fly him to Bern from there."

"Why couldn't he have just flown from here?"

"He said he needed to return an automobile to the bishop there."

Goerdeler looks at Stauffenberg in bewilderment. "Return a car? He had better hurry. Our soldiers are no match for the Americans and Brits, especially with their air superiority, not to mention that we have lost our SS divisions."

"I suspect that Himmler has something to do with that."

"This is becoming a lot more difficult than we imagined."

"Patience, sir, patience. It will all work out."

Von Haeften enters. "Herr Chancellor, Herr Secretary, we have rounded up as many Gestapo, SD, and SS officials as possible. What are we to do with them?"

Goerdeler looks hard at his right-hand man. "This is the decision I hoped would never come. If we keep those thugs alive, they will be a stone in the shoe of a new Germany. We have to kill them, and quickly."

"Herr President, we cannot become what we worked so hard to eliminate. We'll be no better than the Nazi pigs we have overthrown."

"Then, what do you suggest we do?"

Von Stauffenberg thinks and remembers that Strauss asked him to find Wilhelm Canaris. "Von Haeften, send a contingent of the Home Army troops to Spandau Prison. Have them release all the prisoners. Most of them are our friends and colleagues. And let me know if Canaris is among them. Then lock up the people you have just arrested." He turns to Goerdeler. "Anything else, Herr Chancellor?"

"Good thinking; I might have to promote you to vice-chancellor, Claus. But you're responsible for those new inmates."

"I feel responsible for most everything right now."

"Indeed, I understand."

Spandau Prison

"The cells have been all emptied, Lieutenant." The sergeant hands Werner von Haeften a sheaf of papers with names checked off.

"Have you found Canaris?"

"There is an old man left in one cell. We're waiting for the medics to get him. He's not in very good shape. He couldn't even talk, and he doesn't look at all like the photo you gave me."

"Take me to him."

Deep within the prison, the sergeant opens the cell door. A skeleton of a man emaciated and lying in a fetal position, eyes closed, lies on a cot. He is covered with a thin sheet. Von Haeften looks down at the body. He is not sure he is even breathing. He pulls the cover off. The right knee has swollen to the size of a melon. Blackened eyes are shut, and the mouth is puffed up. The hands lie still, mangled and bloodied.

"My God, it's him!"

Chapter Seventy-Four

Nuremberg, Germany

The sky darkens as 454 United States Army Air Force B-17 Flying Fortress bombers approach the city of Nuremberg. The target is the MAN factory complex, a prime manufacturer of gas and diesel engines. At 11:15 A.M., forty squadrons of these heavily armed planes drop over 5,500 bombs on Nuremberg. However, because there is low visibility due to heavy clouds, many bombs seriously miss their mark. Sixty-two homes on the outskirts of the city are damaged or destroyed.

Strauss sees the bombing from 100 KM away on the Autobahn as he drives toward his destination. By 1:30 P.M., he is negotiating the black Citroën as best he can through the streets littered with building debris, burning automobiles, and lifeless bodies. People wander in a daze; some search piles of rubble for loved ones, and others kneel, cry and pray before a destroyed residence, as if it was an altar from Hell. Up ahead, he makes out a damaged signpost; swaying on one eyebolt is the familiar sign: "Lautermilch Tourist Home." He pulls over and parks the car at an angle between a telephone pole and a pile of rubble by the road. It is the best he can do; hopefully, fire trucks, if there are any, can get around the car. He has changed into his black suit, and a new white shirt and tie provided by friends of von Stauffenberg. He carries new papers prepared for him by the provisional government. He is now a Gestapo agent, Ludwig Faller, as many Nazis still control Germany. He hopes he can remember yet another alias; he just wants to be Father Jonathan Strauss again.

Strauss walks the short block up to the house; his mind is flooded with the memory of the interior of the beautiful home. Marta Lautermilch had set the massive dining room table beautifully. Then it was all marred by young Rolf, the brainwashed Hitlerjugen. He saved Lukas Drockler from the Nazis; perhaps he can do the same for Rolf.

The three-story building appears to have taken a direct hit. The perimeter walls are standing, but most of the interior floors are gone, pan-caked onto the first floor. He gingerly makes his way up the steps to the front door, still intact. He pulls out a handkerchief and covers his face from the dust and smoke. There is a faint odor of gas. To the left is the dining room he remembered. He can barely see the massive table beneath wood beams, bricks, and large pieces of plaster, fractured lath still attached on the back. He thinks he hears crying.

"Hello, is anyone alive? Is anyone here?"

The crying gets louder, then a voice. "Here, under the table. Help me."

Strauss gets down on his knees, not caring if he tears his suit pants. He begins to throw off bricks, chunks of plaster, and then a heavy wood beam that takes all of his might to displace. But once out of the way, he sees an opening.

"I'm under here. Help me, please!"

Strauss crouches forward, shoes pushing bricks and rubble out of the way. The great table withstood the onslaught of the floors above. It created a refuge, a cave. In it, staring at Strauss is young Rolf von Heflin. Tears stream down his dirty face onto his torn uniform.

"Rolf, it's Captain Becken. Are you all right?"

Rolf nods his head.

"Where are your grandmother and grandfather?"

"In the kitchen, I think."

Strauss walks backward on all fours, then rights himself and gingerly makes his way around the table to the kitchen door. The smell of gas is very strong. The room is narrow and the floor joists above are still intact, but the lath and plaster ceiling has come down. Heavy wood cabinets full of dishes and glasses have fallen off walls. On the floor is a couple, holding onto each other, lifeless, blood oozing from their heads. Strauss makes the sign of the cross over Karl and Marta Lautermilch. He looks at the massive, black stove and sees the flickering of a flame. He turns and scrambles back to the dining table and the scared boy hiding beneath it.

"Rolf, grab my hand. We have to get out of here!" As soon as he feels the boy's grip, he yanks him out from under the table, lifting him into his arms. With the dazed boy in his grasp, he runs out of the house, down the steps, and toward the car. Dazed citizens look strangely at Strauss and his human cargo. "Get away from here! Get away now!" he yells.

Strauss, winded, gets to the car and drops the boy by the running board; he throws himself on top of his rescue just as there is a huge explosion. Debris flies everywhere, dropping all over him as he protects Rolf. The explosion over, he looks up and dusts himself off. The house is gone, a mass of flames.

Strauss looks at Rolf; he is unharmed. Then he looks at the Reine de la Route. It is covered in debris but is undamaged.

"Let's get you out of here."

Chapter Seventy-Five

Munich, Germany

Eight black and white Lowenbrau stallions, fitted out in polished black leather headcollars, bridles, and stirrups, topped with black ostrich feather headdresses, pull the great beer wagon. One horse is fitted out with a black saddle: A pair of empty boots face backward in the stirrups.

Today there are no beer barrels stacked upon the sturdy oak wagon, sides draped with red and white flags and their black swastikas. Instead, a black catafalque, a meter and a half high holds the coffin of the Führer of the thousand-year Third Reich, Adolf Hitler. It is covered with a blanket of roses designed as the Nazi flag.

The crowds press forward to see the coffin of their dear fallen leader, held back by SS soldiers dressed in black with silver helmets, lining the funeral route. Women wail great cries and toss Edelweiss flowers at the bier. Men cry, white handkerchiefs dab at their eyes. Children wave small flags, not understanding what has truly happened.

As the processional passes the reviewing stand, Heinrich Himmler, Herman Göring and Walter Schellenberg salute their fallen leader, arms outstretched in salute. Behind them, the flag of the new Fourth Reich, designed by the flamboyant Göring, is surprisingly simple. The new flag is all white, save for the black swastika in the center. The white background symbolizes the racial purity of Bavaria, the true ancestral home of the Aryan race, now renamed Germania.

The three men have not assumed titles. After Hitler is buried, that will all be decided. Albert Speer has escaped Berlin and is en route to Munich, where he has been commissioned by the troika to design a mausoleum for the dead Führer. It is to echo the Parthenon in appearance but will be twice the size. The corpse, half a head without an ear, a torso without arms, and a foot, will be entombed in a marble sarcophagus, similar to the one for Napoleon in Paris. There will be an eternal flame, and SS guards will stand in honor twenty-four hours a day. No one will ever forget the martyred leader of the Third Reich. At the entrance to the mausoleum will be a statue of the Führer, fifteen meters high.

Himmler leans over to the former head of the Luftwaffe. "I told you the people would embrace our new order."

"I knew they would. Even now, true Germans are making their way here, from the north, from Czechoslovakia and Austria."

"Our SS troops are also increasing once word went out. We now have over 400,000 men under arms."

"I have commandeered another 230 fighter planes from the Russian front."

Schellenberg overhears the conversation and determined to do his part, speaks. "I have drawn up initial plans for a prison and work camp to deal with our enemies. Speer will help me with the details when he arrives."

"I trust it will be similar to Auschwitz and have de-lousing showers, Herr Schellenberg?" Himmler is curious.

"Of course, three large ones."

"I told you, that one day, I...I mean, we, would all rule Germany." Himmler turns his attention back to the passing wagon. He tries to shed a tear but cannot.

Göring smiles and thinks, *"We will rule Germany? No, I will rule it..."*

The Kremlin
Moscow, USSR

"Comrade Chairman, the KGB has informed us of a tremendous explosion in a forest region of East Prussia, not far from the town of Rastenburg. We sent reconnaissance planes to fly over the area and discovered a large group of buildings. We believe that it is a forward command post for Hitler. Other sources have heard rumors that he was present when the explosion happened, and he may be dead."

"I have heard. The American spy chief, Dulles, called and told me of these rumors. I hope that it is so." Josef Stalin looks over a map of eastern Germany and puffs on his pipe. He does not look up at his aide.

"Chairman, if that is the case, there can be peace at last."

"That is what Dulles hopes, too. But you are both wrong."

"Comrade Chairman?"

"After Moscow, after Leningrad, and after my own city of Stalingrad was destroyed? We have lost over 8,000,000 soldiers, and 15,000,000 of our civilian comrades. Hitler's death means nothing to me. We will advance to Berlin. Then I may stop, or I may not. I will tell you this. It is too late for a conditional surrender. Hitler wanted Russia. Well, I want Germany!"

Downing Street
London, England

"Prime Minister, I have an urgent call for you from Bern, Switzerland. It is Mr. Alan Dulles."

Winston Churchill is pacing about his office with his usual nervous energy, a glass of scotch in his hand. MI6 just delivered a Top Secret communiqué from German Intelligence that has been de-coded at Benchley Park. It reads:

> "*Reserve Army in full control of Berlin and surroundings. Opponents in custody. Report on situation in Paris immediately. VS*"

Churchill puts down the telegram. "Mr. Dulles, how are you? Well, I trust. What news do you have about the situation in Germany?" The prime minister goes to his ever-present decanter and pours more scotch for the conversation to follow.

"Prime Minister, I received a call from one of our friends in the Black Orchestra, Claus von Stauffenberg. He straight up told me that after four years, they have finally succeeded in assassinating our Nazi friend. He requested a parlay in Lucerne as soon as possible. The Germans would like to discuss a cease fire, and then terms for peace." Dulles's voice tries to be matter of fact, but he cannot help sounding upbeat.

"They have sought our help and failed many times. Lucerne: is that where they want it? How can we be sure that this time they aren't pulling our collective leg just to stop the war?"

Dulles puffs on his pipe, choosing his words carefully. He can tell the head of America's principal ally almost anything, but not everything. "Sir, I am waiting for verification that what he told me is indeed true."

"From whom?" Churchill is annoyed that he is not being told more and takes a deep sip of his daily tonic.

"Mr. Prime Minister, I'd rather not say…"

"Dulles, you will bloody well say. If it helps, we picked up a cipher from Berlin. It says the Reserve Army is in full control. It was signed by VS."

"That helps put the puzzle together. 'VS' is von Stauffenberg. He is designated to hold a high position of state should Hitler meet an unfortunate end." Dulles hopes Churchill will drop his demand to know how the OSS will verify the death of the Führer.

"Dulles, how will you be sure if he's dead!?"

The head of the OSS in Europe relents. "One of our best agents is embedded with the Black Orchestra. He was involved in the plot and the attempt. I am waiting for his report. He'll be here tonight at 9:00 P.M. Until then, I'm afraid we'll just have to wait."

Churchill is impressed with the fledgling spy agency. MI6 has tried for years to get a spy into the nest of German conspirators. The best they could do was secure information from Wilhelm Canaris. "Bloody good, Dulles old boy, bloody good. Frankly, I am amazed."

"Prime Minister, every once in a while, even a blind dog finds a downed bird."

"Yes, not bad for a blind dog! Call me later; I will be wide awake, I assure you. Goodbye, Dulles." The portly prime minister hangs up the phone and looks at his guest who has been patiently waiting to discuss the war with him. "I'm sorry, General Eisenhower. Tell me, sir, would you like to go to a meeting regarding a cease-fire?"

Chapter Seventy-Six

The Episcopal Palace
Strasbourg, France

Father Jonathan Strauss maneuvers the Citroën Reine de la Route into the courtyard drive of the Episcopal Palace. It is nearly six o'clock; he hopes there will still be a plane to take him to Bern. Rolf gets out of the car. He is trying to be brave and a good soldier of the Hitler Youth, but the death of his grandparents has shaken him.

"Why are we here?"

"This will be your new home, Rolf. There is a good Catholic school that you can attend here."

"No! I am old enough to fight for the Führer. The American bombs killed my family, so I must fight for my country."

"Rolf, Adolf Hitler is dead. The war will be over soon. I'm sorry to have such bad news for you in one day."

Rolf rounds the car and kicks Strauss in the shin. "I don't believe you! You should be shot for desertion! You are not a real soldier. Otherwise, you would cry for the Fatherland."

"Believe me, I have cried for my country. Come on now. There is someone I want you to meet." Strauss opens the trunk of the car and reaches for the suitcase Canaris gave him. He closes his eyes for a second and thinks, *I'm sorry, Michael. This boy needs the money more than you do. At least you won't grow up a Nazi.*

"Johan, I have to admit that I never thought I would see you again, or the car for that matter. I thank God for your safe return." Bishop Ruch moves to the small bar and picks up the bottle of Black & White scotch and refills Strauss's glass.

"I'm sorry about the dented grille. I tried to fix it as best I could." Strauss savors the drink; he hasn't had a cocktail since the pleasant evening with his friend, Admiral Canaris. He is saddened at the thought that he might be dead.

"Think nothing of it. I'll have it fixed in good time. Rolf, would you like some more cream soda and cookies?"

The young man has cleaned up both his face and his uniform, and even done his best to polish his shoes. His yellow hair is combed back, and his blue eyes light up at the question. "Yes, please! We never had this drink in Nuremberg."

"Thank you, Bishop, for accepting Rolf into your school. I hope the money is enough to pay for his tuition, room, and board."

"Indeed. For many years! He will have a home here. We happen to have a fine boarding school run by the Franciscan Brothers. Rolf, what grade will you be in this fall?"

"Eighth grade, sir, but I have to get back to Germany and join the Schutzstaffel and serve my Führer."

"Why don't we all have dinner and then we can discuss it tomorrow? You've had a hard day. It's not everyone who can say they've survived an American bombing run."

Strauss interjects, looking at his watch. "Bishop, the dinner sounds grand, but about the plane. I need to get to Bern tonight."

"Of course, time has flown by. Let me get someone to drive you. Oh, and I forgot to tell you. I received a call from Colonel von Stauffenberg. Our friend, the Admiral, is alive. Barely, but he'll live with crippled legs, and minus a few molars that he didn't need. He was about to be executed at Spandau Prison when the Home Army stormed it and freed all the prisoners. He's at a hospital in Potsdam and his staff is watching over him. So, your mission is already bearing fruit."

"That is the best news. Otto and Karla will take good care of him." He turns to Rolf. "My son, this man and the brothers will make you into a kind and strong man. Hitler would have only made you into a killer. I must go. Godspeed, Rolf."

Rolf gets out of his chair, walks over to the priest, and hugs him around the chest, tears running down his face. "Thank you for saving me."

"Johan, let's get you to the airport." Ruch motions toward the door.

"I'm not looking forward to telling the boss what happened." Strauss downs the last of his scotch, and heads for the exit.

Chapter Seventy-Seven

23 Herrengasse
Bern, Switzerland

The driver pulls up to the three-story building with a mansard roof in the fashionable neighborhood high above the river Aare. It is 9:10 P.M. A tall figure exits the car, dressed in black. He stares at the front doors of several residences.

"It's the townhouse at the end. You'll see a sign by the door: Allen W. Dulles, Special Assistant to the American Minister." The cab driver has been here numerous times before carrying all types of intriguing people.

"Thank you. Have a nice evening." Strauss struggles to adjust his eyes to the night. Dulles has arranged with the local utility to have the streetlight in his cul-de-sac turned off, so his many visitors will have some anonymity. The OSS priest makes his way to the door and rings the bell; he can barely make out the sign. He stands back. The residence is imposing, five windows wide. He can tell that each of the three floors must have high ceilings; he cannot even make out the cap of the mansard roof.

The door opens; the foyer is ablaze with light. "Hello, I'm Allen Dulles. You must be Agent Trommler, right?"

Strauss steps into the large entry hall. "Yes, though I've had so many aliases I hardly know my real name. Right now, I think I'm supposed to be a Gestapo agent named Faller." He looks around. The foyer is large, with classic New England décor. There is a large open staircase that he wonders if they will shortly climb.

"Really? I've had many Gestapo agents come by, usually through the back door to offer me all sorts of information. Most of it was useless, but they needed money for their women and their liquor. How was your trip from Berlin?"

"Tiring. I had to drive to Strasburg first, by way of Nuremberg." He looks at the head of the OSS operation in Europe. The man doesn't look like a spy; he could be a college professor. He is medium height, thin, gray hair, and mustache, wire-rimmed glasses from which peer blue eyes; Strauss can tell they are sizing him up. Dulles wears a wool-worsted sport coat, dark red tie, and gray slacks. Then there is the ever-present pipe. He could have just concluded a lecture on 19th century English history at the local university.

"Bishop Ruch told me that he loaned you his Citröen for your trip to Berlin. He was pleasantly surprised that you brought it back. A very kind gesture, Trommler. Come, follow me; my office is upstairs. I've been eagerly awaiting your news."

The two OSS agents walk up the staircase that ends in a large midfloor landing twenty feet long, then left and up another flight of stairs. A pair of six-panel wood doors open to Dulles's office. While there is an actual OSS headquarters located at 24 Dufourstrasse, occupied by one other operative and clerical staff, all the real intelligence is gathered here, at Dulles's residence. It is a well-known house in Bern.

Strauss stops as he walks through the door. Seated in two comfortable chairs are Brendan Galloway and Jack Lawrence; unexpected.

"Monsignor Strauss, Jonathan, it is wonderful to see you again. You had us all very worried." Galloway is up and immediately shakes Strauss's hand, giving him a great bear hug. His words are genuine.

Lawrence remains seated. "Strauss, good to see you." He speaks with a lack of conviction.

Dulles goes to his desk, re-lights his pipe, and looks down at a singular file on his desk. Swirls of blue smoke rise and permeate the room with aromas of wood and cherry. "Tell us, Father Strauss, what happened. Is he dead?"

"Director, he is certainly dead. I saw it with my own eyes. It was an immense explosion. The ground shook. There were three windows in the room where the meeting took place. Flames shot out of them, and the building, solid concrete, was damaged. It was Hitler's personal building. I saw him the day before. He's not nearly as tall as..."

"Thank you, Strauss. We know all about him."

"Yes, right. Well, Von Stauffenberg had two packages of plastic explosives in his case, plus the detonators."

Dulles is curious. "Tell me about the detonators."

"They were thin copper tubes containing some sort of acid. They also had a wire inside and a firing pin. Von Stauffenberg had to squeeze the tubing to release the acid, which ate through the wire, releasing the firing pin."

"Ah, yes, British made. But tell me, how was he able to do that? He has no hand."

"His left hand has a thumb and two fingers. It was no easy task. He asked me to come along the first day..."

"What first day?"

"The meeting was originally scheduled for Saturday, the 19th, but it was canceled. Apparently, Hitler did that all the time. The next day, only von Stauffenberg went into the bunker. I said Mass."

Dulles looks at Strauss; the tobacco in the pipe has gone out. "What? Mass? Is that why you failed in stopping the assassination attempt?"

"No, sir, that's how we got the bombs into the Führerbunker. I switched cases with Claus. My chaplain's case contained the bombs and that's how I was able to get them into the compound."

Dulles looks at his errant spy and says in a flat voice: "Agent Strauss, Trommler, your assignment was to stop von Stauffenberg from killing the man by any means necessary. Was something about those orders not clear to you?"

"Mr. Dulles, I'm sorry but couldn't go through with it. The man deserved to die. I apologize. I know I won't get the reward you promised me. But my son will be all right."

"You apologize? Strauss, there were many important and complex reasons we wanted Hitler alive."

Jack Lawrence looks at Galloway. "I told you he couldn't go through with it." Galloway waves his comment off, wanting to hear more.

"Johan, did you see his body?"

"No. We got out of there right away. Werner was shot in the arm during the escape."

"Werner?" Galloway isn't aware of any plotter named Werner.

"Lieutenant Werner von Haeften. He is von Stauffenberg's attaché," Dulles says as he puts a match to the bowl of his pipe again.

"Then how can we be sure he is dead, Alan?"

"How much explosive was there, Strauss?" Dulles studies his report looking for an answer.

"Each brick was over two kilos. I put them in the case myself. They were roughly seven inches by four inches, and a couple of inches thick. They barely fit in the chaplain's kit."

"Brendan, I'm pretty certain he's dead. Those plastic explosives are very powerful stuff." Dulles has had experience with the potent mixture before.

"Let me understand this. You brought them into the Wolf's Lair in your chaplain's kit?" Galloway is confused.

"Yes, well, it belonged to Father Cletus, who was shot trying to warn Sister Paulina and me about two SD agents. The case had a secret compartment…"

"All right, enough, Trommler." Dulles is tired of the back and forth. "You'll spend the night here, and in the morning write a full report. It's all very confusing, but I think the main point is that Adolf Hitler is dead, and we have a new government to deal with. They want a meeting in Lucerne immediately to discuss a cease fire and terms. Stalin refuses any surrender; he wants revenge. And it appears that hardline Nazis led by Himmler and Göring have set up a new Reich in the state of Bavaria, except they are now calling it 'Germania.' The Czech leadership will certainly want their country back. Austria doesn't know what it wants. We have a lot to deal with thanks to von Stauffenberg and our agent here, Trommler."

"Then, if you don't mind, I'll leave you gentlemen to discuss the new situation. I'm very tired." Strauss gets up to leave.

Lawrence stands up. "The fucking 'new situation' that you created, Strauss, by failing at your mission! I told Winslow Gardner you weren't the man for the job. You're a priest, for God's sake. How is a priest going to kill anyone?"

Strauss turns and looks hard at Lawrence. "I got Hitler killed, didn't I? Mr. Dulles, do you think I might get dinner?"

"Certainly, Strauss, certainly."

"Thank you." Strauss goes to the door and turns. "Oh, and Lawrence, you're a jackass."

Dulles smiles and opens the file on his desk as if he were opening an original Gutenberg Bible. "Okay, let's look at what Agent Trommler did accomplish. First, though coerced, he agreed to serve his country on a dangerous mission. In Italy, he was a chaplain for the 36th Infantry Division in several bad skirmishes on the way to Rome. On that trek, he carried twenty pounds of explosives, which he delivered to you, Galloway. You gave him further orders to deliver them to some Partisan fishermen in Livorno. While on that fishing boat, he blew up a German gun boat. Then you told him to check on a war atrocity in, let's see, Sant'Anna di Stazzema, if I'm pronouncing that correctly. He did, and we have identified the German and Italian brigades that perpetrated that horrible act, so we can try their leaders for war crimes."

Lawrence interrupts. "But he failed to stop the goddamn assassination of Hitler!"

"Bear with me, Agent Lawrence. There is more. In Milan, he risked his life to protect innocent people dining in a restaurant, almost blowing his cover. In Strasbourg, he made contact with the Black Orchestra, including our friend Wilhelm Canaris, whose life he helped save, and embedded himself into that group. That alone is very impressive. On his journey to Rastenburg, he killed several of the enemy, six, to be exact, and then he managed to get into the Wolf's Lair. And Ruch told me he saved the life of a young, orphaned boy in Nuremberg. Finally, he aided in the killing of our archenemy, Adolf Hitler."

"Exactly! He failed! And now look at the raft of political shit we have to deal with, Alan. A martyred Führer, a rogue Nazi country called Germania. A New Republic of Germany that wants peace with conditions. Strauss should be court-martialed!"

Dulles looks stoically at Lawrence, his pipe lit and smoke rising from the bowl again. He gets up and goes over to a sideboard. From a decanter, he pours bourbon into a glass. "Jack, will you excuse us for a moment? I need to talk with Brendan, alone."

Lawrence's face reddens. "Okay. Fine, of course." He gets up to leave.

"And please, shut the door, Jack."

His shoulders slumped, Lawrence departs, slamming the heavy door.

Dulles lifts the decanter toward Galloway, who nods. The OSS chief pours two fingers in another glass and walks over to his senior officer. "Lawrence is right. Strauss failed us. But perhaps he was successful in the greater scheme of things."

"The situation has changed, Alan. It's now de-stabilized."

"Brendan, it was pretty de-stabilized two days ago. The Nazis were intent on fighting to the bitter end. We've taken heavy casualties in Normandy, and V-1 flying bombs were wreaking havoc in London. At least they've stopped, and the Germans are retreating. So now we just have another situation, a new future to create. The history of this world can turn on a dime. What if George Washington gave up and didn't attack Trenton? What if Hitler had not stopped the German army from pursuing the British at Dunkirk and destroyed the entire army, 300,000 men? And if we had not cracked the Japanese codes, we would never have known about their planned attack on Midway

Island. Because Nimitz put all his hopes on a codebreaker's thin supposition, we sunk four of their aircraft carriers and the Japs are on the ropes. Strauss didn't do the wrong thing. He merely took it upon himself to steer history in a different direction. By doing so, I'm sure many lives will be saved, countless lives. The poor Jews being gassed in the Third Reich's concentration camps can be liberated. Our bombing of German cities can stop. So we have to deal with it, but it's not all bad."

"I see your point. And deep down, I'm happy he got rid of that son-of-a-bitch."

"As am I, Brendan, as am I. We just have to continue to deal with the rigid ideologues that see the world and history as a straight line."

"Anyone come to mind?"

"Jack Lawrence, Stalin, maybe even Roosevelt."

"I'll pretend I didn't hear that." Galloway finishes his drink. He hasn't had bourbon since he was back in the States.

"How much is the bonus we promised Strauss if he succeeded?" Dulles asks.

"You mean tuition for a Catholic high school and college? What's that, $10,000? He had a son out of wedlock before he became a priest. We told him we'd foot the bill and nothing more would be said about it."

"I read about that in his file. And we blackmailed him over it. We're almost as bad as the Gestapo. So, $10,000. That's a pretty paltry bounty for the head of Adolf Hitler, wouldn't you say? Get him paid and send him back to New York for some good R&R. Then get him back here."

"Why, Alan?"

"I think you need an assistant in Rome. We're going to be busy. We have a lot more moving parts to deal with now." Dulles goes over to the decanter and raises it. "Another, my friend?"

Chapter Seventy-Eight

St. Peter & Paul Catholic Church
Bern, Switzerland

The church is no larger than any in Europe. It is certainly not a cathedral. The interior is cool due to the thick limestone walls of its Romanesque design. And it is in Bern where the average temperature in July is in the mid-seventies. Monsignor Jonathan Strauss sits in a pew mid-way in the nave. He is admiring the Swiss simplicity of the building. Minimal adornment is the rule. Dulles has given him directions and it was easy to find, no farther than four blocks from the residence at 23 Herrengasse.

He reflects on the morning. He had slept until 9 A.M., and after a hot bath, a large breakfast awaited him. Dulles's residence is like a four-star hotel. The cook served him an omelet with ham, cheese, and vegetables; rösti, a potato pancake; and a basket of gipfeli, Swiss croissants. Then he got down to work. By noon he was finished with his sixteen-page report written in longhand. Dulles appeared just as he was finishing the top-secret document.

"Let me get this straight. You said Mass to the German troops just so you could bring in the explosives in this chaplain's briefcase?"

"It is a small suitcase and it had a secret compartment. As I mentioned last night, Father Cletus, the pastor at St. John's, was shot by the SD. But it was me they were trying to kill."

"Kill you?"

"Yes, Canaris had been tortured and must have told Schellenberg that I was on my way to Wolf's Lair."

"Is this in your report?"

"Yes, sir all of it, it's very detailed."

"All right. I'll read it later. Father Strauss, I'm giving you the reward we promised, even though you failed in your assignment. You did a good job, and you deserve it, and more importantly, your son deserves it. But, as Lawrence said, we have 'a raft of political shit to deal with' now."

"I'm truly sorry about that, sir, I truly am."

"In the end, Brendan and I think you did the right thing. You and Stauffenberg have probably saved a lot of lives."

"You would like him, Mr. Dulles. He's a fine person."

"I'd like to meet him someday. Now, as for you. Take the day to enjoy Bern. Tomorrow, around noon, there is a train to Lucerne. From there, a train leaves for Rome. Stay a few days if you like."

"I'd really like to get back to New York, if that's all right?"

"Certainly, let me work on the arrangements. You'll need to get to Naples, and I'll see about a troopship. I'll have your tickets and letters of passage by this evening. Do you have any money?"

"About 200 Reichsmarks that Stauffenberg gave me."

"Let me get you another hundred and a couple hundred lira. Inflation has started as the rumors spread about your accomplishment." Dulles smiles.

"Sir, again…"

"Father Strauss. Please. Thank you for what you did."

Strauss looks toward the front of the church. He gets up and walks to a pew closer to the apse so that he can admire the beautiful crucifix above the marble altar, draped in fine French linen. Sliding in, he sits down. Across the aisle, an elderly woman is deep in prayer. In front of him, a young man says his rosary. Early afternoon light filters through the narrow, arched windows, but the interior is still somewhat dark. It is quiet and peaceful. He sits, not praying, no longer thinking about his earlier conversation with Dulles. He stares at the crucifix, then the votive candles, flickering like a hundred stars. He sighs and realizes that he is at peace. Peace with himself. Peace with his life. Peace with the world he is a part of. He sighs again and smiles. He is a priest and a spy. So be it.

The sign above the quaint shop said: "Verkäufer, Neue, Uebrauchte und Seltene Bücher." Father Jonathan Strauss can see through the window that it is indeed a bookstore, a very well-stocked one. He opens the solid door and a little bell rings, announcing his entrance. The shopkeeper is arranging some books on a table near the door.

"Guten Tag. Kann ich dir helfen?" the woman smiles at the tall man with the Roman collar.

"Yes, please. I was wondering if you have any books by American authors."

"Yes, we do, in the back. Follow me. Which one?"

"Hemingway, Ernest Hemingway."

"Oh, yes, he is very popular these days. Is there a particular language?"

"I don't suppose you would have *A Farewell to Arms* in English?" Strauss looks around the store. He could spend hours there.

"English is very difficult to find. Here we are." The shopkeeper moves her finger along shelves titled "Amerika," slowing as she arrives at books beginning in 'H.' "There you are, Mr. Hemingway. We have *For Whom the Bell Tolls*, and *The Sun Also Rises*. Ah, here it is. *A Farewell to Arms*. Oh, I'm sorry, it is in Italian. I suppose because the novel takes place in Italy, no?"

Strauss smiles. "Italian? Italian is fine. I'll take it. It will fill the hours of my upcoming trip." He follows the shopkeeper to a counter at the front. "How much?"

"What type of currency do you have? We get so many."

"Reichsmarks." Strauss is sure that will be acceptable.

"Yes, very well. Forty-two marks then. It is so hard to keep track as the value fluctuates every day. And now, that the war may soon be over...Did you hear that Hitler may be dead?"

"Yes, I heard the rumors."

"Thank God. I hope it is true."

"Let's hope so. Have a pleasant afternoon, fräulein."

"And Godspeed to you, Father. Have a nice trip."

The Bern train station is spotless. Even so, several workers are sweeping the floors, wiping handrails, and cleaning glass. Strauss carries the suitcase given to him only a month and a half ago by Marcello, Galloway's assistant. Today, it is surprisingly light, even though he still has a gun, a knife, his breviary, and *A Farewell to Arms* inside. He is wearing his cassock; freshly dry-cleaned, it shows off the red piping. Dulles has given him one of his hats, a black fedora. Strauss wants to look American, and fortunately, the hat fits.

He proceeds to track four, and a shiny, sky-blue train awaits him. In typical espionage style, the ticket is first class, as are the tickets to Rome and Naples. And he will once again have his own cabin on the troopship, the *USS R. L. Howze*. He has been invited to eat with the captain and officers every night during the voyage to New York. *"Finally, a true holiday,"* he thinks. Strauss boards car number two and makes his way to cabin number six, opens the doors and stops.

"Brendan, what are you doing here? It's great to see you." Strauss is astonished and pleased.

"My visit with Alan is done, as well. There is much work to be done in Rome. Have a seat." Archbishop Galloway reaches into his briefcase and takes out a bottle of Johnny Walker scotch and two glasses. There is a small folding table against the outside wall. He lifts it, snapping it into place. In a small compartment behind it are hand towels and a cloth doily. He places the white crocheted napkin on the small table and sets the scotch and glasses on it.

"It's a long trip, Jonathan, so let's talk about your next assignment with the OSS."

Chapter Seventy-Nine

Governor's Residence
Gibraltar, Spain
British Overseas Territory

The tiny protectorate is sovereign British territory. Churchill has decided two things: He will set the terms and agenda for this parlay, and it will be on Allied ground, not on neutral territory like Switzerland. The Germans give in, reluctantly.

The dining room of the governor's residence is grand, suitable for banquets of visiting dignitaries to this island that has been in British control since 1713. During the war, the island has been evacuated and turned into a mighty fortress and an important naval base for the British Royal Navy.

Hitler's plane, an Fw200 Condor, its swastika tail emblem removed, has been permitted to land on the island, carrying representatives of the provisional government of the New Republic of Germany. They are met without fanfare at the airport and escorted under heavy guard in several armored cars.

Another table, not as wide or as long as the main dining table, has been brought into the room. Chairs are arranged on one side of each table, facing the opposite table. If they had guns, the parties could shoot across the room at one another. Churchill has selected the governor's residence, known as the "Convent," due to its original use by Franciscan sisters dating back to 1531, as the location for the meeting. Having it in the territories' Parliament Building would lend an improper air of legitimacy to the new German government. This could still be a clever ruse by the Nazis.

It is 10:00 A.M., Sunday, August 6, 1944. Ever being the good host, Churchill arranged for the German delegation to have a fine dinner the night before in a smaller room used for conferences. There was quail, short ribs of beef, smoked sausage, potatoes, leeks and squash, and plenty of champagne.

The German delegation is comprised of Karl Goerdeler, Chancellor; Ludwig Beck, President; State Secretary to the Chancellor, Peter von Wartenburg; Minister of War, Friedrich Olbricht; Secretary to the War Minister, Claus von Stauffenberg, and Commander of the Armed Forces, Field Marshal Erwin von Witzleben. Additionally, several male and female aides and secretaries have accompanied this august group. They have brought new flags with them, to be arrayed behind the seats. Gone is the red and white banner with a swastika. The new flag is the same flag that flew over the country from 1922 to 1926. It is comprised of three bars. Black at the top, a white center bar, and a red bottom bar. In the center, the Weimar Republic German eagle has been added. It is a strong and proud flag.

The delegation lingers, and watches are checked. It is now 10:25 A.M. The gamesmanship has begun.

"They are purposely making us wait. I knew we should not have agreed to Gibraltar. It has set a bad precedent." Olbricht, the War Minister is fuming.

"We made the French wait in 1940 at the railroad car. Turnabout is fair play, my friend." Claus von Stauffenberg speaks in a calming voice. A door at the far end of the room, usually used by servants, opens. The Allied delegation has arrived.

The group is an unusual one. There are no diplomats, save one. Churchill has decided this is about a cease fire, nothing more. It is headed by the Supreme Commander of SHAEF, Dwight Eisenhower, Field Marshal Bernard Law Montgomery in support, along with General Omar Bradley, and curiously enough, General George Patton. The sole diplomat is Churchill's eyes and ears, the uninspiring Anthony Eden, Foreign Secretary. America's Secretary of War, Cordell Hull had hoped to attend, but the distance from Washington and the immediate timing of the conclave has prevented it. Besides, Roosevelt is skeptical. He wanted Hitler to see his downfall and accept unconditional surrender. This new cast of players will want more.

Eisenhower speaks in his calm, monotone Kansas voice. He does not know what to expect but is curious. "Gentlemen, as you requested this meeting, I welcome you and turn the meeting over to you."

Goerdeler speaks: "Thank you, General, and thank you for your hospitality. Simply stated, the New Republic of Germany seeks peace. To initiate that, we are asking for a cease-fire to commence one week from today on August 13, 1944, at noon. In the intervening week, I can assure you that no offensive actions will be taken by our armed forces. With a cease-fire in place we ask for a fair, merciful, and just peace treaty, the foundation of which will be the conditional surrender of Germany..."

Day Three
Cease Fire Conference

The German delegation is drinking beer, champagne, or whiskey in their designated meeting lounge. For some it eases the pain of the onerous Allied terms; for others, it fuels anger.

"This last condition is unacceptable. A Board of Governors, made up of American, British, and French representatives, to oversee us in running our own country?" President Ludwig Beck is angry.

"Ludwig, we've come a long way in three days. We started with just a cease-fire proposal. But the Allies are taking us seriously and now we are negotiating terms to end the war." Goerdeler, the chancellor and diplomat, has no illusions about the outcome of the meeting. After all, the New Republic of Germany is not exactly dealing from a position of strength. "The Board will only exist for five years."

"We've already accepted a return to our borders as they were in 1939, plus returning the Rhineland. It's too much."

"That only seems fair. We don't deserve to rule the Netherlands, Luxembourg, or Belgium. As to the Rhineland, the Allies agreed to a plebiscite in 1948 by the occupants to determine whether they want to return to Germany."

"And we had to give back the Sudetenland to Czechoslovakia."

"What did you expect? It was an embarrassment for Chamberlain when we marched into the remainder of that country. He called the annexation agreement 'peace for our times.' It didn't exactly turn out that way."

"Goerdeler, you are not much of a negotiator." Beck takes a drink of the American bourbon. It is quite good.

"I don't have a lot to negotiate with. Look on the bright side. The Allies are recognizing our government, not that group of Nazis in Bavaria. A state of war will exist with the Nazis in Germania, and the Allies will put a siege in place to ultimately starve them into submission."

"I guess that's something." Beck is coming around, thanks to the bourbon.

"And we convinced them to help us in defending the Fatherland against the Bolsheviks. All American and British forces will join with us now to protect our eastern borders from the advancing Red horde."

"We can thank Patton for that. He hates the Russians." Beck pours another bourbon.

"Churchill weighed in as well. He knows all Stalin wants is as many countries as possible under Soviet domination." Goerdeler pours himself some more champagne. "So, can we accept the Board of Governors, Beck?"

"Hell, accept everything. I want peace."

"We all want peace. More importantly, we need peace."

Chapter Eighty

ONE YEAR LATER
AUGUST 8, 1945
Neuschwanstein Castle
Füssen, Germany

The motorcade of limousines proceeds up the winding road from Füssen and crosses a narrow bridge. They funnel through the massive entry portico into the large courtyard. Generals with batons of office, field marshals bedecked with medals, black-booted SS officers, and women in elegant evening gowns slowly exit from their motor coaches, the car door held open by attendants dressed as medieval knights. Their eyes are drawn to the magical and imposing castle, once the home of "Mad" King Ludwig II of Bavaria. Tonight, his Excellency Grand Führer Herman I, is hosting another lavish ball.

As the guests enter and make their way to the throne room, they walk through an arcade flanked by marble statues of Roman emperors, plundered from Italy. Priceless Van Gogh paintings adorn the walls, along with the irreplaceable works of art by Rembrandt, Monet, and Vermeer. On a large wall in the throne room is a 16th-century Flemish tapestry removed from the Berghof by Göring. He decided that the Alpine home of his former leader was far too bourgeois for the new Führer of the Fourth Reich. This majestic, fairytale castle suits him fine.

The Grand Führer surveys the assemblage, musing, *"This is how you rule a country!"* He thinks back to the day in late September 1944 when he reprised the Night of the Long Knives. Eleven years earlier, in 1934, he had personally orchestrated three nights of mayhem and murder that killed eighty-five rivals and opponents of Adolf Hitler, which consolidated Hitler's power over Germany. Reprising it a second time was easy. While Göring sat drinking a beer in the Eagle's Nest, Himmler was shot in the back of the head. Schellenberg was given a gun and told he had three minutes to kill himself. The mayor of Munich was strangled to death. And forty-three other potential adversaries were disposed of, never to be seen or heard from again. A week later, Herman Göring placed onto his head, the crown that once sat on the heads of the Hapsburg Imperial Dynasty, and decreed that he was now Grand Führer Herman I.

Tonight, Herman I is dressed as Ludwig II once dressed, like an ancient king, complete with a white ermine cape. A garland of gold leaves sits upon his head. His shoes sport gold buckles, raised heels, and silk lederhosen stockings. He drinks Liebfraumilch wine from a golden goblet.

The procession continues. The men and women bow deeply as they reach the throne, the same one that once belonged in the Kaiser William II of the House of Hohenzollern. Herman I nods, smiles, or orders his goblet to be filled with more wine. The line of adoring subjects is long, and he is thirsty.

Germania has been fortunate in the last year. Other than a partially effective blockade by the Allies, and not being recognized as the true German nation, the country has done quite well. Rebuilding is on pace, and imports from Austria and the Balkan states are satisfying the wants and needs of his loving subjects. A servant approaches the throne and bows deeply.

"Excellency, come. You must see this. On the balcony. Please, hurry." The servant sweeps his arm and points the way. The Grand Führer follows his retinue in tow. Off the throne room is a large, cantilevered stone balustrade affording views of Germania and its capital city, Munich, in the distance. It makes the views from the Berghof look like a modest country scene.

"What? I do not see anything."

"Up in the sky. Look, several huge silver planes."

"My God, I see them. They're beautiful. And look at the massive contrails. They must be flying at over 25,000 feet. Whose planes are they?"

"I do not know, but I think the lead plane is flying over Munich, Excellency."

"I think you're right. Look, it's descending rapidly. My, what an aircraft. Look at its wingspan! We must design one for the new Luftwaffe."

The plane levels off, flies straight for a short period and then turns sharply toward the west as it ascends rapidly. The other planes follow.

There is a brilliant flash of light as if a second sun has been created. Herman I steps back and covers his eyes. He can almost feel the air move. Then a massive white cloud slowly forms and rises from the lands above Munich. In a moment, it begins to resemble a huge mushroom. He feels the wind pick up; it is hot and unsettling.

"Excellency, what is that?"

"I don't know. I don't know. We must get back to the guests. But I think the party is over."

THE END

EPILOGUE

Eleven Years Later
October 23, 1956
Vatican City
Rome, Italy

Monsignor Jonathan Strauss crosses Vatican Square on a brilliantly sunny fall day. He is headed for St. Charles Palace and the Vatican Information Office. He is the director, and if his workload is light today, he wants to take the afternoon off and visit one of his favorite spots, the gardens of the Villa Borghese. But first he has a meeting with the CIA station chief in Rome, at his office. He looks at his watch. 8:55 A.M. He will just make the nine o'clock meeting. He does not like to keep Jack Lawrence waiting. Twelve years later and the man is still an ass.

"Excuse me, Monsignor, I seem to be lost." A handsome young priest walks up to Strauss. His hair is brown, eyes blue, and he is as tall as the man he has approached. His accent betrays America, New York City in particular.

"Yes, son, where do you need to go?"

"I just arrived from New York, and I am on vacation. I have a ticket from the Archbishop to attend the weekly audience with the Pope. Where is the conference center?"

"By the Vatican Museum." Strauss looks at his watch as he turns. "It's back in that direction. I'm sorry, I'd take you there myself, but I don't have time. New York, huh?"

"Yes, Monsignor, the lower west side."

"I'm John Strauss, I work at the Vatican Information Office. I'm also from New York."

"Michael Wagner, Monsignor. It's nice to meet a fellow countryman."

Strauss does a double take. He looks at the young priest. It is like looking in a mirror thirty years ago. Feelings stir inside him. Could it be?

"What is your name again?"

"I'm Father Michael Wagner."

"Really? Vacation? How long will you be here?"

"One week, then another in Paris, and then one in Germany."

"Do you drive, son?"

"Monsignor, I'm from New York. No one drives; we take cabs or the subway."

"I know of a few church officials here that are in need of a driver. Maybe we can extend your stay in Rome. One week is hardly enough time to see all of Rome. I'm an excellent driver myself. And if you can drive in New York, you can drive in Rome."

"But…"

"But, nothing. Look, you need to get to the audience. The conference center is that way. You'll see the signs. After you're done, come back to that yellow building. It's the St. Charles Palace. Just ask for me, John Strauss. And I would love to have dinner tonight with a fellow New Yorker."

Michael is taken aback. "It sounds wonderful."

"I know a nice restaurant. I'll drive. See you later and we can discuss your extended stay here in Rome, Father Michael…Wagner."

"But I have to get back to St. Patrick's."

"Don't worry. I have a few connections."

In the corner of his eye, Strauss sees a monk trying to run in his clumsy sandals toward him. He is coming from the St. Charles Palace.

"Monsignor Director! Monsignor Director!"

Strauss looks at Father Wagner. "I'm sorry. That's my assistant, Brother Paul."

The fat monk reaches Strauss panting.

"Yes, Brother Paul, what is it?"

"The Hungarians have just revolted against the Communist government in Budapest. The people are rising up. The Hungarian Revolution has begun!"

POSTSCRIPT

I have always been fascinated about the "What ifs" of history; events that might have turned out differently if some small detail had gone in another direction or because circumstances changed at the last moment.

As Alan Dulles recalls in Chapter 77, what would have happened to the British Expeditionary Force if Hitler had not issued orders for the Wehrmacht to stop its Blitzkrieg pursuit of them as they retreated to Dunkirk? Destroyed, would that have meant the end of Britain in the war, so dispirited by that defeat?

What would have happened if George Washington, with his ragtag, half frozen army of patriots, had decided to sit out Christmas night and not attack the Hessians at Trenton, New Jersey? We might have lost the Revolutionary War, and still be an English colony.

Dulles mentions the Battle of Midway. Six months earlier, the Japanese had devastated our naval fleet, air force and port facilities at Pearl Harbor. We missed all the subtle signals of that attack. Now, the U.S. was on the ropes, and Japan was on an aggressive march throughout Southeast Asia.

But our code breakers had deciphered the Japanese naval code. The messages were cryptic at best. We put the pieces together and determined (a logical guess, really) that an attack was coming at Midway Island. Admiral Chester A. Nimitz took the gamble. We surprised the Japanese with our fleet of three aircraft carriers, outnumbered by the four of the mighty Japanese fleet. When the smoke cleared, all four Japanese carriers were on the bottom of the ocean, and they had lost 242 planes and many experienced pilots. The tide of the Pacific war turned on that one hunch.

For me however, the assassination attempt of Adolf Hitler is the greatest event in history determined by a few minor details. In the fictitious scenario you have just read, everything goes according to the plan devised by Claus von Stauffenberg and the fictitious character of Father Jonathan Strauss. The meeting with Hitler takes places in the Führerbunker, which had bomb resistant six-foot-thick walls. There was nowhere for the bomb blast to go but to reverberate within the room. In reality, because the day was very warm, the meeting had been moved to the Lagebaracke, a hastily constructed wood building. The blast was able to explode outward and destroy the building. Many of the occupants, including Hitler, survived, although four people died, one immediately, a stenographer, and later, three officers from wounds sustained in the blast.

In the actual attempt, (which took place on July 20, 1944, with the bomb exploding at precisely 12:42 P.M. The day was Thursday, not Sunday.) Stauffenberg was rushed and could only arm one of the packages of explosives, not the two he had in his briefcase. He had excused himself to use the facilities, but because the meeting was starting, had trouble squeezing the detonators. If two bombs had gone off the damage would have been, obviously, twice as great.

*Note: The fact that von Stauffenberg had only one hand with three fingers is also a remarkable fact. Try squeezing a pair of pliers with three fingers. I did, and it is quite difficult.

Lastly, and perhaps the smallest detail, is the placement of the bomb in the conference room. Von Stauffenberg placed it near the solid wood leg of the table, toward Hitler. That is, the leg was not a post, but a solid slab of oak, several inches thick, and the entire width of the table above. As planned, he was called out of the room for an urgent phone call. General Brandt was seated at the table, with the briefcase at his feet, and it got in his way. So he moved the case with the bomb to the outside of the oak slab. That caused the blast to be deflected away from the Führer. If the briefcase had stayed where von

Stauffenberg placed it, the blast would have certainly killed the leader of the Third Reich.

Such is the turning of history because of the smallest details.

Finally, it has been great fun thinking about what would have happened if indeed, Adolf Hitler had been killed, and a new government formed. Grand Führer Herman I indeed!

This much is certain:

Over 1,000,000 soldiers would have not been killed in the period from August 1944 through April 1945.

Over 1,000,000 Jews and other "undesirables" would have been saved from the gas chambers and by other means of murder or torture. It is a fact that the Nazi extermination machine ramped up its efforts in the final year of the war.

Dresden, Germany, would not have been destroyed and with it, over 20,000 civilians. From July 1944 through January of 1945, almost 14,000 civilians were killed every month by Allied bombings. That would have been avoided. (Note: I am not suggesting that Allied bombings were wrong, only that they would not have occurred with the war ending in August 1944.)

The Warsaw uprising by the Poles (which Sister Paulina planned to be a part of) would have not taken place, killing 16,000 Resistance fighters, and between 150,000 and 200,000 civilians. It is likely, however, that the Soviet Union would have moved against Warsaw anyway, exacting a high number of casualties.

The Battle of the Bulge, Hitler's last desperate gamble would not have taken place. Therefore, 89,500 American troops would not have been killed, wounded or captured. And 63,200 German soldiers would have lived.

It goes on and on.

One last comment. The German officers and patriots who plotted to kill Adolf Hitler, while not Nazis (some had been at the outset of the war), were still German nationalists. They would have dug in their heels at many of the certain rigid demands of the Allies. Von Stauffenberg hoped that Germany would be allowed to keep the Rhineland and parts of Czechoslovakia. Others would have demanded that the army remain in force (which it does in my scenario, so that the combined German, American and British armies can take the fight to the Russian Communists.)

President Roosevelt and other Americans in Washington were quite adamant about unconditional surrender. The Secretary of the Treasury, Henry Morgenthau, Jr. proposed *The Morgenthau Plan*, which called for the elimination of all German industry and would make Germany a purely agrarian society. A study of the plan estimated that, if implemented, 25 million Germans would have starved to death. It was never taken seriously by Roosevelt, and less so by President Truman. He enacted the much wiser and compassionate *Marshall Plan*. So, we will never know whether a conditional surrender could have been achieved at my fictitious Gibraltar Conference. In the end, Germany accepted all Allied terms and did surrender unconditionally.

The following Explanatory provides more information and details about the actual events that take place within the fictional context of the novel, followed by photographs of the people, places, and objects that I found as a part of my research.

Thank you for reading.

R. J. Linteau

EXPLANATORY

Prologue

On April 7, 1943, while driving from one panzer division to another to direct their movements, von Stauffenberg's column was strafed by a P-40 Kittyhawk, most likely from the No. 3 Squadron of the Royal Australian Air Force. He spent three months in a hospital in Munich, having lost his left eye, right hand, and ring and pinky finger of his left hand. He jokingly remarked to friends that he never really knew what to do with so many fingers when he had all of them. He was awarded the Wound Badge in Gold and the German Cross in Gold for his courage.

Chapter One

The Polish estate of Helmuth James von Moltke, located in the small town of Kreisau, Silesia, was the center of activity for a resistance group known as the *Kreisau Circle* (see photo). The group was comprised of about twenty-five dissidents, mostly intellectuals and professionals of both conservative and liberal leanings, who opposed the Nazi Regime. They did not favor a violent overthrow of the government but rather discussed how a new government would be organized after the end of the Third Reich. That alone was sufficient grounds for their arrest. Von Moltke was arrested in January 1945 and executed later that month. (In the novel he is arrested in May of 1944 to integrate him into the plot.)

Both the Black Orchestra and Kreisau Circle were aware of each group's activities. The second most prominent member of the

Circle was Peter Graf Yorck von Wartenburg. In a new government, planned by the Black Orchestra, in real and fictional circumstances, he was slated to be the secretary to the new chancellor, Carl Goerdeler.

Chapter Three

The Pentagon was completed in January 1943. For the purposes of the story, I have it being newly completed in late January of 1944.

Chapter Six

Brigadeführer Walter Schellenberg and Admiral Wilhelm Canaris were indeed friends in the same business, but rivals. They both loved to ride horses and did so often.

Chapter Eight

The planned assassination attempt on Hitler by Rittmeister Eberhard Breitenbuch was to take place on March 11, 1944, at the Berghof. The circumstances of the attempt were as described here. There were a total of forty-two plots to kill Hitler, and probably more. The July 20, 1944 assassination attempt came closest to succeeding.

Chapter Ten

General Friedrich Fromm was head of the Reserve Army. He toyed with becoming a part of the conspiracy to kill Hitler but refused once von Stauffenberg returned to Berlin to set operation Valkyrie into motion. As such, he was placed under arrest, and General Olbricht took over as head of the Reserve Army. Hours later, when it was discovered that Hitler had not been killed, Fromm, with the help of loyal soldiers in the Reserve Army, arrested the conspirators. To demonstrate his loyalty to Hitler and avoid being arrested as a collaborator, Fromm had them all executed on the same day. It didn't help. He was tried, convicted of cowardice before the enemy, and executed on March 12, 1945.

Those executed included Claus von Stauffenberg and Werner von Haeften. As Stauffenberg was about to be shot, von Haeften jumped in front of him. He was killed and then Stauffenberg was shot, saying: "Long live sacred Germany!"

Chapter Twelve

In 1943, Wilhelm Canaris was brought blindfolded to the Convent of the Nuns of the Passion of Our Blessed Lord in Paris to meet with the local head of the British Intelligence Services, Colonel Claude Oliver, whose code name was "Jade Amicol." Canaris wanted to know the terms for peace if Germany got rid of Hitler. Oliver conveyed the message to MI6 and two weeks later, Churchill responded "Unconditional surrender."

Operation Foxley, and the other assassination scenarios, were seriously considered by the British SOE, a secret branch under the Minister of Economic Warfare

Chapter Sixteen

The White Rose was an organization of students at the University of Munich who opposed the Nazis and Hitler. They were non-violent and succeeded in distributing over 15,000 leaflets condemning Nazi policies. Most of the members were arrested in February of 1943 and executed by guillotine after brief trials, where the defendants were not even allowed to speak. The two most prominent members, the founders of the group, were a brother and sister, Hans and Sophie Scholl. They became martyrs for a democratic Germany.

Chapter Seventeen

The Via Rasella attack by Italian Partisans against the Nazi occupiers of Rome took place on March 23, 1944. A column of the 11th Company, 3rd Battalion, SS Police Regiment 'Bozen' organized to intimidate and suppress the Italian Resistance, was ambushed by them. Sixteen Partisans used eighteen kilos of TNT filled in iron tubing. In all, thirty-three Germans were killed. In retribution, the Germans rounded up 335 Italian prisoners from all walks of life and of all ages. The number was five over the number called for (ten Italians for each German casualty). The Germans transported them in truckloads to caves located in Ardeatine. There the prisoners were marched into the caves, forced to kneel and, one by one, shot in the back of the head.

Chapter Twenty-Nine

The massacre of 560 innocent people took place on August 12, 1944, in the hamlet of Sant'Anna di Stazzema in Tuscany, Italy (see photo). The events are accurately depicted in the book. In 2005, those involved were sentenced "In Absentia" to life imprisonment by an Italian court. Extradition requests from Italy were rejected by Germany. In 2012, a German court failed to convict a group of seventeen soldiers involved because of a lack of evidence.

Chapter Thirty-Five

Platform 21 was the secret underground platform located in Milan's Central Train Station. Between December 1943 and January 1945, twenty trains carried 1,200 Italian Jews to Auschwitz and other extermination camps (see photo). The platform was re-discovered in 1995 and it is now the site of a museum and memorial to those that left from there to go to their certain death. In total, over 8,000 Italian Jews were killed in the Holocaust.

Chapter Thirty-Nine

The experiments on murdered Jewish people by the Reich's University in Strasbourg, to prove that they were a sub-human species, are accurately depicted in this chapter. These experiments and the autopsies were conducted by Nazi physician and war criminal, August Hirt.

He conducted the experiments on racial anatomy at the *Institut d'Anatomie Normale;* it was there he planned the Jewish Skeleton Collection.

Chapter Forty-Three

In this chapter, the Nuremberg Rallies are accurately described (see photos). They took place from 1933 through 1938. The grounds where the rallies were held covered eleven square kilometers with eight buildings. The event was held over four days, usually in September of each year. The principal rally was held in the Zeppelinfield with its massive Tribune reviewing stand structure. The huge swastika atop of it was blown up in 1945.

Chapter Forty-Seven

Wannsee, Germany was the site of the Wannsee Conference (see photo), held on January 20, 1942, organized by Reinhard Heydrich, head of the SD, and later, the Gestapo, (later succeeded by Walter Schellenberg after Heydrich's assassination by Czech Partisans in June 1942). The meeting included all of the ranking ministers of the Nazi government to coordinate a plan for carrying out the "Final Solution" of the Jewish question, i.e., the planned extermination of the Jews of Europe by starvation, being worked to death, gassed or shot en masse.

Chapter Fifty-Four

Soldau Concentration Camp was located in Dzialdowo, a town in northeastern Poland, part of the province of East Prussia. Some 10,000 to 13,000 prisoners, perhaps more, died there. The description in the book is a composite of several extermination camps throughout Poland. The camp had three sub-camps, one of which was located in Ilowo-Osada (see photos). There were no gas chambers at Soldau. Mass killings were conducted in the nearby Bialucki Forest, where prisoners were brought by truck and shot to death alongside five large pits. In addition to Jews, Polish intelligentsia, priests, and political prisoners were secretly executed here.

Photos

Colonel Claus Phillip Maria Schenk Graf von Stauffenberg
Public Domain

Von Stauffenberg with three of his children
Associated Press

*Von Stauffenberg (left) with Hitler and Field Marshal Keitel (right) at the Wolf's Lair
German Federal Archives*

Admiral Wilhelm Canaris, Chief of the ABWEHR
German Federal Archives

Carl Friedrich Goerdeler
Designated Chancellor of the new government
German Federal Archives

Ludwig Beck
Designated President of the new government
German Federal Archives

Henning von Tresckow
Architect of Operation Valkyrie
German Federal Archives

*Friedrich Fromm, Commander of the
Reserve Army
German Federal Archives*

*Brigadeführer Walter Schellenberg, Head of the SD
German Federal Archives*

Oberleutnant Werner von Haeften, Stauffenberg's Aide
Gedenkstätte Deutscher Widerstand

Von Moltke Estate. Home of the Kreisau Circle.
File:Krzyzowa4.JPG

Entrance to the Berghof, Obersalzberg Germany
By Bundesarchiv, Bild 183-1999-0412-502 / CC-BY-SA 3.0, CC BY-SA 3.0.

Hitler and Eva Braun at the Berghof
By Bundesarchiv, B 145 Bild-F051673-0059 / CC-BY-SA, CC BY-SA 3.0.

The Berghof, Obersalzberg, Bavaria
Public Domain

U.S. Troopship, same as the U.S. General H.O. Ernst
By US Navy - http://www.navsource.org/archives/09/22/22134.htm, Public Domain

American soldiers march on Rome along Route 6, June 1944
By U.S. Army - Public Domain

American troops enter Rome, June 4, 1944.
By U.S. Army - Public Domain

*Field Marshal Erwin Rommel inspecting the Normandy beach defenses.
By Bundesarchiv, Bild 101I-719-0243-33 / Jesse / CC-BY-SA 3.0, CC BY-SA 3.0.*

*Rommel (center) reviewing the locations of defenses in Normandy,
France with his field officers.
Keystone, Getty images*

An inflatable dummy tank modeled after the Sherman tank. The phantom First Army Group was under the command of General George Patton. U.S. Army Public Domain

The Führer Study in the Reich's Chancellery. It was over 4,000 square feet in size. Photo: Hugo Jaeger

*The Grand Marble Gallery, Reich's Chancellery 1939.
It was longer than the Hall of Mirrors at Versailles.
By Bundesarchiv, Bild 183-K1216-501 / Hoffmann / CC-BY-SA 3.0, CC BY-SA 3.0.*

*Members of the Italian Black Brigade
File: Pavolini and Costa, Milan, 1944.jpg, Public Domain*

The aftermath of the Via Rasella Attack. Italian civilians are rounded-up for reprisals. The next day, many will be murdered in the Ardeatine caves outside the city. Bundesarchiv Koch CC By SA

An elderly survivor in the village square, Sant'Anna di Stazzema, December 1944. Photo taken by the U.S. Army, Public Domain.

Entrance to Platform 21, Milan, Italy Central Railway Station
Creative Commons: Fcarbonara

Young members of the Black Brigades. Note the skull and crossbones pin on the boy's unusual cap.
Public Domain

*The Führersonderzug, Brandenburg, Hitler's Private Train.
German Federal Archives*

*The Brandenburg, Hitler's personal train was pulled by two locomotives.
It was sixteen cars long. It was named Amerika until January 1943.
German Federal Archives.*

Hotel Lutetia, Paris. ABWEHR Headquarters in France
https://creativecommons.org/licenses/by-sa/4.0/deed.en

Episcopal Palace, Strasbourg France
Photography: Ji Elle, Public Domain

Blood Flag Ceremony, Nuremburg Rally.
Bundesarchiv, Bild 102-04062A / Georg Pahl / CC-BY-SA 3.0

The Cathedral of Light, Nuremberg Rally, 1935.
The "Tribune" reviewing podium is in the distance.
Bundesarchiv, Bild 183-1982-1130-502 / CC-BY-SA 3.0

The faithful salute their leader, Adolf Hitler
Nuremberg Rally, 1935.
German Federal Archives

Bombing of Berlin July 1944.
By Bundesarchiv, Bild 183-J30142 / CC-BY-SA 3.0, CC BY-SA 3.0
Note the German women carrying two suitcases walking past the destruction.

Hitler Youth at Summer Camp
Hulton-Deutsch Collection/Corbis via Getty Images

Decorated Hitler Jugen flak helpers during a war rally and medal ceremony held amid Germany's declining fortunes.
German Federal Archives

*Captured soldiers of the 12th SS Panzer Division.
Of the 20,000 original young recruits, only 300 survived.
German Federal Archives*

*Sixteen-year-old Willi Hübner being awarded the Iron Cross in March of 1945.
By Bundesarchiv, Bild 183-G0627-500-001 / CC-BY-SA 3.0, CC BY-SA 3.0.*

*The estate where the Wannsee Conference was held January 1942 Wannsee, Germany
By A. Savin (Wikimedia Commons · WikiPhotoSpace) - Own work, CC BY-SA 3.0*

*Processing building of Soldau Concentration Camp
Ilowo-Osada, Poland
Photo: Beax*

*Jews being loaded onto cattle cars bound for Auschwitz.
Public Domain*

*Bodies being pulled out of a train carrying Romanian Jews.
By An unknown journalist - Cartea Neagr , Public Domain*

Auschwitz Birkenau concentration Camp. Hungarian Jews are being selected for labor or extermination. May / June 1944.
By Unknown. Several sources believe the photographer to have been Ernst Hoffmann or Bernhard Walter of the SS - Yad Vashem: "Jews undergoing selection on the ramp. Visible in the background is the famous entrance to the camp. Some veteran inmates are helping the new comers." Public Domain.

Dormitory at Auschwitz Extermination Camp.
Credit: China Crisis

*Hitler's concrete bunker at the Wolf's Lair, East Prussia
By Avi1111 dr. avishai teicher - Own work, CC BY-SA 3.0.*

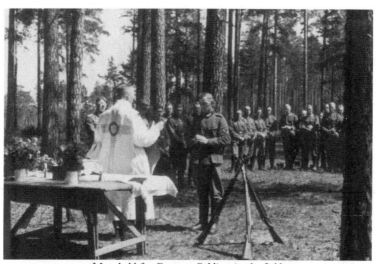

*Mass held for German Soldiers in the field.
By Bundesarchiv, Bild 146-2005-0193 / Walter Henisch / CC-BY-SA 3.0, CC BY-SA 3.0.*

A Chaplain's briefcase.
Public Domain

Alan Dulles, Head of the OSS in Europe
By US Government - Prologue Magazine, spring 2002 (NARA, 306-PS-59-17740), Public Domain.

*Alan Dulles's Residence at Herrengasse 23, Bern, Switzerland
By Sandstein - Own work, CC BY 3.0.*

*Neuschwanstein Castle, Füssen, Germany, Bavaria
By Thomas Wolf, www.foto-tw.de, CC BY-SA 3.0*

Bibliography

Ambrose, Stephen E. *The Wild Blue: The Men and Boys Who Flew the B-24s Over Germany 1944–45*. Simon & Schuster, 2001.

Ambrose, Stephen E. *D-Day: June 6, 1944: The Climactic Battle of World War II*. Simon & Schuster UK, 2002, 2016.

Beschloss, Michael. *The Conquerors: Roosevelt, Truman and the Destruction of Hitler's Germany, 1941–1945*. Simon & Schuster, 2002.

Breuer, William B. *Unexplained Mysteries of World War II*. John Wiley & Sons, 1997.

Cowley, Robert, Editor. *What If?: The World's Foremost Military Historians Imagine What Might Have Been*. Berkley Books, 1999.

Jones, Nigel. *Countdown to Valkyrie: The July Plot to Assassinate Hitler*. Amazon Books, 2008.

Larsen, Erik. *The Splendid and the Vile: A Saga of Churchill, Family, and Defiance During the Blitz*. Crown Books, 2020.

Natkiel, Richard. *Atlas of World War II*. Barnes & Noble Books, 1985.

New American Bible, St. Joseph Edition. New Testament. Catholic Book Publishing Co., Imprimatur, August 27, 1986.

Bradsher, Dr. Gregory. *Alan Dulles and No. 23 Herrengasse, Bern, Switzerland, 1942–1945*. National Archives. Uploaded November 9, 2012.

Patton, George S. *War as I Knew It*. Houghton & Mifflin & Co. 1947.

Payne, Robert. *The Life & Death of Adolf Hitler*. Praeger Publishers, 1973.

WIKIPEDIA Articles (partial list):

"Alan Dulles"
"Allied Bombing in World War II"
"Ardeatine Massacre, Italy"
"August Hirt"
"Auschwitz Concentration Camp"
"Band of German Maidens"
"Battle for Caen, France"
"Bauhaus School of Architecture"
"Beer Hall Putsch, 1923"
"Bendlerblock, Berlin"
"Berghof, Obersalzberg"
"Blood Flag Ceremony"
"Bombing of Berlin"
"Bombing of Nuremberg"
"Carlingue"
"Cherbourg, France"
"Claus von Stauffenberg"
"Carl Friedrich Goerdeler"
"D-Day"
"D-Day Advances Timeline"
"Episcopal Palace, Strasbourg, France"
"Erwin Rommel"
"First Army Group"
"French Surrender, World War II"
"Forte dei Marmi, Italy"
"Friedrich Fromm"
"German Chaplains, Wehrmacht"
"German Extermination Camps"
"Germania"

"Gestapo"
"Gibraltar, Spain"
"Hans Oster"
"Helmuth von Moltke"
"Henning von Tresckow"
"Herman Göring"
"Hitlerjugen (Hitler Youth)"
"Hitler's Food Tasters"
"Hitler's Personal Train"
"Hitlers' Personal Airplane"
"Hitler's Study, Reich Chancellery"
"Hellmuth Stieff"
"Hotel Lutetia, Paris"
"Hungarian Revolution"
"Italian Black Brigades"
"Josef Müller, CSU politician"
"Kreisau Circle"
"La Spezia, Italy"
"Lehrter-Bahnhof Train Station, Berlin"
"Liberation of Rome, June 1944"
"Luxembourg, World War II"
"Livorno, Italy"
"Ludwig Beck"
"Margot Wölk"
"Memoriale della Shoah"
"Milan, Italy, World War II"
"MI6"
"Milice Police"
"Military Chaplains"
"Monuments Men"
"Munich Beer Halls"
"Natzweiler-Struthof Concentration Camp"
"Nazi Party Rally Grounds"

"Netherlands, World War II"
"Neuschwanstein Castle"
"Night of the Long Knives"
"Nuremberg Rally"
"OSS"
"Occupation of Rome"
"Operation Barbarossa"
"Operation Foxley"
"Operation Overlord"
"Operation Valkyrie"
"Platform 21, Milan"
"Pentagon, Washington, D.C."
"Rastenburg, East Prussia"
"Reich's Chancellery, Berlin"
"Reich University Strasbourg, France"
"Reserve Army, Berlin"
"Sant'Anna di Stazzema Massacre"
"Schwarze Kapelle (Black Orchestra)"
"Soldau Concentration Camp"
"St. Charles Palace, Vatican City"
"St. Patrick's Cathedral, New York"
"Strasbourg, World War II"
"Tiergarten, Berlin"
"Timeline of World War II, 1944, 1945"
"Theodor Morell"
"Types of Allied Bombs"
"Victory Monument, Berlin"
"Vatican City"
"Vichy Government"
"Volkshalle, Berlin"
"Walter Schellenberg"
"Wannsee Conference"
"White Rose"

"William J. Donovan"
"Wolf's Lair"
"Wessel Freytag von Loringhoven"
"Wilhelm Canaris"
"USS *General O. H. Ernst* (AP-133)"
"12th Panzer Group"
"20 July Plot"

(I am indebted to the group of researchers and writers who work at Wikipedia. Their articles are amazing in their detail and thoroughness. I could not have written this novel without the help of this resource.)

Other Articles:

Callan, Paul. "The Day My Dad Tried to Kill Hitler." *The Express*. October 1, 2014.

Duff, Mark. "The Italian Jews Deported from Milan's Hidden Platform." *BBC News*. March 3, 2011.

Greenspan, Jesse. "The July Plot: When German Elites Tried to Kill Hitler." *History*. July 30, 2019.

Ilany, Ofri. "The Secret Society that Inspired a Nazi Officer's Attempt to Kill Adolf Hitler." *HAARETZ*. March 21, 2019.

Lewis, Andy. "Sheep Among Wolves or Part of the Pack? Men of God in Hitler's Armies." Student Research Paper, USCB. Spring 2004.

Patterson, Tony. "Hitler's Former Food Taster Reveals the Horrors of the Wolf's Lair." *The Independent*. September 14, 2014.

Stockton, Richard. "Killing Hitler. The Countless Plots to Overthrow the German Führer." *All That's Interesting*. March 11, 2016, Updated December 6, 2017.

"The Chaplain Kit," Germany, website.
"The German Officer Who Tried to Kill Hitler." *BBC News*, July 20, 2014.

Film:

Singer, Bryan, dir. *Valkyrie*. Starring Tom Cruise, Kenneth Branagh, Terence Stamp, Tom Wilkinson; Written by Christopher McQuarrie and Nathan Alexander. Metro-Goldwyn-Mayer, 2008.

About the Author

R. J. Linteau's inaugural novel, *The Architect*, is available in bookstores and on Amazon and Kindle. It was published in March 2021 by Dorrance Publishing Co. He has also written two screenplays and a number of short stories. In high school, he wrote short stories that he sold to fellow classmates for a senior English assignment. It turned out to be very lucrative.

Linteau lives in Marietta, Georgia with his wife. He has two children and two grandchildren. He and his wife enjoy traveling to Europe and vacationing in Key West, Florida and Saint Simon's Island, Georgia.

Please send him your comments at: **RJLinteau.author@gmail.com**

Advance praise for *The Black Orchestra:*

- A fascinating alternative history about real German conspirators and a fictional New York priest who tries to stop them. ...an exciting mixture of simple ingenuity and a rewriting of history. Clarion Reviews.
- Well, he has done it again. R. J. Linteau has produced another page turner which is meticulously researched. I couldn't put the book down! Linteau has the ability to grab you and hook you from the first page. Can't wait for the next book. Suzie H. G.
- If you think history is only about boring places and dates, think again as history comes alive and pulls you in with the turn of each page. The book...was hard to put down. David A.
- This book was a delight. Your take on the familiar subject was excellent. Thoroughly enjoyed your masterpiece...you are an extraordinary literary talent. Robert F.
- The characters were compelling, brave and terrifying. The history came alive with the great storytelling that kept you on the edge of your seat, cheering for the good guys. Kay O.
- You've created a very engrossing storyline. The history and the use of a fictional character lead the reader through the story and events...very impressive. James V.
- Wow! The author did a great job of words, emotions, characters and settings. I was very into the story the whole way. I read it twice! Alice B.

- Masterful plot development; full of surprises, including the ultimate one. Amazed at the research. A page turner for sure. The author has the gift; he is a very good writer. Thomas R.
- *The Black Orchestra* is definitely a page turner. The story really held my interest. The author blends his knowledge of the settings with the action of the book. His awareness of these areas is so detailed that it adds to the feeling of being there. Thomas B.
- A great fictional history with a twist in the ending. Riveting in detail, description and interspersing of facts. Edward L.